Cary J. Lenehan is a former trades assistant, soldier, public servant, cab driver, truck driver, game designer, fishmonger, horticulturalist and university tutor— among other things. His hobbies include collecting and reading books (the non-fiction are Dewey decimalised), Tasmanian native plants (particularly the edible ones), medieval re-creation and gaming. Over the years he has taught people how to use everything from shortswords to rocket launchers.

He met his wife at an SF Convention while cosplaying and they have not looked back. He was born in Sydney before marrying and moving to the Snowy Mountains where they started their family. They moved to Tasmania for the warmer winters and are not likely to ever leave it. Looking out of the window beside Cary's computer is a sweeping view of Mount Wellington/Kunanyi and its range.

Warriors of Vhast Series
published by
IFWG Publishing Australia

Warriors of Vhast Book 4

Scouring the Land

by
Cary J Lenehan

Scouring the Land

Book 4, Warriors of Vhast

All Rights Reserved

ISBN-13: 978-1-925956-51-1

Copyright ©2019 Cary J Lenehan

Printed in Times and LHF Essendine font types.

IFWG Publishing International
Melbourne

www.ifwgpublishing.com

Introduction

We are now up to the fourth book, and so the adventure is half over—you would think. I am not saying that there will be more books added on to the end, because the rest of the story is being told in the short stories and novellas through Patreon under my name and these provide details of what is happening elsewhere on Vhast. These, along with the maps, the recipes, the plants and animals, and the Tarot deck, are what will continue to extend the story.

The books only talk about one part of The Land and the areas around it. The Land is one of the seven continents of Vhast, and it is also the smallest of them. The Patreon stories also provide back story and historical context to the books, with tales running back over 10,000 years into the past to the creation of the world.

I hope that I continue to entertain you with my conception and that you keep reading my words, sharing my world with your friends, and posting reviews.

Again I say that I do appreciate feedback from my readers and I look forward to meeting, or talking to, you all at one stage or another.

Cary J. Lenehan
Hobart

A cast list, glossary of terms used in this novel, and a detailed breakdown of the village of Mousehole can be found from page 349.

Once again I thank Marjorie for the support and help she has given me over many years and again I have to thank my friend and beta reader Pip Woodfield for the help that she has given me.

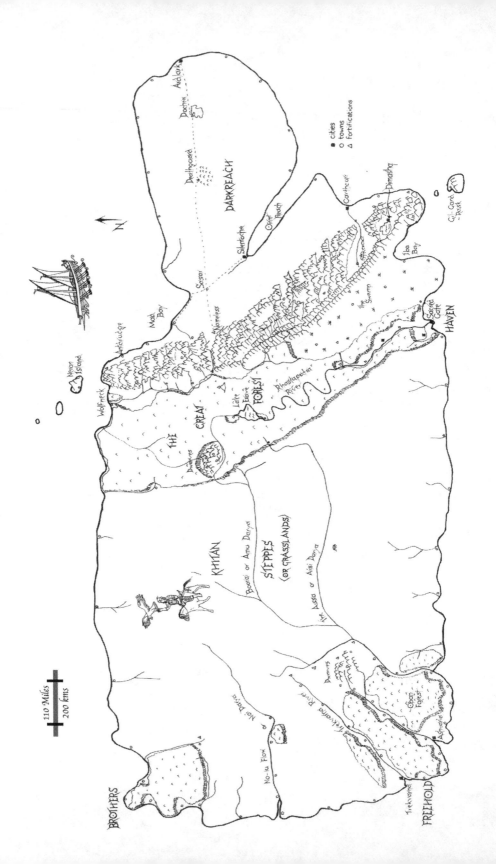

Strike hard to remove that which is plain
Just to reveal a new dark tier again
Layer on layer like an onion we peel
Til 'now we have won', it is a refrain.

As slippery to seize on as any live eel
The evil we fight will yield to our steel
Out plain in the open or hid right away
All the pain that we see, it adds to our zeal.

Come from the shadows or in open affray
Will we e're run out of dire foes to slay?
To wrest free all our lives from the fell foe
Both treasure and magic alike we outlay.

From one person wandering our numbers they grow
Soon armies to war o'er the plains they do flow
With chariots shattered and our enemies slain
We bask warm in the feeling of victory's glow.

Theodora do Hrothnog
Some jottings in her journal in the form of a quatrain

Map of the Lands
East of Lake Erave

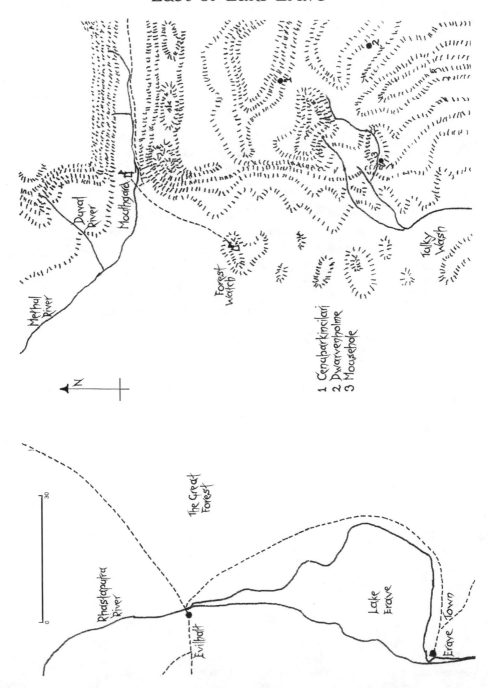

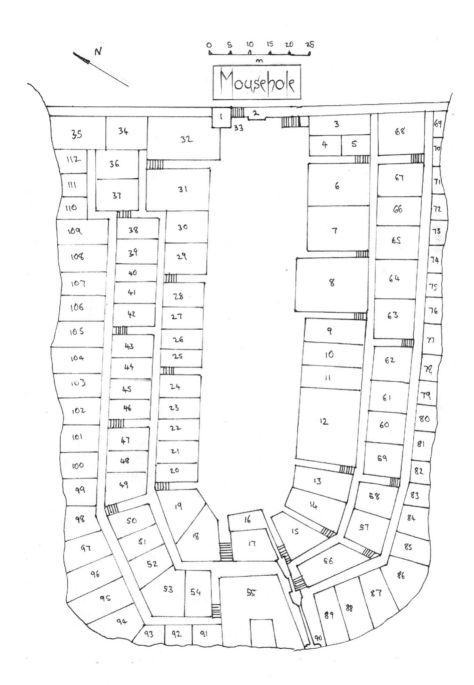

Mousehole's details can be found at page 365

Prologue

The Dragon of the Mountains was dead, and all of the Mice had survived. What is more, it turned out, much to the relief of their wives, that neither priest had become addicted to the Sleepwell potion…this time. Now, with the dragon gone and the treasure recovered, Thord quickly set out to return to Dwarvenholme with the tale of exactly what had occurred.

Their village was only a small one. The Princesses realised that they needed to continually reinforce their power in the minds of anyone near them in order to survive. By now word of Mousehole and its deeds could even be getting to the Caliphate and the Swamp, and the Princesses wanted all of them to think twice before they tried anything against the Mice. They wanted, if anyone thought of the Mice at all, to think of mice that could roar and bite like lions.

Chapter 1

Rani Rai
3rd Undecim, in the Year of the Water Lizard

The next thing that we have to do I have been putting off doing for quite some time. If we are about to go out into the world with a lot of our force, it can be put off no longer. In order to secure our back, we have to visit Aziz's old village of Dhargev and so impress them with the power of the valley that it will break forever the hold that the Masters have on them.

She paused and listened to the happy sounds of children and poultry outside her window. *We must make sure that never again while we are away, the village of Mousehole fear an attack from the Cenubarkincilari, the Hobgoblins of the Southern Mountains. It will be even better to make them our allies, but that may be asking too much.*

During the winter Rani had thought hard about how to make sure that this would happen and had sat down with her wife, as well as Aziz and Verily and Father Christopher. They had brought in Ayesha, as she spoke some Hob, and Astrid because, as Aziz put it: "she monster too". They had hammered out the issues and a plan had been devised for when it was needed.

Now it is time for us to put that plan into effect and see if it works as we hope it will.

Rani
Before dawn on 4th Undecim

"The watch very careless when I left…may be different now," said Aziz. "Masters just appear or send someone, otherwise we have strong stone walls all around village and who silly enough to attack Hobgoblins? Must pass through valley first anyway and someone notice. Hobs attack others…they not attack us…may have changed some after raid here, but not likely much."

We are travelling with the carpet and all of the saddles. I wish that I had not let my wife talk me into wearing one of these kilts. Most of the others have them from their time as slaves or from the wedding, but this is the first time I will be wearing one in public and I feel so…exposed. Theo-dear keeps pulling my arms down to stop me crossing them over my breasts, but others should not be able to see them, just her.

I have never appeared in public before with so little on my body. To make it worse there is still a chill in the air and my nipples show it and with nothing under my kilt… it even feels worse…and more naked to have all of my jewellery on, and as for this…paint.

Aziz had been very careful to paint them all with certain designs, in charcoal mixed with fat and different earth pigments. "This is the paint for peace and trade, not war," he said as he critically looked at his efforts. "It look much better on our grey skin than on your pink and brown. But they understand. We very careful with how we paint ourselves. It let others see what you are there for."

The carpet was flown by Eleanor and had Theodora and Rani seated on it. *Eleanor has to be very careful flying the carpet because behind my wife and I, and with us both holding on to it to help keep it steady, is standing the drum that had been made for Aziz and Verily's wedding, with Kāhina ready to beat it, and some presents and trade items stacked and secured around it. It would be so easy for us all to tip over.*

On the saddles we have Astrid and Basil, Aziz and Verily, our chief priest and Bianca and then Hulagu, Harald, Ayesha and Anahita. Verily and Astrid have their children with them, and Harald is dressed as a Dwarf, the only one of us not in a kilt. He is dressed. Why can't I be? Mind you, the paint markings are even harder to see on his armour than on my skin.

Astrid the Cat

I know that Aziz said that it will be safe, but I would prefer not to make a *mistake. I have my children here.* The Mice came in late at night, near to dawn, and kept low. When they were just outside the clearing of the village they set down and Ayesha and Basil, equipped with the invisibility rings and Astrid's anti-magic charm, were sent out to deal quietly with any watch. *It is almost an anti-climax.*

The sky has scarce lightened at all before my husband is standing on the wall above the gate waving at us. Astrid signalled for them to move forward. "Saddles first." *He wants us to land up on the wall?*

He is right. Not only is there enough space there above the gate to land the carpet, but it gives us the high ground. Now we wait, as the sky grows pale in the still morning. It is a beautiful crisp morn with a tickle of wood smoke and the smell of animal dung lying heavy in the air. Only the chickens, scratching between the buildings, are stirring.

Astrid looked around. *There is a fair size village, perhaps a thousand people. In the centre is a large beehive-shaped building of baked brick with stairs curling up around the outside of it. Aziz says that is the granary and a watch point they hardly ever use. And only three other really large buildings: the biggest is a hall, then there is a house for the chief with a barracks for his chief warriors and a large dormitory for the unmarried men. We need to get ready.*

"They will be up soon to tend the animals. We had better proceed and, once again, I just have to say that I don't like this bit. There are too many things in it that can go wrong, and you two are far too exposed...in so many ways." She grinned. *It takes just one glance at Rani, and she starts to cross her arms again.* "I can parry a few missiles, but only a few and Rani is not wearing her helmet...or much else."

I could not resist that. I admit to being uncomfortable walking around like this, but I can bluff it and it makes it easier to have someone even more uncomfortable than me. She is as easy to poke as her wife and now she is not even trying to resist covering her boobs. Theodora has to pull her arms down again. "I still think that we are better coming in during the day."

"We have made the plan," said Rani. *She may be pretending to ignore the way her nipples are being obviously made firm by the chill air for all to see... but her fluttering hands betray her.* "And if I am made to be in this ridiculous... dress...we will go ahead with it." Astrid looked around to check on everyone.

Theodora and Rani stand on the carpet, with Aziz in front and to the right and me to the left. Eleanor sits ready to take off if needed and Aziz and I stand with our saddles beside us, both openly armed. Aziz has his scimitar and shield, and I have my spear. Thankfully, the children are asleep in their carriers on the saddle.

Aziz and I each have a wriggling tied-up sentry in front of us. Kāhina stands behind the drum. All of the others are mounted on their saddles...stationary and a few paces above the wall. Except for us at the front, all weapons are at hand but not drawn. Rani is looking around. She nods to Kāhina, who begins to beat out the rhythm that Aziz has taught her to make.

Astrid suppressed a giggle. *Once again Rani has promptly and without thinking crossed her arms over her breasts, and her wife has glared at her and grabbed her right hand and held it tight so that she cannot do it again. Now I need to face the front and look serious.*

It was not long before first heads and then Hobs started to appear. *Most have weapons in hand, but it seems that the drum beat, and the paint are telling them that we come in peace, for no arrows are headed our way and children and women are appearing as well, and mixed in with the warriors. Several are pointing at Aziz and there is much nodding of heads and quiet conversation.*

None of the Hobgoblins are coming too close and none want to step forward. Aziz is looking among the Hobs as the Hobs look at us. Once he waved briefly at someone, but it is obvious that everyone is waiting on someone to appear. Here we go. A young Hobgoblin, perhaps one only as old as Aziz, is pushing his way through the others.

He is coming from much further into the village and others are still coming from even further away, but he must be the one we wait on, because Aziz has held his sword hand up and Kāhina has stopped beating the drum. I need to get ready to quietly translate to the Princesses.

"Saygạnzạmrat," he said. "Is that you? What are you doing up there? Why are you with these yadci, these strangers? Where are the sentries?" *Aziz points down and the young Hob nods on seeing the bound men.*

"Greetings, Nacibdamịr," said Aziz. "You must now be chief, but I no longer have my child name, so my name is no longer Saygạnzạmrat, it is now Azizsevgili. I am no longer your playmate and the unmarried son of a poor hunter. I have killed an enemy and am now an adult and a warrior of the tribe of the Mice.

"This is the tribe who defeated my old tribe, your tribe. I see my mother there. I tell her that I am now a married man, I am wealthy, and I have twin grandsons for her to be proud of. What is more I no longer follow the spirits of the tribe. I follow the most powerful of the gods of the soft ones. I am here to tell you that the spirits betrayed us and led us to attack my new tribe.

"I now know that for too long the spirits were just voices of the creatures that held the old home of the Dwarves. Many died that night the tribe attacked my new village and I was captured. Do you want to know who killed, in single combat, all of the warriors that were not killed by arrows or by magic?" *There is a nodding from below, particularly among the women. My turn to show my bad accent then and see how well my keeping Verily company in learning has worked.*

"It was me." Astrid stood with legs apart, left hand on hip and her spear planted firmly on the ground near her foot. *The Hobs must have understood me because they are all looking at me.*

"But you are a soft one and woman," said the young Hob.

"Nice you notice," *I think my sarcasm is lost with my accent.* She raised her spear and waved it. "I am also mother and hunter and warrior. Today, I am the chief warrior of Mousehole...of our village."

"Women cannot be warriors," declared the young man firmly.

"Would you like me to wash this paint off and come down to talk to you about that?" She smiled and showed her teeth. The young Hob involuntarily took a step backwards. *He is not used to soft ones with real teeth. My teeth may be small by Hobgoblin standards, but they will still rip a throat out and are much more than other soft ones usually have.*

"I have already *talked* with more than twenty of your people who did not come home. I have talked with others who were far more dangerous in battle than you look to be. I am still here, and they are not."

"What are you? You are neither one of the soft ones, nor are you a green-skin."

"I am both and so is my husband," she waved in the direction of Basil, who waved "and Aziz's children are half soft one and half grey-skin. I am a woman and a warrior, and I will bet I am a better warrior than you. Among our tribe women can do anything that a man can do. I can be both mother and warrior at same time." She looked around at the women before her. *I can see a few approving looks from some of the women, particularly the young ones.*

Aziz sounds a bit like the Princesses as he starts again. "I bring you the rulers of my village. These are the Princesses Rani and Theodora," he pointed at each of them and they nodded on hearing their name. "We come in peace to talk to the leader of Dhargev about trade and about no longer making war." He turned more directly to the young Hob in front of him. "Nacibdamır, were all of your brothers killed and are you now chief or do we wait for someone else?"

"I am now the chief of the Cenubarkincilari," said Nacibdamır. *He sounds unhappy and several of the older Hobs looked sideways at him when he said that.*

Aziz continued. "You still have your child name, so are you properly anointed? Have you completed the rituals?"

I was not sure that it was possible, but this Nacibdamır looks even more unhappy than he was before. "No, we do not have any priests left. We only have two apprentices and they say they cannot do this for me. One has gone north to the Zangindoyuushzcu to look for a priest to come and teach and to be our new priest, but he has not come back. We are going to send someone else in a week."

"Then I have good news for you," said Aziz. "I can get you a new priest and a new religion. It is a religion that will not fail you like the old one did."

Another young Hob burst forward. *Hello, who is he? He is very slight for a Hob and has very pale grey skin. Not a warrior then.* "It did not fail us. We were betrayed by setanyi, by demons. Did you help them do that?"

"I see you, little Dindarqoyun," said Aziz. "Are you all they have left as a priest? The tribe has fallen on hard times then. You are right about the betrayal, but the setanyi did not mean to betray you. They really wanted you to win. They betrayed you by corrupting our priests and our old spirits and making them face my new tribe who have right, and might, on their side. We have killed many of the tribe.

"You might have heard of the Dwarves coming back to the mountains..." Astrid looked around. *Heads are nodding everywhere. They have heard all right.* "The old home of the Dwarves is where the setanyi lived. First, we killed the old chief of the Cenubarkincilari, then we killed most of the setanyi, and now we have killed the most fearsome of their servants.

"Three days ago, we killed the dragon of the mountain that has been here longer than our tribe has, and that has eaten armies, and has pillaged our flocks for all of time, and has killed many of our people. The spirits that I used to worship bowed to the setanyi and the dragon did the bidding of the setanyi, but my new god helped me kill the ones who held your village as servants. You do want Dhargev to be friends with my new village...don't you?"

He looked at Nacibdamir and then around at the other hobs gathered in front of him. "We are rich and powerful. Look at the magic here. Have you ever seen such magic as the things that we ride through the sky? My wife is one of the soft ones..." he waved toward Verily. *Now she is landing her saddle behind the wall, near to the Hobs, below and in front of us, and dismounting.*

Verily got off her saddle and picked up their sons, Saglamruh and Sunmak from the baby quivers on the side and held them on her hips. "See the necklace of jet that she wears. Could any of the women here own anything like that? Look at the warrior Astrid the Cat. See what she wears...this village mines garnets...those are rubies."

It is not hard now to hear the whispers. My rubies are impressive. "Look at my Princess Theodora..." *Theodora has her jewelled collar from off her court costume around her neck.* "And my Princess Rani..." *She is wearing a diamond in her nose and a necklace of small and large diamonds pale against her brown skin* "And me and the other soft ones." *We all have jewellery that is designed to impress and as such as has probably not been seen in Dhargev before.*

"My Princesses want to be at peace with Dhargev and to trade with you and bring wealth. What is more, the Dwarves of Dwarvenholme are growing in number and they need food, and they will pay you well for cheese and meat and grain. If you are at peace with us, you can trade with them. If you are at war with us, even while you survive, and it will not be for long, you will not be able to trade."

He stopped at looked at the young chief. "Well Nacibdamir, will you listen to Dindarqoyun, who is not yet a man, or will you listen to me, who is? Will you let my priest talk to people about the true religion, so that they can leave behind the one that has failed the village, and now cannot even anoint you?"

Now Nacibdamir is thinking. He is looking up at those on the wall and he looks at Verily, who stands right before him, and what she wears and the children she holds. It is obvious that they are part Hob. He looks at Dindarqoyun, who is hopping from foot to foot in an agitated fashion and is not looking very much like he is in control of himself, let alone the situation.

He is thinking about the choices he has. I can see his brow has creases in it. Stand straight. He is looking at me and my boobs, and only then at my spear. He tries to balance those up. Now he turns and looks at the warriors he has, some look like strong men in their prime but mainly it is young men or old ones, the best of those who are left to the tribe. I think it is an easy choice, but not one he wants to make.

"I have decided," he said. "I will talk with your Princesses about peace and trade. Your priest may talk to me and to the village about his religion, but..." He held his hand up towards Dindarqoyun, "Every time he talks of religion Dindarqoyun must be there to hear and, if he can, counter any argument that your priest makes." He turned to Dindarqoyun. "Is that fair?"

The young apprentice priest is looking glum. I don't think that he is very sure of his ability to argue about gods with our priest. What is more, I really don't think that he wants it to be a fair argument. He is not being given a choice though. He is not a happy Hob at all.

"Good," said Aziz. "Now my mother should meet her daughter and her grandchildren, and like a good son I have a small present for her, and a pouch of gold so that she may buy things for herself." He pulled an arm torque of gold shaped like a serpent from his pouch.

I helped choose that. I hope she likes it. It is cunningly made with its details picked out in mithril, and the serpent goes around for four coils and has eyes made of ruby. I can hear the reaction to it from the women around him.

'This is a chief's gift...' 'Any son who gave that to his mother is a good and wealthy son indeed...' 'Pity he is married...' Verily heard that one as well. She is glaring at the woman. He also pulled out a leather pouch that made a nice heavy chinking noise as it was pulled out. He came down the steps from the wall, and gathering Verily, went to see his mother.

"My turn," said Father Christopher quietly, as he landed his saddle near Dindarqoyun. Bianca landed near him. While they have been teaching Aziz both Greek and Latin, both he and Theodule have been learning Hobgoblin in return. *He said that he thought that perhaps this opportunity might come and that he had best be prepared for it. He said it was a chance that came to few priests. It looks like his prayers will be answered.* "I am Father Christopher," he said to the young Hob. "I priest of the One True God and this my mate Bianca. We need talk."

Rani got Eleanor to land the carpet inside the wall and waved Ayesha over. Nacibdamir approached the Princesses. "Can you speak to me?" he asked.

"They not speak Hob," said Ayesha, "but I speak little. You speak Arabic or Darkspeech or other tongue?"

Nacibdamir shook his head and said in Dwarven, "Only few words."

"Then we try my Hob. If no understand we go ask Aziz…"

Chapter II

Father Christopher Palamas
Late on 4th Undecim

It is proving to be an interesting day. Doing Orthros, in a mixture of Greek, Latin and Hobgoblin, for my flock and before a fascinated audience is… different. Then we move on to being a physician. For the Hobs these are the same thing; they don't have secular healers.

They had difficulty understanding when I called Basil and Ayesha to help me with binding and dressing wounds and lesions and to look at the sick. They had already worked out that neither was a priest…and what is more, they knew that Ayesha is not of the same religion as me. She had been there for Orthros, but she had also had her own sunrise prayers.

I seem to have to spend a lot of time explaining to Dindarqoyun that healing is not the same as being a priest, although many priests are also healers. It grew worse when Ayesha discovered that there was a village apothecary and dragged her into the discussion. To the Hobs it is much more than just customary that only a man could be a priest and a healer, and only a woman could be an herbalist.

"What about midwives?" asked Ayesha. "You have them, don't you?" Two more Hob women were produced. "Do you heal?" she asked. The women looked sidewise at the young apprentice Hob priest and then at each other and at the herbalist.

"We are not supposed to," said the eldest of the three, diplomatically.

Astrid

A strid spent her time talking to young Hob women and men. *Many of the women are larger than me and, without my magical aids; many would have been stronger as well. Almost all of the men are both bigger and stronger.* The men were dismissive of her as a warrior and she had to find Aziz and see if there was a way she could prove her skills to the young men without killing them.

It turns out that they use wooden swords and spears for practice and can accommodate me readily. I note that the more mature men are just sitting back and watching the young ones make fools of themselves, but none of the young men can touch me with their wooden swords and several are indignant that I am able to sidestep their charge, trip them, knock aside their shields and poke them in the stomach or back almost at will.

She had to lay one young Hob out cold as he came back time after time and refused to take his hits. This got several of the other males upset, but the situation was defused by the young Hob women who made such crude suggestions and comments about his impetuosity and lack of prowess that even Astrid nearly blushed.

Even more than home, Hob custom does not prevent sex before marriage, indeed, it encourages it. At home it is usually just once you are engaged. Combined with the normal working clothes of the tribes, this leaves few secrets hidden about a Hob's shortcomings in any matter.

The young men found my prowess even more disconcerting when Freya and Georgiou decided that they needed to finally come out of their baby quivers to be fed. A female warrior had been bad enough for the poor dears. One who takes time out from fighting to breastfeed is far too much for some of them. However, at least it cements the younger women to me and now I don't have to worry about the babies when they are not at breast.

Nacibdamịr

I hope that none can see it, but I only feel relief about this visit. I was not supposed to be the village chief. I was the fourth son of my father and it was unlikely that I would even have gotten married, let alone been in control. I was destined to spend my days as a hunter and a fond uncle of my elder brothers' children, and I was happy with that.

I learnt how to hunt, not how to rule, and people want me to make decisions that I know nothing about. There is so much that I need to find out from these Yụmụkimşe, Soft One, rulers. It is hard for us with such different tongues, but I need to keep asking. They seem to know what they are doing, perhaps they will help me

A treaty sounds like a good idea to me. We need to grow again. We have lost nearly a third of the adult men of the village and not just all of my relations. I do not want to lose any more men in battles that we cannot win. What is more, I am the last of the family of chiefs. If I fail, then I fail not just for myself, but for all of my ancestors. At least I am used to taking counsel from women. They have kept me from making too bad a mess of it so far.

Rani

*H*e thinks that we have not noticed, and I need to keep our influence. I *need to talk in Hindi. I am sure that none of them know that.* "I am glad that it is not just me who feels lost. It is fine for those of you who are born to it, but to the rest of us this ruling is very hard work."

"And what makes you think that I am not just guessing?" asked Theodora.

*I*t turns out that there is a women's council for a Hobgoblin tribe as well as a *chief and, while they do not formally have any power, the way Nacibdamịr defers to its head, I suspect that any chief who ignores what the women say will have great difficulty getting anything done. He is a smart boy; he just lacks experience.*

The Princesses were introduced to Boyọkụrek, the current head woman of their circle. *Who turns out to be Aziz's mother, and she is the opposite of Nacibdamịr in many ways. She is used to asking questions and being obeyed.* She joined the group with her grandsons.

"They take after their mother too much, they both have this ugly hair, but they are big and strong and two sons from one birth is good," she said. She looked at her daughter-in-law standing beside her husband with her eyes downcast. "She seems a nice meek obedient Soft One,"

Theo-dear could have been subtler with disguising a splutter at that comment as a cough. She drew a pointed look from Boyọkụrek. "And she shows the proper respect for a mother and she is making my son happy, so I will keep her as a daughter." *Now she is looking at us and weighing us up. Who won the battle? I think it was us.*

"You two I am not sure of. You hold hands all the time and kiss. Do you not have proper husbands?"

Theodora blushed. "We are in love with each other," *This is so much harder with an interpreter. I hope that this was all not a misunderstanding.* "And we are married before God. We have adopted one child and we may get more. A ruler only needs children to succeed them, and while our daughter Fear is not the fruit of our loins, she is our daughter and will succeed us, even if we cannot work out a way to have children ourselves."

"How can you have children? You are both girls?" was the gruff reply.

"Women, not girls…look at my wife's eyes."

Boyǫkụrek did. She shrugged. "You people all have different eyes. That one," she pointed at Basil, "is the only one with black eyes like a Kharl. That one," she pointed at Bianca, "has eyes like winter sky and your girl with the spear who pretends to be a warrior has eyes like spring grass. What difference does it make that this one has gold eyes?"

"It is not just your grand-children; my wife is also not fully human…a Soft One. Her great-grandfather is Hrothnog." *I don't need to speak Hobgoblin to know when that was translated from the look on Boyǫkụrek's face.*

"Our village is not part of Darkreach, and we do not want Darkreach to come into the mountains. We have a Treaty with Hrothnog that they will leave our area alone, which means leaving you alone." *Ayesha has to call Aziz over for help to translate most of that. He is staying…great, more people to hear all about our private business. Still, it seems important to be honest if we are to deal with these people.*

"We saw him a little while ago, and even if we, and we are both strong mages, cannot work out a way of doing something, I think that he offered to help us. I have not given up on the idea of us having children of our own, although Fear will always be our first daughter."

Astrid brought a mature Hob up to Rani and Theodora when they had finished their negotiation and were just wandering around with Aziz showing them the village. "This is Gukludạshiyicisi. He carries things around the valley for other people and he has packhorses. He has heard we have things to trade with us and he wants to look at them and make offers."

"Even better, he wants a letter from you so that he can trade with the Dwarves. He speaks a little of many languages. If I have it right, he not only has Hob and Goblin but even a few words of the hidden Ogres, of the Giants, and of the Trolls and even a very few of Darkspeech. However, he has no Dwarven tongue and nothing much in speech that is useful for trade outside the valley among those who count themselves as cultured."

"So, I think that he needs you to write out what he is going there for. He figures that, if he looks peaceful, they will not shoot him. Once they know he is there for trade they can work out the money later as they can always just cope with signs for that. I think that they will welcome him as they have had a good harvest here in the valley and have lots of grain as well as cloth."

"More importantly he tells me that traders come here sometimes from Darkreach and from the Caliphate to buy their garnets and their turquoise. They have one mine for each hidden in the valley. I asked Ayesha, and she tells me that she has never heard of any trader coming here, and her father's town is the closest in the Caliphate to here."

"What is more, I am sure Carausius would have mentioned, once he saw Aziz, if he knew of any coming from Darkreach. I wonder if these traders who come here are real traders or if they are really servants or spies of the Masters? We need to find out. I have let Basil know and he will, when next Carausius calls, send a message back to Darkreach, but what do we do about the Caliphate?"

The Princesses looked at each other. *My wife is as puzzled as I am.* "We don't know," said Theodora. "Thank you for bringing this to our attention. We will think about this and talk again with Nacibdamįr."

That night the Hobgoblins held a feast. *It turns out that Dhargev has a bard, Pąrlakmugąni or Bright Singer. This has gotten both Ayesha and my wife excited and it is fortunate that we brought musicians to keep everyone distracted, as he is being almost monopolised by them. At least Ayesha told the story of Dwarvenholme and the story of the Dragon, and Aziz had translated both, before they all disappeared.*

While Kãhina and others drummed, and Verily juggled, and songs were sung that none understood, the three actual bards sat outside the hall. *They want to hear his songs and tales…and he wants the same from them. I am best leaving them alone. It seems that he is the most skilled person with languages in the valley and can use Goblin, Darkspeech, Arabic and Dwarven acceptably, as well as having a few words of some of the other mountain languages, and he knows many songs they do not, and vice versa.*

It looks like there will be one trade item here that both sides want. I am sure that my wife is already promising to return before we even think of going.

Rani
5th Undecim, the start of Diwali

The next morning, before they left, Dhargev had a treaty with Mousehole. *We have given Guklud̨ashiyicisi two letters to take with him to the Dwarves. I hope this will be enough. The first one is for the first Dwarf he meets. It simply asks for him, as a favour to Mousehole, to be passed on to speak to Thord.*

The second has Thord's name on it. He needs to know that we have a Treaty now with Dhargev and with a copy of that treaty to show the Dwarves, and asking him to take Guklud̨ashiyicisi to the Mayor to explain his purpose and what the village has to offer.

The would-be trader already has a large pack on his back, and two shaggy mountain horses fully-packed and laden with bags of grain for his first trip, and is taking his wife and children with him—all of them with packs, but also all carrying a weapon of some sort. It seems that he hopes that the sight of little ones will show that they are peaceful, but he is prepared in case it is decided otherwise.

Christopher

Now I have to promise that, until I find a priest for them of their own, *either Theodule or I will fly up to Dhargev at least once a week. Once the Hobs discovered about confession, they have become quite eager to embrace the ideas that I bear. For some reason it strikes a chord with them, the idea that, by telling someone else about them, their sins can be forgiven.*

I have to admit that many take great solace from it. It seems that their normal religion is not very big on forgiveness, and I have to keep explaining why we have not just killed all of the Cenubarkincilari and taken their mines for ourselves after the tribe had attacked the village. They had been expecting this to happen, and so had not ventured another attempt on the Mice in case they were away when it happened.

I hope that I am not losing something in the translation, but it does look like a good start for me converting the whole Hobgoblin tribe. Some want to confess on the spot, and then I have to explain again and again that they have to be Christian first and they need to learn more about Christianity before they can convert.

Even young Dindarqoyun seems interested in the idea that he can leave his doubts and sins with someone else and start out fresh all over again. He is not suited to the role that fate seems to have cast for him.

Chapter III

Christopher
5th Undecim

Both Theodule and I now speak some Hob, but the Dhargev valley is going to be a large and long-term effort. It will need its own full-time priest…at least one…and more would be better. I have to admit that the idea of adding this many to the flock in one mass conversion is exciting. Seeing that the Mice are about to start heading off again after the Masters, we do not have the time for this project ourselves on a long-term basis.

This means a quick trip up to Greensin, to again broach the subject of husbands, and to see if we can find at least one priest who is brave enough to start a new church with a flock that, at least in legend, is more likely to eat the priest than the Eucharist. I think that it is time to gather Theodule and go to see the Princesses.

"This time the trip will be quicker as we can use the saddles. We only need to fly in and then come back the next day."

"Firstly, only one of you can go," said Rani "And secondly you will take," she thought for a moment, "Astrid, Aine, Lakshmi and Tabitha. Lastly, you will do exactly what Astrid says." The priests looked at each other and then agreed.

Verily I Rejoice in the Lord Tiller
5th Undecim

I needed that trip to Dhargev. I have never felt more relaxed. I love Aziz, but I was very worried about meeting my new family. I just did not know what to expect. Having a mother-in-law who is a woman of consequence, and who accepts me as her son's little soft one. Once again, I have been accepted for who I am…and again despite my appearance and not because of it.

It was such a relief to her that when she realised it, she went and had a small cry to herself while she fed her sons. *Gradually, since my marriage, my sleep has been getting better and is less disturbed. I rarely wake myself up with nightmares now. I wonder if, after this visit, my sleep will get even better… and I needed that cry.*

Now it is time to drive out some more demons from my system. She went and fetched her hammered dulcimer that she had bought on the trip to Darkreach. *I bought it on an impulse and have not touched it since we came back from Ardlark. With the children both down and asleep for a while, they both being sound sleepers, it is time to work on some of my childhood feelings. This is the way to do it…with the music of the past.*

She took the dulcimer to the Hall and started practicing. She was trying to play an old hymn that she sort of remembered, but it was not working. *I really am hopeless with this, but it is the one pleasant memory of my childhood and I am going to keep going until I get it right…even if I have to inflict it on anyone in listening range. After all, the Kharl who had sold it to me seems to have taught himself, so I should be able to…eventually.*

"That is not how you do it," said an unexpected voice. She looked up. Make, the unrepentant Brotherhood girl, stood in front of her with an armload of linen and an odd look on her face. "Has no one shown you what to do?"

Verily was so surprised that she said nothing. She just indicated to Make that she should sit beside her. The girl put her linen on the table and sat primly upright and took the dulcimer. "First you are holding the hammers wrong…it is like this…then this is how you strike it." She started to play the instrument.

It seems to me that, totally out of the blue sky, this strange girl is actually an expert in playing it. What I was making a mess of is now the sweet melody of the remembered hymn. It fills the room and people passing by are poking their heads in to see what miracle has happened. Make went on to another piece with an odd absorbed expression on her face and then another. Verily just sat and watched what she was doing. She had finished five pieces when she came back to awareness and realised where she was.

"I am sorry. I have interrupted you. This is yours. I should get back to work before I am punished," and she went to stand.

"No…you sit there. It may be my dulcimer, but I cannot play it…you will not be punished for not working. You would not be punished anyway, but I will go and see Sajāh with you and explain what you are doing…no, I won't… she is standing here. Sajāh, I need Make to teach me how to play this. Can I borrow her please?"

"Of course," said Sajāh. "I can put that linen in the cupboard."

It was a couple of hours later, when Danelis came to say that her babies were awake that they finished. Verily had made Make promise to keep teaching her. *Now, I really can feel pleased with myself. This is the first time that Make has volunteered to do anything as a part of the community of the village. Nothing else has ever worked.*

It might have taken a return to our old familiar background to do it, but it may just be the wedge that splits open the log of her resistance. After all, in the cell it only took Aziz saying how much he liked to talk to me to start me opening up to him.

Astrid
6th Undccim

"Do we hide or are we to be open with our travel?" It was early in the morning, and they were packing food and gifts for the Church in their saddlebags and were about to head off.

"It is time for us to stop hiding," said Theodora. Rani nodded in agreement. "If the Masters hear of your trip to Greensin then it will also make them think that we are headed in that direction again, when we intend to strike the opposite way. It is what Basil got his man to hint at in Darkreach, and this will help to confirm it to a listener."

Astrid nodded and gave Basil a kiss. *He is making sure the babies are secure in their quivers, but there is no choice but to take them.* "Unless you can start feeding them, they are coming with me. Now, I will see you again tomorrow night. Stop fussing. Take a night off…see if Goditha or another of the men wants to get drunk, or if Theodora wants to beat you at chess. You never know, one day you might actually beat her."

He kissed her back. "Actually, I think that I might have an early night and a quiet sleep…one without any interruption from anyone." Astrid poked out her tongue as she mounted and called her little expedition to order.

They flew out of the valley, waving as they went to a group that was heading up the cliff to the body of the dragon. *We are still digging gems out of its flesh and taking its flesh to eat and preserve, but we will soon have to stop that as it grows too ripe. At present Hagar is making a major experiment in making dragon salami. If it works, we will have, at least while it lasts, a unique trade item.*

Once they had left the entrance to the valley, they immediately went high seeking altitude, flying in a wedge with Astrid at the front. *Unless a watcher is observant from the ground we should look like a small flock of geese or other birds. Hopefully they won't notice that we are a bit astray in direction and timing…and very fast.*

Astrid brought them down on a small knoll in the forest east of the Dwarven hills to stretch their legs, and to eat and take a break. "Heroes in the sagas never seem to have to feed and change babies," she said.

Lakshmi smiled. "It is women who have always done that work and it is usually men who write the stories. Besides, most of the heroes do not seem to have sex, or if they do, they lack being proper men and have no children. At any rate, if there is no sex, then there are no babies to change. I will see what Harald thinks about that idea when I get home." She smiled and continued innocently. "Will you ask Basil the same?"

Astrid laughed. "I don't even like that idea. Why should he?"

Chapter IV

Astrid
Late afternoon on the 6th Undecim

They arrived at Greensin in the afternoon, flying down out of the clouds that were gathering, swooping low through the village and alighting in front of the Metropolitan's house. *It is less scary seeing him after Hrothnog and knowing that he is another Basil, just like my Basil. The guards are alert. They have seen us coming and the Metropolitan is already coming out to see us, his secretary at his heels.*

Christopher had made sure that they all knew what to do as they flew and they all made a bow by reaching down and touching the ground with the right hand, rising then placing the right hand over the left with their palms upward. "Bless, Your Eminence," said Christopher.

"You are back," said the Metropolitan after completing the ritual. "You have more news? Where is your Princess? Have the three men I sent to you arrived? Have these ladies come to compliment me or to complain? For that matter, what are you flying?"

Christopher looks a little confused. Sometimes he is still the priest I once rescued. "Your Eminence, it seems that they have not yet arrived and only two of us are unmarried…and they will both be very upset if men arrive while we are away. I am not sure why…men only lead to babies and Lakshmi and I have already been complaining on that point today, not that we don't love our children you understand."

"I do. But what are you here for?"

"May we talk quietly? We have a big favour to ask and Father Christopher and Father Theodule are so excited by the prospect that they have quite lost their wits." *Well might the Metropolitan's eyebrows rise like that.*

"Sorry, I am being a poor host, come inside. Andronicus, get us refreshments please." Removing the children and the gifts from their saddles the Mice all trooped inside, the girls who had not been there before looking around them as they went.

This is a far grander building than even the Mouse Hall. It has rich carpets on the walls and the floors, well-polished timber panels on the walls. The floors almost shine with the candelabra of magic and crystal, shedding soft light over all and banishing the gloom even from the corners of the room. I want this at home. We have the money for it. People bustled around looking busy and servants came to try and help them with carrying things.

After the gifts had been presented and gratefully accepted, and they were seated, the Metropolitan returned to business. "Now, let us start again. If the men have not arrived yet, what are you so excited about?"

"Your Eminence," said Father Christopher, "we told you about the Hobgoblin attack and how we gained a new convert from a prisoner and how he has married one of our girls." The Metropolitan nodded. "Well, once we killed the dragon...oh yes...we have eliminated the beast...we then went to see the village he came from, the village of Dhargev.

"Last winter we killed many of their menfolk and the survivors want to make peace with us. We now have a Treaty with the Cenubarkincilari, their tribe, and a Treaty with the Dwarves. Part of the Treaty with the Cenubarkincilari is that we can preach to them. I have started doing that already but we have to send them a priest at least once a week, and Theodule and I need help, as even with our saddles, we do not have time to go there along with everything else that needs to be done. We need two priests at least, and they need to learn Hobgoblin, but we can help them with that with Aziz...we have written down the words that we know..." he trailed off.

The Metropolitan was holding up his hand. *Now that Father Christopher has started talking, he doesn't know when to stop and he scarce drew breath during his last sentence.*

"You want me to send missionaries to the Hobgoblins?" asked the Metropolitan. "That has not been tried for many years as it has, in the past, just led to martyrs."

"Before he starts again, I will speak," said Astrid. "Yes, Your Eminence, we do. It would probably be best to send two, as there are over a pair of hands times a pair of hands filled of Hobgoblins in the valley. You may even need to send more priests than that, but it is a great opportunity.

"They are filled with doubt over their gods because of what has happened to them and Ayesha's people will not be slow to send their priests once they find out. Whoever you send will need to be open-minded as the Hobs mainly dress in clothes that show the breasts of the women and they have their own customs in other areas as well.

"If I can give you some advice, the Princesses think that it may be best to leave as much untouched with them as you can. It will make it easier for them to accept change. Ayesha says that their language is like Goblin and I saw that, when they write their language, they use runes, as we do in Wolfneck, and as the Dwarves do, if that is any help to you."

The Metropolitan nodded and smiled. "You are right. This is a great opportunity. I can see the church of St Fergus or of the Saints Cyril and Methodius being established very soon. Perhaps both." He rubbed his hands together and smiled, and turned back to speak over his shoulder. "Andronicus…" As usual, the man was nearby. "Send to the Abbott. I need to consult with him. Explain what it is about and tell him to bring lists of those whom he thinks would be suitable from within our see. Do not tell anyone else until we have acted. We may need to call in priests from some villages and replace them with others. Should we send them with an escort?"

That is a good question. "It will be a good idea to get them safely there. What with the normal hazards of travel, and the servants of the Masters up to the Lord knows what, it will be dangerous for men of God to travel unaccompanied. But, and this is important, they must come and see us in Mousehole before they go on to Dhargev.

"It will only add a few days to the trip, and we will have to show them how to paint for peace before they go in. You will send some of the Basilica Anthropoi? Will they take off their armour and wear paint on their faces and chests if we tell them to?" *He nods. He must think that they will. I hope that he is right.*

"It is good that they be seen in the mountains but it essential that they do wear paint because if they do not, they will be attacked and all of the work we have done will be wasted. This is one of the strongest customs of the Hobs apparently.

"We had killed many of them and we knocked out their sentries and landed right in the village uninvited and yet, because we were properly painted, they accepted straight away that we were there to talk with them and that they could not attack us just as we would not attack them. If we had not been painted with the right patterns, we would have been attacked regardless of our intentions.

"I also have a package of papers for you. They are copies of Treaties, the location of the other patterns of the Masters, all sorts of things that should keep Andronicus happy for some time, and a list of more contacts of the Masters in the villages of the north. It might be good if you see to them.

"Now, if you do not need us anymore, I think that I will show the girls around while you talk with our priest. Also, can we go to your mint and change a lot of money? We have lots of gold in Mousehole, but very little else. We need much more coin other than gold and mithril if we are to deal with outsiders. At present we cannot even charge visitors anything to use our inn as we probably cannot give change for what they offer."

Arrangements were made and the women were blessed and left, leaving Father Christopher deep in conference. *It is unlikely that he will even notice that we are gone. After all, he has to arrange for the conversion of the entire tribe of the Cenubarkincilari. No one has borne that sort of responsibility within many cycles.*

After doing some shopping, and changing a small bag of gold to many bags of smaller coin, the Mousehole women were shown a place to spend the night. After going to the Hesperinos service, it being Krondag, they decided that, rather than have food brought to them they would go to the best tavern in Greensin, the oddly named Pious Smith, to eat.

They ate, and Aine and Tabitha decided that they would stay out and spend some time looking in the taverns of the town to see what they could find out. Astrid and Lakshmi decided that, with the babies, a quieter night was in order, so after warning the two other women to be careful, they returned to their rooms.

The pair came back rather late that night. *Tabitha is supporting the smaller woman. I have never seen her drunk before and now she can hardly walk.* Aine had some difficulty climbing the two steps to the entrance veranda and the two nearly fell. Tabitha had to be helped in her task and the brewer was finally more carried in to the guesthouse than she walked.

She was more than a little drunk and also still very loudly critical of the local beverages. "I had to test them all you see…to give them a fair go…they are not as good as me," she said proudly and loudly, despite Tabitha's efforts to keep her quiet.

"Next time we come here to visit I will make sure that some of my produce is brought for the Metropolitan instead of the swill they serve here. He gave us the good Fathers so we should look after him." With that she consented to be led off to her bed where she collapsed heavily, already asleep and still fully dressed. *She will regret this in the morning.*

Chapter V

Astrid
7th Undecim

The next morning, they headed back to Mousehole. *It is a fairly quiet group that we have here. Father Christopher is very tired. He must have been up talking with the Abbot and the Metropolitan for most of the night. Aine started by complaining about how bright the morning is and how much noise we are making, and has been silent since and keeps shading her eyes from the light in the east.*

As they were heading back, Astrid noted something she had not seen on the way up to Greensin. *There is a small group of people on the road up from Evilhalt. If they keep a normal pace, they will be at our village in three days. I count five men and three packhorses. I am sure that the Metropolitan had said that there are three men coming. Where did the others come from?*

She closed up and checked with the others as they flew. Aine and Tabitha, having a particular interest in the subject, had especially noted the number.

I suppose that others could have joined them on the way. Still, I want to make sure that I have a chance to check out these men quietly before they note me. Once the men come closer, I will use my ring and amulet and escort them into the village without them noticing and will take the opportunity to listen to what they say.

Ayesha bint Hāritha al-Yāq sa
8th Undecim

Christopher went up to Dhargev early in the morning. He took Ayesha, Bianca, Aziz and Verily with him. *He will be coming back tonight, but I want to go with him to the village. I am not going to miss a chance to get to that bard and hear more of what he has to say.*

I may never get this chance again. His stories and songs come from a completely different tradition to anything I have ever heard before and I want to learn what I can from him. I know many stories of my people fighting the Hobs. Now I want to find out what the stories are like when they are told from the other side.

They came back to the village elated. *Having met Aziz, I should have expected it, but the Hobs seem to be happy that, although their more distant northern cousins have ignored them, this strong tribe, us, their near neighbours, are keeping our agreement and had already made arrangements for them to have new priests.*

We even told them that the priests would have mounted warriors with them as they travelled, but they seemed to expect that as the right thing to happen. It seems that they should have a strong escort, as important men. The soldiers would not stay to rule them, but they would leave once the priests were settled and under the protection of the tribe. This is all as it should be.

I have to say that there are some interesting wrinkles on what happened at the start of this Age in some of the Hob songs. If I have their tongue right, their legends are very different from everyone else's that I have ever heard about. The tribe was not really affected much by The Burning and it is possible that they lost less of their history than many others had.

They knew of Dwarvenholme and where it lay, but they had been so terrified of the Masters, who were there from its fall, that they had never ventured near it. They are also looking forward to seeing if Gukludąshiyicisi returns from the Dwarves. Most are still not convinced that he will and bets are being bandied about. The Hobs rarely leave their valley and, if Guk returns and is going to set up trade, they seem to be happy for him to do so.

If he does, well…they have lots of food to sell this season…and indeed on most seasons. Their valley may lack many other things, such as metals, but it is rich in the amount of food that it produces. This season they had lots of maize, but they always had plenty of root crops and onions as well as an abundance of goats and sheep. The Dwarves will love them.

Christopher
Later that night

"Father, I need to talk with you about my faith and my marriage," Bryony said.

"Of course, but shouldn't Stefan be here as well?"

"He doesn't know yet and I am not sure when to tell him," was the reply.

Chapter VI

Astrid
10th Undecim

The scout flyers had reported that the men were definitely arriving on Tetarti. Astrid farmed out the next feed of her two *(one advantage of having so many babies in the village at once, it is not hard to do, if you didn't mind the discomfort of a build-up of milk)* and headed out into the afternoon. She had her ring and amulet on, and a talker.

It was Runl's idea to do it that way and I approve of it. This way I can hear what they say and, if necessary, report back to the lookout. Only Stefan will be seen to be visible there, but in case they are not what they were supposed to be, he has Harald and Aine with him out of sight. There are others going high up on saddles and the Khitan are mounted and inside the valley as well, just in case. If the arrivals are hostile, they will not have a chance. I hope that we have not forgotten anything.

As they were all heading out, Giles called out from where he was working: "Reject them all as useless mouths," he said "Unless at least one, and preferably more than one, is a farmer. I am so much in need of more help here. I would hate to have us needing to buy in food from the Dwarves. My unskilled helpers can only do so much, and I do not have time to teach them if I am to keep us all fed."

"I will see what I can do. At least you don't have to worry about me being only concerned with a pretty face. I am already taken. On the other hand, if they turn nasty...Aine here may miss deliberately if she likes what she sees." Aine began spluttering. "Come on, stop lolly-gagging, I need to get to them before they see you." They went on to the gate and then outside. Spear in hand, Astrid headed up the path at a jog.

Astrid
Soon after

When Astrid came up to the five men she was in for a surprise. *I recognise one of them. In fact, I know him rather too well. It is Ulric, one of the crew to Svein's boat, and both one of his close drinking companions and his bosun. He was one who had heartily joined in the jokes that Svein made about me and he also had offered to help Svein break me in.*

The other four are striding along happily and all, at least, look to be straightforward and upright men. The first one is walking some fifty paces in front of the others and has a bow strung in his hand, but with no arrow nocked. The next two of them are quietly whistling a happy tune as they walk along leading packhorses. They are keeping an eye out, but are obviously not expecting much in the way of trouble. All have their weapons in their scabbards and the first two leading the horses have bows on their backs. The third one with a packhorse has a crossbow handy on it.

Ulric brings up the rear, and although he is a handsome man, particularly by Wolfneck standards, he has a surly look on his face as if he seems to resent being there. He will resent it even more soon, if I have anything to do with it. He is the only one who walks with a weapon out but then he, like me, uses a spear.

He also has a pack and a round shield on his back and a sword at his side. There is quite a space between the other four and him. It is as if they are travelling in the same direction, but are not really together. Soon after Astrid recognised him, he started looking around him as if he were uncomfortable. *Perhaps he senses me as an ambush then. That is interesting.*

The first that any of them spoke was when the last man with a horse turned around. He spoke Dwarven. "Come on Ulric. You do keep laggin' behind. You talked me into comin' to find a wife here an' now it is as if you don't want to come yourself." *I can hear his Dwarven accent easily…or perhaps he is from Evilhalt and joined the others as they passed through there. Yes, he sounds more like Stefan than Thord.*

"What do you mean?" replied Ulric.

"T'last few days it has oft been 'What if t'ey are not as pretty as t'ey said?' 'What if we can't find 'em?' 'What if t'ey don't want us?' I'm a gettin' sick of it. Here am I a gettin' more an' more excited. Word is that Stefan left Evilhalt an' now has a stunnin' woman an' a child an' is a great hero an' rich when he was a goin' to be just another man like me, with nay prospects at home."

"Well, I'm in t'same wagon t'at he was in an' I want to do better as well. You pointed out I could do t'at an' t'at we could join these t'ree who were sent an'you said t'at is a why you left your Warkworth behind. Now, you're a here 'n' you didn't even bring anythin'for your new life. T'rest of us hast, but it is as if you don't expect to stay."

Ulric is slow replying and he is lying about where he comes from. Interesting. I wonder why? She fell in behind Ulric where any tracks that she might make would not be easily seen, but she could still clearly hear what was said.

"It is like this, Arthur. I am just not used to anything being good. I told you that I lost everything to the Brotherhood. Once you have had everything, and then had it taken away from you, it is hard to believe that you can ever have it all again…that is all. There is nothing sinister, I am just being cautious. As for not having anything with me, if they are all as rich as they say, then I will be able to get better stuff here."

"But it would make a better impression if'n you ha' brought somethin' with you. It's almost as if you a want to be rejected an' sent away," said the one she now knew was Arthur.

And that would be a good guess. He is coming to spy on us, find out what he can, and then be found unsuitable and to be sent away to report. I guess they must not know about me or they would not have sent him along to spy on us unless, of course, they just don't care about him. No…they would want information and so I am unknown.

"No…no…I want to stay here. Particularly if they are all as pretty as Aaron insists they are…or at least as pretty as the ones that he and the others say they saw in Greensin. Just keep walking, we must be there soon."

Indeed, you will. Only another ridge to go. She dropped back a little and quietly used the talker. "Stefan, when I finish, do you know an Arthur from Evilhalt. He has a pleasant appearance, is about your age and height and with blond hair. He uses a crossbow and is probably a younger son.

"Another is called Aaron. He is one of the front three and is from Greensin. The last is called Ulric and he claims he is from Warkworth and lost his family to the Brotherhood. He is lying. He is from Wolfneck and he works for my beloved former betrothed Svein.

"In other words, I think he is an agent of the Masters along to spy on us…you had better find out how the Princesses want to play this. I think that I should stay invisible and no one should mention me and remember to tell Danelis not to react. If I remember right, she is from Warkworth. Call me when you know what is going to happen, but be soft. I have my ring on…but they can still hear me." *You have to talk directly into a Talker to be clearly heard, but I can softly hear things being shouted out in the background in the village.*

Stefan came on: "I know an Arthur...Arthur Garden. He's a fifth son on a big farm with no prospects of a inheritin' anythin.' It's big, but not rich enough for him to be a set up in a new assart with all his brothers to be taken care of an' dowries for his sisters an' all. He is a bit of a dreamer an' listens to too many stories...a bit like me I suppose...you should remember him. He were oft from among t'front row of drinkers in Evilhalt. He was in my watch. Is he left handed?"

Astrid looked ahead. His sword was in a scabbard on his right-hand side. "Yes, he is. I didn't even notice that."

"T'en he probably is who he says he is. Not as good with a sword as I was when we started. Good hard worker on a farm an' he plays skittles like me. The girls should like him. Giles will love him."

Now that I am looking again at the man, he is actually familiar to me. I was paying more attention to Ulric; but yes, he is one of the happy drinkers. I hope that he can accept without a fuss the way that a dancer has become a Princess.

In a little while, the one at the front reached the top of the last ridge, just before the slope where they had ambushed the bandits and below the cliff with the dead dragon on top. His eyes went ahead for a moment before he turned and yelled back to the others. "We must be there. I can see a ravine with a bridge crossing it. We were told to look for that. I cannot see a path yet, but it should be there."

He paused for a moment, turning and looking around...sniffing the air. "What is that smell? If that is a dead animal, it may be too late for me to do anything with its skin. If it isn't a dead animal, I am sure that I don't want to know what it is." Astrid looked up and noted that the bones of the wing could not be seen from here as they were obscured by trees.

Just then Rani came onto the talker. "Stefan, stand up and let them see you. Wave at them...we will pretend that we have just seen them, and Aine and Harald can let them in. Astrid, stay close and keep listening. We will try and leave some clear space near your Ulric for you."

"He is not..." *Damn, she just pulled my leg and I reacted as her wife would.* "Right, and make sure that my husband is ready to take him prisoner when I say so, and that Theodora is ready to ask him a question or two under a spell then. Maybe we should do that to everyone who comes in anyway. We need to be damn sure. I am not going to trust these women to anyone who might hurt them ever again. We freed them once. We have to make sure that what they get now is better."

"Like what you organised for Fātima?" Theodora's voice came innocently over the talker but a bit faint and then louder as if she had just pulled her husband's hand a bit closer to her.

"Yes…exactly like I organised for Fātima." *I won't rise to the bait this time.* "I got her exactly the husband that she said that she wanted, and will be safe with, and no, I am never, ever, going to explain that to you or to anyone else. You can ask your ancestor to explain it to you if you are game to do it. Quiet now. Stefan just showed himself. I want to listen. I will put this away now so that it will not be heard when I get closer."

"I told you we were there," said the one in front happily as he pointed. "We were told that there was a lookout. Tonight, we sleep in beds again and we can start courting. I hope they need me and want me. It was an adventure coming here, and that is enough of a story to tell my future children of crossing half the world to try and win their mother without even having seen her."

"Mind you, I wouldn't mind the little one with the silver hair, or the one with the ripe breasts that I did see at the hanging in Greensin. It shocked all the women so much, but as long as I end up happy, and they are all supposed to be beautiful…who cares which one will take me? Come on you four. Hurry up."

Moving quicker now they all headed down along the base of the talus slope to the bridge. *Again Ulric is hanging back from the others and is still looking around him suspiciously.*

Chapter VII

Stefan Ostrogski
10th Undecim, Soon after

Stefan, Harald and Aine stood on the platform. *Most are from the north, so they probably use Greek at home, but I have none of that. Hindi it is then.* "Welcome to Mousehole. You must be t' ones t'at Metropolitan Basil told us about…but he only said t'ree." *Now to sound surprised.* "Who are…oh hello, Arthur. So you have decided to come an' see t'world, an' a look for wife, have you?"

"I must have good chance if'n you have got one. T'ey must not be very discriminating, or else t'ey are all blind," said Arthur.

That is embarrassing. "Well, actually, I'm not married. She doesn't want t'at at present." The five were now gathered below him. "I know who you are, now introduce me to t'others. You four can tell me what you do an' state what you are all here for."

Arthur stood where he could point to them all. "Well, it is obvious why we are here. T'ose t'ree even have a letter introducin' t'em from t'Metropolitan. T'one you first saw is Aaron Skynner. He's a tanner an' apparently he can dance." The named man acknowledged that he was being talked about by removing his hat jauntily and doing a little jig with his feet.

Show off…the girls will like you. "T'at one with all his worldly goods sharing a horse with Aaron is T'omas Akkers, who is looking for a wife an' a safe an' good piece of land to farm, not necessarily in t'at order. He can also play a recorder an' has been practicin' hopin' to charm with his music instead of t'personality t'at he does not ha'."

Thomas waved up to the lookout blushing as he did so. "T' next is Jordan Croker." The named man made a small bow. "He needs a horse all on his own. He heard t'at you need a potter an' he is a cracked anyway. Not content with t'at he also likes to make salami, which we are sick of eatin' by now. Last t'ere is Ulric Godwinson."

"No, it isn't," came in a whisper from the talker.

"He is a fisherman from Warkworth who lost his family an' everythin' else to t'Brotherhood an' has left t' sea far behind to make new start. He seems bit gloomy, but he's a good man who likes a laugh. He is willin' to try to be anythin' you need, seeing t'at you won't need fisherman in t'mountains." Harald and Aine started down the path from the lookout.

"Well t'en, I welcome you all to t'valley of t'Mice. I am on duty out here until lunch, but I'll see you all later. Aine an' Harald 'll see you in to t'valley an' answer your questions. Aine is our brewer and Harald is our miner. T'fact t'at he looks like a tall Dwarf is because he t'inks t'at he is one. We don't tell him he's not…in case he stops digging. It is day time now, an' most of our people 'll be working, but you'll meet everyone tonight."

"T'omas an' Arthur, feel free to have a word with Giles on the way in. He'll be t'one working in t'fields an'complainin' about not havin' enough farmers in t'village…so cheer him up 'n' tell him t'at you are hunters or somethin' t'at is nothin' to do with farmin', will you please. You won't be a marryin' him, so you don't have to try an' stay on his good side."

Harald Pitt

Aine took the lead. *She is wiggling her butt at them as she walks.* Harald grinned as he brought up the rear. *I need to stay back and leave room behind Ulric for Astrid. Evilhalt…so let us talk in Dwarven.* "So, what have you been told is here?"

"Ulric told me t'ere were very pretty girls an' lots of money. I guess it is not real true, but I'm a youngest son of a farmer with no prospects at home, so as long as I can get a farm an' a wife I will be coming out well ahead."

"There is lots of money, but little to spend it on. T' women are very pretty, but t'ey are also very fussy…you Ulric…what do you ha' to offer?

"I have been told that I am good looking, that I am good in bed and I am well-hung," was the smug reply.

"Is t'at all?"

"I have never needed more with a woman," he said even more smugly. Harald just grunted in reply. *I don't want to alert the man at this stage, and there is no other way to answer a statement that is so stupid.*

Aine Bragwr

A ine paused at the gate waiting for it to open. *This one is Aaron, I think*
"Well, what are you looking for here?"

"Like Ulric I have lost everything and want to start again. We lived outside
Glengate and I went away to Evilhalt selling a load of leather and when I got
back everything had been burnt to the ground, killed or taken. I was told that
it was the Khitan but, from what I hear, the Khitan have been getting a lot of
blame that does not belong to them.

"It has been a hard few years, but I was working for someone else in Greensin when the Metropolitan told me that it was time for me to put it all behind
me and start again. I am looking forward to that. I am not as young as the
others and I am not looking for romance.

"My marriage was arranged in the first place and we did not love each other,
but I loved my children, and my wife and I were well suited, and I will always
miss her. We never really loved each other, but she turned into being my best
friend and a good friend is hard to replace."

The gate is opening and the first thing he gets to see is four Khitan on horses
"I guess that I won't necessarily be leaving the Khitan behind then. I know that
there was one with you at Greensin. I didn't know that you had several. Do they
live here or are they just passing through?"

"We have our own little clan growing here now. You will like them. We all
do. The blonde one on the right is one of our Presbytera."

"A Khitan Presbytera?"

"It is complicated." They started walking up the path to the village. *I had
better speak up so that they all can hear me.* "You can see some of our fields
ahead of us. This entire area can be ploughed or used for orchards. We have
water from our river here and the flocks can graze further up the valley and in
our upland meadow.

"You can see how rich the grass is and we are growing marvellous crops.
You can see Giles over there." She waved. "Two are them are farmers, Giles...I
will bring them over later." He grinned and mimed raising his head and hands
as if giving a prayer of thanks to heaven before waving back and returning to
his work. "He will be so glad that you are here."

"Your land," asked Thomas "who actually owns it? If we stay, will we have
our own fields?"

"That is an interesting question. I presume you heard how we started?" *At
least they are all nodding.* "Well, we have always just worked for each other.

I know it may sound silly, but we are really just trying to feed ourselves and be safe and happy. It is not as if we need to get rich. We just do what needs to be done.

"For instance…Aaron, is it?" He nodded, and Aine continued. "Dulcie will be so happy to see you. She is normally our carpenter but because no one else can do tanning she has to take time off to make leather when so much of the village needs her attention as a carpenter.

"She is also the only one who can make pots…and Jordan, please do not laugh when you see one. She is trying so hard. She is going to want to marry you both just for making her life so much easier." *Now, that is a thought.*

"I nearly forgot. Have you been warned about our customs here?" *Damn, now they are shaking their heads.* "If she wanted to marry both of you and you didn't mind, the priests would probably allow it. As well, do not be surprised if you see women who are dressed only in a leather skirt. We have grown used to not wearing much. We had so little when we were slaves and now we are comfortable that way.

"The church knows about our customs and does not mind. We regard it as rude for a man to stare at a woman's breasts…that may take some practice for you. As well, it will be best if you leave it to the women to introduce themselves. That way you will quickest find out who is unmarried and who is interested in men. By the way, in case it is important, I am both unmarried and very interested in men…if they be good ones."

Astrid

*T*he others are all looking at the land and the fields, and looking at their *future. Ulric is looking at the boundaries of the valley. It looks like he is trying to find a way in or out. You are so mine. You are going to tell me all about Svein and what he is up to so that I can take him all unsuspecting just like taking a baby seal out on the ice.*

Aine

B y now they had passed through the village wall. Aine first pointed out her brewhouse, just after the old slave barracks, with its several levels for the malting floor and brewing areas. It even has a tunnel back into the slope for storage. That made it one of the largest buildings. Next door was their bakery and between was their shared chimney.

I suppose their purpose does not really need explanation, the sharp smell of hops, blended with those of malt and yeast makes their purpose readily evident. She then turned to the other side of their single overly wide street, where she pointed out the lookout on the roof of the Hall and then explained about the gong.

"I will take you now to meet the Princesses, and then I will start to show you around the village." *The men are looking all around. It is just a normal day... nothing special, but I suppose that, from their view, they see a village street, one with no apparent shops, but with several workshops in use and several other buildings that are closed up tight. Some looked deserted and in need of maintenance...because they are.*

A few people move about, stopping to look at them out of curiosity. Dulcie and Tabitha are working on the roof frame of one of the houses further up the slope of the valley and behind the workshops. Both are only wearing a kilt. Despite me telling them, the men are finding it hard not to stare, but four of them are trying.

Astrid's Ulric isn't even making an attempt. Oh, Saint Ursula, he just licked his lips! From the Mouse Hall, I can hear Ruth leading a group of young female voices in a recitation of declensions of Latin verbs. I suppose it should all be explained. "We still have many empty buildings that need repairing, so people can move in, as Dulcie and Tabitha"—she waved in their direction—"are doing. We have many spare workshops, but I will show you all of that later."

Basil is up ahead, and he has a large pouch at his side. It will have shackles and such in it. Lakshmi is with him, as if they are just offhandedly talking and our Fathers are standing near them. Ulric stopped when he saw the Fathers, and has casually crossed behind the others to stay away from them. I will bet that Astrid gets Basil to nab him soon. She moved back behind the other two, trying to stay out of their way.

Basil has moved forward to Ulric's left and Lakshmi has gone to his right. How to distract...? She pointed at the roof of the Hall of Mouse. "Up there you will notice that we have our own gargoyle. We picked her up in Dwarvenholme." *They are moving into place.*

Basil silently held out one finger, then two, then three...and he and Lakshmi moved to grab an arm each. Basil had already slapped a shackle on one wrist, and he moved it towards Lakshmi and the other end of the shackle went on the other wrist before Ulric realised that he had been taken. *He is caught between them.*

"Don't be alarmed." *Ulric is starting to struggle and protest, and they are turning to see what is happening and reaching for their weapons.* "He has been lying to you since he met you and he is here under false pretences to spy on us." *Is that calm enough?* Ulric started to make spluttering noises.

"Save it," said Basil to him "everyone come inside, and it will all be explained."

Astrid

*U*lric *is well caught, and the other four are leaving their horses, but they are now moving a little nervously as they enter the hall. The Princesses are sitting on their chairs up front with Nikephorus and Valeria waiting behind them. The attendants are looking timidly at the people starting to fill up the room.*

As they move forward uncertainly, they can hear others entering behind them. They look at Ulric disarmed and struggling in Basil's grip. He is moving the wrist shackle around to keep him off balance. I think that they are noticing that only Aine is standing near them. Even Harald has dropped back, and no one is making any move to threaten them.

"Greetings," said Theodora to the four other men who now stood apart from Ulric, who had been taken to the side. "And if your purpose here is honest, welcome to Mousehole. I am the Princess Theodora, and this is the Princess Rani, my husband. You will get to meet the rest of us later." She waved in Ulric's direction.

"The man with you has been arrested because he is here as a spy for our enemies. We will now let him speak and deal briefly with him and then we can get on to more pleasant matters. You can then introduce yourselves, and the ladies watching from behind you can start to find out all about you."

She looked at Ulric. "Hello, Ulric," she said. "Why don't you tell us about yourself and why you are here?"

Ulric swallowed. "I don't know you and I have done nothing wrong. I made my way here all the way from Warkworth because I heard about the wealth and the women, and was told that you wanted men here. I was obviously wrong so, if you let me go, I will leave here and I promise you that I will never try and return."

"From Warkworth?" asked Rani. "Are you sure that you are not from Wolfneck, where your sword and your jewellery say you are from?"

"I have been there, that is where I bought this stuff. I was a sailor and fisherman and I travelled a lot."

"So, you would know this girl then?" and she waved Danelis forward. The silver-haired girl had followed them in and now smiled at the other four and glared at Ulric.

"She is not from Wolfneck," said Ulric. *Despite having slipped and fallen into the crapper, he still cannot keep his eyes off her boobs.*

"No, she isn't," said Theodora. "Where are you from Danelis, and when did you leave there?"

"I was born near Warkworth," said Danelis "and I was taken from there four years ago and this man may have visited there, because I think that I saw him come off a boat once, but he is not from those parts. It is only a small village on the west coast, and everyone knows everyone in the area."

"She is lying for some reason," said Ulric desperately.

It is time to take off my ring. There is an immediate reaction from the other four, who see me, but Ulric is facing the wrong way and has not seen me appear behind him. Now, I get to scare the shit out of him. "So, how is Svein then?" Ulric tried to spin around as a look of horror appeared on his face. Astrid moved around to where he could see her. "When did you leave him in Wolfneck? How is my hometown? Is my family well?"

"You are dead...I was told..." he spluttered.

"I am sure my darling former betrothed has told you many things. He is so like that...generous in his lies...by the way, that is my husband who is holding you. His name is Basil Akritas and like you and me, he is part-Kharl. But unlike us, he is from Darkreach and is a Tribune — a high officer in Hrothnog's service — and he has spent his life looking for criminals and traitors.

"You are both of those, and you and he and I are going to have a very long talk. You are going to tell us everything you know about Svein, and who he works for and where he goes. To help you and your memory, our Princess will cast a spell on you when we need her to, and you will tell us everything that you thought that you had forgotten about your life. After that we may have to execute you if we think that you have tried to hide anything or if you are evil enough. I do so hope that will prove to be the case."

During this Ulric's knees started to give way. *He knows that he is caught. He is looking frantically at the other four, but they have drawn further away from him with odd looks on their faces as I spoke. Both my words and his reaction to them have told them all that they need to know, and they no longer want to be seen as being associated with him. I don't blame them.*

Rani looked at the priests whispering to each other. Father Christopher spoke up. "I get nothing from him, but Theodule says that he has the feel of evil about him. It is no exact proof with only one of us, but then it is only a feeling anyway. He looked at us and then tried to avoid us when he came in, as if he feared what we might see of him." Rani nodded.

"Thank you, Excellencies. Can we please take Ulric away now and start to renew our old acquaintance? Ulric used to make me many promises…almost as many as Svein did. I am sure that we have so much to catch up on about Wolfneck, and I am also sure the unmarried ladies want to find out about these nice men, and the nice men look worried enough without us cluttering up the room. Ulric is an unpleasantry that you can all do without for a while, but I am far more interested in him than in what the other men have to offer."

"Go," said Theodora, "and call me if you need me."

Ulric was taken out of the room, to be stripped and attached to the frame in the yard near the wall. *We have never gotten around to disposing of it and it is proving useful to have around.*

Theodora do Hrothnog

*E*veryone is watching them leave. We need to make a new start. We don't want to lose four at once because we have terrified them. The girls will never forgive us. I know we will get them to introduce themselves and what they have to offer.*

Several women behind them were very intently listening, and Dulcie, who had also followed them in and still had a bow saw in her hand, gave out a faint cheer when the occupations of Jordan and Aaron were given.

Theodora stood up once the introductions had been made. "Tonight, we will have a welcome feast. You will all get a chance to know these men a lot better then. We will need to find out if they can dance for a start. Aine and Harald will be showing them around the village for the rest of the day, so those of you who have things to do, get back to work and answer any questions they have if you see them and we will see you all later tonight."

Chapter VIII

Aine
A little while later

Thomas and Arthur had unloaded their horses and gone straight out to where Giles was working. *I get to just stand around and listen to them talk soil and ploughing. They are not even interested in my poor vines on the hill.*

They spent the rest of the day with him alternately working, talking and looking over the place, tasting the soil and rubbing it between their hands, looking at the new fruit trees and other things. There was a lot of waving of hands and walking back and forward as if measuring new fields for the plough. What a farmer could bring with him on a horse to a new village was revealed when Arthur came back inside the wall and reappeared with the share of a new heavy plough, a parting gift from his family.

That is welcome. We only have a light one now, and once this one is mounted on a frame, we can use it on some of the heavier soil and so Giles can plough further away from the river flat with its risk of flooding and corn rust.

Thomas has brought his own plough as well as seed bags for wheat, barley, and other corn. He even has some vegetable seeds. The seeds were also a family gift on his leaving as he had spent all of his money on the plough. Giles seems very pleased..

Aaron is just wandering around looking lost. I will dump this lot and go see if I can help him find a place to set up. He was talking to Dulcie, briefly. I notice that she pointed at where she did her work near the valley gate. She has nothing permanent set up and he shook his head at where she

works. Where can I get him to go?

I guess that we'll explore the area outside the valley. He seems happy enough to announce that, if he can get some stonework done, there is a much better place to work below the bridge where the smell of tanning will not float through the valley. While he was out the valley, he casually asked about the smell that was hanging around the entrance and was told about the dragon.

His excitement is evident and while he runs back inside for knives and his horse, I had better grab Harald. I think that we are about to spend the rest of the day cutting and cleaning dragon hide and weighing it down in the river below the bridge where he wants to set up. "Do you realise how much this is worth?" he asked.

Of course, Stefan would encourage him. "I can make, not tan, an if'n you can tan enough," said Stefan, "t'en t'ere'll be new leather armour of t'finest material comin' up for everyone an' all t'same type, not t'hodge-podge of styles an' material t'at we ha' now," he said.

"I'm more used to pouches, but I've at least some experience with armour now an' we don't ha' enough metal for everyone so we can start with t'is. By t'way I hope you can use t'at bow an' sword. I am in charge of training t' militia here an' practice is on every Krondag at least. We've been attacked here before an' it is likely to happen sometime again, even if you do not join one of our expeditions out."

Astrid
Some time later

Well, *Ulric is proving to have a wealth of information.* He was trussed up and stripped and then presented with some of the items that would be used on him. He was told about what had happened to others secured in the same place. He was at first reluctant to talk. "He even lied about his size. How can we trust him anyway?" she said.

Now to use one of Bianca's tricks and sound eager…well, I am anyway. "Can I get Bianca and we will see how long he lasts? I want to try some of the things on him that his master and he said they wanted to do to me." She began to outline a few ideas, and show him some items, until he started looking at her with fear and then he began to talk.

Astrid kept sitting in front of him and playing with the leather strap-on phallus as he talked to remind him. *Bianca is right. Once you have their attention, it is not really important what you actually do to them. It is what they think you are going to do. If they are cowards, then their own fear works against them.*

It turned out that he had been with Svein for many years and was his right-hand man. They really had not known that Astrid had survived as no sign had been seen of her since she left. It was thought that she had died in that first blizzard and her body had never been found. They had heard of a part-Kharl girl with teeth called the Cat, but she was supposed to be from Darkreach.

I suppose that no one ever called me that at home. "Don't worry, dear," said Basil. "If they know little about you then you will come more of a surprise for them."

It turned out that Svein made regular trips to the Shunned Isle. Ulric said that only Svein went on to the land there. Ulric had stayed on the boat to prevent the crew from leaving with it in fear of what might happen to them. They were well paid for those trips. They had also done raids on farms near the coast, sometimes making it look like Khitan work, mainly when they were in Brotherhood areas.

Sometimes it was to look as if it was done by the Brotherhood, if it was outside their land. Occasionally, if she was beautiful, they took a woman…they had taken three to the Shunned Isle over the last year and they had also bought some from the Brotherhood and sold them in Skrice on Neron Island north of Wolfneck.

Unprompted, he mentioned having seen a huge boat with two masts with its hull clad in metal. It had been in a harbour on the Shunned Isle. He had asked Svein what it was, only to be told to be silent and never to mention it to anyone. Basil nodded at that. *That sounds like the big boat my husband was worried about. I guess that he was right about it.*

Basil Akritas

It took a bit of persuasion, but Ulric admitted taking a child from the Brotherhood to the Shunned Isle. No money had changed hands.

Ulric may say that he doesn't know what she was going for, but I don't believe him and what is more I don't care if he is lying. Unknowingly, he has just signed his own death warrant. I haven't told him this and my wife is managing to stay silent. We will encourage him to just keep on talking. Whatever else he has done, he is now on record as a child slaver. That is already established as a capital offence here in Mousehole.

Basil wrote down everything that he said. *It will be compared with what others have told me. He doesn't have any new names, but there are places and descriptions of people. Some of the northern villages are so small that this should be enough, although I am certain that we already knew of most of these and the Metropolitan has been informed of them.*

However, I will add it all to the next package for the Metropolitan in case they were not on the last list. When he seemed drained of information he was dumped in a cell beside Vengeance.

I get to put a naked Ulric away, putting him and his clothes in the cell two away from Vengeance and checking the locks and bars, making sure that the two had food for the night and the other things that are done with prisoners. Meanwhile, my wife gleefully introduces the two:

"Vengeance…this is Ulric. Ulric works more directly for the Masters than you do. He told us of taking slaves from a man who sounds just like your Brother Micah and taking messages to the Masters from one who sounds like your Brother Job. He is guilty of torture, arson, rape, and murder and he knows that they are wrong, but he is a weak and evil man and so he does them anyway.

"Ulric…this is Vengeance. Vengeance works as a Flail of God for the one who gave you the message to the creatures on Shunned Isle. He is guilty of torture, arson, rape, and murder but, unlike you, he tells himself that he is doing the work of God and so he is happy to live with his evil, and is so twisted in his head that he thinks he does good."

The two men are looking at each other with an expression of repugnance on their faces. "We will leave you two alone now. I am sure that you have a lot of mutual friends to discuss and mutual hobbies to compare notes on."

It is time to go for dinner, but I am tempted now to stay. She cannot resist poking people. "That should make for some interesting conversation."

Dulcie ferch Mari y Saer
Early that evening

I like it. It is nightfall, and he has already unloaded his gear into an abandoned workshop, and we are assembling his kick wheel. We have even talked about what is needed in fixing the door and a few other things so that he can live above it. He keeps sneaking looks at my breasts, but at least he looks embarrassed if I catch him.

I have taken him out to where I have built a kiln and he has pronounced it good enough to start work with. He wanted to go off and look at my clay source, and I don't think that was an excuse to get me alone. He was properly disappointed to find that the best source lies in the upper valley and a day's trip away.

At least, he is poking at what I have left wrapped in wet cloths and seems satisfied. From the way he is going about things, whether he gains a wife or not, he is setting up shop in the valley. I approve of his attitude. She moved closer to where he was.

By this Saint Bean that Christopher talks about, he is even making polite noises about some of my plates and bowls, and the best that can be said of them is that they work…if you don't mind them not always sitting flat even on a table. I suppose that he must be flirting with me. I guess that he likes what he sees.

Ayesha

*W*e take any excuse for a party. At least the new men have a chance to see our little village of Mice at its best. Aine has a barrel of new ale of the first brewing brought out and tapped. We get to tell stories, sing songs, dance dances and play music. Especially dances are danced. With Nikephorus and four more men there it means that the women who want to, and it seems like almost all of them, can dance even more.*

*I*am sure there is some sort of plot going on. I am not sure exactly who is a part of it, but it has to involve at least Anahita, Bianca, Kāhina and Astrid. At least Astrid I am sure of. She has a grin on her face that is too obvious. It is the same sort of look that she had on her face when she and Basil were getting the Princesses together.*

The others have a look on their faces that is just too bland. Every time I stand up, I seem to be worked into a dance. What is more, I am usually steered into a dance with Hulagu. I am sometimes allowed to dance with Basil or Father Christopher, but never with one of the new men. Whenever one heads my way, he is headed off by one of the four and taken elsewhere. Perhaps it is the way of Allah, the Wise, telling me not to do these things.

Stefan

That night, during the dance, while she was feeding Aneurin, Bryony nervously asked Stefan whether he wanted to marry her, or if he was happy with just having her. "Many men are happy to just take a woman without any ties, and that is what I wanted and agreed to when we started. If that is what you want, then I am happy to not change anything."

Well, that is a surprise, but a pleasant one. Stefan bent down and kissed her on the cheek and smiled. "I've been wondering an' a hopin' when you'd change your mind. In t' morning t'en we do need to go an' talk with t' Fathers about what sort of ceremony you can accept."

"I have already done that. I hope you don't mind."

"No, why would I mind? 're you goin' to tell me how I am to be gettin' a married or will it be a surprise as well? What did make you change your mind?"

"The dragon. I realised that, if you died Aneurin would be mine, by the law of my land, but he would not really have a father by the rules of yours, and I would miss you too much if you…left…for any reason. I don't have a priest of my religion here now, and the only one who ever was here was one of the bandits and evil. That is not a good way to keep me loyal to what I was taught."

"So, I am going to join you and become a Christian, and we will have a Christian wedding. It seems that we will soon be headed towards Rising Mud and I will be going with you to hopefully clear my home of any people that may be there who are there as servants of the Masters. I know that I would have been given up as lost some time ago, but this way I might be able to come back from the dead for them and be able to show off my husband and my child to any who knew me and to make up for my loss. I hope you don't mind."

He kissed her again. "I did make t'at decision some time ago. I'll take you on whatever terms I can ha' you on. I love you, you silly girl. Now let me try an' put t' heir to bed an' we can go back to t' dance an' make an announcement to head off any of t'ese new men askin' you an' ha'you forgettin' who t' father of your child is…seein' t'at t'ey all seem to dance better t'an I do."

She may have made a playful punch at me, but she has a happy smile on her face.

Ayesha

The biggest sensation of the night, overshadowing a mere wedding announcement, was when Verily brought out the dulcimer that she had bought in Darkreach, and then once it was set up before a chair, brought out the musician who would play it.

Make may be playing a Brotherhood hymn, but few of the audience know that. All they know is that she is making a magical sound from the instrument. The tune is not a complex one, and Kãhina is the first to join in with a drum, then Elizabeth is able to join in on her shawm. Make is asked to play it again and Dulcie joined in with her sackbut, Ruth with a lute and Bianca with a recorder.

It is lovely sounding music, even if Bianca confided in me that there is a crude tavern song parodying it that is popular in Freehold. The new men, accustomed most of the time to no more than a simple lute, or fiddle and drums that are often roughly played, are astounded.

Make played a couple more pieces and then, confused by the applause, fled out of the hall. *The main thing was that at least for a short time, she was away from the kitchen and actually seemed pleased with the reaction. People had actually liked something that she did, and she knows that.*

Ayesha
The middle of the night

May Shaitan take those four women to perdition. I wake up alone in my bed and I am having those cursed dreams again.

Theodule Cephalou
12th Undecim

It is my turn to go up to Dhargev for Krondag services. Ayesha, Aziz, Verily, and my wife and I keep explaining the faith to the Hobs. It is made easier because Gukludqshiyicisi has returned from his first trip to the Dwarves with jewellery, several shields and some weapons.

At least he has shortened his name to Guk for trading with the Dwarves and other outsiders and already has bought another horse. He is busy loading food and cloth for the next trip and is taking orders for weapons and measuring Hobs for armour. I am surprised. He already has a couple of Dwarven words and has left his oldest son to stay with Thord to learn more.

Next trip, he wants a daughter to stay behind, and so on until all his children can speak Dwarven. What do I do about him sending his children to Mousehole to learn other languages? I suppose that I say yes, and hope that the Princesses won't mind. Maybe we can charge people to come to Ruth's school. I know that my wife will be keen on that idea.

That means that the next trip has to be done by carpet to bring back a passenger. At any rate, the fact that the trader has returned to them has been one more proof that there is a new and bright future ahead for the tribe of the Cenubarkincilari. I note that Guk has taken time out from his loading to attend closely to what I have to say in my service, even if he cannot understand it all. He is making sure that he and his family are sitting up at the very front.

Nacibdamɪr

*T*o my surprise, I am happy. There is less grumbling around the village. People are even starting to listen a little to what I say without looking at one of the Women's Council first. I have even overheard people saying that I am bringing them wealth and security by my wise leadership.

I think that I need to keep on doing what Princess Theodora quietly said to me. I have to say little and to let everything go on when it is going smoothly and just sit back and take the credit. I am even having mothers starting to come to me about their daughters. I don't want to rush into that. The first offers will not be the best.

Theodule

"**B**ecause Father Christopher is going out of Mousehole to again fight the setanyii," he says to his congregation, "I am not sure when one of us will be back again, but it will be as soon as we can. I am sure that you all want the setanyii defeated." *Yes, they all agree that it is a very good idea. They certainly don't seem to want the creatures back ruining their lives when* *everything is starting to look so good for the tribe.*

Stefan
14th Undecim

Bryony was confessed and baptised before her wedding. The bride was given away by Rani and attended by Dulcie and Aine, both of whom came from the Swamp as well.

I am attended by Arthur, much to his surprise, and by Hulagu. To my surprise, I have ended up with a beautiful bride. She is dressed in a form-hugging green silk bliaut to contrast with her red hair. It has an unusual plunging neckline that comes down deep into her cleavage.

At least now I know why. The dress needs to be low to accommodate the long necklace of green jade with matching rings, earrings and bracelets that show up against her red hair and pale freckled skin. We may have been lovers for over a year, but I just want to take her to bed all over again as if it were our first night.

Chapter IX

Rani
Late on the 15th of Undecim

*W*ho among the Mice should go out on this expedition to the Swamp is
*a very ticklish question. For a start, Theo-dear has very firmly put her
foot down and declared that I am not going, nor is she allowing anyone else who
was born in Haven to go along.*

*I cannot even reasonably complain about what she has decided. She is comp-
letely right, the most serious brewing conflict in The Land at present, apart from
the ongoing insanity of the Brotherhood, is the centuries old dispute between us
and the Swamp that was not even halted by The Burning.*

*The fact that there is an inherent religious dimension always adds fuel to
any likelihood of war, and taking an unmistakably Havenite face with a group
of strangers into the Swamp at present would near guarantee that an archer
would shoot at us before we can say anything to anyone. We would be seen
as a prelude to invasion—particularly if they somehow identify me as a Battle
Mage. There is no such thing as stripping off and painting your breasts to
show that you have a peaceful intent there.*

*Apart from that, I am not sure what we face in The Swamp, and it is hard
to know what to take if you do not know what you are about to confront. If the
scribbled list in Old Speech is to be believed, there is a pattern of the Masters
somewhere near Rising Mud, even if Conrad had somehow not mentioned
it when he was questioned. It is even possible that he might not have known
about his local Pattern, seeing that he used the one in Pavitra Phāṭaka.*

*With luck it might not even be used at present. That would be too much to
ask for. There are most likely going to be servants of the Masters there, and
probably quite competent and deadly ones. We need to take them by surprise.
We have been lucky so far in that we have been able to take each little group*

of their enemy unexpectedly as they approached us. This has meant that we have suffered no losses so far.

Now we only have a few descriptions of people and some names, which may not even be real ones, from the late unlamented Conrad and his men, but we have no idea how deeply these people are entrenched into the power structure of the area that calls itself The Confederation of the Free, nor do we know what their powers are.

What is worse is that now we are going into one of our enemy's safe places, not them coming to ours. Unless we are lucky, our people may all die. Alternatively, we might even kill our enemies accidentally and not know it. The very name that the villages of The Swamp use among themselves, and which is totally ignored by everyone else, is a clue to how difficult this is going to be.

Each village loftily insists on their individual independence, and they are unlikely to co-operate with someone from outside their watery jungles on the simple, and to them sufficient grounds, that they are Outsiders. For them, it is all about their family being first and only then the village.

Whoever makes decisions in any area will want to be seen to be free of any outside influence. This stubborn independence and insistence on their individual rights over any sense of community holds the area back in so many ways. They are a nuisance and a refuge for thieves and outlaws from other lands, but only Haven has a major issue with the Swamp. They are too fragmented to be a threat to anyone else.

To an extent it is just like the villages and towns around Lake Erave. Even if they come together, they will never be a real threat to anyone, but then those who live around the Lake don't pretend to be a unified people. To an extent, we in Mousehole have faced the same issue of independence because of the dragon.

Theo-dear declined to ask her Hrothnog for help, so that we could be seen by others to be independent and standing free. The problem, as it proved, was one we were able to solve for ourselves, but we hadn't known it at the time. For us though, it was a risk that we had accepted for a longer-term gain and not a matter of principle.

Rani sighed. *Having imposed on ourselves the task of clearing The Land from the Masters, this leaves us with only a few choices as to action. Firstly, we can fly down at night, hide the saddles, and sneak into the town surreptitiously and do what we have to do as quietly as we can…then try to leave the same way.*

Secondly, we could go to the village in force, and projecting all of the power that we can muster, trumpet aloud our quest and hope that whoever runs Rising Mud this year will co-operate with us. This is a very unlikely outcome. It is more likely that whoever is in power there is one of those that we will have to kill.

Thirdly, we can just ignore whoever is in control, go in openly and hope that we can accomplish our mission without too much loss when we fight off a whole village. Anything but the first option means that, unless we get all of the Masters' tools in one strike, it is likely that our descriptions, our strengths and our plans will be revealed to all of the world that is interested.

At present it is obvious, from what little Ulric had known, that we are still a mystery to the surviving Masters. Also the fact that we seem to know more about our enemy, or at least are better at making guesses about them, than our enemy knows or guesses about us, is probably a key to our success so far.

These questions lead to other questions, such as should we take babies with us? If we don't, it will restrict the numbers who can go and will take away some of our most effective combatants. If we do, it leads to the problem of keeping the children safe. If we take the babies and leave them out of the combat, it then leads to questions like whether taking someone to care for the babies is more of a waste than leaving all of the mothers behind in the first place.

There are still other questions. Such as the wisdom of taking Khitan with us if we are trying to be inconspicuous. If we go, it will be by saddle and carpet and that means that we can take no horses. While there are Khitan to be found almost everywhere, finding one that is without a horse is rare. Finding more than one like that is almost unknown.

Rani sighed again, more deeply this time. *I have been thinking about these questions ever since the defeat of the dragon. It is even a similar problem to that posed by the beast. We have limited resources to deploy away from the village. There are restrictions on who can go, and the exact tactics cannot be settled on until the actual situation presents itself to those who are there.*

One thing that is certain is that a priest has to be present so that they can locate and eliminate the pattern. That we need to send a mage is also apparent. That gives two names. If my wife goes, that will mean Basil and Ayesha will demand to go as well. But where Basil goes, Astrid will want to be as well, and she never leaves her children behind. Stefan and Bryony will be going and that means yet another baby.

There are two women from that village, Aine and Dulcie, but while Aine is quite competent with both a bow and a sword, Stefan tells me that Dulcie is still almost useless and can only be used in an emergency.

Astrid has been training Tabitha as both a scout and hunter with a spear and bow, and has already announced to me that she wants to take the girl on the next expedition out as she needs experience before she ends up being distracted by babies...which neatly ignores the question as to whether taking babies on a raid or trip distracts Astrid.

That gives me nine names already for spaces on ten saddles and a carpet. I will go to sleep on my questions and hope to have more clarity in the morning.

Rani
16th of Undecim

*J*ust like every other morning, it is no clearer. Thankfully, while the ideas turn
around in my head, for a few days I can just look at running a small village
with an influx of new residents and a trial coming up. At least Theo-dear looks
after the daily things for us. I only find out about most of the little problems
around the village after they are long past. It seems that my lovely wife has a
flair for soothing our local domestic issues, while I am expected to look after
the larger picture.

On that…what will it mean if we start to bring Guk's children down? What
if we do start a school? If we do that, we could bring in Hobs from Dhargev,
Fātima's children and anyone else that Hrothnog sends out of Darkreach,
young Dwarves from Dwarvenholme and possibly even some of the children
of Evilhalt or Lake Erave.

If we do that, we can mould the children as we want and make people look
at Mousehole, in the long-term, as a neutral place to go to for problems to
be solved. The idea of an education centre appeals to me and fits in well with
what I have planned for my mage school.

Rani was struck by a sudden thought. *We are going to the Swamp and will
be flying straight past the land of the Bear People. Like most of The Land, I
know very little about the odd people of that area. I know that many of them
are thought to be shape-shifters. I know that they are largely druids…but
unlike those of the Swamp, they do not steal and sacrifice cattle openly just
to annoy the people of Haven. I know that they like their privacy. Other than
that, I know nothing. I wonder if the women from the Swamp know any more.
I will ask.*

She pondered if the Bear People were ideal to talk to about their school. *I
am sure that they have their own schooling, but what if we can offer to educate
some of their children? We do have unique opportunities here. Perhaps we
can even teach them to be mages in a safe neutral place with no political
entanglements?*

*We have to be seen as being not prejudiced about different races and
attitudes at least. Surely that has to be attractive. We might have to take a
druid into the village, to bring the people of that religion in, but that will also
give us another possible teacher.*

*I will talk to Lādi and Sajāh and Ruth about how much it will cost, and
how much we can charge and where we will put children and teach them. It is*

just as well, with the new arrivals, that Dulcie can go back to being a full-time carpenter now. She will be kept busy with repairs to the abandoned buildings and she will need Tabitha to help her full-time as well.

After having been sitting and thinking awhile in her study, finally Rani went outside to discover that the usual tranquillity in the village was totally lacking. *Most of the time our people go about their work unhurriedly. Not today. The fact that we have two new workshops to set up, as well as new people to impress, seems to have struck a chord.*

She could see Goditha, Harald, Aziz and Verily with her babies, all dressed for heavy work and with picks and other tools for working earth and stone in a wheelbarrow and headed out of the village gate. *That would be the heavy construction crew then.*

They have the tanner with them and Aine, who normally only concerns herself with her brews and the crops to support them. That is right, I heard them talking about building a tannery downstream of the bridge. I suppose that once they are there Aaron will go on to where he is still looking at recovering skin from the dragon. What is Aine doing with them then?

Rani could hear singing coming from the workshop that was being set up for the spinners and weavers.,, *That is Make's voice. Usually Make is only found in the kitchen. Maybe last night marked a breakthrough in more ways than one for the girl.* She listened to the words. *I only have a few words of their language, but it sounds like she is singing what has to be a Brotherhood hymn. I wonder what the Muslim women who are also working there will think of that or if they even know what she sings.*

Looking down, I can see that Tabitha is working on repairing the door of a workshop while she is being supervised by Dulcie, who is herself working on making a shutter for someone's window as it lies across two sawhorses. I see Norbert and Shilpa hard at work in the smithy, by the faint sound of what is said at the other end of the village they are currently making hinges for Dulcie to then use.

I presume that all of the farmers are out in the fields and that the Khitan have the flocks somewhere. I can hear Naeve whistling in the dairy as she seethes milk in a pan so it can be turned into cheese, and Astrid and Basil are heading out of the village with the carpet rolled up over Astrid's shoulder and carrying an axe each…large axes for felling timber, while Basil has the babies. I wonder if I want to know what that is about. Why would you need both the carpet and axes?

Ruth has the small girls hard at work in their school. I can hear that going as well, so I will go and find Lãdi and Sajãh and see what they think about the idea of a school. As she went, she thought about the school. *One of the faults of the schools that I have been to, and my wife complains about the same thing, is that there is nothing practical in them.*

You come out of them with a lot of learning, but can do nothing practical for yourself. You need servants around to do things for you. I wonder if I should discuss this with Ruth. Our teacher already spends a small part of each day doing sports; making the girls run and throw things and ride and shoot little bows.

What if they spend, say, a half-day each week with a different person doing a trade for a while? Then, if they find one they like, or are good at, they can do that for the half a day each week and so learn something practical. That will not eat much into their book learning and will balance it so that they would not be so…well…as bookish as I have to admit I am.

We will also have to think about who else we can use as teachers. She took a seat on the bench that had been put on the veranda of the Hall of Mice as she thought and leant back. *At the moment Ruth has seven girls to teach ranging from seven to eleven years old and there were sixteen babies in the village and there are sure to be more of them on the way.*

From what my servants tell me, there is at least one on the way now. Within a few years they will all be in school. Ruth cannot teach all of them at once, as they will be learning different things. This will become even more the case if they take in students from outside. I will end up teaching magic.

My wife will have to settle down and learn how to teach. She can speak many languages at least. Ayesha and the priests are about to start work on the children. They already teach adults, now it is time to get them started on the younger ones. Even Lakshmi, with her knowledge of plants and potions will be of some use.

Yes, it will mean that the village will have to re-organise once we achieve what we have to do now, but it will work. It is not as if we have to work to make money. We only have to work to keep ourselves fed and safe. If we have to buy in food, it will not be the end of the world. We may even end up with assarts all around us who rely on us for protection and leadership and give, or sell, food to the valley in return.

Such a plan as I now have in my head will make us very safe as it will be in the best interests of all of the smaller independent areas to keep their children safe. She discovered that she had gone back to ruminating over things, but was now sitting in the sun on the veranda of the Hall of the Mouse as everything went on around her, instead of in her study.

Everyone is working, but none seem to object to the fact that I am just sitting here in the sun. It is as if everyone around me knows that I am also hard at work. My work just happens to be very different to theirs. Rani stood up and smiled. *Now, I have to find those women and talk about what we need to do to put my plan into practice.*

That night she discovered that her idea occasioned a buzz of conversation. After the common meal had finished, and those who had eaten in their own houses chose to join in, there was much discussion of her idea. *People are sitting around working out what they will need to do to make it work and several of the tradespeople are wondering which of the girls will end up as their apprentices.*

She had to smile at the bemused faces on the new men. *Here we are in a tavern full of beautiful women in various forms of dress, with drinks for free just for asking, with cards sitting ignored on a couple of tables, a chess set sits on another, there is a stack of instruments near the stage and people are sitting around talking excitedly about setting up a school.*

It must be almost the most alien thing that they have encountered in their short stay here so far. At least they are trying to fit in. They are not sitting together. Although people moved around, she noticed that Aine generally sat near the entrance to her taproom with the tanner near her. *Jordan the potter is talking mainly with Dulcie.*

The two farmers are with Giles and Naeve and a few of the other girls, Tabitha and Danelis in particular. Although they are talking with the men and drinking kaf, it is mainly the Muslim girls who are missing out. They do not seem concerned though. The arrival of new girls from Darkreach has led them to feel that they have not been forgotten.

And given their culture, they need fewer men to be happily married. One or two good ones, if the women get on well, would be enough. Norbert, Sajāh and Fortunata were proof that that arrangement worked well. Occasionally, as the mood took someone, music would be played, or a dance danced or taught. *It was almost like we are a huge family with everyone home for the night and happy with each other's company.*

During the night, she found out about the axes and the carpet. Dulcie was running out of timber and Astrid and Basil had turned into timber fellers for the nonce. They had taken the carpet to bring trimmed logs into the village from where they cut them. *I am not sure that I approve of this use of something that can be so easily torn, but Astrid swears that she is being careful with it.*

Rani went to have a word with her wife about making something more acceptable that would be sturdier than a carpet. *She was so pleased with her spell crafting for the saddles; let us see what she can come up with now.*

I am rewarded by seeing Theo-dear's eyes glaze over in a familiar fashion. She will now sit for the rest of the night in a corner nursing a glass of Aine's brandy, scarce acknowledging that I exist or even that she has a glass in her hand. She has found a slate from somewhere, and is alternately marking it and revising as she goes or just staring into nothing. No lovemaking for me tonight then.

Rani
17th of Undecim

The next morning, Rani had the solution to the problem of the Swamp. *It has taken many nights of sleeping on the problem. Maybe it was just that yesterday was the feast day of Saint Jude, the patron of lost causes; that had done it for me. Our Christian priest really does love preaching to a theme based on that saint. He makes me think.*

We will take all ten saddles and the carpet to the Bear People, travelling openly as we go. We have no indication that the Bear People are involved in any way with the Masters. No one that we have caught has ever mentioned having anything to do with the Bear People, or even going to their land.

While we are there, we will buy a donkey or a small packhorse and sedate it. Lakshmi has to have something in her herbs to do that. We can put the donkey on the carpet and fly into the Swamp towards Rising Mud. If Basil and Astrid can carry logs on it, then carrying a small animal will be easy. There they can hide the saddles and the carpet can return home, or to the Bear Land.

From there, our people will go on foot as a troop of entertainers and some people travelling with them. Hulagu can go to look after the donkey and we can make up a story about exile. Bryony and Aine will have to wear a mask until they choose to reveal themselves. It will be best for them to dress as women of the Caliphate.

That means that Ayesha will have to wear a veil as well, and so will Theo-dear. Ayesha has become very used to wearing just a headscarf. Now it is time for her to go back to a veil. As for my wife, well it is time for Salimah and her black eyes to come out again. She went out to find the ones that she wanted to go and set up a meeting with everyone for that night.

We also have to deal with Ulric, and we really have to make up our minds as to what to do with Vengeance. We cannot really hold him forever. We don't have the people for that and there is always a chance that he may escape and hurt someone.

Chapter X

Rani
17th of Undecim

*T*his is the hard part of being a Princess. No one talks about things like this in the stories. Ulric had been brought out to the frame and, despite his struggles, shackled into it. Some people came to watch, and Make and the new people were made to, but none except Astrid had a personal grievance against him, so there were not as many present as usual during a questioning.

Vengeance was also compelled to attend, but he was very well shackled and had guards in constant attendance on him. He was put where he could clearly see and hear Ulric. Theodora addressed Ulric.

"Basil tells me that he has gotten a lot of information from you and this would normally work in your favour, but he tells me that, among your other crimes, you have confessed to selling children into slavery for sex. We regard that as a capital crime here, regardless of where you committed the act. Before we execute you, I am going to see if there is anything else that you can tell us."

Despite his pleas and crying, Theodora cast a spell over him and quietened him. *It was a waste of time. The only new things we are getting from him are that he did know what the girl was being taken for and that the person who had given them the packages to take to the Masters was named by Svein as Brother Job.*

Svein told him that the whole Brotherhood worked for the Masters…whether they knew it or not, and that when the Masters took over everything his crew would be placed high in ruling The Land, and that he had been told that the Brotherhood would not be. They were just there to provide troops and to cause trouble.

Svein also told him that it was one of the Masters that had appeared to their First Prophet in a magic circle, and that the Masters made up their entire religion.

Despite his predicament, Ulric thinks that this is very funny. Vengeance was shaking his head. *His faith is still unshaken, and he keeps up a string of prayers in his own language, to try and stop himself hearing the truth. Make, however is sitting very still and has gone quite pale.*

When they had finished, they untied him and sat him down in shackles until the spell wore off. "Do you want to make confession before you die?" Theodora asked. Not surprisingly he did, and it was quite some time before Father Christopher indicated that he was finished. *Now we walk him to his death.*

With his head hung low and crying he was led, still chained, occasionally trying to struggle. He was walked out along the path towards the river with Basil behind him. Without warning, Basil suddenly pulled his head up and plunged a shortsword into his brain. He was unshackled and his body then dumped into the river. Christopher said prayers for him, but he was to go unburied.

Vengeance has been returned to his cell. I have made up my mind on his fate. Now I have to let him know. Rani went along to the cell and looked at the man. *His eyes are filled with hate as he returns my gaze.*

"I have decided that you have committed enough crimes against other people for us to justify executing you. I had nearly come around to deciding that, and listening to what I just heard confirmed it. I now agree with Father Christopher that it matters little that you think you are not sinning. That is not an excuse, but just a piece of logic that has no morality attached to it. What you have admitted that you have done against women and children is a sin punishable by death anywhere else apart from in your perverted land. Is there anything that you have to say to me that may change my mind?"

"He was an evil and a deranged man who had been told lies," Vengeance said. "I do not know who he spoke to that posed as one of our leaders, but it would not have been them. The Prophets spoke directly to Archangels and they still do so regularly.

"When you do murder me, I will go straight away to sit on the right hand of God as a martyr to the True Faith, so why should I try and change your mind? I regret that I have unfinished business, but I tried, and my failure will not be held against me. I do, however, want you to bring me the slave girl. I need to talk to her before you murder me."

"No, you will not," Rani said. "Your wants are no longer important if they conflict with the needs of others. She is starting to show signs of sense and I am not having you trying to further confuse her. I will give you tonight to collect your thoughts and to pray to the so-called Masters, the devils who you think are angels. Tomorrow we will take you out to the river to die after you have had breakfast."

Vengeance just nodded in reply. Rani looked at him. *He is very calm, far too calm for a person who has been told of his death. He is going to try and escape or to kill someone before he dies. We are going to have to do something about that.*

Rani
18th of Undecim

*H*e has finished his breakfast without issue…good. Now he is standing there pretending to be meek and waiting to be taken out. His hands are opening and closing. He is definitely waiting to try something. Basil and Verily are just standing and waiting for him. He is looking from one to another of us and we look back…there it is…

Suddenly Vengeance gave a lurch and then went down to his knees. "We knew that you were going to try something, so your food has a distillation of ghost mushrooms in it," said Basil. "You will be unconscious soon, and then we will carry you out and open your veins, and kill you before you wake up again and dump your body in the river. It is very merciful and much more so than you deserve."

That Vengeance was planning something is clear. He is struggling to move and failing and there is a look of pure hatred on his face as his consciousness slowly begins to slip away. I have to admit that I will be glad when he is gone. His was a wasted life.

Chapter XI

Rani
18th of Undecim, Saint Arthur's Day

*W*ith unpleasant tasks out of the way, the expedition to the south can be *gotten underway. Stefan, Bryony, Christopher, Theodora, Basil, Aine, Ayesha, Astrid, Hulagu and Tabitha will be going into the Swamp and I will be going on the carpet with them to the Bear People. There, I will stay and talk with the people.*

While I am there, Goditha can take the carpet, and the donkey, into the Swamp alongside the saddles and then come back for me. It seems to be a good plan. It remains to be seen how it will unfold in the light of day.

The only one of them with any real training in the geography of the Land was Bryony, and although she came from just next door to the Bear Folk, she only had a vague idea where they were going.

She thinks that if we follow the road that leads past Mousehole we will eventually reach one of their settlements. The maps that we have are just as vague. At least they indicate that one village is on the Tulky Wash, well upstream of where it joins the Rhastaputra River at Garthang Keep. Another, the one we will aim for, is supposed to be on one of the tributaries of the Tulky.

Bryony had read Simon's book, and he had visited the Bear People, but he was uncharacteristically very vague with the details of his visit. She thought from what he did say that the village might be on the Oberon River. Ayesha had told her that she had seen fires when she had left home, and that would be about right.

"We will leave in two days time on Firstday." Rani said. "This will allow a last trip up to Dhargev for a priest on Krondag and will let me fly along the route that the trader Guk will be taking. I will take Aziz with me and see what Guk thinks about a school. If he is agreeable, we might bring one of his children back to Mousehole straight away." *This has an advantage, right from the start. It will let us see how well the girls of Mousehole will accept an outsider coming in to their school.*

Rani
19th of Undecim

While Father Christopher performed the service and talked to the Hobs, Aziz loaded his mother, Boyokurek, on board the carpet and Rani took her for the flight in search of Guk. *I hope that she will be useful in persuading the trader and I also hope that Aziz's mother will get some pleasure from the trip.*

When they found Guk he was on the way back from the Dwarves again, and once he had the idea of a school explained to him, was delighted with it and almost visibly began swelling with pride. *His wife may have opened her eyes wide when I told him how much it will cost, but Guk has just thrust a purse of Dwarven money at me.*

He is looking over his children with a calculating eye, and saying that until he has more horses, he cannot send a son or one who could carry a good load. So we get his third daughter as the first from outside the valley at our school.

He is a very smart man for a simple trader. Now we are hearing how his prestige will rise further in the village from this. He may be unsure of how long he will leave her with us, but at least I made him promise that it will be at least to the end of the year of the Water Butterfly. His daughter will have at least a full year of learning, and then he and his wife can see if they think that it was worth their while to have more schooling for her.

When they left the trader, with the Hob girl riding on the carpet with Boyokurek, Rani got Aziz to ask her what her name was. *There is a lot of talk backwards and forwards as Aziz flies alongside the carpet. It is a lot more talk than just asking a name.* Rani was starting to get impatient when eventually Aziz answered her.

"She is called Zamratejedehar," said Aziz. "It means Emerald Dragon. You can call her Zamrat. She does not understand exactly what is going to happen to her, but then I am not sure her father did either. I am trying to explain to her, but us Hobs do not really have schools. We listen to the stories of the bards and of the priests at night when the work is done."

"She thinks this is going to be very easy for her and will not believe me when I say how hard it is, and that I must do it when I finish my work and she gets to do it all day instead of work. We will see how hard she finds it when we get back."

"You do realise, don't you, that you are going to have to help." *She is a very big girl.* "I don't even know how old she is."

"Help only when I not out on hunt or fighting Masters," replied Aziz. "That my job. Maybe Verily help, if Ząmrat trust my soft one. Until you have others for school, she not sleep in barracks alone, she stay with us. I ask age already. She seen seven years. Hobs get big quick…even girls."

It turns out that Aziz's mother enjoys flying very much, and now we have returned, she adds to the benefits of their new arrangement by excitedly describing her flight to the other women of the village. Being the first of their village to fly, before even any of the men, goes far toward enhancing her prestige in the eyes of all.

Rani
On the flight home

How do we fit Ząmrat in with the other girls? Maybe I should have thought this through better. Our first student speaks none of the tongues in general use in the village. Which one should we teach her first? Should we just teach her all of them?

It is obvious that Verily will be sitting down with her a lot to bring her to where she can understand what is going on without needing someone there all of the time. Luckily, Verily is one of our better linguists, and apart from the mage languages, speaks fluently most of the main tongues except Greek…and she is working hard on correcting that deficiency.

As they came into the valley, Dulcie was on duty at the lookout with one of the new men, the potter Jordan, and waved to them happily. *It is good to see that they are being shown that they will have responsibilities here. That is if that is what he is there to be shown. At least he has a bow with him, his sword at his side and a shield on his back.*

When they arrived at the village, her doubts about the young girls accepting the Hob evaporated like mist in the morning. That they would bring someone back must have been expected, as Ruth and Verily had all of the young ones out in the courtyard and everyone was wearing their kilts. Ząmrat started talking to Aziz when she saw this, and he replied. Rani looked quizzically at him.

"She ask why they dress like Hobs, not like soft ones," he said. "I say they do this to welcome her and honour her. She very happy with this. It very Hob thing to do. I take her now and introduce her."

Not much work is being done for the rest of the day at the school with Zqmrat being shown the village, and Verily being asked to explain things to her, and then Fortunata measuring her so that she has other clothes rather than just a kilt. We even have to explain that to her.

That is one reason she was ready to leave straight away to come with us. The only clothes she has ever owned are her kilt and her cloak and she had both of those on when we visited the family. Everything else she owns is either on her or in her pouches.

Chapter XII

Astrid
20th Undecim

A nice early morning and we are already further south than we have ever been, despite the carpet holding us back. Astrid scouted ahead as they flew, sometimes taking Hulagu and sometimes Tabitha with her. She would speed ahead and then, leaving someone on sky watch, come down to look for tracks on the path and near it. After landing for an early lunch, and to feed and change the babies, they went on following the old road.

Our road is obviously less used down here than it is near Mousehole. All we are seeing is animal tracks. It is so little used that we nearly missed a turn-off that leads up. It is probably the road up to the Caliphate. Now, it is just a track that has probably not been used since the fall of the bandits.

After that turn, the main road had grown even more disused than it had been before. From the air it could be seen, but from the ground it would have been hard to make out for most of its length, even if someone just stumbled on it. There was even a small Whitey-wood tree growing in the middle of the actual roadway after the turn-off, and the whole length is covered in dirt and grass and small shrubs.

It was obvious that with what we are doing, just our own traffic on the road around Mousehole will soon give away our location on its own without any other signs, as the roads are gradually cleared of the vegetation that still grows here.

It is just as well we are in the air and some of us staying high, for the same can be said about the Bear Folk village as can be said about the road. It is very hard to make out. It is built some way off the road down a slope in a large secluded forest dell. It is not, in any way, like a normal village that we are used to.

From the ground it would have been possible for most people to walk straight past it if no one was about. It was located on both sides of a small river, and the bridge over the river was the only normal thing about the settlement that could be seen. Almost all of the buildings were either built into the hillsides themselves, and so were only visible as doors and windows, or else were under mounds with grass growing over them.

At least they look a bit like some of the old buildings in Wolfneck. They are rounded like small hills but with an entrance just like the burial mounds in Darkreach, except that there are living people coming out of them to look at the riders in the sky. Still, despite the curiosity there is no sign of menace from below and Rani is sending Bryony, who speaks some Bear-tongue, to go down and ask if we have permission to enter the village.

Bryony ferch Daffyd

I wonder where I should land. I can see a couple of uniform and tended groves of trees with people in robes coming from them. Those would be the sacred groves then…better not land there.

Ahead is a group of tents with quite a few people around them. They don't look like the sort of tents that people live in. From what I can see they look to be set up inside like shops. Perhaps the tents are there for shade only or maybe if there is a shower of rain. If it is a market, then that would be a good place to land. More slowly she approached, making sure no one was beneath her.

I cannot see any signs of anyone acting aggressively towards me, and although there is a group of archers hurrying in my direction with bows like Astrid's in their hands, they have all of their arrows in quivers. Some of the people with robes are also hurrying towards me. I am going to wait until they all arrive before I complete my descent. They look official.

With a glance up to where the Mice waited in the sky, she started to look around at the people near her. *Most look more or less the same as people anywhere would look, but the adult men all have big beards and everyone wears very loose clothes, including some in voluminous plaid kilts.*

They all, both men and women, have long hair held back in a simple ponytail or a braid. I cannot see a lot of weapons on people's belts, but this is the middle of their village and they might not feel threatened. If they are really skin-changing Bear People, there are none in bear form at present that I can see, but there are lots of other animals around.

There are packs of dogs, some pigs running around with a young swineherd trying to keep order and even… She gave a start. *…In some of the nearby trees, some very large cats the size of a panther or of a leopard. Despite these animals, it all seems very calm and quiet. What with the little girls, it is often noisier than this in Mousehole, and we have far fewer people there.*

Speaking of which… Aneurin chose this moment to wake up and decide that he needed feeding. *I have a choice between having a crying baby or else possibly offending the people approaching by feeding him. Bugger them…* Tossing a mental coin, she unlaced and opened the top of her jerkin and pulled aside her top and took Aneurin out of his baby quiver and started feeding him.

She had only just got him settled and feeding when the bowmen arrived with one of what she thought were priests. *He is a large and very hairy man, and if anyone is going to turn into a bear right in front of me, I will bet on it being him. It is time to see if I learnt this tongue well enough to talk to them.*

She used her knees to steer herself down the last leg of the flight and gave a nervous giggle to herself as she did. *At least they will not see me as threatening.*

"I bring you greetings from the Princesses Rani and Theodora of Mousehole. My name is Bryony ferch Dafydd. I hope that I do not offend you in this, but my son Aneurin chose this moment to seek food and babies are not to be denied." *Actually, looking at the faces in front of me, if there was anything to see written there, it is approval.*

"You are from the Swamp," said the man in the robe who was at the front in a deep rumbly voice, "but you speak for some Princesses that we have never heard of before. Before we go any further, I will ask you to explain yourself."

I suppose that was to be expected and he reserves his welcome by not giving his name. I had better be good. Here comes the history of the last year in a few words. "I do not know if you are aware of this, but there is a road that runs along the foot of the mountains from the old days. It lays only a short walk out of your village here." She waved her free hand.

"Several days journey north on foot there is a hidden valley. I know not if you have lost anyone or anything over the last few years in an unexplained fashion in that direction…" *The man in robes and one of the men with bows are exchanging looks that do not need to be explained while several are looking at a young girl.* "I see that you have. Our village, which is called Mousehole, used to belong to a group of bandits, almost a small army of them actually."

Bryony continued without waiting for a reply. "These bandits worked for the creatures who held Dwarvenholme, and they sowed strife and violence and discord. Although we do not know why, it seems that they want The Land to dissolve into war…and it has almost worked.

"I was one of the many slaves from all over that they held thrall in the valley. A group of people, gathered by prophesy, came and set us free. They have now joined with the freed slaves and we now all call ourselves the village of Mousehole, which was the name of our valley before the Burning. We are now called the Mice." *That is the first real reaction I have had from them. Why would our name get them looking at each other?*

She went on. "Our liberators then went on to find and to free Dwarvenholme from those who held it. The Dwarves have now returned to their old home. We have also slain the dragon of the mountains, and defeated and then befriended the Cenubarkincilari, the southern hobgoblins." *I certainly have their attention now.*

"Despite our success these creatures, who call themselves the Masters, are not yet finished. They still hold sway in the minds of many evil men and seem to almost rule some places. We, that is the Mice,"—*again there is that reaction*—"wish to rid the world of these so-called Masters.

"We are an unusual group of people in many ways, gathered from all over The Land, but we are very strong in our valley. Our people come originally from the far west to the furthest east of The Land and from the cold north to the hot south. We are not all human."

"Our Princesses are in the sky, and seek permission from your rulers to land and to explain further about us and to discuss many things, including a school that we are setting up to teach the young of any land who wish to learn, including those who wish to learn to be mages. Did I mention that our Princess Rani used to be a Havenite battle mage and our Princess Theodora is a great grand-daughter of Hrothnog?"

As I speak, the look of caution that had been on the faces of the ones with bows is relaxing. They must have had some trouble here. I don't know what it was, but I seem to be explaining things to them. Eventually the man ahead of her spoke.

"I am Cathal, and I am the Magister of this village of Birchdingle. The Chief Magister of our people is Calgacus and he is approaching now. Call down your people from the sky. We lack a palace, such as Princesses are used to, but we can retire to a tavern, if that is acceptable, to have discussions. I must ask. Do you have those saddles for sale? I have never seen so many people in flight before. It must be…useful."

Bryony waved up to those above and turned back to Cathal. "It was what allowed us to defeat the dragon…that and our other magic and great bravery, but I will let one of our storytellers tell you about that. Do you like storytellers?" she asked innocently. *I am fairly sure of the answer to that question at least.*

"We regard it as one of the greatest arts. We look forward to hearing from them tonight."

Astrid

A strid led the Mice down. *I thought that I saw Bryony feeding her young-ling. Well, if seeing one warrior with a child at her breast was unexpected enough, seeing two will be even more unusual. I only have Hindi to use on them.*

"Greetings, I hope someone understands this tongue and I should point them out, but my arms are both occupied. I am Astrid the Cat." *Why would a simple introduction from me have so many people looking at each other?* She continued.

"The one sitting on the carpet in the silk is the Princess Rani and the one with the golden eyes on the saddle beside me is the Princess Theodora. Now, I can leave you lot to sort things out and be diplomatic while I get back to business. Is there somewhere where I can clean some diapers that greatly need changing?"

Rani

T he Mice were led off to a building built into a nearby hillside. *It is not obviously a tavern until one notices tables and benches outside it in the shade of a stand of the medical hop bushes. There is no sign outside. Even at home we have the owner's name.* Rani stayed silent. *My wife is being pleasant to the locals. Let us see if they can resist her Darkreach Court charm offensive.*

Rani looked around. *I suppose that, like Mousehole, when you have only a limited number of people, everyone knows where everything is and you don't need signs. Mind you, although it is hard to tell because of the way the village is built, from the air it looks like there must be at least a thousand people in this one and possibly even twice that many.*

That would make them another interesting trade partner, if it comes to that. With four different communities only a few days or at most weeks travel apart, whoever got in that quickly, and found out what each group has, and is best at making, and what they want from the others, will rapidly become very wealthy.

It seems like Guk has gotten the right idea very quickly. It is a pity that we don't have enough people in Mousehole to spare to set up a trade circuit, seeing that any traders would have to travel past our door unless they choose to go up to the Caliphate first and I think that will be more out of the way rather than more direct.

I wonder if Eleanor might want to have a go at it. We certainly have enough packhorses for the job, if someone can pry them loose from our Khitan.

She was still weighing up the alternatives when they were sat down, and she was asked what she would like to eat or drink. Having asked for local delicacies, whatever they were going to be, she noticed that, except for Astrid who had been taken somewhere, all of the others had been sat down as well, and that Goditha had rolled up the carpet and brought it with her.

"You don't have the look of a diplomatic group," Cathal said in Hindi to Rani, as he waited for another person attired as he was to arrive. "Except for yourself and the woman with very short hair and the carpet, the rest of you seem dressed for both travel and war."

"That is part of why we are calling on you." *There is a sudden tenseness. Perhaps I could have phrased that better.* "We are on the way to make a raid on some of the Master's servants at Rising Mud, and thought that it would be impolite to fly past you without an explanation…" — *and they relax again.* By this time the other person had arrived. *He looks very similar in appearance to Cathal. They were probably related.*

"This is Calgacus," said Cathal. "He is the Magister for the whole of the Bear People. It is he whom you need to talk to first if you wish to deal with us." Introductions were made as Calgacus insisted on greeting and hearing from every one of the Mice.

Christopher

*H*e is trying to judge us by our tone and our grip. I saw a huge stone circle from the air so, if he is religious, and he looks it, he must be a Druid or perhaps a type of Shaman. Let us see how he reacts to Hulagu.* Hulagu was the last, except for the absent Astrid, to speak.

Instead of saying that he is a Wolf, Hulagu has introduced himself in Hindi as being of the Horse totem. Both of their priests look surprised and they are exchanging looks of concern. I wonder what that is about?

"The Horse totem of the Khitan no longer exists in this world or the other," said Calgacus. *He is a shaman then.* "Why do you claim a totem that no longer exists?"

"The valley of the Mice has its own grazing lands in the mountains — rich grazing lands. I have children, and my sister has children and we have, for various reasons, been led to claim the lands afresh, and seeing that there are four adults from three totems, we thought it best, as did our spirits when we consulted them, to call back the totem of the Horse from the Twilight Plains.

"My Su-Khan and the Tar-Khan of the Dire Wolves know a little of our intent, and I have spoken some with the chief Shaman of the Dire Wolves in the real world, but the Kha-Khan does not know this from us directly yet, and we have yet to present ourselves at Dagh Ordu to make formal claim, and as yet we have no Tar-Khan of our own.

"We will do this when our prophecy is fulfilled, but we know not when that will be. In the last Age, the Horse totem was powerful. It has been born again, and will rise to be small but important as this Age reaches a climax. But the free-running Horse will be subject to the Mouse, and although we lay claim to and use the grazing lands of the mountains, we will live most of the time within walls and fly rather than ride."

What is Hulagu was talking about? I know that his sister is Bianca, but apart from that I am in the dark. Does this mean that he no longer seeks husbands for his köle or is that something else? From the faces of the Princesses they are just as mystified. However, from the looks being exchanged between the two shamen of the Bear People, it all seems to make perfect sense to them.

Hulagu continued. "What is more, as a sign of this, although I could be a shaman, I am not. I study to be a mage as the walled ones have mages. Our totem lacks a shaman and the signs are not clear if we will ever have one, or if we are all to take some of that role. If we do that, it will not be me who does, nor will it be my sister, who is the wife of this priest and a Christian."

Hulagu has finished and now we all sit in silence while the two men exchange looks. Finally, Calgacus spoke. "What you have said is in accord with what we have seen in the real world and in the prophetic dreams. It is only in this shadow life that it is confusing. I take it that the valley of these Mice is the fixed area just to the north that we cannot see into, in either the real world or this one?"

"Yes," said Hulagu, "so my grandfather, Nokaj, has told me when he sought to see there and to speak to me."

"In that case," said Calgacus, "our dreams and prophecies are reaching a conclusion." He looked at Rani and Theodora. "It seems that I am to fall into your wishes. This visit was foretold. I am sad to see you as you bring both peace and strife for our people. You will open us up to the world and we will never be the same again. What may we do for you?"

Rani

*O*f all the reactions I had been expecting, this is not one of them. They settled in for the night, telling the story as it has evolved to this point. Calgacus raised his hand early on and sent messengers to bring people who were introduced as Odhamnait Teítldottir, Inis Éadoaindottir and Eithear Reodarson. The first two were women and all three were bards.

Calgacus insisted that the story be told again from the start...*and in full. I fear that it is going to be a very long night.*

Rani
21st Undecim

I am very tired, and my wife has had barely an hour's sleep, and even with kaf she needs a lot more than that to function well. We are all too tired to go any further today. Hulagu has already gone to select a packhorse. I think that we will continue tomorrow.

It seems that the cat is one of the totems here, and Tabitha, it seems, gets along not just with the stable cats. She is already playing with a black panther and her half-grown kittens, rolling around in the grass with them.

To everyone's interest, Freya had crawled away from her mother as she lay resting in the grass, and went up to the mother panther. Astrid was made aware of her absence by a gurgling and giggling, as the panther held her daughter between her paws and licked her clean. "It is my fault," said Astrid to Basil. "I called her the Kitten."

Christopher

*D*uring the second night, Rani and Theodora were introduced to two boys and a girl who would be going back with them to the school. Their fees for the next year were quickly paid in full. *It seems that the idea of the school is a good one. Ruth will be pleased.* Father Christopher was also introduced to someone who, to his mind, was even more interesting than anyone that they had met before in this village.

"Father Christopher," said Cathal, "this is Father Simeon. Although he is one of us in truth, perhaps he belongs with you instead of with us. We are not rejecting him, you understand, but he has no co-religious here and is not likely that he would ever have them."

Christopher looked at the man in front of him. *At first glance he looks just like many of those around us. He is not overly tall, but he is bulky and very hairy, but he has a rosary and a crucifix at his side.*

The man coughed as if clearing his throat. "On the other hand," he said, "I am not sure that you will accept me. I am not of your faith, but am Catholic. I know nothing of what important differences there may be between what we believe, and I need to say even before we start to explore that issue that I am a shape-changer. I was born a were-wolf, and from a long line of such and I was not born in The Land."

The women have been talking about other lands. I remember them discussing the land to the west and how Freehold had probably colonised it. "You will be from the western land then?"

This Simeon looks more than a little surprised. "Yes…we call it the New-foundland…but I thought it was a secret here, as travel is forbidden between the two for most people. Until you spoke, no one that I have spoken to has known of it, and you are here in the middle of The Land and yet you speak almost casually of it. How do you know of the Newfoundland? As it is, I am only here due to a long series of miracles."

"We Mice," said Christopher, "have many sources of information. I think that I can safely say that no one else here knows but us. We know that it is only one of many lands that lie over the ocean. One day we may have to visit some of them. We are not sure where they all are, so that should be an interesting task…but I digress…you say you are a shape-shifter. How do you come to the cloth, and as a priest of the…the Catholics? That cannot have been easy. Didn't they object?"

"I will tell you my story at another time. It is very long. The short answer is that yes, some of them did, and that is how I am now here. I think that officially I am now excommunicated and so would be grateful if we could talk about my future."

Christopher rubbed his hands with undisguised glee. *I may not have understood that business about horses, or what had Astrid so excited with what is happening with her daughter and the large black cat, but these subjects of excommunication and of proper theological questions are meat and drink to me.* "In the name of Saints Cyril and Methodius, let us find a place to sit and talk."

Eventually, it was decided that Simeon would go to Mousehole on the carpet when it returned, and once there, would talk with Theodule. "I am not concerned about you being a shape-shifter," said Christopher. "If God accepts you as a priest, and that would be evident immediately from whether your prayers are accepted, then who am I to deny or even to question Him and His choices?

"I am more concerned with you being able to accept our village…I must explain…firstly" and he began ticking things off on his fingers "our Princesses are married, before God and to each other. They are not our only such couple. The young girl who has the carpet is married in a like fashion.

"Secondly, our services are attended by people of many faiths and we do not pressure them to convert. Thirdly, the dress of our people is not normally seen anywhere else among Christian folk… Fourthly, we have one Christian man who is married to two women in the eyes of God, and one of the women is a Muslim. Fifthly, many of our people are not human, and we have several marriages, and children, among these.

"Astrid and Basil" he pointed, "are one of these couples. Both are part Kharl, but she is from Wolfneck and he is from Darkreach. Sixth, we have excellent relations with Darkreach, and have found that we have not had the truth about that strange land given to those of us who have been raised west of the mountains.

"One of our people has married Hrothnog and is now its Empress. Seventh, my wife was born as Catholic, but has become Orthodox…at the same time she has been adopted as Khitan, and is a part of this Horse totem…and no, I don't understand that part and am not privy to those secrets. There is more, but those are possibly the main things. Can you accept those?"

This Simeon is looking more and more stunned as my list comes out. When Christopher had finished there was a pause, as the Catholic priest digested what he had heard before he replied with a smile. "I am not sure, but it sounds as if I have been seeking your village for a very long time indeed, conceivably, for all of my life."

Chapter XIII

Bryony
22nd Undecim, Saint Aemigdius' Day

They set off before dawn the next day with a small, and heavily sedated mountain packhorse, similar to those Guk had, complete with pack-frames and packs, lying on the carpet. *It will be a long flight and we fly high. We have taken a lot more sedative for the horse as it will be unlikely to stay quiet for the whole trip.*

I am nervous about heading back to Leidauesgynedıg. What ıf I am recognised? At least this part should be safe. Luckily, there are not likely to be many who are going to see us, unless we are unlucky, and we are seen by a carpet flying from the Caliphate.

As far as I am concerned Leidauesgynedig lies on the Buccleah, but Ayesha calls it the Ziyanda Rūdh. She keeps correcting us. "You should only call it the Ziyanda Rūdh since you are going to be appearing in your Caliphate garb," said Ayesha. "It is the river that Ta'if is built on. We have, however, not followed the river.

"We women are to be escaped slaves and that escape is how Hulagu lost his horse. We have come direct from Yãqūsa down through the mountains. I have told you some things about Yãqūsa, now you will have to remember it. Remember that it is walled and a sort of circular shape. It lies next to a major ford on the Khãbūr Rūdh, which flows down into Darkreach.

"You also know my father's name," Ayesha continued. "But I am now his former slave, not his daughter. If it is possible, I will try and answer any questions that people ask about my home."

They had to land twice for the horse to get more fodder laced with herbs to make it sleep again and for toilet breaks. *Some things are hard, or at least intimidating, to do from a saddle that is flying high in the sky.* Late in the afternoon Bryony glimpsed the area around Rising Mud. *We are still several days of slow foot travel out, but now we need to come down to where we are less visible.*

Here they came down to a low altitude and flew, now at tree-top height, until they were only a bit over a day's walk out, but still beyond the first sets of assarts. *At least these spread along the rivers rather than far into the jungle. I could have brought us closer, but…*

"It is important," Bryony said, "that we come in looking as if we have travelled through the jungle, so do not try too hard to avoid getting dirty. It would be very suspicious if we arrived there looking fresh. We will hide the saddles and end up spending two nights in the jungle."

I will bring them into the same side of the village as my father's farm was near the hamlet of Iwerddon. They found a ruin. *I remember it from hunting trips, there are lots of old stones around here…now to hide the saddles.*

Goditha, once she had the horse off her carpet, bade them farewell and immediately headed back with the carpet to pick up Rani and the others. She would be retracing the low flight over the jungle until it was dark. Then she would climb and head north. She was planning on flying all through the night until she arrived.

She would sleep only when she descended safely in the land of the Bear folk. Once everyone was returned to Mousehole she would fly back to the ruins to wait for the returning raiders. Between her sword and her growing stock of spells it was thought she should be safe.

Tokotak Hulagu Jirgin

They had set up three watches. *I am now classed as one of those who cast magic and so have to fit in with the more powerful casters, Theodora and Christopher. I have first watch along with Ayesha and Aine; Christopher takes the second with Tabitha, Astrid and Basil, while Theodora has the third with Stefan and Bryony.*

Ayesha

Allah, the Compassionate, please take pity on me. Why is Astrid in charge of these things? Even here she manages to get me to be with him. Sex and relationships are all a game to her. She would do very well if she decided to change career and become a matchmaker back in the Caliphate.

Astrid

T   *he sounds that I have to get used to in this forest are very different to those near Mousehole and even more different to those of the north. The silence of the boreal forests that I grew up in does not exist here. Even at night there are screeching noises and a lot of running about going on in the trees all around us. Odd thumping noises fill the air and there are large numbers of sounds from what I hope are frogs of different sorts.*

It seems that, if anything, the night is noisier than the day had been. Animals move about and feed and argue all around us. Bryony was not sympathetic when we woke her up. "Most of what you are hearing is from possums, and while possums can steal your food if you are careless, they are essentially mostly harmless."

Mostly…she said mostly. I will concentrate more on what I can see and smell rather than what I can hear, as even with all of the noise, there is very little to see. There is far too much to smell though. There are the sweet smell of flowers, dank and rotting smells, the scent of animals and many other unidentified things.

At least, even with all of the trees around us, it being clear weather and only three days past full for Terror, there is plenty of light. There is some shaking of foliage, but that is all the explanation I have for all the noises. At least there is nothing large coming towards us.

Astrid
23rd Undecim, Saint Cecilia's Day

I   *have discovered one thing about camping in the ruins. I have been spoilt by living in the village and sleeping in beds. I am not used to spending the night on cold wet ground that I share with insects and I am even more used to the relaxed watches that we keep at home, with a warm kitchen nearby where I can get kaf and soup at nearly any hour.*

"Soft…we are all grown soft…I am becoming Rani." Astrid muttered to herself after her watch as she coped with two very young children who had never had such an experience before and were very sure that they did not like it.

"I prefer to think of myself as civilised," said her husband loftily. "Unlike some people, who I could name, I prefer to only go as far enough out of town that I can get back in time for a warm bath, not stay out in the wilds until my clothing needs to be discarded when I take it off."

"You will be discarded if you do not allow me to wriggle up to you."

Astrid

Next morning, Basil lit a fire, and they had breakfast and set off. *Seeing that it is her home area, although she is dressed as a Caliphate woman, Bryony can lead off. Next it will be me, then Tabitha, and then Stefan. He is followed by Theodora sandwiched tightly between Basil and Ayesha; then comes Christopher and Hulagu with the packhorse and lastly Aine.*

Each kept checking ahead and behind. They were wearing leather rather than metal and Christopher was back to looking like a mercenary, rather than a priest. The supposed slave women were dressed in travel clothes, but they had dancing gear packed away if it was needed. *Their travel clothes at least leave a good deal of concealed places for weapons and wands.*

Theodora

It is nice, in some ways, to slip back to being Salimah, with my mask on, my hair orange, even though it is concealed by my hijab, and my eyes black. I have no responsibilities and am off on a grand adventure. I may still be clumsy eating with a veil, but I am a mistress of the art next to some of the others.

It is amusing to see Aine and Bryony, who have never worn one before, putting as much veil in their mouth as food. This is what the women in the Grey Doe saw when I first arrived there. Surely, I was not that bad. However, she knew, in the back of her mind, that this was not just a simple adventure for her that came with no consequences.

On this trip we could easily die. If we make a mistake here, my lovely husband might never find out what had gone wrong…just that something had, and we have not returned. I have been sitting back, so far, and Astrid seems to have taken charge. For a moment she thought about being the Princess and running things.

Astrid looks at me when she makes a decision, but it is nice not to be the one everyone looks at. I am out of my depth here. Here my store of knowledge is completely useless. I know all of the wrong things. This is the sort of thing that my hunters, Astrid and Bryony in the field, and Basil and Ayesha in the town, should look after.

Surely this is the essence of leadership: to let the right people do their job and not interfere. Theodora took to nodding at Astrid to endorse what she was asking when she looked her way. *I think that Astrid takes this as confirmation and becomes more confident in giving her orders.*

Bryony

A s they moved out, Bryony pointed to some of the orb-spinner spiders in their beautiful dew-clad webs stretched between trees to catch insects and, in some cases, small birds. The hand-sized and larger creatures sat in the middle of their webs, glistening with the morning dew. *I think that they are beautiful, but Theodora, in particular, is not impressed with them.*

"They are mostly harmless," Bryony said. "Just brush them off if they get on you. However, watch out if you sit for any little black spiders with a red dot on their tail. They are dangerous." She used a broken branch to brush aside an orb-spinner web that was across the path before continuing.

"It is very important to check above you as well…there are a number of hunters that live in the trees and some are smart enough to wait until everyone has passed and to then drop down on the last person. When you stop, remember to look above you for the drop bears, in particular. They are not bears…they are sort of possums…but these ones are dangerous.

"They are not common, but few survive their attack. If you have a spear, and are not moving, always keep the butt grounded and the point in the air. Before you sit down—look carefully at the branches above you, and if the rock you are about to sit on is the only one around—don't sit on it. It isn't a rock."

The land they were moving through varied greatly. In some places the trees stood in eerie silence on a ground thickly covered in rotting leaves, and it was possible to see for a good bowshot, but when the land sloped down to a creek, and there were many of those crossing their route, the understorey of the vegetation grew denser and, in some places, it was hard to force your way through.

I have not seen the giant lizards for so long…and there is another through the trees.

Once there was even a small herd of Rearing Lizards, beasts that made a herd of mammoths look small. *They move slowly and push aside the smaller trees as they walk. From the crashing noises, more of the forest giants of some sort can sometimes be heard, but are too far away to see. Vines draped from tree to tree and, even worse for Theodora, sometimes spider webs do the same thing. But it is home to me, and I have missed it.*

Astrid

*T*hose we do not have in the north. One large spider sat on a web that was stretched all the way across a small clearing. *Its body alone is far larger than my whole hand. Even Bryony wants us to avoid that one. The day is hot, and as it grows later the air is getting more and more humid, and the babies are showing more and more discomfort.*

The air in among the trees is quite still and it smells of damp and of vegetable rot. I have to allow the babies to have some laudanum while feeding or else the noise that they make will alert everyone to our presence. "I love them dearly," she said to Basil, "but they are getting weaned and left behind in Mousehole as soon as I can possibly do so."

While they were having lunch, the discovery of the first leech by Tabitha led to a frantic search by everyone of their body and that of the person beside them, and the babies and horse as well. *No more have been found yet, but it seems only a matter of time.* Theodora kept turning in circles to make sure that one was not trying to get to her from a plant and she totally refused to sit down again.

Bryony had just pointed out a pitcher plant beside where Astrid sat and told her to drop the leach into so that it would not bother them again. *She may think it fascinating, but I don't.* "Enough already. Let us get this done and get back north as quickly as we can. Everything in this place wants to eat you…even the plants. Let's finish here quickly and go back to where we are the hunters and not the hunted."

As the afternoon draws on, and the afternoon rain begins, I don't need Bryony to tell me that we are coming close to a settlement. There are stumps where particular trees had been felled and torn areas where they have been dragged away. There are even patches that have been cleared, and a few years crop wrenched out of the soil before it had to be left to grow back its jungle.

Bryony explained it. "Much of this land is too poor to farm in properly without building the soil, so many farmers just work the land that way. They work for a few years, and hunt the area around their farm and then move on and chop down another area. It is not a good way to get rich, but you can easily raise a family like that.

"The rich land is harder to get, although it floods and gets fought over, but this" and she waved a hand around "is free and anyone can start a farm in it without let. A younger son will always start out in these uplands and most will set up a farm before they can attract a woman. I would have been on one of these farms myself with Conan if things had turned out differently."

Bryony

The first occupied assart came into sight just before it was time to start thinking about cooking, if they were going to stop for the night. Bryony waved to the people there and they waved back, but she kept going. "Why aren't we stopping here to sleep?" asked Theodora.

"They didn't ask us to," Bryony said. "Unless someone waves you over, you do not impose on them. All of the people here pride themselves on their privacy and their independence, and so it is impolite to force yourself on them.

"This will work in our favour when we get to Rising Mud. Unless we provoke an official enquiry from the Sherriff, if we keep quiet and to ourselves…except if we have to entertain…then people are not likely to ask questions. They may suspect that we are not who we say we are, but usually they will be polite and not ask about this.

"So, with hidden faces on those of us who need it, we have a fair chance of being undisturbed. Of course, we have to be careful of people stealing from us. As outsiders anyone can do that to us without any dishonour at all. It is not like they would be stealing from the neighbours as we have no local friends or relatives to back us up, and even if we did catch the thief, we are unlikely to hang around until solstice or equinox to settle the matter."

"Isn't there any law at all?" asked Tabitha.

"There is more a strong set of customs in place than there are laws as other places have them," Bryony replied. "There are people who will argue a plea for you in front of the Sherriff and the Assembly for money, but they are not really lawyers. The people of the Confederation of the Free do not like to be cramped and laws are usually seen as an imposition on their freedom.

"They also don't like to be taxed, and avoid those if they can, even ones they have voted for. However, it is also always important to remember that if you kill anyone, you must be sure that you can afford to pay the fine. It is why I insisted we bring so much money with us.

"We may even get away with killing anyone that we need to kill if I am willing to stand up before the Sherriff and prove that whoever we killed was responsible for the death of Conan and my family, and my enslavement. The business of the bandits and the Masters will not be seen as important, but the personal matter of retribution for the wrongs done to me would be."

"Aye," said Aine, "and if I can show the same…well, I have a butcher's bill to present as well. It is time for me to collect on this even if we have to challenge someone to do so. The interest on this bill has grown, although it is turning out well in the end for me there are many that did not make it, and although custom says that I have no right, I want to collect for them as well." *I can agree with that.*

Ayesha

"To think that I thought that my husband was being harsh in her judgement of this place," Theodora quietly said to Ayesha, shaking her head as they set up for the night in a fairly open area, one with a few old charred patches in it, probably an assart that had been recently abandoned. "I thought she was just being herself and judging from within her upbringing. She was right, wasn't she?"

Ayesha could only shrug. *I am finding it harder and harder to judge places by the standards that I was brought up with and I am still not sure of the ones I have now. I need to go back and talk with Iyād ibn Walīd in Ardlark. I still have not talked much with Christopher or Theodule, as I am not comfortable asking them religious questions. I need to discuss this with a holy man of the Faith who I also trust as a good man. Allah, the Merciful, will surely guide me on the right path.*

That night passed much as the last had done, but this time the sentries were a little more relaxed about the noises that happened all around and above them. The humid night passed, not quietly at all, but at least without a serious incident. *By the end of this night, I am sure that all of us, except those who grew up here, are willing to pray all possums into perdition where they will be joined by all leaches as the servants of Shaitan that they really are.*

Bryony
25th Undecim

The land began a gentle slope downwards. "This marks the slope down to the river land," Bryony told everyone as they paused for her to explain. "Where we have been, that we call the upland, cannot be permanently farmed. If you are careful, the riverbank land can be.

"Now we have to be more judicious about what we touch, or do, as we come out of the places where everything is free to all people, into the places where everything has someone who thinks that they own it. Make sure you break no fences, and as soon as we find a track, we go onto it and do not stray from it."

It took another hour pushing through heavier and heavier understorey, complete with tree ferns and tangled vines with hooks on them, before they ended up on what may have been more than a game path. It took another half an hour at the faster pace they could maintain on it when they were not cutting their way, to be sure that this path had an increasing amount of traffic on it.

This is not a path I remember, but it is a path and other small paths are starting to join it and there are the wheel marks of a cart. Soon they started to see clearings of increased size and fences. Houses, usually fenced with tall solid fences, some with sharpened stakes on the top, started to appear and each farm, with its buildings joined by these fences, was looking more like a small fortification than a place to farm.

"Remember that we have the animals of the jungle to contend with. Having a thunder lizard stealing your goats is not nice, and down here there are even plants that can move about and can kill. It is best to be protected," Bryony explained.

Hulagu

Walking plants...I always thought those stories were made up. Now, having been here where the stories started, I am not so sure of my doubt. Bryony speaks so casually of them.

Bryony

Eventually a broad brown muddy river came into view ahead of them through the trees. Branches and other things could be seen floating in it and sometimes the water swirled as if something stirred the water underneath or took an insect from the surface. "The...Ziyanda Rŭdh" She pointed downstream. "See? To the right...out in the middle...that is Rising Mud."

They all looked along the river and could see, still a way off, a series of islands. There was a bridge leading out to the first and there was a fair amount of traffic along the river as boats carried goods along.

"This is the main river road here, with Dolbarden and then the Haven fort of Garthang Keep below, and Eastguard Tower and then the Caliphate village of Ta'if above. Even Dulcie and Aine's village of Bathmawr can be reached by river from here, and although travelling on the rivers has its own dangers, it is far safer to use them rather than to travel far on the land."

They continued along with Bryony pointing things out. In particular, she pointed at something that looked like a log on the river bank. She had just started to explain what it was when the 'log' opened its jaws. "Anywhere that connects to the sea can have these. They are rare in this river and this far up, but Rani would see more of them where she is from. You do not ever swim in our rivers unless you are very careful."

"It is time now for me to be an escaped slave." They shuffled their order around. Ayesha, Theodora, Bryony and Aine put their larger weapons on the horse, although they kept daggers hidden about their body. They then took up their places walking meekly behind the horse.

Theodora

I may never have carried weapons in Ardlark, but now I find myself missing them. My hands keep nervously feeling for the wands that I keep concealed. Astrid took point, followed by Stefan and Basil. Then Christopher and Hulagu came with the horse, the 'slave' women in a gaggle around them and lastly Tabitha brought up the rear.

Of those who were not posing as slaves, only Stefan and Tabitha had a little Faen, the language of the area. *We may not look like traders, but we certainly don't look to be a very military band of people and I suppose that is really the point of it all. Once again, I must use Astrid's Darkspeech to call it a maskirovka.*

Chapter XIV

Astrid
25th Undecim

*B*ryony said that there would be a guard at the end of the bridge. He is a *fairly useless sentry, standing there with an unstrung short bow hanging on a peg, and with a quiver and a sword at his belt. He has a shield just propped up in the tall shed beside him. It looks like he doesn't like leaving his rain shelter.*

What he is guarding I am not sure, as he is just looking at me and holding his hand out. I have the toll ready. Hopefully it has not changed. She gave him one silver ten-penny piece, seven pennies of mixed silver and copper and a single tin ten-mote piece. *It is worn and bent to almost look like a thimble.*

We got all of these in Greensin. Nothing is new and some are as worn as we have. He is counting us, and counting the coin. I don't think that he is very good at adding up. The sentry waved them through lazily, putting the coin in a pouch on his belt. *He has said nothing and yet I sure do not look like a local. As far as he is concerned the money, on its own, seems to be a complete explanation of our presence. What an idiot.*

I am not so sure about this bridge. We may have none at all at Wolfneck, but I am now used to the stone bridges at Mousehole, and at Mouthguard and up the Methul River. They all seem solid and almost part of the land, rooted in it. This bridge stands a full four paces above the water, yet it is made of wood that is rough under my hand and only just wide enough for a small cart.

It looks like they expect that it will be washed away in a flood and will have to be replaced. Through an occasional gap in the planks that made up the surface they walked on, she could see the brown water flowing lazily below. At each side of the bridge was a single rail set on top of the posts that held the path out of the river.

They are like fences a lazy farmer might put around a field to show that they own the land, but also that they are not expecting them to be useful at keeping anything in or out of the field. She leaned nervously against it. *It seems stout enough for casual use, but it would be very easy to break. I hope that our horse doesn't put a hoof through it all.*

She looked back at the horse. *At least it is not just me having problems with where we are treading; the horse seems to be picking its way very nervously forward as well. It is not even just the bridge. The river smells of mud and there are those river reptiles and plants floating in it.*

Looking at the village, it could be seen that it was built on several islands of varying sizes. *From what I can see there is timber driven down into the mud surrounding the islands. The timber serves as a revetment. The mud has been brought up in buckets and packed behind the timber.* She knew this to be the case because she could see a work crew repairing a section ahead of her.

It looks like it is a constant task, and I can see another crew in two boats under our bridge working on it. The others are working, but one person is just watching the water around them, with a spear in his hand. Someone coming this way is passing unconcerned above them. We should try and do the same.

Just before they came to the first island, she crossed a section that obviously opened up. *There are counterweights at each end, and an arrangement of ropes so that something with a mast that was up to about six paces wide will fit through, if everyone is careful. I think that it is a good idea to be well off the bridge if a boat is travelling through it. I don't want to rely on the care that they might take.*

They came off the bridge and Astrid started looking around. I am looking for a sign with a little red devil riding a horse on it. *According to Bryony the Horse and Imp is a trader's tavern.* She saw one with a picture of a bed…*that is the Enchanted Bed and more expensive without having much more quality.*

There was one with two women facing each other…*that is the Cat's Argument and a brief glance at the clientele sitting outside confirms Bryony's opinion of it. There are some wolf whistles and a shout, which sounds like an offer of money, presumably for one of the women. I will just ignore them.* She walked further into a plaza and looked around. *There it is on our left.*

She called Stefan and Tabitha up and pointed. *Those two will get us rooms. Hopefully, it will be quick. The babies are getting restless; looking around and starting to wriggle. They are sick of being in their slings and I am sick of carrying them. My back is sore, and my boobs tell me that the children want feeding soon.* Stefan nodded and entered, as Astrid gathered the others with Tabitha there to fend off any questions. *Thankfully, none are coming.*

Stefan emerged, and addressed them all in a simple Dwarven so that most understood. "I pay for two nights already. Translate later for t'ose who don't get t'is. Hulagu, go with boy, you stay with horse…safer." Hulagu grunted and followed a stable boy. "Rest come with me. One room for all of us. We have Salimah's snores again, but beds. Find room, unload horse."

They headed into the inn. *It seems to be about the same quality as The Slain Enemy in Evilhalt. A few curious eyes are following us, weighing up the women in particular and maybe wondering if the men can defend them. I will resist the urge to smile at them… Tabitha is trying to stare them down. If she had a tail, it would be all fluffed up now.*

They were shown to a room and entered. *It is large, and has three big beds, and two windows on the front wall and one on the side. It must be taking up half of the front of the building.* Theodora was about to say something when Basil put a finger to his lips and started to move around the room, first checking the door, finding that the key they had been given worked, and then tapping things and peering under other items.

Astrid and Bryony sat on beds and started to care for children while he was doing this, and Stefan took Ayesha out and they went to find Hulagu, but the rest just stood in the middle of the room, looking around and waiting.

Basil

*S*tefan *and Ayesha are back with a load off the horse before I am finished with my inspection. Good, the others are waving them to silence. They can wait as well.*

Just then Basil finished. "I cannot find any places where someone can listen in, of course with magic they can spy as they wish, and we cannot block them without being conspicuous. You can speak now."

Stefan spoke up in Hindi. "Hulagu will stay t'ere," he said. "He's happy with t' horses an' he says t'at he doesn't trust t' stable-hand. He said t'at he was looking at t' packhorse as most boys look at some sweets t'ey were hoping to set free from, t'cook an' he wasn't happy when Hulagu started to set up to stay in t'stable. He don't think t'at he'll ha' trouble if he sleeps light. We can take turns seeing him, t'at way we'll all learn how t'place is laid out."

That makes sense. "Father…what do you need to cast to find the pattern?"

"Just some bare floor, my son. I brought chalk with me. Remember, once I have cast this, I cannot get rid of a pattern, if I find it, or heal anyone until tomorrow." He looked at Theodora, who nodded back.

"Best if we find out if it is in the village now," she said. "It could be outside in a farm and then we will have a totally different problem." Christopher nodded. They dragged beds and chairs around, and cleared a space for him to work in the middle of the room. When this was done, they sat or lay on the beds until he was finished.

As he started work, he explained. "I think they believe it will be safe enough for them to operate in the village. In Ardlark and Greensin they were outside because of the number of priests around who have a good chance to tell if they are good or evil. Here, it is less of a problem for them. Druids are not as good at telling these things as priests are, and witches, like shamen, cannot do it at all. Bryony, you said there was a church, one of my sort, that is…here somewhere."

"Yes," said Bryony, "it is on an island two across from here."

"We will go there after I do this. I need to check on the priest anyway. I am sure Metropolitan Cosmas would want that. Anyway, it is likely that I will need to wander around and see which actual building the pattern is in, if I find it." He returned to his chalk, humming a kyrielle as he worked.

When he had finished drawing, he plopped himself down on the nearest bed and looked at everyone looking at him. "I think that we need to do Divine Service first. I will start by taking confessions in the corner over here. Please whisper to me unless you want everyone to hear," he grinned "…And that might count as the sin of pride."

Once he had shriven those who wanted it, he conducted a quiet service and then, placing himself in the diagram on the floor, cast the miracle that would tell him where the pattern of the Masters was…if it was nearby. *It must be very close.* Christopher leapt straight out of the circle and went to the window. He looked out and nodded. Drawing back, so that he would be shadowed from the outside, he gathered Bryony and pointed. "That large, dark yellow-painted house on the next island with the yellow painted shingles, beside the water with a small boat beside it…do you know who it belongs to?

"I was wondering if that is who it would be. Cuthbert was a friend of his and one of the men Conrad described sounded like him—even if he had his name wrong. He is Glyn ap Tristan. He is a mage. I don't know how strong he is, but most of them seem to be about the same here." She turned to Theodora. "He couldn't do anything that you and Rani do."

"Well," said Christopher, "now we will go to the church. Bryony, can you come with me and carry something to makes it look as if you are a slave?"

It is time for me to take charge. "This is the sort of operation that I used to do for a living. I was good enough at my job that I ended up here. Father, please let me organise this. Ayesha will go as well and they can carry that box," he pointed. "Put it down to rest yourselves near his place. It looks like you will have to pass it anyway. See if you can find anything interesting about how to get in, or anything else of significance."

Basil continued. "I am going to take Stefan, and we are going to sit in the sun in the plaza before the rain starts, and we are going to have a drink and he will listen, and I will watch. Stefan, we need to sit where we can see that house. Tabitha…you speak some Faen. Take Theodora and a basket and go find some shops. Find out when the market is…" He held up his hand to forestall an opening mouth.

"Yes, Bryony, I know it is Deutera and Dithlau, but I wouldn't know that if I didn't have you here…we need dried food…yes that will do…we have been on the road for a while, and so we need more supplies. Do not take any nonsense, but keep an eye out for people trying to cut the bottom from your purse."

"Keep it inside your jerkin at all times when you are not using it. It may not be elegant taking it out from under your breasts, but it is safer. Aine…feed Hulagu, and organise some food for us in this room when we get back. See if you can get anything from the tavern servants. Puss, my dear…you get to look after the babies…think of it as quiet time." He grinned.

"Quiet time. With three babies who are starting to move about…and to try and talk…and who are starting to get teeth. You get out of here. You will have quiet time for a month once we get home," said Astrid in mock severity.

"And you will join him if you say one word except 'Yes, dear'. Do you hear?" said Bryony.

"Yes, dear," said Stefan meekly as he left the room. *He spoilt that image by grinning broadly at me as we left.*

Basil

Stefan and Basil took station outside their tavern. *Not the worst way to go on guard and to keep a look out for wrongdoers.* The beer arrived…*and that is weak, but not too bad either. It cost more to have it cool, but it is worth it. Now we will start a conversation about our supposed travel down from the mountains, and the local spiders, and other nuisances and how glad we are to be again sleeping in beds instead of on the ground.*

They kept their entire conversation going in Hindi, despite that being the tongue of the local enemy. *It is obvious to any who look at us that we are not from the same place originally, and so many people speak Hindi as a second language that to do anything else would have been odd.*

Besides, I want people to hear this talk and while some of our listeners might have some Dwarven, Darkspeech is unlikely to have been heard here at all and using it will give far too much away. As it is, our talk is just to serve as a distraction.

Bryony

Christopher headed across the bridge, with Bryony whispering instructions to him. *Astrid is right. Take him out of his church and he really can get lost anywhere. I am glad he is our priest and I love him and everything, but he really is not meant to be anything else. How Bianca puts up with him when she is so sensible, I don't know.*

They went over the first bridge to the next island. *The first island that we are staying on may be far larger than this one, but Ynys Cyslltu is the hub of the village. You have to come here to get anywhere else—there are four bridges that go out from it. One we just crossed, one leads to another island, which in turn leads to the land and the other two lead to the other islands, one upstream, and one downstream. These two have no connection to the riverbank at all.*

The house we are interested in is just here next to the bridge, but someone inside of it can keep track of almost anything that passes through the town if they want to. The women had been acting as if the chest was heavy, although they had emptied it of the provisions that it had held before they left. *It now only has a present of money in mixed coin from different lands for the priest, and now we are in front of the suspicious house it is time to put it down.*

Ayesha called to Christopher in Arabic. *He didn't even hear that. He has wandered on and only noticed that we are not there, when he realised he needed to know which bridge to head towards and turned to ask me. He scurries back.*

Ayesha

They were resting on the chest, and Ayesha continued to upbraid him for leaving them, again speaking in Arabic. *Our Christian priest does not understand a word of it, but an onlooker will not know that.* In the meantime, she was having a good look at the house.

It will not be easy to force a way into it. The door is stout and looks like it will resist any attempt to enter it by force. The occupant is a mage, and the apparent means to get in are probably trapped, and besides, there is a boat tethered outside for a quick escape.

An interesting problem, but my teachers made me work with far harder ones, hoping that I would fail. For a start, the house is all made of timber and that provides far more chance to get in than stone and iron does, and by leaving the boat at a dock, he has left a back door that he will not be expecting the locals to use.

I expect though, that the dock itself, and possibly its surrounds, will have an alarm on them. She looked around. *There is a lot of bird life. By the will of Allah, the Provident, the alarm will have to take account of that. This will be fun. I will have a good look at it tonight. I have enough to work with for now.*

Christopher came over. He spoke quietly in Hindi "Sorry, I forgot about that bit. It is the smaller building behind the house near the boat that we want. We cannot see it from here, but I could see it well from the square. Is that important? Do we go on to the church now?"

Bryony

Bryony looked at Ayesha, who nodded. *I will use Dwarven as we agreed.* "Yes Fa...Christopher." *I really should learn some Darkspeech. It would make conversations easier in the village. It is a tongue that so few people speak outside of Darkreach itself, that most of the time we could talk freely and openly in it, without any problems.*

Christopher

The church here looks more like a large, single-roomed hall with an attached house than anything else, but it has a small sign out the front proclaiming it to be the Church of Saint Mark written in a number of languages. The patron of thieves, robbers and ferrymen...how appropriate it is for this place. The priests that serve here must have a sense of humour at least.

He looked around. *The church is obviously neither popular nor prosperous. It probably just caters to a couple of locals and any passing travellers. My 'slaves' will seem unusual, but I could be a traveller from where they are a more common sight.* He went into the church. *It will, at most, seat forty people crowded together...there is a priest up front.*

The man turned around suddenly putting his hand to his side, as if he were reaching for a weapon to defend against an expected attack. "Forgive me for startling you, Father," Christopher said in Greek, "But can you spare me some time?"

"I can," said the priest cautiously, in the same tongue.

"Ayesha…please keep watch for us. Bryony, let us talk to this man. Greetings, Father. I am Father Christopher from the village of Mousehole, and despite the way she is dressed, this is one of my parishioners, Bryony ferch Dafydd. The Caliphate woman is also one of my parishioners, if not one of my Christian parishioners."

"We need to talk, and not just about Saint Cecilia, who's Day it recently was…mind you, as she is patron of bards, you may think that I speak with her in mind." *At least he looks curious about my words…and an attacker is not likely to know about Days and patronage. That should serve as enough of a shibboleth.*

"I am Father Kessog and I have never heard of your village," was the reply. Christopher smiled again. *He has named himself after the patron of those who fight against monsters on the land.* "But at least you know more of the saints than any of the people who live here do, including all of my parishioners, and so welcome to my parish and in the Name of God, pray tell me why you are here to see me."

Ayesha

*A*s they do, the priests have fallen into discussion. We will not have their attention for a while. Bryony may be paying attention and answering questions, but I am not interested in sitting inside tamely and just waiting on them.

She moved and sat just inside the church in the cool gloom, and looked out of the door that she had deliberately left open behind her. *I am interested to see if there are any passers-by who are interested in us. I have not noticed any so far, but you never know.*

She sat quietly. *People walk across the square in front of me and even down the street beside us. From what I can see, smell and hear, there is a stable down there on the tip of the island. At least no one even looks twice at the church, even if they could see anything when looking from the bright sunshine outside into the gloomy shadow inside a building.*

Ayesha

*W*e *are going to be the last back. The priests have talked long enough, and from the look of the sky, the rain is about to start.* She grabbed Christopher and dragged him away from the church and back to the inn. *Bryony looks relieved to be rescued. She needs to learn. Even Bianca does not just sit around when her husband finds another priest to talk to.*

Theodora

*N*one *of the shops we are interested in face the plaza, which would be the home of the market, on the same island as us at the Horse and Imp. There is a wharf alongside the marketplace and that tells me how goods will arrive and sometimes leave. The house we are interested in is across the water from here.*

As she left the tavern, Theodora looked at the house. *It is right next to the water and painted yellow.* She looked around her at the other buildings. *Very few houses are painted with more than a sign of what the occupants do... although a few are whitewashed. I am willing to bet that this Glyn is a water-mage. Good. That puts a limit on what he is best at.*

If what I learnt at home is the same here, then most village mages are about the same strength, unless they have occasion to fight or struggle hard and so grow more rapidly...and so that should give me something to work with. That meant he could...no...I will think on that tonight. I need to get back to what we are here for.

They began to move around the winding streets, eventually finding the store they wanted hidden with a hard to find entrance. *You would think that a beautiful woman with one blue eye and one green one, who is armed with a hunting spear, and with a Caliphate slave who is taller than her would occasion some comment, but then you would be wrong in Rising Mud.*

Tabitha, even with her limited Faen is able to shop without any problems and without anyone asking questions. From my experience in Ardlark, I am sure that she is being overcharged, but that is to be expected. She had to smile behind her veil. *Here I am, a Princess shopping...really my first time since Ardlark...and I am the one carrying the basket.*

She silently appreciated the irony and kept her senses as sharp as she could. *I have a better than even chance of feeling if there is magic passing me by, and a good chance of picking up something invisible, and while I am not seeing the second, I am picking up lots of magic around me. It is all low-level magic, according to my senses, but there is plenty of it about. A village this size, I would expect to support at least two hands of mages.*

Most of it she sensed, as she allowed her senses to feel out what they could, was around weapons or pouches. *I am seeing more than a few women with necklaces, and when I look carefully and try and pierce the veil, I sense that many are disguise spells, such as I am wearing myself. Common enough, particularly with older women, and I certainly qualify on that count.*

Given that I have already seen several such charms, this means that there is at least one good air mage locally. He probably makes a good living for himself from making those charms. I have had heard that many do.

On the other hand, our target is probably going to be a water mage, and given the location of the village in the river, surrounded by water, and with it close at hand the whole time, I doubt that we will find many earth or fire mages at all. The location is not likely to suit them. They would have to fight the prevailing elements too hard in their everyday casting.

That means that, if they were enchanting weapons they would have to work as hard at it as I do, and my husband's fire wands...I have two of them on me now...will not be likely to pass as being locally made. Luckily, there are very few people who can easily tell the sign of made magic just as Verily can.

Basil
Late in the afternoon

They all met back at the Horse and Imp just before the rain started. *We have them sitting on beds and chairs around the room as food is produced from the shopping and added to what we already have with us. Now to find out what we know.*

Basil looked around at the room full of people. "Start eating now and make yourselves comfortable, because we may be a while here and then busy later. Aine...you can start with your report, and then please relieve Hulagu so that he can tell us if he has found anything out."

Aine stood up. "Umm...I have very little to say. The inn has just the ground floor and the one we are on. There is no cellar. No buildings here have them because they would fill up with water. They have a cool room out the back and that is one way the local mages make money...a lot of it judging from a complaint that I heard."

"The servants were not very curious. In fact, they are even less curious than when I was here as a wine trader, admittedly that was many years ago. I was actually kidnapped near here, you know, after a good sale. I thought that they just wanted to rob me…at any rate, the servants give you curious and sometimes sad looks, but they do not ask questions."

She paused and thought a moment before continuing. "It is as if they have learnt not to ask any questions about odd strangers. They are even less curious than they used to be. I think that is all that I have to say. I will go down to Hulagu now."

"Good report. Be careful. Make sure you are armed…take a sword under your cloak, and I will send him straight back down. Next, I will report. The beer here is not bad…" His wife threw a nut at him and it bounced off his head, which he rubbed, "And there is little for me to report as well. I should mention that on operations like this the words 'little to report' are heard a lot."

"You just have to mention anything, no matter how small, that looks odd. For us, the little things were that two people went into the house we are interested in. One was probably the mage and the second was probably a servant. I think that he was a servant because he went out to the dock later and threw some rubbish into the river."

Basil looked around. "He was very careful to stay back a little from the steps leading down to the water so I bet that the top step, at least, has a ward of warning on it. When he went into the house from outside, the servant had a basket of what looked like food."

"The mage had come from this island, and had been drinking and he was more than a little drunk when he got home. I could not see into it, but from what little I could hear, there is a courtyard behind his house, and I think that even after he had come home, he sat there drinking for the rest of the afternoon. Now, Stefan…"

Stefan was sitting there with his mouth open. "I'm sure t'at I sat beside you t' whole afternoon. I didn't see or hear any of t'at. I had a nice drink. I listened to t' locals an' t'ere is talk of war agin Haven. T'ey had been hopin' t'at Haven would attack t'em, but t'eir army pulled back away an' people are saying t'at t'ey be cowards for not comin' into t' Swamp…personal I would call it sensible…so t'ere is open talk of a sendin' people soon to cut off t'eir trade with raids an' to force 'em to attack." He sat back.

Basil nodded. "Next, let us hear from the shoppers."

Theodora nodded and stood. "Just for a start, Tabitha is far worse at shopping than I am. I just want that on record because, Basil, I know what you think of my ability to bargain." She went on to detail what she had worked out and concluded. "So, we can see that any magic traps are likely to not be as good as Ayesha might be used to, as water mages are not good at traps."

"They can, however, do spells that have special efficacy over humans, which means that Basil, Astrid, and myself will be less affected by them, as none of us are fully human. Any traps are likely to just stop you, stun you, or to cause sleep rather than harm you. I think that is all," and she sat down.

"I haven't had much of a chance to shop in my life," said Tabitha, in her defence as she stood. "But I got all the food we need. It is hard to find. Someone is buying up all of the preserved food. That was part of why it cost so much. I guess that fits in with people being sent elsewhere to fight." She sat down.

There was a knock on the door and Ayesha went to it. "Who is it?" she asked in Khitan. "A horse," was the answer in Hulagu's voice. She opened the door and let him in.

"Anything to report?" asked Basil.

"Only that if I want to sell the packhorse there is a ready market, and if we leave it alone for any length of time it will somehow manage to walk out of the locked stables. And no one will have noticed it going. I have had two good offers so far. I will get back straight away. I don't want to leave Aine there on her own." He nodded, grabbed some more food and left again.

"Father Christopher…you are next."

The priest stood. "We will have the Hesperinos service once this is over. It is a little late for it, so we will then have Apodeipnon next, and I may do a midnight service, which usually only monks do, and we will do Orthros in the morning as usual.

"I have conferred with Father Kessog, who is the local priest. We need those services. There is much evil in this town, and it is growing. He keeps losing parishioners, particularly those with pretty women in their family, or who might oppose a war with Haven. He only has two families left out of his flock, and they both live well out of the village itself.

"The whole village is starting to live in fear, as others who are opposed to war die or disappear. I will let Bryony tell the rest. I gave him funds and told him what is happening in the rest of the world. He has a young son and daughter. I will not be surprised if they appear in Mousehole soon as students for the school, and to get them away from this place. The problem will be getting them to us." Christopher sat down. He looked tired.

"I guess that I am next then," said Bryony. "Father Kessog knew my father, although we were not of his flock. Apparently, we were the first family to be targeted. Many have been targeted since then. There is a group who call themselves the Patriots, and our target is a main leader of it here."

"He has even spoken publicly in the marketplace, calling anyone who does not want war with Haven a traitor to the Free and probably in the pay of them. Last week, he suggested that anyone going on this raid might have their expenses paid for by public-spirited people. The leaders met today and Basil probably saw him returning from that meeting."

She continued. "I don't know if it will all collapse if we kill Glyn, but he apparently has a lot of good money to throw around and money will always buy you some support." She sat down and Basil looked at Ayesha.

"I reached the same conclusions about traps as the Princess," she said. "The house is in the middle of everything, but there is a short laneway beside it, and the house behind is set back. I was just going to scout his house tonight, but I now think that if he has been drinking, he will be fuddled and we should take him tonight.

"I don't think that there is any doubt about his guilt, and if you do not want to question him, this is what I am trained for. I don't want to capture and question him, as it makes it all more complex and makes us more likely to be caught. What I propose is that I go out after midnight, after Christopher has slept, with Astrid...you can climb can't you?" Astrid nodded.

"We both wear our jewellery with the invisibility glamour. I go in, and she stops anyone leaving the building. After a count of time...we will work out how long...she comes over the roof from the front. We kill anyone inside and then open the door. Basil, as soon as you see the door open you bring Father Christopher over quietly."

She looked around for nods of agreement. "Get rid of anyone that you see on the way there who objects. We dispel the pattern and then come back here. If we are still unseen, then first thing in the morning, we leave." She looked at Basil. He thought briefly and then nodded, and was about to speak when Astrid spoke.

"Don't you want my report?" she said.

"But you were inside."

"Yes, dear," was the reply. "And I was bored when the babies slept, and I was upstairs, and I had a window that you can see some of the dock from, and am also used to watching prey...at least six largish river boats under oars, and full of armed men...very few women at all that I could see...arrived at the main dock of the village today from upstream."

"A couple of horses in the wells, but not many...mostly foot. If we don't act, they may go on tomorrow, possibly with Glyn. I am willing to bet anything that they will be in the pay of those public-spirited people with the money, and he may have the money if he is the local leader. If we do act, we will either have to leave very early in the morning with them after us, or else sit still and try and resist a truth spell because we will be the hot suspects."

"Then it is confirmed. With your Excellency's approval"—Theodora nodded—"we will do as Ayesha suggests, but with the following changes. Stefan, when we finish here go and stay with Hulagu. It may be dangerous for him to be on his own. Be ready to leave with the horse prepared first thing in the morning, as soon as there is a glimmer of light."

"You said that we are paid up here, didn't you?" Stefan nodded. "Good. Theodora...Princess, when we leave, you are to take up a position at this window with your wands. Try and avoid it, but use them if you have to. Aine and Tabitha, you will do the same with your bows at the other front window. Do not use explosive arrows unless you really need to, and they would be best used on a mage or to bring down a bridge."

"Father Christopher...you can start praying. I think that you are right. We may need all the help that we can get before the next day is over. You will be doing a very early Krondag service in the morning. We leave this town as soon as it is just becoming light, and before anyone else would be expecting it. As we go out of the inn, if any try to say anything, we knock them out, tie them up and bring them back here. When we go, we just leave them."

"I want to be there when he dies," said Bryony flatly.

Bloody hell. I was hoping to avoid this...now to sound apologetic and divert her. "I really don't think that will be possible. Of course, we will see if Ayesha can leave him alive for you, and you can come over with Father Christopher and me, but I will leave it to Ayesha's judgement if it is safe to keep him alive until you get there."

She is about to object. "Yes, I know that Lakshmi held a mage for us in Mousehole, but it only worked there because she had lots of support handy, and it was not on his home ground and...well...you don't want Ayesha putting herself in danger, do you?" Bryony shook her head sadly. "She will do her best to keep him alive for you, but do not be disappointed if she cannot." *Ayesha is looking relieved.*

After the services, Aine was left on watch and the rest tried to sleep. The experienced ones actually did, but Bryony ended up sitting and staring out of the window at the house for the whole night.

Chapter XV

Theodora
26th Undecim, just after midnight

*B*ryony is waking us…it must be midnight and time for Father Christopher's *service and then it will be time to go. We have no lights. We must rely on the waning half-moon to see what we must.*

"Ayesha," she said, "Don't forget what happened at Mousehole. He will have at least one contingency cure in operation, and he may have a teleport set up to somewhere with a diagram. Oh, and don't be surprised if there is one of the lesser undead around somewhere. Water mages are good at making them and they are ideal as cheap guards. Remember that he is a mage and may be able to see through the glamour of your rings. Do not rely on them."

"I never do. We never had them when we trained. We were told that they made you lazy," said Ayesha as she and Astrid held hands and put on their jewellery. *Both have disappeared from view and the door is opening and closing. Basil, Christopher and Bryony sit on the bed nearest the door ready to go, and Aine and Tabitha are taking up station near the window with me. Silence fell on the room.*

There they are. "They are crossing the bridge." They looked at her. "I said that mages have a way of seeing through such glamour…for once I can see them. Astrid has taken up a place on the veranda beside the door, and Ayesha has her daggers out and is working her away along the wall above the water"

"Now she has disappeared. Not actually disappeared…I mean that she has just gone out of sight into the yard."

Ayesha

*I*t is strange walking along invisible and holding an invisible hand. It is even stranger being on such a mission with a partner. It is both riskier and safer. Safer because you have back-up, and riskier because you have to co-ordinate your actions. Even something as simple as that silly thing with putting the jewellery in place with one hand out of action is harder than it should have been.

It is nice holding hands as you go though. It sort of makes you less nervous knowing that someone else is there.

Except for some faint noise from another island, probably from a tavern or someone having a celebration, all is silent. The village seems almost deserted. They reached the house and she went to let go, only to be pulled closer and to receive a kiss on the forehead and a whispered "good luck" from the air before being released. *Well, at least she cares…that is nice…and never happened during training.*

Astrid

*A*strid looked around her at the porch. *It is nice and solid. It will be very easy to get from this on to the roof when I am used to climbing trees that have branches that begin well above my head.* She settled down to wait until she had made her count. *I can just put my spear up there and then lift myself until my leg can go up on the edge.*

Ayesha

*A*yesha felt her way along the side of the island and the building. *This sort of thing I am an expert in. My teachers said that, and they are not lavish with praise.* Her toes in their soft boots were dug into cracks between the logs and timbers and she kept her balance with daggers stuck hard into the wood and the cracks between the timbers.

She drove them in hard and also kept a fair amount of her weight on them as well. *At least I need not worry about leaving a trail tonight. Just get in quick and undetected, and do the job as Allah, the Just, requires.* She reached the gap in the wall for the dock.

It is just so open and inviting as a way in. It is trapped of course, but what else is? They would be expecting normal thieves, not a ghazi, and thieves would come by boat. I will not risk putting a foot down wrong, and will keep going the way I am until I am around the corner. I want to be well away from the opening before I risk putting my foot onto the ground.

There were two doors into the house. The main one was closed fully—and was probably trapped—but she could see that the other, probably to the kitchen, had not been properly latched. She moved over there, and using just her lockpick, began opening the lock.

I am right...it is the kitchen. She moved through into the next room. *Servant's quarters will probably be at the rear...Shaitan take it! There is a servant of sorts. Theodora was right.* Standing in the next room was an undead. *A zombie perhaps, from the look of him...I could take it out now.*

No, she decided, *it has probably been told to guard the back door and so it will do nothing on its own. It is looking in that direction. I can probably safely leave it there for later...and it will be quieter that way. Undead are good for many jobs, but you have to be very careful with what you tell them to do, as they obey your words exactly.*

She moved through the house exercising all of her normal caution, and found her target by following his snores. *He makes our Princess sound silent.* When he came in view, she could see a skinny, beardless man with a large nose and a very receding hairline.

From the hair lying on the bed beside him, it looks like he pathetically grows it longer on one side and flings it over the top to disguise the bare top. Despite being a lot taller, he will weigh a lot less than I do. He is sprawled part-dressed across his bed...not a good look from here. Part of a cover was across him and the rest trailed on the floor.

There is spilt alcohol that has run from a knocked over jug on the floor, and a puddle of vomit lies beside the bed mingling with it. The smell in the room is...intense. Her nose wrinkled in reaction. *Glyn is not at his best tonight.* She looked at him from the doorway. *The door stands open, but the entrance could have an alarm on it. Not likely, but possible.*

I need to take him so that he does not get a chance to do anything first, and to minimise problems if he has a contingency teleport operating. His Adam's apple bobbed up and down in his skinny neck as he snored and swallowed, and that made up her mind.

Ayesha drew her kukri, and noting where the puddles were so that she didn't tread in them and slip, she moved quickly beside him, and with all her strength, brought it carefully and quickly down on his exposed neck, cutting between vertebrae as another snore was cut short. Her other hand moved the head away by his hair as it was severed. In reflex, his body arced, and his cure spell kicked in.

I have achieved what I want. His head is not attached to his body anymore, and although he is alive again, his eyes are glaring at me, and his mouth is just opening and closing uselessly from where I hold it half a pace from his body. A cure like that won't work for long if the parts are not attached to each other.

Blood is cascading in a fountain out of his neck, and his body is thrashing around and groping blindly for its head…too late to find it now. The body fell back onto the floor with a crash. Blood now mingled with other liquids on the floor. She looked and prodded him with her blade, but there was no more movement. *Oh dear, I forgot to see if I could keep him alive…that is such a shame. Now, let us see what that noise brings.*

It brought nothing. *How long has it been? I probably have some time left.* She went around the rest of the house. Next door she found a room that was obviously his treasury. *From the amount of ready coin that I can see in bags and boxes, this is the pay for those going to attack Haven. We will take that with us.*

It will conveniently muddy the trail behind us if some think that it was just a robbery and a robbery is always going to be a chance here. Except for the zombie, the house is empty. The servant must sleep somewhere out the back. I don't blame him. I wouldn't want to sleep with a zombie around. I suppose that even zombies have to eat, and it might get hungry in the middle of the night.

The zombie is next. She wanted to avoid touching it in case it had some powers placed in it, so she used the same method on it as she had used on its master. A faint buzzing noise started running through the house from the bedroom as she attacked. It started to move to defend itself and it took several blows as its neck was tougher and she could not get such a good angle for her blow. *Unfortunately, that makes even more noise, particularly when it finally falls.* She waited.

The door started to open ahead of her, and she moved to the side and started to strike only to stop herself. A spear had poked into the room followed by Astrid. Ayesha took her ring off.

"There you are," said Astrid. "The servant slept out the back," she said "And you were not very silent. I heard the first kill. Luckily no one else did. I came straight away and just as well. If you look over there…" She pointed out at the courtyard. "There is a gong just like we use at home. He was about to beat it when I put my spear through him and wiggled it, and then tossed him in the river and held him under with it until he stopped struggling. He didn't get more than a strangled yelp out before he was in the water." Astrid cocked her head to the side. "I see that I set the alarm off with that. Anyway, I didn't hear or see him come up, and I watched for a while before I heard the second noise and came in."

"Thank you," said Ayesha. "I will keep looking around. You go out the front and wave at them. Open the door with your spear if you can. It may be trapped."

Astrid

A strid did as she was told, but nothing happened. *It isn't even locked. He must really have been drunk when he came home.* She waved at the tavern and got a wave back from the window. She waited and saw three figures come out the door.

Basil and Bryony are strolling as if they are out for a night walk, but Father Christopher is a caricature of someone trying to be stealthy and he just ends up looking suspicious. She sighed. *We really are going to have to take him in hand at some stage and do some sort of training with him if he is going to come out with us into the world.*

The three arrived as Ayesha came from the back. *She has that buzzing thing…and throws it in the river. It brings back a blessed silence to the house.* Closing the door behind them Ayesha showed them the body and the treasure. Bryony kicked the head and then turned back to the door. "At least his head doesn't look happy. I will drop this in the river when we go. Well, let us get on with the rest of it," she said.

Basil spoke up. "Unless you need me for something else, I will keep these two with me and we will pack up the treasure and anything else that looks interesting. Ayesha, take the Father and get rid of the pattern."

Ayesha

A yesha took the priest's hand and led him through the house. As she was about to leave the back room, she noticed a key hung on the wall behind the door. *I have my lockpick, but a key is always better.* She grabbed it and turned to discover that she had to stop Father Christopher from bending down to examine the dead zombie. They went out to the back.

There are three buildings. One has an open door, and there is a sword lying on the ground and a dark stain is clearly visible in the light shed by Terror near it in front of the gong that Astrid mentioned. The second is just a small shed, so the third, solid looking one by the water must be the one I want.

She went up to it. *Allah is kind…my guess was right.* The key fit the lock and she cautiously opened the door. *It is obviously well used and opens silently. There, in the centre of the room is a pattern and a mirror was on the wall ahead of it, just like it had been at home.* "There you are Father. I will stand guard out here. You can get rid of it and then we will go as quickly as we can."

I will just listen to the night and see if I can hear anything interesting. The priest set to work with his chalk, and within half an hour, the spirit of released mana could be seen leaving through the ceiling with a silent scream on what was almost a face, and leaving a shrill high noise in their heads. Hurriedly, they rejoined others. They had a chest and two very heavy backpacks waiting.

Basil

"**A**strid and I will take the box. Father, you will take one backpack and Bryony will take the other. Ayesha, you have to cover us. If you need to, kill anyone who sees us and looks curious. Now try and look innocent." Quickly they filed out of the house, and Ayesha pulled the door behind them closed with a click. *She has tried it again and it is not opening. She is nodding at me...it must be locked.*

As they went over the bridge, Bryony dropped Glyn's head into the waters. *It is bobbing away in the current. It bobs like something is already starting to peck at it from below. Without the parts, there will be no resurrection for him then.* They returned to the inn, apparently unseen and undetected, and once the treasure was distributed and a sentry set, some tried to get some more sleep before morning.

Christopher

In the pre-dawn gloom, I start to wake them up to begin my service. My flock are still sleepy, and we have to deal with babies being fed, and people eating and putting on what little they have taken off, and readying their weapons. I am sure that this is not the normal lot of a priest.

Once Christopher was finished, they all headed for the door and down to the stables. *We have done what we came to do—and have somehow even collected more treasure while we were at it. Now we just have to get safely home, and I look forward to that.*

Chapter XVI

Astrid
26th Undecim

I *see what Hulagu means. It has to be admitted that even though all of the staff are mostly hiding their feelings very well about the visitors, the groom in the stables is openly surprised that we are leaving even before the sky is more than tinged with light.*

He may not be used to guests leaving this early and without warning, but he obviously knows that we have paid, so after a futile attempt to delay us, and with a last reluctant look at the now laden packhorse, he has let us out of the stable door. He is closing it behind us, and I will bet that he is off to discuss the matter with the other servants.

The morning was still and quiet, and for Rising Mud, it was relatively cool. A faint mist rose steaming and quiet from the river, but that would burn off as soon as the sun properly rose. *There are only two people visible, and they are hurrying over the bridge from the island where the mage's house is to this one, as if trying to reach their home before dawn officially happens.*

The Mice headed across the bridge that led back to the shore, leading their packhorse. *On the bridge is where we are the most vulnerable. There is nowhere for us to run to, and if there are more of those giant crocodiles around, nowhere to swim to either, that is for those who can swim...in other words, Stefan.*

They reached the shore and turned east. *There are two men at the end of the bridge on guard, but they are making no move to follow us or even to ask us anything. Probably only two so that one keeps the other awake. It seems that people are free to leave the village whenever they chose to. There are, however, very curious looks on their faces.*

"A long trip needs early start," Stefan volunteered, quoting an old trader proverb, and one of the men nodded, their curiosity lessening a little. *I fervently hope that neither of the guards knows that this is the direction that we came from when we entered the village. Apparently, they don't…or if they do, they don't care…either response is quite possible here.*

They made haste along the riverbank, trying to move quickly without giving the appearance of guilt or of fleeing anything, just moving as people would who had a long day ahead of them, which they wished to see over quickly.

They had gone about a thousand paces, and were temporarily out of sight of the bridge when Astrid paused. *There is a small group of people standing beside the road.* She was about to react when one stepped forward.

"Father Christopher?" came the voice.

"Father Kessog," was the reply. "What are you doing here?"

"I thought that your business with us might be very brief. Your business here in the village will stir up a hornet's nest won't it?"

We need to cut this off. "Well yes," Astrid replied, "but you would perhaps be best not knowing what it was and thus staying as innocents."

"I suspect that the way things are going here in the Land of the Free, being innocent will not keep us alive," said Father Kessog. "I am taking my wife, and we are going with all of our people who are left, and we are all fleeing into a place that I know of in the forest. We will be safe there. We will stay there for some time until it all dies down."

"Once it does, we will then come back and use the money you gave us to rebuild our homes and lives, and to build the church again if need be. These are our children Cadfael and Angharad." He pushed forward a boy and a girl of about ten to twelve years of age. "They are not coming with us. We think they will be safer with you, so we want to ask if you will take them with you to your school and keep them safe there for us."

"But we…" started Theodora, who had just come up.

"What she means to say," interjected Astrid, "…is that we would love to take them with us, and we will work out a way to keep them safe and look after them for you."

"God bless you all," was the relieved reply as their mother kissed the children goodbye and hugged them, giving them final instructions.

"Hello." *They are standing there with small packs on their backs and looking a little lost.* "I am Astrid, and these babies are Freya and Georgiou. I hope that you can move quickly, and obey and do what we tell you." *The children are both nodding. They have serious expressions on their faces.*

"That is good, because people will soon be trying to kill us, but we will keep you safe if you do exactly what I, or this woman…" She pointed at Bryony. "…who is from your village, tell you to do." She turned to Father Kessog and his wife.

"Go straight into the bush, and when you hear the pursuit come after us, stay still and hide until it dies down. They will probably see us and head straight for us...I hope. Remember that they will return at some time as well, so stay off this road and keep well out of sight of it." She turned around again. "It is time for us to get a move on." They headed off down the road again.

Stefan

They were half way along the river path to where they had joined it from the jungle when there was uproar from the village behind them. A gong could be heard, possibly the one beside the rear entrance to the house of the late unlamented Glyn, and the noise of an angry mob grew. It could be heard to rise, even from so far away.

It took some time but Tabitha, who walked in the rear of the group, reported that horses were being led across the bridge, and that a group of about twenty horsemen were setting off in pursuit of them along the river.

"T'ey canna be t'at stupid." Stefan turned to look back. "Bryony, does'n your village use horse bows like Hulagu an' Ayesha do?"

"No, they don't. Some use longbows, but most use normal bows. Why?"

"Because, unless t'ey're very lucky, t'ose twenty're about to die. T'is is real battle now an' without Rani here, I'll take charge. We keep a-goin' until t'ey're half a hand of hundreds away an' t'en t' archers'll turn an' prepare. T'rest'll stand ready for if'n t'ey manage to close."

"Archers'll start shooting at'n two hundred on my call. Only use explosive heads when I call, or to stop any t'at look like fleein' or any t'at look like t'ey're mages. Princess...you're to use your bow with t' others, but you a-keep watch for any mages an' be prepared to take t'em out by any means you want. If t'ese 're all t'ey hast sent, t'at may be all of t' horsemen in t' village. Astrid, were t'ere many horses on t'ose boats?"

Astrid paused before answering. *She mentioned some.* "At most one, maybe two, per boat, but that is all. I am not sure if there were even that many."

"T'en t'at couldst be all t'at t'ey ha'. If we kill t'ese ones, it'll be easier for us to evade 'em later. For now, just keep goin'."

He had just finished when Tabitha called forward again. "There are now a large number of footmen coming along as well, and there are two more horsemen with them."

"T'ey'll be officers or mages, or both. When it comes time t'ey'll be priority if t'ere is a chance. If'n t'ey really are t'is stupid, we may be able to call halt to t' comin' war afore it starts. We've a-taken one of t'eir leaders, an' t'eir means of communicatin' with t'eir masters, we've a-taken t'eir pay, an'now we'll take a nice piece out of t'eir raiders."

Stefan

The horses pursuing them stayed bunched together. *They are more used to raids on traders and isolated farms than to a real conflict. I would say that the men behind us are not very well aware of the actual tactics of a battle. It seems that they think that they will just run down the mostly female group fleeing in terror ahead of them.*

I may not have been in a battle either, but we have books and leaders with experience in Evilhalt, and I read and listened. In fact my aim is to separate the cavalry even further from the foot behind them and expose them even more to archery fire. The time came when Tabitha halted them.

Stefan took Cadfael and Angharad aside and gave them the packhorse to hold onto. Bryony and Astrid hung the babies' slings from the horse as well. "Stay backed into the scrub and keep him between you and them," Astrid said. "Do not try and peek around him, and if I call out…then run into the trees and take the horse." She waited, looking at them, until the two children promised.

Theodora removed Rani's helmet from her pack. "It doesn't fit very well," she complained.

"Then why are you wearing it?" asked Astrid as she placed arrows into the ground.

"Because it stops arrows," said Theodora. "I am going to be at the front, and hopefully if any of them fire a bow, they will fire at me instead of you. As well, if any are mages, I will resist their attack better than you will."

Astrid nodded. *That was an unusually sensible analysis of a battle plan for the Princess, even Basil and Ayesha are not objecting.*

Theodora took the front position as she had stated, and behind her Bryony, Astrid, Aine, Hulagu, Ayesha, and Tabitha lined up. There was only just room for them across the path. Stefan stood behind them and then Christopher stood behind him with his sling. Stefan looked and called out "Princess, Bryony, Aine and Hulagu, you will fire when I call 'odd'. The rest when I call 'even'."

The riders came on. *It looks like most of them have lances ready although some are waving swords. At least two seem to have a short bow that can be used from a horse, although not as well as those of the Khitan.*

"Nock."

"Draw."

"Odd—fire, reload." Four arrows streaked out and found targets in man or horse.

"Even—fire, reload"

"Odd—fire, reload"

Although there were only a few of them firing, the co-ordinated volleys were already showing their effect. Even though several of the pursuers wore armour, their horses didn't, and four were already down. One pursuer looked like he was drawing a wand, but the archers were watching for this.

On the next volley he was hit by three of the four shafts—and two of the archers had used exploding heads. The rider toppled off his horse, dead or dying, to disappear under the hooves of those behind him. Further back in the pack a horse tripped over his body, further adding to the chaos. The horse screamed.

The riders kept coming and Stefan kept calling and the arrows kept flying. *As they draw closer our arrows are having more effect. It seems that there are at least a few archers among the riders as the shorter-range shafts of their lighter bows are starting to appear near the line...but Theodora was right. They are taking the easy course and aiming at the person in front. No one has seemed to notice that their arrows are falling out of the sky rather than hit her.*

Stefan kept calling. *Horses and riders keep falling, but the riders are either very brave or else foolhardy or even arrogant. At any rate, they are not very observant of what is happening around them. The cries and other noise from the fallen are growing louder.* Closer they came, and Stefan and Basil began preparing their martobulli. *There seem to be no more mages.*

Eventually their courage failed, and the front riders started to try to halt and turn on the narrow path. At first, they were forced on by the others behind them, but eventually they all halted in a knot around a hand of hands of paces away unsure whether to press on or run. *Let us help you decide.*

Stefan and Basil started throwing their heavy iron darts as soon as they stopped, and the attack of these joined in the assault from the bows to terrible effect. *Some, now on foot, are starting to flee, but it is too late for them.* The last were cut down before they could escape out of range.

Stefan looked back down the path and judged distances. "Forward and glean shafts. Dispatch the wounded, even the horses. We don't want to meet them later." Except for the priest and the children, they went forward to recover their arrows and darts. Gradually, the wounded were silenced. After they had picked out all the arrows they could find and worked out which could be reused, they returned and sorted their shafts out to the right owners.

"I found which one was the mage," said Theodora. "I have his equipment, or at any rate the bits of it that felt magical."

"And I found their purses," grinned Astrid as she held up a small sack which seemed to be fairly heavy. "Some of them must have been wealthy. They won't be using these to pay the mob now."

"Good. All ready? Then let us a-continue. The rest haven't slowed, but we still have good lead and we've had chance to catch our breath." They kept going and eventually reached the turn-off from the river that led into the jungle.

They continued past the assarts they had seen on the way in. *Again, the people ignore us as we go by. This time the local habits really aid us well, as any of the inhabitants who see us know nothing of the pursuit behind, and just look on or wave as we pass.* Eventually, they reached the solid wall of jungle as the more lightly encumbered pursuers had started to gain a little on them.

When they had gone some way up the path, and around a covering corner, Astrid pulled off from the lead, handed Basil the babies in their slings and her spear, and started digging in a pack saddle on their horse.

"I am going to set something to give them pause," she said to Stefan. "I thought that I might need this, and I brought a surprise package." She removed a box from her pack, and from it carefully pulled a molotail and a ball of cord. "Take the box and hurry on. I will catch up. I thought of a nice way to adapt a hunting trap."

Fifteen minutes later a loud explosion and a chorus of screams rent the air. Soon after, Astrid came running up from the rear and rejoined them just as a faint flicker of fire could be seen through the denseness of the forest. She laughed. "Yes," she exclaimed. "I laid the trap then stepped back around the corner and put a couple of shafts into them to bunch them up a bit and then ran off. It seems to have worked."

As far as I can see, from the occasional glimpses that I get, the pursuit is keeping up all day. Around them the noise of the jungle continued, oblivious to what played out below. Although they saw some of the beasts of the jungle, the very fact that they were moving much more quickly and noisily guaranteed that most would be scared away from their path.

Every now and then, when there was enough clear space to see those behind them, Astrid would drop back from the main group and fire a couple of shafts into the pursuers and then duck back onto the path through the solid jungle. This forced their pursuers to slow and search for any traps as they continued.

She reports that they definitely have only weaker bows and none of their shafts are coming close to her. "Basil can keep the babies. I can keep this up all day. I guess that I will actually have to do that. It is a pity that I only brought one of the molotails, but I didn't think that the chance to use a second was very likely."

Eventually they drew ahead of the pursuit. *It is hard to tell, but either the villagers have given up, or they have taken a break to eat and will continue the pursuit later. As far as they know they have many days to go before we even leave the jungles. The pursuers know the area and can even move forward in pursuit at night if they wish.*

A pursuit always takes a long time to reach its end, but usually the advantage lies with the pursuers to set out the terms of it. Those who are fleeing, and who also have the smaller numbers have to run as fast as they can. Any rest for them is a danger, particularly when there is only one path that they can take. However, unknown to the pursuers, we are only travelling a short way and that changes the rules of the game.

The Mice ate as they walked, only stopping briefly when they needed to attend to nature and taking every chance to open the gap between themselves and their pursuers. *If we can get to the saddles and fly away before we are seen, it will add to the mystery of the attack and leave our opponents with even less knowledge of what we did.*

As far as the Swamp will know, we could even have come from the Caliphate, we could be mercenaries, we could even be disguised local thieves, and not only are none of us of the right appearance, but we are travelling in totally the wrong direction to have come from Haven. It will likely remain a complete mystery for Rising Mud, unless Father Kessog is caught.

As they went on weariness became a problem. First, the children had to awkwardly ride, one at a time, on the pack frame, and then Theodora had to take a break. *I remember Basil saying something about stamina. We will need to work on this when we train before we go out more into the world.* The children were even fed as their mothers walked.

Just before dusk Stefan called a halt. "We feed, we relieve ourselves an' we sit an' stretch. No a-sleepin'. Make sure t'at you hast somethin' to drink. We're a-travellin' fast. Bryony, you know t' area. If'n I'm right, we should reach t'ruins in an hour or so, t'at be right?"

"I think so", she replied. "That last creek looks familiar."

"What do we do when we get there?" asked Tabitha. "We have the children now, and it is a day early for Goditha to be back."

"You an' Aine, you can take t'em in your saddles an' ride double. T'e saddles should ha' more t'an enough lift for t'at."

"What about Dzlieri Guli?" asked Hulagu. Everyone looked at him. He patted the packhorse beside him. "Dzlieri Guli. It is what I have called this one. It means 'Strong Heart.' He is good packhorse, not big like my sister's Sluggard, but he works hard and with no complaint, and held still when arrows flying. We not want to lose him. Good horse to take on raids."

Bloody Khitan and horses... "But we canna put him on saddle."

"Why not? He is small. We still have medicine to knock him out. We sling him with rope between two saddles, or better still four. Tie ropes to his girth and packframe. We fly low until we know it is secure. Saddles carry that much I am sure. Theodora will know." He looked at her.

She had an expression on her face of thought. "If the lightest people do it and they have nothing else on their saddles, not even weapons, it should be quite safe if we use four. Astrid has made everyone practice flying and staying in formation. It is just as well, but it will take some time to rig it up, won't it?"

"Then we should hurry," said Hulagu, standing up.

Why even try and resist? "Yes... It is time to get a-goin' again." To a chorus of groans, they stood and set off into the growing twilight.

Astrid

The short jungle twilight had faded into dark by the time they found the ruins. Quickly they began to unearth the saddles and prepare them. *It is time for us to delay things a bit.* She gathered Bryony and went back down the track a little way to an area where the jungle had a very open space under the canopy to see if their followers were close.

We need to confuse things more and erase as many tracks as we can. They had just started to see some movement, and Astrid had sent a shaft that way and was rewarded with a cry, when they were called back to the ruins. Stefan was the last there with their saddles. "Time to say farewell," he said as they mounted and flew off after the others.

They flew for a few hours north and east towards the mountains, and then stopped to eat and sleep.

Theodora
27th Undecim

Next morning, they went on to Birchdingle, arriving before Goditha left. *My beloved is surprised. Not only are we all safe, but we have brought the horse back, two children, and even have enough treasure with us to pay for a small army. We can add that to the already overflowing coffers of Mousehole... as if we needed more.*

Waiting with Rani and Goditha were Arlene Caelfinddottir, Fullon Ógánson and Ir Baethson, the three children who would come back to the school. They were introduced to the two children that had come from the Swamp.

"We are not going to all fit on the carpet," said Rani.

"Children will travel on carpet with Goditha, and you will ride my saddle back," said Hulagu. "I will walk with Dzlieri Guli and most of the treasure. When you get back send my köle with horses for me. They will find us on the road. Tell them to be quick. I have walked far enough already.

"I am Khitan. We are not meant to walk. That is why the spirits invented horses so that we only have to use legs for dancing." He smiled.

"Admit it," said Astrid. "It offends you as a Khitan, once you have a horse in your possession, to ever let go of it for any reason unless you are made to. You will do almost anything to add to your herds. Isn't that true?"

Hulagu answered with a grin on his face. "This I will not bother to completely deny, but he is a good horse nonetheless."

Chapter XVII

Chief Predestinator Gamil
12,789,387,1300L

I *am very excited. Despite all of our working and planning, the checking and the re-checking of the calculations, it is just not possible to predict everything that will happen when you get down to details. Who would have expected the Renegade to take the part that he has chosen, and to get involved in the whole matter as subtly as he so consistently has this time around?*

It is almost as if he intervenes without intervening. He is almost acting as I act, just poking and prodding and motivating and enabling. It lies completely outside my calculations. The Daveen must be wrath. What will they do? What can they do without breaking the Rules? Will they indeed break the Rules again?

They broke them before when they thought that they had needed to, but the consequences may have been so severe then that, despite their desire for control of Vhast they may think twice, or perhaps even more often, before doing so again. Exquisite…it is exquisite.

She turned her mind back to her screens, waiting to see what would perhaps happen next. *It is lucky that my people need very little sleep as it is more exciting to watch things unfold live rather than seeing a recording the next morning.*

I just wish that, whatever they have done in the valley, I could see through it and hear properly rather than just deduce what is going on there. I know that the technical people are behaving like primates over this, jumping up and down and making agitated sounds, but it is having no effect. We have to rely solely on visuals taken from too far away to be of any real use.

Unless something happens inside one of the buildings, and a lot does, we can just see, roughly, what is happening in the valley, even if we often cannot tell who does it. We sometimes cannot even tell a man from a woman. What is worse, we cannot hear a single thing, and so we do not have any idea why anything happens even when we see it.

Any remotes we have sent disappear off-screen on their final approach, and so they have not been able to help either. None have even been recovered. It means for imprecision in the calculations, but still I am feeling very pleased and in great hope of final success.

Chapter XVIII

Ruth Hawker
28th Undecim

*H*aving our raiders return to Mousehole with a carpet load of children for the school is a bit of a surprise. Suddenly, I have thirteen children instead of just the seven residents. I may be looking a bit harassed; after all, what language do I even teach them in?

Each of the local children (except Repent, the youngest of the local girls, and also the one with the least grasp of languages) was given one of the new children as a study partner. It was that child's responsibility to help their partner learn.

I do not know if it is better or worse that the Princesses have decided that there will be three main languages taught here. It makes sense to have Latin, Hindi, and Darkspeech as a start, although as they get older, they will, like the adults, be expected to learn more. People from the west of the Land usually have at least some Latin, the east speaks Darkspeech and the rest usually have some Hindi.

The role that Princess Rani has outlined in order for Mousehole to prosper demands that we be able to communicate with anyone we come across, and I concur. We will always be small, and to succeed in the long term we will need to be traders, diplomats and teachers.

Princess Theodora added that it is hard to quickly gain someone's sympathy and trust if you cannot talk to them in their own language. All of our local children, those who were brought here by the bandits, lack one or more of these main three, and so they will have to work harder to learn them themselves in order to help teach their partner.

Presbytera Bianca the Foundling

A nahita and Kāhina are to be sent south to fetch Hulagu. As they get ready, they joke about him walking, and wonder if they should forget to bring him a horse or else just stay ahead of him, out of bowshot, so that he has to walk the whole way back. That is wrong. It is time for me, as his sister, to put my foot down.

"Do I have to come with you and make sure you do not do that and bring dishonour on him? He is doing this to add to our herd, not because he has lost his horse or because he likes walking. He is trying to add to your honour, do not take away from his."

Now, chastened at being lectured like this by one not born of the tents, they are suddenly quietly packing and riding off down the track with spare horses trailing behind on leads. Now, at last, they move quickly.

Chapter XIX

Rani
28th Undecim

Once they were all settled again, and she had left her wife and Ruth to make the introductions for the children, and to the sound of much noise and chaos to see about barracks rooms being prepared for them, Rani sat down in her study to think with some tea and some candied fruit that her wife had returned with.

I need to consider where next as a target for our expeditions out of the village. We have cleared, or at least neutralised in the case of Darkreach, six of the pattern locations. We are halfway there. We cannot rest on our efforts so far. We have to keep going. We now need to move quickly, and to do as much as we can before our advantage of surprise is lost, and before the Masters can mobilise another force to send against us.

After a long time of thinking she sighed deeply. *Much as I hate to contemplate it, the next place that we have to strike out at is to eliminate the pattern that is in my home city of Pavitra Phāṭaka. It is the next closest pattern that we know of, and while it exists, it is the pattern that poses the most direct threat to us.*

As she sat and inhaled the hibiscus scent of a fragrant tisane in one of Jordan's new cups—*a cup that doesn't wobble when you put it down*—she contemplated what lay ahead. *Going home openly will plunge me back into the everyday politics of caste that I left behind when I decided to follow my prophesised destiny.*

The rulers of Haven may have known for a long time about my destiny, but they are obviously uncomfortable with it. They could have done a lot to prepare me for my task, but instead they waited, and they kept me ignorant.

Once my destiny became apparent, they hurried me out of Haven as quickly as they could. They did so politely, and with all the assistance that they could give me and still remain silent, but nonetheless they had done it. It was done so quickly that I was not given time to think about what was happening, or what would happen to me, and I thus had no real chance to refuse.

Now…I have changed. I have changed a lot. When I go back, who I can talk to, who I can touch, what I can eat and do, will suddenly become important again. If I take Lakshmi or Parminder with me and admit their caste, I cannot even talk to them in front of my parents. I can talk to Shilpa, but cannot allow her to stay in my parent's house.

If I take my wife, how will I introduce her to my family? Should I lie? Her being a woman, while not a negligible problem in itself, is of far less actual importance than the fact that she is paradēśī, an outsider, a foreigner and so unacceptable as a partner.

Fear will never be accepted as my daughter because of her birth and she will not understand that at all. Theo-dear defiantly took me to meet her dread progenitor without knowing what his response would be. Come to think of it, why did my wife want to know if I had brothers? One thing at least, although it is very unlikely, is that if my family decides that Theodora has a caste at all it will be the same as mine if not perhaps slightly higher.

Getting back to the main problem, it is a mystery how the Master's pattern has been concealed for as long as it has. Admittedly, it lies on Anta Dvīpa, End Island, and not many people, or at any rate, not many people that I know have even been on that island.

It is almost entirely, as far as I know, inhabited by the Sudra and Harijan castes, and so in theory, Shilpa will be best person to look into its secrets, as she is a trader and so Sudra. The island lies beside the only channel of the Rhastaputra that leads to the sea without any bridges.

Being the only route from the river for an ocean-going vessel, the island is an ideal place from which to slip in and out of the city by sea. Bridges span every other channel, although many Brahmin or Kshatya only use boats to move around the city on rather than risk the contamination of the streets.

The only bridge from Anta is to Vyāpārī Dvīpa, Merchant's Island. Again, there is a Sudra connection. Anta is at the end of all of the bridges and ferries. It is the last place in Pavitra Phāṭaka…in so many ways an isolated place in a crowded city.

I have been mulling over the two ingredients that are probably the key to the Master's pattern lying concealed for all this time. Firstly, there is its isolated location. Such a menace should have mainly the Brahmin or the Kshatya looking for it, unless someone in Haven has some group like Basil's people working in it…and I have never heard of that.

However, the Brahmin caste are hardly ever seen off Rājā kē Dvīpa,

Vidvānōṁ Dvīpa or Mandira Dvīpa, Rajah's Island, the Island of Scholars or the Temple Island. If they even visit Vyāpārī, it is with their heads held high and their eyes averted from everything. They are blind to anything that they do not want to see, and they only seek to avoid ritual pollution. I know. I was the same way such a short time ago.

More importantly, my caste, the caste of rulers and warriors, has been lax in our duties. It is our job to protect Haven, and it seems that we have failed in this regard. We have, in our pride, only looked for the obvious external threats to Haven such as are presented by the bandits of the Swamp or, at the most, have looked for the threats that might come to our trade routes.

From the perspective I have now, it is not clear why we did that. It is not as if Haven can do much about the latter, as the trade routes lie largely outside Haven, and without the ability to send a force there quickly, are largely beyond their control.

The last time I heard of an attempt to send a force outside Haven was when some Freeholders stole an army payroll and fled back west across the plains. The thieves defeated all of those little forces that had been uselessly sent after them, until a thug had eventually gotten to them once they thought they were safe back in their home in Trekvarna.

Haven still hadn't been able to recover the payroll, and the attempt had more than slightly soured relations with Freehold for quite a while, as the same people had been of some use to the Queen there. Even the people living in the towns along the coast had not been happy with the troops that had been sent.

My best tool to find out what is happening, and who went to where the pattern is, and even who the tools of the Masters are now in Haven, will be to take the Harijan Lakshmi with me, and to simply lie about her caste to my family when it is needed.

She shuddered at the religious consequences to her doing this. Having admitted to herself that this may be the best course, then it was also possible to admit that Lakshmi and Basil, between them, could probably ferret out the truth.

If they have a mage to back them up. I probably cannot take on that role in a city where I am known, but is Parminder advanced enough to do the job? She is learning, but is she learning fast enough? Will she be in too much danger? Will any of the women who come from Haven want to go back to what they have left behind?

Here, they have status and friends and few restrictions. In Haven, they will be looked down on, and have all sorts of restrictions placed on what they can do and where they can go. What is more, Parminder will have to leave her sister Gurinder, and her daughter Melissa. At least Gurinder is going to school, and she can stay in the barracks if Goditha feels she cannot look after her on her own.

Is it important that Parminder is now Christian? I don't think that changing religion affects your caste. It is not a subject that has ever come up for me before. If it doesn't affect caste, then despite being a mage, and one who is a rare mage of the elemental spirit, and with gifts of the mind that even I envy, she is still Harijan and not even eligible to enrol at the university or become a mage.

She will be regarded as an abomination and none of the mages in Haven will even talk to her. Some might even try to have her eliminated. Lakshmi is now Christian also, and she might not want to leave her son George behind either. Just because Astrid and Bryony took their children to the Swamp doesn't mean that anyone else will want to take theirs into danger.

In fact, Astrid may have made it harder to get one of the mothers to go out of Mousehole, for even in the short time since they have returned, she has been loud in saying how hard it is with a baby outside, not only keeping them safe from flying arrows, that part she is dismissive of as a normal fact of life, but in keeping them quiet, feeding them while trying to scout, getting clean nappies in the field and such other things that most mothers do not have to cope with in their daily life with children who are safely at home. She is now actively looking towards weaning her two as fast as she can.

If we do not go to Haven openly what can we do? If we are hidden, it will mean that we cannot count on the open support of the Maharaja, although I can still use my letter if I need it. Also, we will not have the backing of the Mages at the University, but that may be more of an advantage than a hindrance. I realise now that they are so rigid in their thinking…as bad in many ways as Darkreach.

The only thing that I have been trained for is to be a Battle Mage. I have been taught spells for war and for killing. I have not been encouraged to think of new uses of magic, but just to get better at my job, and learn by rote and become comfortable with casting more and more powerful killing spells, most of which have been written down and prepared for many turns of the calendar.

Compare that with my wife, who is not only more powerful than most of the mages in the University, but can also sit down for a while and become totally lost to the world, and when she re-emerges to reality, will have come up with new spells that are unheard of and have major implications. There is only one old water mage at the University that I know of who would get lost like that… and his mind wanders anyway.

Nothing like the spell for the saddles and the spell that hides the valley has ever existed, to my knowledge, and while they would not have been able to be cast by anyone I have ever known before, Theo-dear worked out how to do them when she really should have failed. No, not having the mages on my side, as long as I have my wife with me, is not really a problem for my planning.

I should go back and think at a more basic level. If we go to Haven, we can go there one of three ways and each has its own limitations and advantages. We can go by land, by water or by air. In the same way we can return by each of the same methods, but some ways of going exclude other ways of returning or other options of action.

For instance, if we go by land that will mean riding, as the chance of getting the Mice to walk that far is, except for Astrid, Aziz and perhaps Tabitha or Bryony, negligible. If we are riding, we will not be able to take the saddles. Not having the saddles will mean that we cannot return by air. If we go by air, we will have to be open.

The chance of secretly flying through a city that has more mages than anywhere else in The Land, without being detected, is absolutely zero. If we are flying, we will have to declare ourselves. It will warn the people we are coming for, and it will restrict who can go. It will also restrict how many can go. There are only ten saddles and one carpet. That places a very small upper limit on how many people can be used.

If I rule out going by land and through the air, that leaves going by water as the only option, and there are three variants on that. We could come from the east, the west or down the river. If we come from the west, then we will have to get to one of the independent villages of the plains and then find a trading vessel heading east to travel on.

We can count on Metropolitan Cosmas for support there, and possibly the Khitan, but it will still mean a lot of travel. If we come from the east, that will mean going to Darkreach and then getting a ship from Southpoint. I am sure that Hrothnog will give us a ship and Basil would love to see his parents, but that will also not be very inconspicuous and will take a very long time.

I have never seen anything on the subject, and so I am not sure when the last Darkreach ship was seen in the waters around Haven, but I am almost ready to swear that it was not a friendly trader and we would ourselves be travelling on one of their ships of war.

That leaves coming by river. It is possible to get a river trader from Erave Town. We could either hire one or buy one. If we hired one, we would not have as much control of it. If we bought one, we would have to crew it, and of all of the people in the valley, I think that only Astrid knows how to sail. Would that be important? I wonder how hard it would be to learn.

Can Astrid teach us enough in, say, a couple of weeks for us to use a boat? We already have experience with her teaching people in the sky, so people are at least used to listening to her. As well, just how hard can it be to sail down *a river? I will have to talk to Astrid. If we go by boat, can we return the same way?*

I suppose that it will be harder to come back up the river, instead of just float down it, but I presume that my wife, an air mage, can produce a wind if she wants to, and on the way down we can perhaps learn the skills that we need to sail back up.

It is spring and will be summer soon. The wind in Haven comes mainly from the southwest in those seasons, and we will have to travel north with the wind to return home and go against it when going down. Will that be important? I know nothing about boats. Again, I will have to ask Astrid. How many can we fit into a boat? Can we hide away the saddles and take them with us?

If we go by river, with the judicious use of my letter, we can perhaps conceal our numbers and who is on board and so come almost un-noticed into Pavitra Phāṭaka. Perhaps, if we can just look like river traders, we can take more people.

I am unsure how many will fit on a boat, but perhaps we can even take who-ever we want, and if who is on board is unknown, we can almost ignore caste until we emerge into the city, and we can perhaps do that at night. It will all depend on how many people and what other items we can get in a boat and what it can do.

Rani realised that it was now time for her to come out of her study. *I have spent most of the day here and can go no further just sitting and thinking. Going to Pavitra Phāṭaka by water looks to be the best option for us at the moment, but I really do not have enough information to work with to create any sort of plan.* She sighed. *Everything I have thought about leads me to go and ask Astrid.*

Rani
A little later

*A*strid seems very pleased with the idea, perhaps too pleased. Travelling on a boat seems to her to be the best option of all. She will have a place to put the babies to sleep and she will not have to be near a horse. As for what they could do with a boat, at least she admitted that she was not sure. She has not seen much of the boats of the south.*

She says that she is used to coracles and wherries and skerries and knorr and drakkar, whatever they all are…they sound more like animals than boats.

Astrid said that she will need to see some from the lake up close. That means going to Lake Erave and seeing what is available. She is already rubbing her hands together in happiness.

It is easy to see that she wants to buy a boat. I should have expected that. Asking Astrid whether to buy or hire a boat is a bit like asking Hulagu whether to buy or to hire a horse. Well, at least money is not a problem Astrid is taking some time to give me an answer on whether she could train a crew.

"Give me a week with them on the Lake and I will tell you if it can be done," she said. "They will not be sailors in that time, but if they are going to be good enough to not sink us, and to know what to do if I call an order, I will know. It will take at least another week, maybe two or three, to get them to where I am happy with them, and we will have another week as we travel down-river.

"That will be easy for them. This new priest, this Simeon, can I use him as a sailor? He probably has at least some experience with sailing to have gotten here. I will ask him." *She has now slipped into the same, only half-there, talking to oneself mode that Theo-dear often does when contemplating spells.*

"We will need a strong light that can shine ahead from the bow, to sail at night. We will need a way to call up winds as we need them and…I will think about what else. Oh…that is one thing…if we are in a boat already…there was that Gil-Gand-Rask place that has a pattern of the Masters. Is that nearby? Can we just sail on to it?"

She turned to her husband. "Basil…you will love this…it is so much fun to be on a boat. It will be even better in the south with its flat seas." *Basil doesn't look very convinced despite the eagerness as she speaks. Astrid picked up on that very quickly.* "Your sister likes them," she added hopefully.

Rani left Astrid excitedly planning and thinking and wondering what she could get into a boat on a river. *The woman has, as usual, left me with more questions than I started with. They are different questions, but there are more of them. However, it at least looks like it has a chance to work if we take this path.*

Rani
31st Undecim, early in the morning

A strid came up to Rani. She was dressed for travel and she and Basil had one child each in a sling. She opened with, "Father Simeon can sail a bit… he worked his way across in a trading boat of the Latins. That will give me someone who can be my coxswain, so we have a better chance of success." *She is looking at me as if she is expecting an argument.*

"I want you to give me some money, actually I want you to give me a lot of money. I am taking Basil and we are going to take some saddles and fly to Evilhalt, and if need be, go on to Erave Town to look for a boat. If we find the right one, we will buy it on the spot before they have a chance to think over the deal and ask for more."

Rani was set back on her heels. *Here I am carefully planning each step, and Astrid is jumping in with both feet. Astrid can obviously see this on my face.* She continued: "Even if we don't use it now, it may come in useful later, and even if I can buy one that I like, it will probably need to be re-built. It will either be a normal fishing boat or a small trader.

"You will want something that is more like a smugglers boat with hidden places, and places under cover, and places we can put saddles and large sums of money, and a flat bit to put one of your magic patterns on, so that Theodora can call up winds and all of those other things…weapons storage…a safe place for molotails…able to carry a couple of horses if we need to.

"I am not going to be able to buy a boat that has everything we need, but I will buy one that can be made to have most of what we want. I am tossing up whether to go for speed or manoeuvre. Have you decided whether we are going to this island? That will affect the amount of freeboard I want it to have, and whether it has a flat bottom. Even a drakkar has a keel and sideboards for the open sea."

Dealing with Astrid is sometimes a little like dealing with a monsoon rain. There is something unstoppable about her sometimes. "I am not sure, but prepare for it…mind you, I don't even know what freeboard is—I presume that boats come with it, or do they have to have it added?—let alone most of the rest of it."

From the grin on Astrid's face, I have just said something incredibly stupid and even Basil has a faint smile on his face. It must have been a really spectacular stupidity, and I cannot even point out my greater knowledge in other areas. Astrid will cheerfully admit her ignorance on most other fronts. "Go to the mine and get what you need for money. How long will you be?"

"I was going to take Stefan and Bryony. They don't know it yet, but he can see his family, and it will help us in the town to be seen as being a bit more local, and both Basil and I are not really good at speaking Dwarven. His family can fuss over the baby and over Bryony. I think that she needs some fussing over as well."

"I can have a good bath in the pools under the Enemy," she continued. "I do so wish that Goditha had the time to get our bathhouse finished. It is the only way to feel clean and we have the hot spring. As well, we need to settle down for a bit, because Basil wants some time to see if anyone is asking about us.

"We also want to take Lakshmi with us. She wants to talk to someone about making rosewater, and Basil wants her to have some more experience on what he calls police work in someone else's village before we go to Haven. I am intending to take at least a week.

"We will all be very innocent and well-behaved, just three women with babies. Do you want us to take any messages? I am sure that Sigihevi, and Cynric if we go to Erave Town, will want to hear from you. It is what rulers do with each other, isn't it?" *There was a studied innocence that she used in that last question.*

Chapter XX

Astrid
A little later on the 31st of Undecim

*D*espite the light showers that are running up the mountains, we are setting out before something else gets added to the list of things to do. I have letters to deliver, not just to Sigihevi and Cynric, but also, once Father Christopher heard where we are going, to Father Anastastias and Metropolitan Cosmas as well.

I want us to look less military than we usually do, and so while we have our weapons, they are strapped on rather than carried in our hands. As they were about to set out, Theodora came out. *We have been caught again.*

"Good, you are still here," she said. "I want you each to take one of these in case you need them. Keep them concealed." She started handing out wands to them. "They are mine, so they use air bolts, which means they are safe to use indoors. Only use them if you need to. Now, Astrid, I need to know how much wind you will want and for how long you want it to last."

"Every Captain's desire...controllable wind," she smiled and then turned serious. "We need it to last as long as you can, but having it when needed would be best. If we need to call up wind it will be either because we are becalmed, or because we need to get more speed than someone else." *What is best...it is hard to say.*

"If it is because we are becalmed, we will need it fresh...say strong enough to raise horses on the waves...you know what I mean?" Theodora nodded. *Unlike her husband, at least she has been on a ship.* "That will need to last longer. If we are escaping, we will need it stronger...strong wind, enough to pick up waves and make the spray fly. We might not need that for as long though. Can you do something for both?"

How about the reverse? "Something to calm a storm would also be good, if we are going to cross an ocean with an inexperienced crew."

"Out on the ocean? In a small boat?" *That last almost came out as a squeak. There is a look of concern on Theodora's face.* "How small?"

"I have done it lots and lots of times. It can be quite safe. I take it Rani didn't tell you that part. Better if you have a word with your husband. It is time for us to go now. Babies only last so long quiet. Bye." *It is time for a quick exit.*

Astrid jumped on her saddle and waved her group into the air. *Rani had probably guessed Theodora's reaction to that part and avoided bringing the subject up.* She turned as they flew over the village wall to wave at Harald standing guard on the Hall. *Theodora is heading quickly back to her house.*

Astrid

*I*t is like a Holy Day fair. We are going somewhere without anyone to kill when we get there, and with lots of money to do some shopping. I am looking forward to the rest. I grabbed a lot of money, probably far more than we need. I have enough with me to buy a boat or two, and to have them modified as I want…and then enough for each of us to just have fun with as well. Glyn and the horsemen who followed us will pay for it all, and Stefan has to impress his parents after all.*

She turned in the air to address the others. "What does everyone think about this…we will have to stop to feed and change the babies, so can we do it somewhere comfortable? Let's go to the Darkreach outpost and give them something to report. I brought some stuff along with me, in case the weather is good enough for a picnic on the way and the showers clear.

"They must get bored sitting there on their little mountain. It will mean an early stop for us, but this will be a good excuse for us to look at one of their forts and see how it is set up, and to see what they can see from where they are. If they get huffy, I can introduce the Tribune to them."

Basil was about to say something, when Stefan called out above the wind of their passage. "Basil may object, 'cause he hast two duties, but I be t'inkin' it good idea. You never a-know when we might a-need 'em in some way, an' it'd be nice to know what be t'ere. Basil, do you know what be actual t'ere?"

"No, I don't, and you are right. It is prudent, while we have spare time, to check it out."

Astrid curved them off to the right.

Memrin do Modlin

*O*h dear, this could be interesting. I had better make sure that I am right… *it would not do to make a mistake here…it is too easy for a Primus to lose that stripe over an error.* She applied her eye to the telescope again. *Yes, I am sure…now to try not to sound nervous.* "Sergeant…" He looked up. "The flying things from the valley…"

"Yes, we know all about them." *He sounds impatient.*

"Well, some are coming here," she said.

"What do you mean coming here?" *Now he sounds nervous.*

"Five of them left the valley some time ago, and I noted it down as we are supposed to, and then I ignored them because they started by heading down from the hills towards the lake, but a little while ago they changed their direction and are now coming directly here."

I guess that the clatter behind me on the ladder leading up here, the platform for the lookout and the signal beacon, means he is coming up to check…and the second lighter clattering means my sergeant is coming up as well. Then there is a third That must be our druid too. It is marvellous what a bit of excitement can do to our usually sleepy garrison. It is getting more than a bit crowded up on the platform now.

Nargrit dol Katuch

*N*o post commander has had this problem for a long time. We never have *visitors here, but there is nothing to say that we cannot have visitors. It is just that no one ever wants to visit here. We are a thousand paces above the forest and many thousands from the nearest settlement. You have to use a telescope just to see the nearest settlement.*

There are only five of the flying things approaching, but that is half of the number of riders who took out the dragon. He looked at Mü-lin, his second sergeant. *She is no help. She is looking at me with a look of studied innocence that must have taken hours of practice to acquire when she was a recruit.*

Our druid is no better. He can do the minor healing that we need on garrison duty in a quiet spot, and he can run our services, but that is about all. He is an insakharl and this is his first independent duty and, while as a priest, he nominally outranks me, priests don't usually insist on the distinction, if they have any sense. *That look of innocence and cluelessness on his face is almost certainly genuine.*

He leant out of the tower and looked down. *The entire garrison is looking back up at me.* "I want one of the riders on her wolf," — he pointed at one coming out of the stables — "you will do… Get hidden out of sight outside and down the hill as soon as possible. You are to observe and only come in if I call you or send this Primus for you" he pointed at Memrin.

"If this is a trick, and we are attacked you are to wait until night and then head for Mouthguard and let them know. The rest of you…we will treat this as if it is a visit from some senior officer. I have Standing Orders from our Strategos to co-operate with them, so we will see what they want…now make this place tidy. It is time we had a proper inspection anyway."

What else should we do? "Cook…see about some refreshments." He looked at the dots for a little while before continuing. "You have perhaps half an hour. Parade uniforms all around." Below the garrison erupted in that state of chaos that only military bases have when orders like that are given.

He turned to the sentry. "Go and change, and get straight back here. I will do duty until you return." Memrin jumped and slid down the pole to the ground.

The sergeant looked at the other two. *Mü-lin is looking at me as if I am mad and the priest is still looking innocent.* "What are you two waiting for? You can get ready as well." They slid down the pole, the druid nearly falling off as he did so. *Priests…they really do need to get out in the world more often.*

Astrid

"I see people standing near a giant crossbow, two of them actually…but they are just standing there like a guard."

Basil grinned. "They are called ballistae and they are like a guard. They are in an inspection position. So much for you surprising them, I doubt that they stand like that all of the time. They are treating us like we were high ranking officers."

"Well, you are. If that is the way they want it…come on, let us land. There is enough flat space above the gate. We will put down there."

Astrid

"**G**reetings, I am Astrid the Cat from the village of Mousehole. You have probably seen us flying around. I was in charge of the fight to kill the dragon. This is Stefan, he and his wife Bryony do not speak much Darkspeech, but he made the final blows that killed the dragon. The other lady is named Lakshmi and she also speaks only a little Darkspeech, she is our village apothecary. This is my husband, Basil Akritas. He is also a Tribune of the Antikataskopeía reporting direct to Strategos Panterius."

That is better. Every spine that is visible…except that one in the robes, the only one that is not a Kichic-kharl, is visibly straightening. The one in front of them, if I am reading the insignia right is a sergeant, now has a small smile on his face and his eyes have flicked at another smaller sergeant. He called it correctly and the others didn't.

"Sergeant Nargrit of the Border Regiment, your Excellency," he turned and saluted Basil with his fist on his heart, "Sir. We are ready for inspection."

Basil

I'll bet you are. Damn it, I cannot disappoint you and Astrid did want to have a look around. If I have to play like a proper officer, she can do it as well. Time to give instructions… "Lead on, Sergeant. My wife and I will follow you." He then tried to act like he had seen officers do when he was last in barracks as a recruit, even if his wife sometimes made that hard.

I am actually impressed with how well organised they are. It is easy for isolated units to become slack, but it seems that this Nargrit does not believe in that. He was even prepared enough to have someone outside in case our visit turned bad. That is good to see.

After the inspection the cook produced some biscuits. *Good shortbread… the cook must be from Axepol. Astrid's presentation of a hand of bottles of Aine's wine and one of her brandy to the garrison went well. I wonder if Aine knows that they went missing? I have never been to one of these border posts, but from the smiles all around, this is a rare luxury for them.*

They were shown the telescopes and how far they could see, which was a very long way in a clear sky around the mount, and were even asked to sign the logbook. Basil added a note of commendation above his signature and saw Nargrit visibly grow in stature on noting it. *I'll bet that page ends up framed on the wall.*

Astrid

*I*t is nice to have a chance to see which roads can be seen from here, and how much of them. At least until it was cleared, the road to Mousehole from Evilhalt is almost invisible. They do know about it, unfortunately, but that is all. At least a request to my husband to go leafing back through the records shows that our first trip up to Mousehole had not been seen, but then the bandits managed to move un-noticed as well.

The garrison used the visit to practice their grasp of Dwarven and Hindi and Latin—*all of them poor*—on their guests. The saddles were also demonstrated to the troops. In particular the wolf cavalry were impressed. *Wait until I tell Hulagu and Thord that half of the garrison at Forest Watch are wolf-riders… although these are wolves like Hillstrider is a sheep.*

We are perhaps spending longer than we meant here, but we have no time limits on us, and it is good to show the neighbours that we are nice people…and to impress them at the same time.

Chapter XXI

Astrid

O n leaving Forest Watch they flew straight on down to Evilhalt. They reached the ford late in the afternoon and were let in. *I think that we will be firm from the start.* "Send a message to Baron Sigihevi please, and we will be pleased to come and see him and Father Anastasias, once we have settled in and fed the babies. If they need us more urgently, they will have to come and see us."

It turned out that they had plenty of time to feed the children and get them to sleep. Lakshmi accused them of bringing her along as a baby sitter, but she agreed to wait with them until they returned.

Astrid

I *wish that we had brought a Princess with us...this is turning out to be far more than just a courtesy meeting.* The news coming out of the Swamp had not been good, and the Lake towns had been expecting to have their trade routes disrupted all over again when they were just starting to return to normal after the destruction of the bandits.

They had not been looking forward to it happening, even if they were now fairly sure who was to blame. There had been some discussion as to whether to actually ally the towns with Haven, although Haven had not been told this. *Although it remains to be seen if our raid had actually worked, it seems that they are grateful to us for our intervention and perhaps making any war unnecessary.*

The news of the death of the dragon had come to them as rumour and been *discounted. I don't blame them…and I was there. They are more than surprised to find it to be real.* The priest and the Baron looked at each other when Astrid said she wanted to buy a boat. "Do we want to know why?" asked the Baron.

"I think that we might find it useful for some things that we have to do, and it will not be used here for more than trading anyway as this is where we will keep it."

"It will be perfectly deniable and have no connection with you…although I doubt that it will get up to anything that you would disapprove of," added Basil. "The saddles are very conspicuous as a means of entry into an area; that is all."

That satisfies them and we can close the meeting…oh yes "Our Princesses have taken it into their collective heads that they are going to open a school. I know that most areas have schools, but this one will be different. For a start, the children will be in school a lot more each day, the same as ours are now.

"They will learn many languages, and get a good teaching in geography and the customs of many lands. We are in the best position of any place to do that. They will be tested, and if they pass, they will get training as mages. Each child will also be kept healthy with exercise and training, depending on their talents. They will, of course, learn to use weapons.

"Also," she continued, "it has been decided that, in case they forget every-thing that is useful in the real world, they will rotate around the village, working with different people until they find something practical that they are good at, and then they will train in that as well for half a day a week."

She grinned. "We expect all of the children to go to bed very tired every day. One of the things we are going to offer is a chance to meet with children who will return to their own cultures, often as leaders. We already have a child from the southern hobgoblins." *The expression on their faces is worthwhile in reaction to that, now for part two…* "And three from the Bear people." *I was right; they are shocked.*

"Father Kessog, from Rising Mud, has also entrusted his children to us for a while, but they are not being charged anything. We expect some Dwarves, and even some senior children from Darkreach. Even if none of your civic leaders want to send any of their children, it will be an ideal preparation for anyone of your people who want their children to be a trader. I can assure you, although I cannot explain myself, they will have some unique training opportunities,"

I cannot mention Ayesha, but I can talk of other things: "For a start, think of the bards we have that you know about. We have a lot more than that to offer now." They took their leave as they left the Baron and the priest deep in conversation.

Stefan took Bryony and they collected Aneurin, and went on to visit his parents and to show off the grandchild and Bryony's wedding jewellery. Astrid and Basil looked in on their offspring, who proved to be still asleep. Astrid collected Lakshmi and told Basil it was his turn to look after the children, and went to show Lakshmi what a real bathhouse was like.

Astrid
32nd Undecim

The next morning Stefan arrived back at the inn without Bryony. "She be still with my mother an' being fussed over, an' much be made of t' first grandchild."

Once the others were ready, he took them out of the south gate of Evilhalt and they went downstream of the ford along the shore towards the Lake itself. *I saw a large shed there, probably for drying timber, and something being built beside it as we came in to land.*

There it is. It is not a type of craft that I know well. I have seen its like once in the north when it came up from Freehold, but I have never seen one out of the water on a slip and never thought to see one on the lake. It is caravel built and not a river trader at all. This craft is not what I was thinking of.

I am totally unfamiliar with the rig, but I would have to talk to the builder... besides it probably isn't for sale. It has the look of something that has been built for someone. Perhaps it is being built in secret for someone from the lands to the west, and it is almost complete. Three men, a woman and two lads are working on it, that I can see.

"Master Jacob," called Stefan in Dwarven up to one of the men working on fitting the rigging. *It has two masts, and from the look of the yards, the sails are going to be very different to anything that I have ever sailed...square rig and fore-and-aft as well.* A man poked his head over the rail and looked down.

"Stefan, you've returned. Come to a-look for job, ha'you?" said the man gruffly.

"No," replied Stefan with a wide smile. "T'at be one t'in' t'at I don't be a-need'n. I've at least two jobs an' whole new village now. I am simple here to visit my parents, an' a-show off my wife an' child, an' to help my friend here, who now also a-comes from our village of Mousehole."

"She be a-wantin' to buy boat. You might remember her be a-leavin' with us. She be t' hunter, who helped bring t' new Gospel from Greensin, t' one known as T' Cat. She doesn't speak much Dwarven. She original be from Wolfneck." *The boatwright is looking a little puzzled at me.* She smiled at him. He nodded stiffly to her. *He remembers me now.*

"What does she be a-needin' ship for? Can she be a-sail'n one? I t'ought t'at she be hunter?"

"She's from Wolfneck an' has sailed up to t' ice more t'an once afore. Her father be shipowner, so a-course she has sailed. She hast decided t'at we need boat to be goin' to Haven an' beyond. T'at is all. You'll have to ask her any more t'an t'at. I be soldier an' leatherworker, I be a-knowin' nothin' of boats."

The man started climbing down from the boat, leaving instructions behind to the workers as he came. He came over to the group and looked coldly at Lakshmi and Basil. *Lakshmi is smiling at him with her warmest smile, and you can almost watch the hardness of his features melt, despite the baby on her hip.*

"Be t'is your wife?" he asked.

"No, I'll a-meet you together later." He then switched his language to Hindi to do introductions in. "Master Jacob, t'is'n be Lakshmi. She be our village apothecary, an' also trader in herbs an' gems. T'is be Astrid t' Cat, who you met before. She wants t' boat, an' t'is be her husband Basil. Basil be Darkreach Tribune. He be high officer, who be sent to organise t' guard on one of our rulers." *Be polite and nod as we are introduced.*

"Greetings," said Jacob, also in Hindi. "Stefan didn't a-know, but what do you be a-needin' boat for?"

"For my part, I haven't had a chance to sail since I left home, and I want to occasionally go from here down to Sacred Gate and then perhaps further," *Keep a straight face. I am getting good at making up a story as I go. I must remember that.* "Lakshmi here wants some plants that grow only on the southern islands and even perhaps from south Darkreach, for her potions and, in the long run it would be far cheaper to get a good supply for ourselves when we need them, rather than buy them from traders. We can then also sell them on the way back.

"Basil has a report to prepare on the possibility of basing a Darkreach trader here and of having him trade down the river. So, he wants to see the river. I thought, why hire a ship when we can afford to buy our own and fit it as suits us? That way we are not beholden to someone else, and can go where we feel like. Besides, I miss sailing and want to play on the water sometimes."

"You can be a-buyin' ship on whim? As toy?" *Now, that is a lovely shocked look on the man's face. Even Rani could not match it. Let us add to it.*

"Haven't you heard? We wiped out the bandits of the plains...and took their treasure. We found Dwarvenholme and killed the creatures in it...and took their treasure, and then we killed the Dragon of the Mountains...and took its treasure.

"If I want to buy a town on a whim, I can do that. Stefan can have one of his own as well...but it would have to be a different town if I've bought mine. Now, having said that, I am not going to be gulled by shoddy goods or overcharged, but I will pay good money if I can get what I want. Do you have what I want, or do you know where I can get it?"

Master Jacob is glancing back at the boat behind him and nervously rubbing his hands. He seems quite a bit meeker now. He wants to sell this one, doesn't he? He may have built it for someone, but something has gone wrong.

"Well, ma'am, it be like this…you a-see t'is one behind us" he waved at it bulking large over the conversation. "It be done on commission. T' man who ordered it, he did bring plans, an' said it be for coastal trade, but he didn't want it be a-built in Freehold. T' plans, t'ey came from Freehold though. T'ey be all in Latin, an' it be not for coastal trade."

He tapped the side of his nose with a calloused finger and winked. "I'll be showin' you a-why later. He a-brought me man from Freehold with experience in t'eir boatyards to help me, an' he gave me some money. He be supposed to return with more money t'ree months ago, but he hasn't, an' we ha' run out of money to finish it proper. I be havin' to spend my own money to just keep up t' work, but we aren't workin' very hard an' I could be havin' lot more people on t' job."

If it is a smuggler, our skin-changer priest may know what to do with it. "I have never sailed one like it, but we have someone in our village that may have. What do you call it? Why is it so deep in the hull and where are its sideboards?"

"Oh, she'll be a makin' great trader all right, but not for shallow water. She be havin' deep hull, so she does not be needin' sideboards. You see t'ose rocks over t'ere?" He pointed at a large pile of flat rocks. "T'ey supposed to go in t' bottom under deck, an' t'ey stop her fallin' over under all of her sail an' she'll be takin' lot more sail t'an you're used to."

"She be called a brigantine. T'ere be not many of 'em around apparent, even in Freehold. I been a-hearin' of 'em, but t'at be all. Lucky t'ey were a-good plans he brought us. She can be doin' long trips under different winds an', with t'at hull, carry' round forty tonnes," he said smugly.

Although the ship is about the same length as some that I am used to, this is a lot more than four times the cargo capacity than even a big knorr, but she will need a larger crew, although she could possibly have longer range as well, and be more comfortable. She looked along the hull.

I am impressed. But if I want to buy, then I cannot let him see that. "Let me be showin' you," he added. They climbed up a ladder leaning against the rail of the boat as it sat in its cradle on some wooden rails. *The familiar smells of hemp and timber, tar and oil.* She listened to the sound of the breeze in the ropes that were already rigged. *I have been too long on land and I have sorely missed all of these things.*

Stefan had taken the chance to excuse himself to go back to his family, and Lakshmi and Basil ended up learning a lot more about ships and boats that morning than they really wanted, or thought that they needed to. They went all over the ship, including climbing up into the rigging.

This is something I am not used to. If you have to clear some tackle, you climb a single rope hung loose from the mast, you don't have a rope ladder going up there. This is luxurious. They even went down into the bilge, *Basil thinks that it is just the bottom of the boat, but he can learn better.*

Now comes the fun bit. Lakshmi is better at bargaining than I am. "So she may be available if I leave money, say with the church, for what this Freehold man has left as a deposit and pay you the rest. Is that right?"

"Perhaps we could be a-reachin' an agreement. I be just showin' you t' boat out of interest."

"I am interested, but I need to fly across the Lake and look in Erave Town to see what is available there, and then I want to discuss it with the others, and if we decide to go ahead, Lakshmi will probably come back to negotiate with you. How long would you take to finish it, and could you do some minor modifications to the fittings once she is launched and I am practicing with her?"

Jacob thought for a moment. *He clearly doesn't like the idea of me going elsewhere. He has been facing a loss and being left with a ship that no one among the locals will want. She is too unfamiliar a craft for anyone he knows, and although she will take a huge cargo, she is not the best fit for a ship that will just be used on a river or a lake.*

Even though both are probably deep enough for her, most river traders and fishermen want a flat-bottomed hull that they can ground at the riverside if they need to, and that is less likely to have problems with a mud bank. It is very clear that he doesn't want a possible buyer to walk away.

"I'll be a-gettin' some more men an' can have her finished in week an' I can be a doin' any modifications you want, an' Peniel, he be t' man from Freehold who be helpin' me, he'll help you learn how to sail her if you be wishin'. I be sure we can find some way to reach an agreement."

I think that we have him. "I will let you know if we need that—we may not." She dug in her money pouch and looked at what she had pulled out. *There are two gold talents and three smaller gold hyperion, all from Greensin. That would be more than enough money and gold coin always impresses.*

"Here is some money for you to finish her quickly. If we decide to take her, then that can come off the price, if we don't…well regard it as an expression of interest." *The cold reserve that the man had on his face when we first arrived has totally evaporated in the sun of the gold that he has just been given, and Master Jacob now cannot do enough for us as we take our leave. Having money is fun.*

Astrid

The three headed back to the village and Astrid looked around to make sure there was no one who could hear. "Unless there is something really good in Erave Town, I want her. Once I learn how to sail her, we can take her out into the deep sea safely. She has a compass built in, she has a lot of the stowage that I was expecting to have to ask for, and she even has…and I have always wanted to play with a boat that has one…a wheel."

She looked expectantly at Basil and Lakshmi. *They are just looking blankly at each other and back at me. I can see them both thinking 'boats have wheels?' Didn't they pay attention?* "Remember the round thing at the back on a post with the spokes that came out past the rim? It turns a rudder. Most boats have a steering oar on the side. They work, but they are hard to use in a heavy sea. Some have a rudder with a long pole attached, a tiller."

They still look blank "They work better, but they are still hard labour to use if it is bad weather, and they take up a lot of room on your deck and under it. With a wheel you can steer her better." *I am not getting through, am I?* "Oh, I give up. Just accept what I say, She will be safer at sea and easier to steer. That is all you need to know."

Astrid

After lunch they poked around the village, and Lakshmi went to have a talk with the local apothecary about making rosewater, while Astrid and Basil took their turn to care for George. *Lakshmi has come back with notes and sketches to show Bilqīs the sort of glassware that she wants. The girl will need to get a lot better in her work to make those.*

Now what do we do? Evilhalt had seemed so grand to me when I first came here, and the town is about the same size as home even if there are a lot more people around it, and there is really nothing here that we do not have at home…except the bath.

They went and bought some wine, cheese and fresh bread, and went looking for Stefan and Bryony. *Of course, they are at Stefan's parents, and from the look of relief on Bryony's face, in some need of rescuing, or at least of having someone divert attention away from her.*

Diverting attention is something that I am very good at. But, how best to do it? It seems that we are going to be eating here. I don't think that Anka, Stefan's mother, is giving us a choice on that, so I have plenty of time. Well, I am not a real storyteller, in fact none of us on this trip are, but I have been told I am good at the comic.

She launched into a story that would be guaranteed to impress Stefan's parents with his connections. She told the story of the Imperial wedding in Ardlark. *After all, it is one of those events that rumours about penetrate to every land…even those that have little to do with the place that they happen in.*

Astrid emphasised that the Empress was one of their people, and eventually realised that, even though she had interrupted herself to feed the children, not much dinner was getting cooked, as everyone was listening to her tale. By the time she finished, by telling of her kissing Hrothnog goodbye, from the expression on people's faces she had thoroughly distracted everyone's attention from Bryony.

"You kissed Hrothnog?" asked Stefan's younger brother Amos, "but he is…"

"Yes, he is. Up close, he is everything that you can imagine. He is not human, but what he is I do not know, and he has eyes that glow gold, just like our Princess Theodora, and he reads your mind most of the time, and he is very, very powerful as a mage. I only kissed him because I act on impulse sometimes…it surprises people and can keep you alive in battle and…well, Basil knows him a lot better than I do. He has talked to him a lot more than I have."

It is time for my husband to have some attention. She grabbed a goblet of wine. *I am right. Every eye is now on Basil, sitting quietly in the background, taking babies when they are handed to him and doing what he needed to do with them. He is looking up in surprise. Now he realises that he is supposed to say something.*

"I have only seen him a couple more times, when he sent me out to guard his granddaughter and when I report to him." *Well, that casual comment just increased their interest in him.* "He is, or was, I am not sure which applies now, my Emperor. As my wife said, he is terrifying and more so the closer you come to him, even if he likes you. He likes my wife and I think he likes me, but it can almost make your bowels turn to water just standing in his presence."

He is looking around. "It is easier to face the unquiet dead with just a short-sword, or to face down a mighty swordsman on your own—and I have done both of them—than to have a relaxed conversation with him…and this is not a suitable conversation for before dinner. Astrid, tell them about how the dragon was killed."

Oh well, it was a couple of minutes rest. She launched into the next story. *I wish I could do these tales justice. At least this time Stefan can answer some questions once I am finished. He is the main player in this story anyway.*

Astrid
32nd Undecim

Next morning, they headed off across the lake to Erave Town. *As we dip to wave to Master Jacob and his team at the boat, I can see that another couple of people are already working hard on it and there are a few more walking that way with tools. Jacob must have called in the local carpenter as well as a few others.*

It didn't take long to cross the lake.

Our visit with Mayor Cynric, Metropolitan Cosmas and Captain Leonas is interesting. I expected it to be that way after Evilhalt. They went there first, out of courtesy and handed over the letters for the Mayor.

The first matter was going through the details of the raid into the Swamp. The men were glad to hear of this as they had also been getting all sorts of rumours of war and had not been looking forward to having their trade disrupted all over again. The first disruption of trade from the bandits had hit the town hard enough.

"Although you want to allay fears in your town, can you let the news come out by itself please? It should not be too long. We don't want any stories floating around that connect our visit to the news. We are sort of trying to avoid them working out who may have done the raid."

Before they left to look at what there might be available in boats, they were asked to not go tomorrow until they had come back to see Cynric.

It seems that there are no suitable boats or ships in Erave Town that can be bought. It turns out that the sail maker there has already made and delivered one set of rig for our ship-to-be. We will not be calling at ports used to this type of craft, so I should order a second set as spares and a third mainsail and jib, just in case, and pay for them after Lakshmi has arrived at a price.

You always needed spare sails and the quality is at least fair. We can pick them up at some time when we are practicing our sailing or even when we leave the Lake.

Basil

It is my wife's turn to look after the children. I want to spend time with Lakshmi in The Fisherman's Arms, and then circulating through the other taverns to listen to rumours. Lakshmi is a natural at this task. I can sit in a corner and just keep an eye out. Men are falling over themselves to tell her their life stories.

Over a few games of cards, which she plays well, she must have heard every rumour in town. Although many of the rumours concern the Swamp, and the possibility...nay the certainty...of war, there are none yet concerning what we did there. I suppose that it is still far too early for them to have arrived.

People are speculating on what the town will do about the situation. Many of the locals want to declare war on the people of the Swamp to keep the trade routes open, although others think that they should just stay clear of everything.

They even went to visit Saint Sophia's, Metropolitan Cosmas' basilica, for a service. *I am no longer used to going to church in a real church that does not later become a feast hall. It is so very different to what we are used to at home. It would be nice to have a real church for ourselves, with mosaics and paintings on the walls and the ceiling.*

Basil
34th Undecim

Next morning, they went to see Cynric to be met with Stefano, the nine-year-old son of Leonas, who had with him a small pack of clothes and his tuition money.

"He is bright, but he has not found something he is interested in here," said Leonas. "His mother and I think that it is time that he was fostered away from here to see more of the world anyway. This will give him a good education and it will give him a better start if he knows more of the world outside than he has seen so far. After all, I never meant to end up here. Who knows where he will go? I am sure that he will fit on one of your saddles with you."

"We will see how this works, but I expect that we will send at least one child a year to you. We also expect to hear that they do well," said Cynric confidently as he patted Stefano on the head. *Stefano doesn't look quite so certain about his prospects, but at least he is obeying meekly.*

They returned to Evilhalt across the Lake, skimming across the waves. Stefano rode with Basil, and he was sure that at least he enjoyed this part of his exile. On returning, Basil headed to the tavern to listen to rumours while Stefan and Bryony were again taken by Stefan's parents. This time they had to visit around the extended family and be shown off.

Astrid

Bryony cast a pleading look at Astrid as she and Lakshmi left for the boat-wright's yard. *I hope that my answering grin lacked enough sympathy. At least I get on well with Basil's family. What is more, his family are fun, not dull and provincial like Stefan's. No wonder Stefan wanted to escape Evilhalt.*

Lakshmi had her instructions and went straight into negotiation with Master Jacob. *He might be a master builder of ships, but he was clearly outclassed at negotiation.* As Lakshmi said later, "I could have gotten it for a lot less, but you told me that he had to show a profit. I had not realised how much using my wiles to stay alive had added to my trading skills. Men are just so easy."

Six old platinum eagles, whatever they were really called…at least they were of that weight…from an unknown nation that were in the dragon's hoard were handed over, as well as the money that Astrid had already paid.

Master Jacob is looking at the coins in his hand. He does not know what to do with them. I guess that he was expecting a large bag of gold and he has never seen so much money in so few coins before. Now he has to work out what to do with it…he is already muttering something to that effect.

"You have a moneylender who lives here in Evilhalt, don't you?" Jacob nodded. "If he is honest, then go and ask him how much he will pay you each year for a loan of this money."

"Why would he be a-doin' t'at for?" asked Jacob puzzled. "He be money-lender. He lends money. He not be a-borrowin' it."

"Because people do come to him to borrow money and, if he has more money, he can lend more and even if he has to pay you something for the money, he will make more. Trust me about this." *He looks dubious.*

"I don't understand it myself, but Ruth, who is one of our Presbyteras and who used to be a trader, and who seems to know something about everything, tried to explain it to me one day when I asked what we could do with all of our money. She said that if we were in a normal town, that is what we would do. I didn't understand much of what she said, but that is the essence of what I could understand. If you tried to do it, it wouldn't work because you are like me, you don't understand money. He does it for a living, so it will work for both of you…as long as he is honest."

They went to go away when something occurred to Astrid and she ran back to thrust a couple of extra gold talents at Jacob. "She needs painting. Get that done straight away. Her hull should be dark green, forest green, like the forest she will sail through and her name should be written in gold on the stern. I think it should be written in Hindi. She is bigger and will be stronger and faster than anything else this river has seen, so she will be the River Dragon. I will be back for when she is to be launched with a priest to bless her."

The rest of the day was quiet, and they had decided that, despite the hot bath under the hotel, it was not worth staying in Evilhalt until the boat was finished. *I want to get back and to see if the new priest knows anything about this sort of boat, or if I have wasted our money. We also need to start to work out who we have for a crew.* In the meantime, Basil took Lakshmi out looking for anything of interest.

Stefan

I nearly forgot…I had better call in on Arthur's parents and tell them that he has arrived.

It turned out that they had been anxiously awaiting his call on them. To them, a trip that far into the mountains was a very dangerous one to make and they had been nervous about him arriving. They were reassured to know that he was there and starting to plan how to set out fields and talk to the girls.

"But t'ey used to be slaves didn't t'ey?" said his mother. "T'ey won't have dowries…and be they respectable?" Stefan sighed. *By now, I am sure that mothers are the same everywhere.* "Have you seen my wife? She be another one t'at we rescued. It be not her fault what happened to her. T'e shame be on t'e people who allowed it to happen, or who made it happen, and we now are a-fightin' wit' t'em all over the land."

"As for dowry, did you hear about our Cat a-buyin' t'e boat t'at Master Jacob hast been a-buildin' and how much she paid? She bought t'at just for us to sail around in for fun. Have you heard about the jewellery that Bryony got for our weddin'?" Arthur's mother nodded.

"When your son gets a wife, she might ha' enough money to buy like things t'at if she wants to, and she will…all our brides do…get jewellery similar to

Bryony's when they marry." *The prospect of lots of money seems to reassure parents.*

Stefan

He had another parent waiting for him when he returned to the inn. She was a large woman dressed in a dense woven black wool robe worn over a fine woollen under-robe couched with designs in gold thread. She was hung about with golden chains and had jewelled fingers and a familiar long pouch hung at her side.

It is a wand pouch made by my father and is of his very best work and he had taken a long time over it. Stefan gave a respectful nod to the most powerful of the mages in Evilhalt, Sonia DeMage. *Of course, I know who she is, but I have never actually met her to talk to before. Until I met Theodora and Rani, she was the most powerful mage that I had heard of.*

She is standing there waiting for me with her son and his wife…I know them from militia, and a young girl. Seeing that she is a local girl, I have probably seen her running somewhere around the village, but I cannot remember her at all. She would be six or seven years old. "Young Stefan," the mage said.

"Yes, ma'am?" *Old habits die hard. I am nervous, and feel as if I am about 10 years old and been caught in an orchard with a tunic full of apples.*

"You be a-havin' powerful Darkreach mage in t'is village of yours, an' also teacher from t' University in Haven?" she asked.

"Yes, ma'am." *At least I am sure about that answer.*

"An' you be a-openin' school where anyone a-havin' talent can be a-learnin'?" Stefan nodded. *I am relieved. I know where the conversation is going now.* "Good. It be about time someone did. When I be a-goin'to Sacred Gate, t'teachers, an' everyone else there made me feel like dirt."

"It be time for my granddaughter, Tiffany here…" the young girl smiled nervously, "…to go away if'n she be gettin'a proper education, an'I definite do not want her to be goin' t'ere if'n it can be helped. You be takin' her with you if'n I approve. I be wantin' to meet t'rest of your people t'at are here to see if'n they be t'sort t'at I be lettin' run my daughter's life."

"Yes, ma'am." Stefan took them all inside, and went to install them in the downstairs room where they used to meet, while he sent Ava to find the rest of the Mice and to bring some tea. He told her to pass on why.

The first to arrive was Astrid. *Oh great…now she and Sonia are looking each other up and down, as if they were each planning on making a purchase and neither is sure if what she is being offered is right for the job. Surprisingly, it is Sonia who gives way first. It must be many years since she was been judged like that by anyone at all.*

"Hello," said Astrid, to the girl's parents once she had won. She spoke into the uncomfortable silence that had hung around waiting on the two women to finish. Astrid was balancing one baby on the hip as he tried to wiggle free. "My husband will be down in a moment when he finishes changing our daughter. You want to find out if we are suitable to look after your granddaughter, I hear."

Her directness took Sonia back. "T'at is correct."

Astrid nodded. "This may help, or it may not. The last time that I talked with Hrothnog he asked me if we would foster and teach his new children when they come along."

She received a stare in return. "Which Hrothnog?"

Astrid gave a theatrical shudder. "There is more than one? That is a scary thought. The one I know is terrifying enough on his own. We will be fostering the next children of the Emperor of Darkreach in our village. Is that good enough for you?" *Basil and Lakshmi have now arrived, and Bryony is in the corridor behind them.*

"Your directness be a-refreshin.' Be you like t'is with him?"

"Yes, ma'am, she is." *She turns to see who is interrupting.* "And he said more or less the same to her. She even kissed him goodbye when we left. As a rod for my back, I am her husband, sometimes Tribune Basil Akritas, and sometimes in His Imperial Majesty's service."

"This is Lakshmi, who is our village apothecary, and at the back is Stefan's wife Bryony. She is, like my wife, one of our hunters and helps on the farm. We are a small village, but strong. Part of the key to our strength is that everyone does several things, mainly for the love of it. We all practice our weapons, even more so than Stefan tells us is done in this village, and we are all still in school, either as a teacher or a student or both, even our Princesses."

"I am learning both Greek and Dwarven, and I am teaching some aspects of my former work. I don't know if you are aware, but we already have students from the southern Hobgoblins, the Bear folk, the Swamp, and now Erave Town as well as our own young girls. The school is up and running. Will your granddaughter be joining us?"

"Be it t'at she will indeed, young man. As well as what t'rest of you will teach her, I be sure t'at your wife can show her how to a-stand up for herself. T'at can be more important t'an all of t'rest of it put together."

Chapter XXII

Basil
34th Undecim, the Feast Day of Saint Vitalis

They flew back next day. *We will have quite a surprise for the village. It now owns an ocean-going ship and there are two more students for the school. I wonder how many we are going to take. Between births and students there will soon be more children in Mousehole than adults.*

They arrived home to an even bigger surprise. They entered the village as was normal and, having handed the new children for the school over to Ruth, went to put the saddles away. They were just doing so when a woman's voice called out sternly: "Kutsulbalik...why was I sent here?" Basil whipped around. *That is my sister's voice.*

"Olympias...what are you doing here?" *Sent?* "...And what do you mean sent?" *My sister is coming over from the hall. Behind her is a large Boyuk-kharl with smooth olive-green skin and bright orange hair that stood up in a narrow crest that ran from the front to the back of his head. He is dressed, like Olympias, as a sailor, with a falchion and main-gauche on his hips, and he bore the rank marks of a sergeant. Both of his bare, and large, arms are completely covered in the most elaborate tattoos that I have ever seen.*

"I thought that it was only you who received Imperial summonses," said Olympias. "But no. You get me to go along to the Imperial wedding. I get noticed there, and then I am called up in the middle of the night by your Strategos, and told that I am to pick an experienced coxswain and given half a day to get ready.

"Then we are equipped with new weapons, good ones at least, and then sent here...mind you, actually sent here, into the middle of the mountains... as far from the sea as you can be. I am a sailor. Denizkartal is a sailor. Oh, Denizkartal is my...coxswain." She waved in his direction and he nodded.

Astrid

*B*asil might have missed the slight pause, but I didn't. He is more than a coxswain to her, and she is unsure what to say about it. She sized up the big Boyuk-kharl. He is more handsome than Aziz, about the same as Basil really, but he is a very different colour and much taller. *I might have to take Olympias aside soon to find out the full story there.*

"We end up on a mountain path with instructions to head south until we are stopped at a bridge. We do that and we find ourselves hailed by a sentry and sent into a valley where the largest piece of water would float a canoe…if it was a very small canoe. I am going to repeat myself only once. Why was I sent here?"

His sister has always intimidated him and now Basil is stuck for words. Astrid cleared her throat. "Hello…Olympias. That would be my fault then. I bought a ship yesterday, and although I have enough experience with one of ours from Wolfneck, I probably do not have enough to sail this one." She smiled.

"I guess that His Imperial busybody found that out somehow when he was looking around, and realised that I would be taking his granddaughter to sea in it, and decided to interfere and do something about that. Of course, he would have kept it in the family and so he sent you. I think that he thinks of families first and your brother is already here, so…sorry.

"We really do have a ship and it is nearly finished in a place where it can sail down to the sea, and we have a mission for her, and the River Dragon is lovely. Can you two train a crew who have never been on a ship before to sail one in a few weeks?

"You would be welcome if you could. I wouldn't even mind not being the captain of her. I had better explain to the Princesses what has happened and why it has happened." *And that is as meek as I get.* Olympias and Denizkartal exchanged looks.

Theodora

*M*y husband has taken it well, and I suppose that what upsets me the most is that it looks like we are being spied upon when we go out of the valley and there is really nothing that I can do about it. My Granther may have said that he will not directly interfere, but this surely comes close.

One thing is sure; we will definitely have to step up on teaching people how to speak Darkspeech. Olympias has very little of the outside tongues and her coxswain has none of them at all. I understand sending Olympias, as Basil's sister, but surely Granther could have sent someone better than the Boyuk-kharl along.

Astrid

A strid and Basil had started showing Olympias and Denizkartal around when Astrid noticed Father Simeon talking with Father Theodule. She excused herself and went over to him. "We have not had much of a chance to talk, but you did come from the land to the west, didn't you?"

"Yes, daughter, from the Newfoundland, I did." His Latin has a definite accent, like Bianca's but far stronger.

"I know you worked your way over, but you can sail then?"

"I heard that you were buying a boat. Yes, that I can. I managed to escape and came here on a small brigantine trader as a crewman. It is a long story. I am not a great sailor, but I know how to set a sail and tie knots, and I know what everything is called and what it is for."

"A brigantine, that really is tremendous news." She turned to Father Theodule. "Can I steal Simeon from you, please." Theodule nodded and Astrid dragged Simeon over to meet the latest arrivals.

"Sister..." *This changing the language I speak all the time is going to get tiresome, now to Darkspeech.* "...this is Father Simeon. He is a Catholic priest, not like ours, but similar. He is also a were-wolf." *And then we go back to Latin.*

"This is my husband's sister, Olympias. Like Basil and I she is part-kharl. This is her...coxswain Denizkartal, which means Sea Eagle."

Olympias has a little Latin, and I deliberately paused before introducing Denizkartal...and the reaction is? Yes...a faint blush. Why is she keeping it secret? Of course...you shouldn't bed your crew. Screw that. This is Mousehole. You sleep with who you want...except for Hulagu and Ayesha of course, but they don't know what they want. Now...back to the subject at hand.

"Olympias has come to be captain of our new ship, the River Dragon. She needs crew. You will need to learn Darkspeech, but do you want to go out in the world again?"

"I will go if it is needed, as long as I have this village to come back to. I have been hunted for far too long and I need a safe place to call home."

Switching languages again, Astrid turned to Olympias. "Father Simeon came here from another Land across the ocean on a brigantine. Apparently, I have bought a small brigantine, so he knows what to do on one, but he cannot speak much that is useful. He is willing to be crew, so you have me and him at the moment."

"What makes you think," asked Olympias, "that I am going to be your Captain?"

"Firstly," Astrid, held up her hand and began folding down fingers, "are you going back to tell Hrothnog that you refused?" She looked at Olympias and paused. "No, I didn't think so. Secondly, your brother and I would be disappointed if you refused…and thirdly, here you can marry your coxswain, or just sleep with him if you want, and no one will care about you being in charge of him."

The expressions on the faces of Basil, Olympias and Denizkartal are classic. Astrid grinned widely. "I was right about the last one, wasn't I?"

"You were," said Denizkartal with an answering grin. "I told her that when we came, but she still said no. I will ask her again now."

"You can ask all you want, but until you get a place of your own, our house currently has only two sleeping rooms fixed up and the babies will have to sleep with us for a while and you will be sharing one room and one bed, so I hope you are not too noisy."

Astrid

That night, before they went down to Evilhalt next day, there was some resistance to everyone trying out as crew on the River Dragon. "We were sent here to be spinners and weavers and, hopefully, to find husbands," said Yumn. "Why are we going on a ship? I have never been on a ship before and it could be dangerous."

"It will almost certainly be dangerous," said Astrid. "However, it is important, because it is part of what we do." *Of course…the original people in the valley know what this expedition is all about. They had been slaves, or they had fought the slavers and the Masters. With all of the newcomers into the valley, we have forgotten to pass on this history already.*

No one had explained what had happened. All they had were the casual references and comments that they heard around them. They should have been given it long ago, but now, suddenly, it is important that people have the full story of Mousehole to draw upon. She ran around and gathered together all of the new people; the adults that is, even Make and Maria, who knew part of the story, into the Hall.

I will talk to Ruth and organise a separate session for the children from the school, but they need to know the whole story as well...although perhaps not with as much of the gruesome detail in it. This is something that we will need to do over and over again as new people arrive and join our village. We have to do it; so that why we do what we do becomes a part of everyone's lives. We must never forget.

When she had them gathered, she looked around and began. "I was asked why it is that we have to go out of our safe valley and seek combats and risk death. It is the same reason that here we do not just work, we spend most of our free time training and learning and practicing, and getting better at what we do even though we are already rich."

"Here, anyone can learn to be a mage, if they have the ability. You can learn things from Basil and Ayesha that most people do not get a chance to learn. When Thord is here, and most of you have never met him yet...he is our Ambassador to the Dwarves...you can even learn to walk up cliffs."

"We are not just doing this for fun. We are doing it because it is our destiny, and if we do not do it we fear what will happen. You have not just come to a valley looking for land or a partner or wealth. You have come to take part in a saga...whether you realised it or not."

"I am not going to tell you the details. I make stories sound funny, and ours is not really a funny story. Ayesha is going to tell you the story of Mousehole from the start, and then Verily and Sajāh are going to tell you their stories. Please wait with questions until you are asked. Make yourselves comfortable and I am having food and drink brought for you. You will be here for some time."

Theodora

I was wondering what that annoying girl was up to this time, disrupting the village and gathering people up. She has all of the new ones and half of the others in that room. She collected Rani and followed, and ended up listening to Astrid from outside the room where they could not be seen, behind the listeners and around the corner of the wall.

"Our Cat is growing up and becoming a leader," said Rani. "One of us should have thought of this. I would say that someone has come to her with a problem and she has decided to solve it. We will leave her to it. It is perhaps best that this is coming from her, rather than from us."

Theodora stayed quiet outside and listened. *Yes, Astrid is right. While the new people have each heard little bits and pieces of the story, they really did not know what happened and how it had been for the women here. They do not have the context of the prophecies nor had they heard before what the people who had been captured had to tell them.*

When all of the others had finished there was a brief pause before Astrid started again. "Now that you know the story of our valley, you can understand why many of us are like we are and why we do what we do. I don't want my children to grow up in fear of the Masters coming back here."

Her legs weary from standing that long; Theodora peered around the corner to see what was happening. Everyone was sitting and paying attention. "Now, if you think that you came here for an easy life and you want to reconsider why you are here, then I understand. This is a terrifying life that we have ahead of us until we feel that we are finished."

"I am sure that we can find somewhere else for you to go to if you wish to leave and I will talk to the Princesses for you. If you think that this means you, come and talk to me afterwards." *Astrid is thanking the others. Verily has been left crying in Aziz's arms after she went through her story.*

The newcomers are talking softly among themselves and some are looking at Verily, but I note that none are going to see Astrid. Eventually they went back to their work or to prepare to go down to Evilhalt. I can see thoughtful expressions on many of their faces and there seem to be no objections to what they have been asked to do.

Father Simeon Alvarez
4th Duodecimus, the Feast Day of Saint Sezni

The launching of their ship had taken place on the feast day of Saint Sezni, the fourth of Duodecimus, a fact that Father Simeon found particularly auspicious.

I know that this is the Holy Day of my particular devotion, him being the patron of skin-changers, but I am still a Catholic priest, and yet I get to preach the homily. I have to say that the people of my new village are rather strange. At least the ship is now in the water and officially ours. I suppose that, from now on someone will always be on board to keep watch on the River Dragon.

Olympias Akritina
4th Duodecimus

*I*t is much more orderly in an Imperial shipyard. The last week has been a
madhouse of ferrying people down to Evilhalt and back again, and throwing
money at people to get the work done. I have this River Dragon modified as
I want…on top of what my sister ordered…and then launched, and people
brought down to try out as crew.

*In the meantime, I learn some new words…and I can never let my sister
tell me the name of things again from the shocked looks from some people.
This craft will take a crew of around fifteen and so a lot of this absurd village
will be needed to crew her, and more will be needed if they are to land and go
places while the River Dragon goes on to somewhere else.*

One of the modifications that Astrid ordered was to the two hatch covers.
Instead of being curved to shed water, as they would be on a normal craft, they
have been remade and changed to being flat so that one could have a mage's
pattern on it and the other could have one for the priests.

*Our hatch covers have already been used. This Princess Theodora had some
presents ready for my ship before she was launched. Astrid apparently asked her
for two new spells to enchant into her frame. The two Princesses combined to place
a spell into the River Dragon's timbers, not just once, but on two consecutive
days each.*

"You can now command those winds that you wanted," said Theodora cheerfully. "I haven't worked out how to calm the seas yet, but give me a few days." Astrid
had to explain to Olympias that she was going to be one of the few captains who
could say how hard the wind would blow with a degree of certainty. *I may
forgive her for teaching me the wrong word to ask people to pull on a rope,
but not yet.*

Theodora was as good as her word, and before they first sailed, the calming
spell was added. "It will only take the edge off things and calm the wind and
sea a bit, perhaps by half and only for an hour at a time. I am sorry, but that is
all I can do. It is harder for me calming the wind than doing it the other way
around." *She sounds disappointed at only giving a calmer wind for an hour.
That much may save a mast in a big blow.*

Olympias

What with the blessing by her priests, and the actual launch, it seems like everyone I have met up there is now down here. I suppose there are still sentries, but I am not sure who. The teacher has even managed to ferry all of the older children down on the carpet in a couple of trips. It seems that, if people don't bring much with them, they can usually travel two to a saddle.

They discovered that it was quickest to bring the carpet down with a load and then roll it up and fly it up with a saddle. *Now, the hard work begins for us all. The first shift of trainee sailors are mine to teach their new craft to, while the rest return home to their normal lives, and to await their turn on the water.*

I have decided that except for this priest Simeon, everyone on our first trial crew will speak at least some Darkspeech. This, if I have all of the names, means both of the Princesses, Father Christopher, Ayesha, Verily, Aziz, Sajãh, Goditha, Parminder, Nikephorus, Rabi'ah, Yumn, and Zafirah, as well as my brother and sister.

Olympias
5th Duodecimus

We have decided not to use the man from Freehold, Penial, in training my crew. Perhaps it is more accurate to say that my sister has decided. I admit that he is not interested in the village and what it wants; he has made that clear. My brother tells me that, if he were to be involved in training, he will learn far too much about the Mice that will be of interest to others. He just wants to take his money and return home.

However, damn Basil's paranoia. I already regret turning down his offer to help with training. As sailors, I have to conclude that many of my new recruits are good farmers. On the other hand, this is not unusual, the army and navy are often seen as an escape from a life behind a plough, particularly when there has not been much combat lately, or indeed in the last hundred years.

I admit that Denizkartal and I are used to whipping inexperienced crews into shape. The small craft of the navy are where sailors usually start out their career. A sailor has to be able to do everything on a small ship. They cannot learn just one job. However, I usually have only a few recruits in an experienced crew, not the other way around.

What is more, I cannot stop having difficulty with yelling at a Princess…I *get into full yell and then Theodora turns around, and all that I can see are her eyes and I go silent.*

They found out early the first day that the best way to run a crew with this many new sailors, was for Olympias to hand out the directions and oversee what was going on and to allow the other three to run things more intimately. *At least this means that Astrid gets to yell at the Princesses…she is good at that.*

By the end of the first day they were exhausted, and Fathers Christopher and Simeon had been called to attend several accidents. *It is not just one thing. There have been falls down the ratlines, the rope ladders leading up the masts, and there was a swinging block. We also have rope burns and minor injuries from the many other hazards that wait in the wings for inexperienced hands.*

Parminder falling overboard led to Goditha jumping in after her, which led to Denizkartal jumping in to rescue them both as neither of them could swim.

The River Dragon had, initially, only moved from where it had been launched because of the flow of the current. The first item that Olympias had to teach them was how to use the sweeps lest the brigantine be grounded and lost on its first day.

The ship has ten sweeps, and once we are actually out in the lake we just rowed around for an hour, changing rowers until I am sure that they have at least the idea of how to do that. This was near sufficient on its own to exhaust many in the crew. This Princess Rani, in particular, has never done so much physical work in her entire life, and I am sure that she is beginning to regret encouraging Astrid in this idea.

They spent the rest of the day learning about sails, not all of them, just the mainsail and the topsail, the two larger sails carried square on the mainmast, the spanker, a gaff-rigged fore and aft sail on the rear or spanker mast, as well as the lowest of the spanker staysails.

I am leaving furled the gaff topsail, the two upper staysails, the jibs, and the main topgallant and the other lesser sails. Handling four sails is enough for the long first day. They are confused enough with them.

While they experimented with the magically induced winds, there was enough of a breeze that Olympias felt they should use what had been provided naturally. Without sailing too far with any one combination, they put sails up and they took them down. They even reefed them.

As the day goes by, the times grow less slow. That is perhaps a more accurate way of putting it than saying that they are quicker.

It was only when the day was near done that she furled all of the sails they had used so far, and unfurled the jib, and used their own wind to nose the River Dragon back to land to dock, for the first time, at the actual wharf at Evilhalt.

The hot baths at The Slain Enemy were well used when they got there, and the new crew slept soundly that night, many with balms on their hands or rubbed into sore muscles. The four experienced sailors were not so lucky. They were closeted in the meeting room discussing what went wrong, what went right, and in teaching Father Simeon key words in Darkspeech for the morrow.

"What happens if I am not satisfied with what they can do?"

"Then we will have failed in what we need to do," replied Astrid, and she went on to describe the tactical situation that they found themselves in as Rani had described it to her and why any other approach was inadvisable.

"We have to be stealthy and close in our actions. You saw our Princess Rani in action as a sailor today…well, trying to be a sailor. If she is seen doing that in Haven, she will lose any prestige that we may have gained so far. Even worse, at one stage I had her and little Parminder pulling on a halyard together."

"In Haven, Parminder would be the lowest of the low, and the two of them working on the same thing and touching would be forbidden and would shock everyone. I think I was told that it would actually be illegal. We cannot fail. If we are to do what we need to do, this is the only way." On that bleak note they went to bed.

That set the pattern of the days that followed, and while the crew were allowed to eat on shore, and to use the hot bath in the inn, they were expected to sleep on the River Dragon. Learning to sleep in a hammock was another new experience for everyone in the cramped conditions below deck.

The complaints receive short shift from my sister, who regales them with stories of how the open knorr, the trade boats of the north, sail in the frigid storms of the Arctic sea, and how the sailors sleep on the open deck wrapped in their furs, and often drenched by waves or blasted by icy spray or covered in snow.

She tells stories of having to crack the ice from your sleeping furs in order to get up, and that silences the complaints. She has made it very clear that she thinks that the Dragon is luxurious in what it provides for its crew, and I suppose that it is. There is certainly more room than I am used to, and I am able to openly share my cabin.

Rani
6th Duodecimus

When they were not out on the lake, Rani spent some time looking in the village, and came back with an object which she took straight to the mage's pattern on the hatch cover. *I need to do some work as a mage again... something I am good at.* Unveiling it revealed a covered lantern, and she worked her magic upon it before taking it below deck into the hold.

She entered with a smile on her face and handed it to Goditha. "Can you please fix this to the mainmast so that it can be opened easily, and yet will have as little as possible in front of it? It may need to be right at the top above the..." *I should know what the right words are by now...ah yes* "...the topgallant spar, but some people...not me...can climb up there easily. It will need to point down a little bit, but only a little."

"That climbing also doeth not take in me," was the reply. "But I wilt see what I can get done for thee by others."

"What are you adding to my ship?" Olympias asked of Rani as she saw what was happening.

"It is a lantern. A lantern wants to shed light, so it is easy to work with. This one is working all of the time, but you cannot see anything from it because it has a shutter. When that shutter is opened, the light will shine out—half of a cone of very strong light, far brighter than daylight, will shine for about three hundred paces ahead and a hundred paces across the base."

"It is so we can see ahead of us at night. I will make another, but not as strong, to be hung over the deck that will be a bit softer than daylight, but that will light up the deck for us when we want to at night, and I will make some more small lights for inside the holds and the area where we sleep. Those are all easy."

Olympias
7th Duodecimus, the Feast of the Saints Cosmas and Damien

At least this feast day has passed without the Saints, the patrons of surgeons, needing to be called upon. That made the Captain less gloomy. *My crew are learning the names of the various masts, and the ropes and sails. They are learning what each person has to do when a particular order is given, and they are even learning how to use the sweeps, and the two rowboats that the River Dragon carries: one slung square from the stern and the larger upside down on a rack on the deck.*

For my part, I am learning to cope with a crew who have to sometimes stop to feed or change a baby. I am even learning a few words of Hindi for my next task, training the second crew, none of whom speak more than a few words of Darkspeech. Now I will have to give my orders to novices who cannot understand most of what is being said.

Father Simeon is, however, much happier and less frustrated. He will still have difficulty in understanding me, but he is improving in that. At least he will be able to talk to some of his work crew. I am glad that Father Christopher will also be staying for this week and so he can keep learning at the breaks.

It seems that the people of the Newfoundland usually only have a chance to learn Latin, and except for his having learnt how to speak to wolves, he has not been exposed to any other tongues, although he now has gained a smattering of the language of the Bear folk while he was there…and that is useless with most of us.

Just before the crew changeover, Father Simeon made his first transformation into wolf form in front of the others. It was the full of Panic, and being the lesser moon, he was not compelled to change, but he was more comfortable doing so. He made the change in public, and spent the night in his wolf form, to reassure everyone that he was not a threat to them.

I admit that is something that I have never seen happen in the Imperial Navy. I am not sure that the regulations would even cover it, and there are many there, often of high ranks, who only think of the regulations and not what they mean. She looked fondly at Denizkartal. *I suppose that I am better suited to this craft that my sister has bought for me.*

Olympias
12th Duodecimus

The changeover of the crew was made, and Bianca, Hulagu, Stefan, Bryony, Anahita, Kāhina, Tabitha, Giles, Harald, Lakshmi, Shilpa and Robin joined the ship. They brought with them a present from Fortunata. A flag was hoisted…with their mouse embroidered on it. As the old crew left, they were happy to make jokes at the expense of the new people, and to show them their hands as proof of how hard they would work.

Wait until they are actually under sail in a heavy storm and then they will soon appreciate this placid lake. Most were glad to be going back to Lãdi's cooking and their own beds. Goditha, now having experienced the hot tub bath in the tavern, vowed that making one for herself was going to be her priority, even over the work she was doing on the new church. Even Father Christopher was inclined to agree with that.

Having had, by the end of the week, a crew who, although slow, are able to obey the orders given to them without too much confusion, it is frustrating to have to go back to the start all over again. This time, the confusion is made much worse due to the language barriers.

I had gotten used to the gibes from the fishermen in the tavern gradually lessening. This time an accidental gibe, which resulted in a snapped rope and hard work for the priests on Anahita as the ship wallowed sideways before the wind, provided much amusement for them.

At least I now know that keeping a jib in place, even if it is not going to be normally needed, means that, if worst comes to worst, some of the magical wind and hard work on the wheel will bring the head around under most circumstances. To my sister's joy, she is the one who gets to spend the most time working the wheel and taking charge of the gaff-sail and the mid-ship staysails.

Olympias
14th Duodecimus, the Feast Day of Saint Barbara

*A*t least we can mark this feast day properly. The Saint for engineers has my man mounting and unveiling something that he has been working on in his free time, in co-operation with the Evilhalt blacksmith and the mason, almost since he arrived here. The River Dragon is now armed.

On the bow, to the left and right of the bowsprit, there are two posts that I got Master Jacob to fit in place there. There are another two posts on each side of the stern and people have been asking what they were for and not getting answers.

When they arrived at the ship, Denizkartal, who had taken the last watch, had a tarpaulin over one of the posts at each end. There was something lumpy under each one. There was another tarpaulin on the deck beside them both. When the crew were all gathered, he whipped the tarp off the rearmost and revealed a ballista. It did not fire bolts, however. Astrid translated for him to the others.

"This is a naval version. It fires these stone balls," he removed the second tarp to reveal a small pyramid of stone balls. "We don't have many of these yet and we will need to make many more. These stones sit in what is called a monkey. They are for putting holes in hulls or walls. This is a medium sized ballista and it can reach out to, say, a hand of hundreds of paces if you know what you are doing with it, and your Captain and I do."

He looked around. "When we have more time to make more, we will train some of you on how to use them. It gives the Dragon a sting of its own in battle. We can put both of them on one side, or both in the bow or the stern as we need. I have talked with Father Christopher and he has prayed over some of the balls and they are kept in this locker and marked."

The locker was fixed against the stern rail and had been empty up until now. Now its purpose was clear. "They will double the damage we do. The bad news is that, while we sail down the river, instead of sitting doing nothing, the crew get to sit and chip away at the rocks that I have in the hold until they just pass smoothly through this," and he held up a piece of timber with a round hole in it. "Each must be made as perfect as possible so that the shot flies the same every time."

Christopher looked at the board and then at his hands. "Let me think about this. It may be possible for me to do something so that they only need get the balls roughly right."

Theodora
16th Undecim, the Feast Day of Saint Monica

The Princesses had been down for two days at work in the small galley. They insisted that the crew had to bring food for the night and that the ship had to anchor well out in the lake. They spent some time casting a spell in the galley on each of the days.

Theodora proudly addressed them. "My husband has just done a spell, like she did for the small stove, but it is much bigger. We no longer need bring timber for our galley stove. It will now heat by itself and we now have the timber store spare."

"I am sure I could have made it better, but I am not used to making spells that do not kill and this one was far harder than the last," said Rani modestly.

Rani

The second set of training is due to finish today, and Olympias and her trainers will decide who will make up the crew for now and I will add anyone else I want for combat. Then we will finally have a list of who will go south on this trip. I do not know much about boats, but even I can see the progress that we have made.

I think that another week of training with the final crew after that, and then a rest day before leaving the day after the feast day of St Catherine, the twenty-fifth. She sighed. *It is the first time I have had serious resistance to one of my decisions.*

Rani had planned to leave on the day before St Catherine's, but she had faced a quiet rebellion from anyone who had anything to do with spinning. This was their special day and they had wanted a special feast for it. Christopher had told the Muslim girls, who made up most of the spinners, of the Feast Day and they had been delighted to discover that there was a special day for them, even if it was a Christian holy day, and they wanted to enjoy it. They had never had a special day before. Rani had relented.

In the end, people were included on board for many reasons. *I want all of the people from Haven to be present. You never know when what they know might be important. This means that Shilpa, Lakshmi and Purminder would be going. In turn Harald and Goditha refuse to let their wives go without them, although Goditha would have been going anyway as the ship's carpenter.*

Others I have included for what they might have to do on shore, such as Father Christopher, Basil and Ayesha. My wife and I are going, and Nikephorus has declared that either he or his wife would be going to look after us and that they have decided between themselves that it will be him. His wife is looking relieved. I am not sure that she ever wants to leave Mousehole again.

In all, the list had twenty-six names on it. *As well as those who have a specific purpose on board, a life using horses and living in often mobile tents has equipped the Khitan well for a rolling deck, Bianca is going to keep an eye on her husband, and to make sure he doesn't get lost at night when he is in thought and walk off the deck. Stefan, Bryony, Verily, Aziz and Tabitha are there to either work the ship or fight, as they are needed.*

Nikephorus came down early, bringing some supplies, and spent a few days stocking the ship with what he regarded as enough food. He was delighted with having a magically heating stove and regarded it as a blessing that he did not have to cope with a fire on a timber ship. He also did not have to start a fire in the mornings, just command it to heat. That meant that he would get more sleep.

173

Hulagu
18th Undecim, the Feast of Saint James the Lesser

It was time for the full moon and the new priest's first involuntary change. *I have not seen this happen before, and he is making the change before us all. It is good to see that my sister's children, Rosa and Francesco, saw a wolf, gurgled happily and started crawling straight towards him. As a man he is not small and, in his wolf form, this Simeon is nearly as big as the wolves of my totem.*

My sister seems glad that the priest has control of himself and his urges as her children have ended up crawling all over him. They ended curled up asleep on the transformed priest. I would expect nothing else of a man of the spirit. Just think how powerful our shamen could be if they were like him.

Apparently, this is the Saint for siblings, so my sister gave me a present of a new jacket and I noticed that Basil and his sister exchanged things as well. I must remember this next year. It is important to my sister.

These feasts happen so often, and they seem to mean so much to the Christians. They say that they do not worship these saints, but it does not seem that way. My sister pays more attention to her fetish of this Saint Ursula than I do to the one around my neck.

Rani
19th Undecim

The second round of training had its own set of problems. For a start the crew had started to get used to working with one set of people and they now had others working beside them. On the other hand, people had discovered roles that they were good at.

To my horror, my wife delights in joining Ayesha and Lakshmi as the topsail hands, the ones who are responsible for the highest sails, the topsail and the topgallant. She declared that it was fun and the three, all with training as acrobats, even sometimes, when the ship is steady, walk along the rope joining the two masts.

I have noticed that even Olympias looks alarmed at this, but she dare not rebuke the others without telling my wife off…and she seems reluctant to do that. The three discard their shoes and spend a lot of their time aloft, even taking bow and arrow quivers and attaching them handy to the small top platform on the mainmast, waiting there to be filled when they were needed for combat.

Basil

B asil took advantage of this stretch for him and Lakshmi to see if, with all of this activity, there had been any more interest in them, particularly from anyone newly arrived in town. *There turns out to be some curiosity from traders, but that is understandable.*

I cannot pick up any sinister intent, even when I got Bianca to check on the intent of people with her sense…whatever it is…or when I brought our priests in to check if the people felt wrong to them. The traders turn out to be as normal as can be expected and they are almost all long-term seasonal visitors anyway, but then that would be the best cover for someone who wants to keep their eye on things anyway.

T he feast of Saint Catherine came and went and those who returned back up to the valley for the feast day enjoyed themselves. Father Christopher chose the occasion to ask for the intercession of the saint in aiding them to make their own supplies of good cloth for the first time as he blessed the looms and wheels. He also asked for a blessing on the enterprise that they were about to embark upon.

Olympias
25th of Undecim

T hose who went up for the feast left on the saddles very early the next morning. Olympias wanted to cross most of the Lake that day. *The breeze is coming from the southwest and I want the crew to gain more experience with tacking into the wind.*

I do not want to get lazy and always rely on our magical breeze. Sometimes doing that might draw more attention to us than we want to have. I think that it is best, seeing that I have been told to be inconspicuous, to use as little magic as is possible and keep what we can achieve as a hidden reserve.

As well, until I am more confident with my crew, I think that perhaps I might want to anchor for the night out in the lake near Erave Town before entering the actual river. Once we do that and start down the river we are committed.

I may still be nervous about my new ship and crew, but in the end, everyone is aboard and I cannot put it off any longer. They are ready or they are not. All of our equipment is on board, including five of these saddles stored in the ship's hold. We even have a magical carpet from this Mouse Hall when it was taken. We can, apparently, use it as a bridge when we need to.

"The bandits ignored it or didn't know what it was, and we also keep forgetting it," said Rani. "We will take it now. If we have to board another ship, or land on a shore where we cannot come right alongside, it will give us an advantage."

With final prayers, they cast off from the wharf and headed out towards the Lake. Some, including Stefan's parents, stood on the walls of the village or on the wharf and watched them go. *I have to admit that, last night in the tavern I heard some speculation among the idlers as to whether we will return from our trading trip, with such an inexperienced crew on the long river transit. Seeing that we are not really traders, a failure to return gets even more likely.*

Chapter XXIII

Olympias
25th Duodecimus

Olympias had spent many hours, with Basil acting as a translator for her, in the tavern in Evilhalt buying drinks for the fishermen. *I now hope that they did not tell me any lies about the lake and its depth and its other secrets. If they have, then I am likely to wreck my new ship on its real maiden voyage.*

All I can do is hope and have Parminder, who after all is, according to my sister, able to sense any personal danger that threatens her, swing a lead in front of the ship as we sail across the lake. I have Bryony who, out of our general lack of knowledge, knows the most about maps among the others, noting the results.

We have been doing this since nearly the start of our sailing, but it is only by doing this for many years that an accurate view of an area is built up. If the River Dragon, an ocean-going ship, is to home port here in a lake, then I need to know for myself how the lake is shaped and what hazards it holds. Later, I will transfer what we have found to join the readings I already have.

I am already gaining a rough picture of the upper fifth of the lake, and I would be very surprised if there are any major problems there, although we still have to be wary of isolated and small shoals.

In the meantime, I also have Tabitha constantly casting the log to check our speed. I had Theodora get the village glassblower, that young girl Bilqīs, to make me a timer glass. But she was unsure how accurately she has made it as she had never made one, or even seen one, before I asked for it.

What I have on board is the fourth experiment in making one, and Bilqīs is reluctantly willing to let me use it, but the speeds will only be very rough for now. At least she seems to be fussy in her work. That bodes well. She also made me a larger one that is mounted in a box that can be turned on an axle and then fixed in place again. It sits under a small bell near the spanker mast. There it can be seen easily by whoever has the wheel and by Bryony with her log chart, to mark the hours.

Bilqīs thinks that it is more accurate, but she is not going to warrant it. She is sure that she needs finer sand for the job. That is on the list of things that are needed when we are shopping. Keeping track of the main glass is also one of Parminder's duties.

She sighed. *Has no one living over on this side of the mountains ever thought of systemic navigation before?* From what she had found out so far from asking around, the answer was probably no.

Even Freehold, from what Simeon has told me, seems to lack a lot of practice in this area. The ships' Masters just seem to rely on their own familiarity with the sea, rather than learning from the experience of others in the past. What they know, they write in jealously guarded books, often using ciphers so that only they can read them. Sheer lunacy, it is. You would think that they do not want to increase trade and make things safer.

Slowly the ship tacked backwards and forwards into the natural wind until they were out of sight of Evilhalt. It was hardest at first, as they only had a few hundred paces of river width to deal with, and they mainly relied on the current and the sweeps to get them down to where the river widened out. After that they had more space.

According to what I have been told, it is twenty-five leagues across the lake and the quickest route is to sail straight to the south-southeast, and then turn to starboard and head southwest. I have not taken them that far in their training yet. I wish that I better knew when to turn, but the inaccuracy of my information, the lack of a precise knowledge of my speed, and a total lack of a chart for the whole lake make me despair.

Centuries of sailing around the shores of Darkreach meant that the Captains there did not have this guesswork. *I might wish for an astrolabe to help me be more certain of my position, but even that will have to wait until we reach Sacred Gate. Hopefully, those barbarians have them and I can buy one there. At least I will not have to worry about the expense.*

My sister said she had never seen one before, but once she had been shown how, she could easily follow the compass rose mounted in front of her and maintain a course. She said she was used to doing that at night using just the stars, but I want to be sure of that before relying on it. I love her as a sister, but you do not allow likes to establish if a person is good at their job. Not if you want to stay alive at any rate.

When they were out of sight of Evilhalt, she ordered full sails set and opened up her strongest wind magic. The River Dragon leapt ahead as her speed picked up and a white wake formed under her forefoot. When the new speed reading came in, Olympias nodded to herself happily. *If we keep this up until we are in sight of the village across the lake, we should tie up well before dusk.*

She had divided her crew into two watches, and now called for those who were not on watch to stand down. *In this case, standing down the crew means that they get to help Goditha start at chipping away at some limestone rocks for our ballistae, if they have nothing else to do.*

Those who were on watch actually had an easier time. Once they had tidied all of the ropes and coiled them out of the way, they were able to just sit on the deck, or in the rigging and wait until they were needed.

Goditha Mason

I am watching my new assistants and feeling a growing sense of horror. "Stop thee now, thou wilt completely wreck them. I doeth only bring a small amount of stone from home, and I don't know when I wilt be able to get more. I doeth know that thee and me needeth them, and it will taketh me a long time on my own, but if thou taketh the large lumps and maketh them smaller lumps—about a hand and a half across and then doeth knock the corners off, I wilt take it from there."

"I have actually worked out how I can take it from there," said Father Christopher brightly and then ruefully continued, "…but I cannot do it in one day yet. It will take me using stored mana, and I will only do that if everything is quiet, and life is rarely quiet for long when we are out of the valley. Soon maybe, I might be able to do it in one day.

"If no one needs my services today, I will use some that is stored and try tonight. I will still need them in lumps like that, but I can make them smooth." Everyone had been looking forward to not chipping stone at all, but now looked disappointed again. "Each time I make eight it will mean that I cannot enhance the same number. I need to talk with Denizkartal and work out which it is best to do. As it is, we don't have many stones of any sort yet, and we may need a lot more than we have now of both types."

Olympias

N ow that they had plain sailing ahead of them, and she need not watch and correct her crew all of the time, Olympias took a turn at the wheel to better get the feel of the ship. She looked up at the masts. *I wonder if I can, or indeed should, rake them back a little for more speed.*

This ship is a good design and fast as it is. I warrant that, whoever had originally wanted it, he was a smuggler of some sort. It is the only thing that made sense for it not to be built in Freehold. It had been taking a risk getting it built by someone who had not built a brigantine before, but from what I have seen around me, only cats and sloops and perhaps a cutter.

Master Jacob, when he built her, may not even have known about raking a square rig mainmast to get more speed from the vessel. Will it be worthwhile for the River Dragon? I guess that there is only one way to find out...when I have the time.

Astrid

Now that she no longer had the wheel, Astrid did something she had not done for a very long time. She baited a hook and dropped it over the side, allowing a float to take it back away from the ship. She was almost immediately rewarded. Hand over hand she hauled up one of the small armoured fish. *It is near half a pace long.*

"Stefan, a gaff...that thing,"—she pointed—"and bring it up. I don't want to break my line." Taking it off the hook, she called for Nikephorus to come and get some dinner. She re-baited and threw the line overboard again. She caught three more of the fish before she had to go back to work.

"Is it always that easy?" asked Ayesha, who was standing nearby.

"No. That was a good result for so little time. It is a pity that more of you do not know how to fish, but it is very easy to learn, and keeps our food supply going and," she grinned, "I just happen to have brought with me a whole basket of lines and hooks...every last one that I could buy in Evilhalt. If we end up going to sea, I do not want to run out of food."

"I have heard it said that Allah does not deduct from a man's span that time which he spends in fishing. I think that a fisherman probably said it, and to his wives, but it does look...calming...unless you catch something." They both smiled.

Olympias

They ran quickly across the lake. For the first time all of the sails were set, except the studding sails. *We have them, but I think that my inexperienced crew will be best getting more experience as sailors with a more normal suite before I make them set those sails.*

We will not get much speed from them at present anyway, as they are mainly of use in a light wind. According to the waves and the birds, there is a very light wind, but it is coming in our faces from the southwest, not from behind us.

With their own strong wind behind them they could ignore this, and would take less than a day instead of several days to cross the Lake. *I could get very used to this. I wonder why Darkreach does not do it for all of their ships, although I know that they do it for some. I will be very sad when others can see us, and we must go back to using what is provided by nature.*

She looked overboard. *The colour of the water confirms what Parminder is calling out. This is a deep lake, and the little mage cannot find bottom with the amount of line that I am allowing her to find the depth. One day, we will have to find out exactly how deep it is—but that is for another day. All we need know now is that we will not run aground.*

If it is as deep as the colour of the water makes it look, then it must be cold down below. No wonder Astrid is catching those armoured fish. They, or at least their ocean cousins, are usually only found in the colder waters of the north. I have never heard of them in a river before, but then I have not been to a large mountain lake in a ship before, either.

Astrid

They made their turn, and the watch was changed and they continued. Deniz-kartal took over command and Father Simeon took the wheel. Astrid went back to fishing. This time she was showing others what to do rather than fishing herself. *We are losing more bait than we catch fish. We even nearly lost a line, but it is worthwhile to have them learning. It is good to supplement our food this way.*

When Astrid went to see Nikephorus, it was to find that Basil had to take over with preparing the fish. Having done all of his cooking in the palace, Nikephorus had never met a whole fish that had to be scaled and cleaned before. Basil had to show him how that was done before he could even start cooking.

He had left the children on deck. The children, all of them (and they had nine on board) now had ropes around their waists, and these were fastened to a jackstay running along the ship at near an adult's head height. *They have to be watched so that they do not tangle or choke each other, but it does make it less likely, with their increased mobility, that one will fall overboard...although they seem to be trying hard to do just that.*

Stefan has started working on making harnesses to take the place of the ropes. From the way they are tangling themselves, it seems like a good idea. Astrid smiled a moment as she looked along the row of children down the centre between the two masts. *It looks like a dog run where the sled dogs are kept in line...although dogs seem to have more sense about the whole thing.*

Olympias

They gradually came in sight of Erave Town. The lighthouse is the first thing to become visible. Olympias looked at the time and the weather. *I will keep running for a while, changing my direction so that, to a casual observer it will look like the wind is stronger out on the lake, and that I am tacking with it.*

It was only when they were a thousand paces away that she changed to the lighter wind and then to what nature had provided. Now they had to wear the ship in earnest instead of just taking on the appearance of it for onlookers, and the watch had to look at shifting sails and, although it was mainly the spanker that came fast across the hull, the others still needed their trim adjusting.

As they came closer to the town, the current in the water picked up as the lake emptied into the river. Olympia had the sweeps laid out and got the other watch ready to take them. We will dock, not anchor. Those on duty will bring the ship in with its sails, if I steer right and the wind holds, but it does not hurt to have the sweeps ready in case they are needed.

Astrid has drawn a rough sketch for me of the moorings, and how she thinks the currents run...but of course, until I feel the water, I cannot be sure. According to my sister, the lake becomes the river around the point clad in stone that has the lighthouse on it. It serves to make a large eddy as the river pushes past. If that is right, I should nearly be able to ride the eddy up to the wharf, and if there is a spare spot, tie up there directly.

The lighthouse made a good navigation point, and with Parminder still not finding bottom, she entered the river. The current picked up and eventually

Parminder found bottom, but still at a much greater depth than they needed, getting a touch at the limit of the line at four fathoms. Olympias looked up as they swept past the lighthouse and the small fort that it was a part of.

The watch can stand up there and look down on us from beside their larger ballistae. From their point of view, the war-like ballistae of the River Dragon will probably be more than balanced by the small children still on deck. What could be more innocent?

Olympias looked at the water and thought about the current. *We may need our own wind behind us to get back into the lake. I wonder how many of the local craft have to be warped around the point. I can see a walkway and bollards near the base of the fort and all the way around it. It looks like that sort of warping happens regularly.*

Astrid has drawn the wharf and the currents well enough. There are plenty of boats tied up, but most are side by side out from the wharf. There is room for us if I can time my approach right. Otherwise we might have to be warped in. She took in sail and inched up.

Olympias had crew standing by with both gaffs and bags filled with wool, while Denizkartal and Astrid each had a mooring rope in hand, and were looking at throwing them onto a bollard and then leaping across to tie up. *We will be coming in on our starboard, but it looks like, with the eddy serving to help a craft, that is how it is done here.*

The quay had plenty of people on it, looking with curiosity at what was undoubtedly the largest ship to ever tie up there. They caught the lines as they were thrown, and the mooring took place without any drama with the woollen pads being put in place to prevent damage against the dock. *One advantage of being on a river…at least I don't have to worry about the tides.*

Parminder called the depth for the last time at three fathoms as they came up to being still. *And I don't have to worry about grounding her. She draws less than one and a half fathoms in her current trim.*

Once they were tied up and a gangway run across to the quay, Shilpa jumped out. *I have designated her as the supercargo, all traders have them. Not that we have much to trade at present, just some rose water, some linen cloth, some spicy gasparin-dragon salamis, and other smallgoods, and this is too near Evilhalt for any of them to be of much interest (except for the salami which is unique) but she is also responsible for any docking fees, and I am sure that one of those waiting will be a tax collector.*

She was right, and Shilpa immediately set to haggling with the man over what little was due. As this was being seen to, Rani and Theodora prepared to go and see the Mayor. Olympias strode around her ship, and saw that the crew went into a docking routine of properly furling sails, and coiling ropes and making sure that everything was tidy.

Basil and Lakshmi are already on their way to renew their acquaintance with the fishing community, and Stefan has mounted a guard at the gangplank while Theodora goes off with some others to collect the spare sails. Stefan has taken duty there himself together with Tabitha. Astrid has taken a position where she could care for the children and yet still answer the inevitable questions from the idlers along the wharf.

Lakshmi Brar

B asil and Lakshmi soon found out that the news of the raid on Rising Mud had come out to Lake Erave almost immediately.

Almost as fast as a person can ride the distance, the lake village has received the rumour that the push towards war has stalled. It seems that the people agitating the most for conflict, or at any rate the ones who were most listened to, were the town mages and our raid killed several of them. It seems that the rest very quickly lost interest after that.

Lakshmi found even more than that in the first place they looked. *I have found the man who brought the news out of the Swamp himself. As a Havenite, I am all full of understandable curiosity about what happened.*

According to the man, he had left quickly as he expected the whole place to fall into pieces and he wanted to be well away. He had ridden hard, before the villages started blaming each other and started fighting among themselves... "Although it has to be the Caliphate who did it—there was this group of dancing girls there, and they fought off a pursuit just before disappearing with all of this money. If they was dancing girls...why didn't they dance? They was assassins, I tell you, and they had carpets to escape."

Between us, we cannot find anyone who is overly interested in our village. It is more interesting for everyone to speculate about the Swamp. Rumours about the death of the dragon are dismissed by the people of the lake town as being made up and just tales. After all, no one can kill a dragon. Dragons killed armies and ate towns. At least that is the way of it in all of the stories.

Lakshmi smiled to herself in a way that didn't show on her face. *I guess we won't have much of a market here for the salami then. Our saddles make for a complete revolution in the way that any fight can now take place, but although they have been seen here a couple of times, no one has added three and three to make a hand.*

Shilpa Sodaagar

When they took sail next morning, they had added a little to the goods that they had on board to sell. *I have a quantity of corn of different sorts: wheat, barley, and maize, I have flour, smallgoods, more (and much better quality) rosewater, and of all things, a goodly roll of the embroidered braid that they use for hemming their northern clothes.*

I am not sure where we will be able to sell that last, but I need to have some goods on board so that we can pose as a trader, and it has been slim pickings in that way so far.

I think that I am beginning to see why Carausius likes coming to see us. We always buy everything that he has, and while we may not produce much in our valley yet, what we do have is all very saleable and we have the cash to make up for any shortfalls against what he brings.

Chapter XXIV

Olympias
26th Duodecimus

T hat day saw only the fore and aft sails being set as they tacked down the river into the wind, close-hauled, and coming about rapidly without trying for too much speed. Otherwise, they went with the current with crew standing to the sweeps and using them as needed.

The river was two hundred or more paces wide at its narrowest with no sign of a disturbance on the surface from shallows, and for the most part their linesman had "no bottom" as her call. When she found bottom, it was only once at less than three fathoms and that was on a wide stretch of the river when she called the odd cry of "mark twain" or two fathoms.

She had no feeling of danger even then, and her next reading was again "no bottom." Once they were past the sole outlying hamlet of Erave Town that lay on the river, they started passing forest that seemed trackless, as the river curved away from the more direct land route. The trees slipped past on either side in seemingly undisturbed solitude.

From the book I was shown in Mousehole, the path that we have to follow makes it over twice as far to get to Garthang Keep by the river as it had taken to cross the lake, and this time we cannot, due to the risk of shoals on an unknown river, travel at anywhere near the speed that we did on the lake.

They ran the log and it showed that, by beating close-hauled, they moved a lot faster than the river. They drifted for a while, and while they did so, careful observation and a lot of guesswork gave them a rough speed of around sixty fathoms every minute for the river speed. Although they could keep that speed up without any effort on their part, at any time they could, if they were unlucky or inattentive, run aground. The lead was cast with as little time between casts as was possible, and Bilqīs and Bryony were the busiest people on the whole ship.

"It took us a little over a week to get up here by horse," said Rani. "How long are we going to take this way?"

"If your barbarian lands had proper maps, Princess, I might know. As it is, as far as I have been able to find out, and Basil and Lakshmi have found out no better in talking to the men who sail the lake and this river, there are no maps here. We are making the map as we go.

"Everyone else does it by experience, and by sailing many times with an experienced pilot before they attempt it on their own. That is why we are taking compass bearings, why we note the depth at corners and along the reaches, and why we are trying to guess distance and speed. Everyone our people have talked to has said we are mad doing this without an experienced pilot and I agree.

"According to Basil, several people were casting bets on us being wrecked on our first trip. On the other hand, I found no pilot willing to come with us, so unless you can come up with a way for us to travel quicker, and we can go much faster, we will take around four days for us to get there, and we are most likely far quicker than the usual boats which run this river.

"However, we will not sail all of the time. I intend to anchor at night. I will not risk us sailing at night, even with your light, on an unknown river. The people that we talked to said there are shoals on the river and mud-banks. I am trying to judge where they might be and avoid those spots. It seems to be working so far." The whole time, while she spoke, her eyes had not left the river ahead of them.

Just then Parminder called "mark twain and I feel danger." Olympias called for the helm to be put over, and the River Dragon went to a beam reach, moving directly across both the north-bound wind and the south-bound river.

Looking ahead I can see some apparent lumps in the river. She pointed. "See, there is one now. To get those lumps it must be only a few cubits deep and, if it is mud, we would be grounded. If it is rock, we would be sinking."

"If what you say is right, it will be at least three days before we come upon settlements again. Why don't you fly ahead on saddles and get the riders to measure how deep the water is ahead of us?" asked Rani.

Olympias felt her mouth drop open. Astrid, who had the wheel said, "My God. I am still thinking like just a sailor and I have been using the things for months." *She is looking at me, waiting for an order.*

"Go ahead." *Sailing in unknown waters has now just been completely re-invented. Astrid has called for Father Simeon to take over at the wheel, and now is making up new leads for the riders and organising four people on saddles.* Astrid took one and grabbed the Khitan for the others.

"We need four fliers to run out straight ahead, looking for any obvious shallow areas, measure and come back to Bryony with the results," she said. It took a while, but eventually she had this running to her satisfaction.

I am looking at what I am seeing in Bryony's book of charts and now instead of pacing nervously back and forward and peering ahead, am smiling and feeling more confident. She looked even happier when the first flier, Anahita, reported finding a shallow patch and the fliers converged to plot its size.

This one would have been very dangerous. It is the shallowest that we have plotted so far at only one fathom, but it is so wide here that there is barely a sign of it on the surface. They had to go within a chain of the right bank to go around these shallows, although there the river was very swift and showed no sign of bottom.

Rani

*F*rom the river, the trees change in the reverse of what I experienced as I left Haven. The forest of gums and deciduous trees are already gradually giving way to evergreen jungle. The few animals that I can see are becoming, for most of the others, exotic and we are seeing more of the great lizards through the trees than we see in the colder north.*

Most noticeably the birds are changing from the mostly drab northern types to the brighter and more raucous birds of the south that I am used to. There has even been a small troop of monkeys making noises at us from the canopy of the trees. I feel like I am coming home.

Astrid

*T*onight, we anchor in the middle of the stream with two anchors. My sister wants a strong watch kept above deck, with at least one person in the main top. We cannot be sure exactly who or what is watching us, and although it is unlikely that anything inimical is; it is better to be cautious. After the hard work of the constant tacking on a close reach during the whole day, we are all exhausted.*

The language lessons all around for the night were fairly short, and the entire ship slept soundly in their unfamiliar hammocks when they were not on watch. The bells were muffled and rung softly, but they still echoed through the stillness of the night. Some of them, those who had worked right through the day, such as Parminder and Bryony, were given no watch to keep and had, except for the demands of their children, uninterrupted sleep.

I am not the only one among those who went to Rising Mud to notice, with regret, that we are far enough south that the possums have already begun to make the night noisy around us. At least, being out in the water, we lack those horrible blood-sucking leaches.

Olympias
Early morning 27th Duodecimus

It is time to set sail again. With the slight morning wind coming up the river behind us, and with the use of the sweeps, we are able to gradually make headway against the current and take up the two anchors.

That day and the next couple passed in the same fashion. The steady wind kept up, only really dropping at night and the crew became more accustomed to their tasks.

Christopher
28th Duosecimus

I am right in my thoughts. I can take the rough lumps of limestone, and by the right prayer, smooth them off as we need, and smoother than they can be done by hand. Goditha is very pleased. I can make eight at a time. She would take nearly that many days to make that many balls.

It is hard and fiddly work when she does them, and it is always a risk that stone chips will fly off and hurt someone. As well, she has to continually run them through her gauge to check what she makes to be sure that they are the right size and shape. It is hard to make sure that they fit and don't get too small.

"I will keep making them," she said. "You never know how many we will need in a battle. It will be like arrows. You are supposed to never have enough… once you are in a fight. However, if you make twice as many plain ones as you do enhanced, we will see how that goes when we actually have to use them.

At the moment these monkeys are nearly empty, and the lockers are fairly bare as well, and we have nothing at all in reserve down below."

Denizkartal apologised to them both. *He needn't. I am quite interested to see what happens myself.* He took advantage of the extra balls to fire one from each ballista to check that their mountings were secure and worked when they were actually in use. *He has been training people in how to serve them, without actually firing the mechanism. I suppose that they need to see what will actually happen when they fire.*

Although either he or Olympias would actually fire them if it were needed, they still require people to help wind them back and put the ball in place. *Everyone is well impressed with the results.* Denizkartal sent the one at the bow down the river to its maximum range of nearly thirty chains where it skipped over the surface a few times before finally sinking.

The other one at the stern he aimed at a tree on the riverbank to check its accuracy, carefully correcting the device and aiming about halfway up. *He is accurate in his shot.* The ball hit the trunk and the wood shattered at the impact point. With a loud crack and a tearing sound, the tree slowly broke in two.

Gradually the top toppled over making a loud crashing noise as it fell through the other branches around it, breaking the vines that were running over the tree and on to other trees, and finally down to the ground to an accompanying raucous chorus of protest from the surrounding birds and some other arboreal animals. A flock of bright-coloured parrots rose up and flew away from the river, complaining as they went.

Olympias
29th Duodecimus

That wind comes nearly directly from the south the whole time. It is blowing strongly enough to let a small river boat sail slowly up the river against the current. Each day we begin with an early service from Father Christopher, and we finish with another upon dropping our anchors, head into the stream. Each time the afternoon service is done during showers of warm rain.

During the day, streams both small and large empty into the river, and it grows wider and wider around us without much changing its depth. Seeing that the width of the river is gradually increasing, where there are no shallows, it does mean that the reaches we can make are getting longer and longer before we have to tack again.

Olympias

The first flights out have reported that there is a clearing just downstream of where we laid up for the night. It is time to bring the saddles in and hide them below decks. They went back to the old ways of travel with someone always aloft in the rigging keeping a watch ahead, and everyone anxiously waiting to hear Parminder's call of the river depth.

As we go past the settlements, it is easy to see that the people of this first hamlet are obviously from Haven. They, in turn, have stopped what they are doing and are looking with curiosity at our ship, one that is very unlike any that they have seen before, and also one that they had not seen come up the river.

The fact that they had travelled far faster with the saddles aloft was apparent to everyone. *At least it is, to a degree, made up for by us not finding as many shallow areas to avoid in this stretch, so we can travel in a straighter path. On the other hand, we are beginning to see islands and I have to make choices as to which way to go around them. It seems I choose the right way each time, as we have no difficulty with any of our transits so far.*

After mid-day, we come upon our first sign of the Haven military. Ahead of them and steering for them was a proa, a large and fast canoe, being driven fast upstream by its oarsman as they knelt on their benches and with an officer standing in the bow. *The Princess Rani has prepared for this moment and we have our orders already.*

All of the other Havenites were sent below decks as soon as it was spotted, with Goditha taking over in the bow for her wife. A section of rail was removed on the port side and a ladder let down towards the water, not that it was a long climb up, more a step or two up from the other craft, but it was a courtesy.

Rani stands on deck at the rail with me and we wait. While they were on a tack the proa saw which side had the rail removed, and it came alongside there as the Mice lowered their woollen sacks and one of its crew threw a line up from its bow. It was tied alongside, and the officer came up onto the River Dragon with a curious look on her face.

Rani

*S*he stops when she sees me. "Shri Rani," she said with obvious surprise in her voice. "You have returned. When we heard no more from you…" she trailed off. *It is obvious what the rest of the sentence is. It is one of the officers that I met on my way north. I had been hoping that it would be. It makes the rest of what I have to do easier.*

"Greetings…I need to show you this." She handed the officer the letter from the Maharajah that had been kept safe all this time…*as I wondered what to do with it*. When it was handed back, she continued. "When you get back on board your craft, you are to return as fast as you can to your base and see your Governor. He has not changed?"

On receiving a shake of the head, she continued. "You can tell him the truth, but no-one else. Your crew must tell no one that they saw us, only what I tell you. How far are we from the keep?"

"Another hour will see you in sight of it," was the reply.

"In that case we will go a little further and then anchor. We will pass by Garthang in the night. What of the river? We need two fathoms…apart from the islands are there any mud banks or other obstacles that we need to know about when running at night?"

"No, from here on down, if you do not get too close to the banks, you should have a clear run all the way to Pavitra Phāṭaka itself and can run all night."

"Good. You have not seen the River Dragon." She indicated the ship they were on, "You can say that a small river trader, one that you have seen many times before and that you have talked to on the river, will pass you in the dark. Anything else anyone says is just a rumour. Now, tell me, what do you know of what happens in the Swamp?"

The officer is again surprised, this time by a total change of direction in the conversation. "Pandit, we were expecting to be attacked. After what we were told you found in the north, we had pulled back, but the cattle-killers were continuing to provoke us, and we have been expecting our trade and our settlements to be attacked at any time for a year now.

"All of a sudden it was as if the threat had never been. We have even started to get traders from the Swamp again, and they make no mention of any trouble at all. It is as if there had been none in the first place. It is very strange."

Rani nodded. "The would-be leaders of the war died, and I suppose no one else wanted to take the role lest they die as well. It all collapsed. Once I have returned, if it looks like it will grow again you are to send a fast message to Evilhalt addressed to me. If this ship is there, you can give it to the captain."

She stopped for a moment. *How much should I say?*

"Until I pass this way again, neither you nor your Governor are to repeat a word that I say to any person at all. Once I give the word, you may send news to Pavitra Phāṭaka, if I do not tell them when I am there." She then launched into a very short version of what had happened.

She concluded: "Now there is something that must be destroyed in Pavitra Phāṭaka itself lest the malignancy that caused the problems with trade, and in the Swamp and elsewhere grow within the heart of Haven.

"I cannot tell any of this to anyone I do not trust as I do not know who is involved within Haven. I can probably trust your garrison and its officers, as no word of me and my mission went out to the Masters, but I trust no others until I have proof."

This officer is looking quite shocked at that. "After we have dealt with the issue in Pavitra Phāṭaka, we must sail on to Gil-Gand-Rask, so do not expect us to return soon. Do you have any questions?"

Apinaya Sarin

I have so many questions. She looked around her. *Beside the Battle Mage is a grim-looking woman with faintly greenish skin and black eyes dressed in an unfamiliar uniform. Shri Rani waved at her as the Captain. She has a falchion and a main gauche at her waist.*

Further away is some sort of kharl dressed and armed the same as her, beside him is a much larger and even more hideous grey being, and scattered around the deck are people dressed as if from almost every land that I have heard of. The women are all beautiful, even if the men are not. All of them are heavily armed; even the woman nursing two babies has a spear on the deck beside her.

Looking up, I can see that even the ones that are aloft, all women, have weapons with them. It is all so strange that it has to be true, and it fits with the few rumours that had come in about the Dwarves and the happenings in the mountains. Between the letter and what I see, I have to just stay silent and obey.

"I have none, Pandit. I will convey your words to the Governor, and we will eagerly await your return to us when hopefully you will be able to tell us more."

She saluted and leapt back down into her proa. "Cast off and return home." *The oars flash with the water coming off them in the afternoon sun as my fast craft speeds ahead like a dart and rapidly outpaces the large ship, leaving it lumbering in the scant wake of my smaller vessel.*

Olympias

W*e will continue on for another half a glass before setting just a single anchor and waiting in the middle of the river until the night comes. With my glass, on the distant banks, the giant crocodiles of the sea can be seen sunning themselves while on our ship sailors do the same while they go about lessons and chores.*

They ate an early meal and said their prayers while a watch was kept. The sun sank into the uninhabited jungle on the west of the river and the sky grew darker above them. *Although the moons are both waning as we move towards the double new moon of the New Year Eve, there will still be light enough for us to proceed if we are lucky.*

Olympias (that night)

Once Olympias deemed it dark enough, they took in their anchor and silently slipped down the river with no lights showing. They came upon the keep and even those from Darkreach were impressed as its solid bulk slipped by on their port side.

It would be as hard to take as Nameless is said to be, particularly with a river at its back. I can see in the moonlight the glint of light off water-filled fields ahead of it. They alone will stop an advance and keep most artillery a long distance away until firm roads could be built.

They passed it by and then immediately passed the mouth of the Tulky Wash behind the keep, where it came in to the Rhastaputra River from the Swamp. *I can feel the added force of that river as we are pushed toward the other shore. The officer is correct so far. Despite my worries, I evidently have nothing to fear from this river.*

Rani
32nd Duodecimus, the Feast Day of Saint Irene

They continued down their path, still anchoring at night, as the jungle along the river margin started to disappear and the cultivated fields spread more and more extensively to take up the whole length of the shore. They went past Peelfall and Vinice, with its huge red walls of baked brick enclosing the town.

If Astrid is right, then these towns once had other names. What had these towns been known as in Old Speech that has given them such names that, even to the people who live in them now, still sound strange? Had there once been a people who lived here before Haven. People whose names still lingered when they didn't?

They didn't stop at these towns, nor did they stop at the next town, Shelike. As they passed there, Rani pointed out the elephant stables and their breeding areas.

At each village or town, even some of the smaller settlements, we can see the temples, very different to those the others are used to, and they have nothing like the ever busy ghats with people coming down into the river to bathe fully clothed, keeping a close watch out for the giant crocodiles as they do so. They all are curious about the funeral fires as well. To me it is a return to the normal...and brings with it other problems.

Christopher

Saint Catherine was the last day that was special to us in our valley. This is another. It is also the last of the feast days for the patron saints for the year.

"Harald and Goditha," Christopher called as he began to prepare his service, "Can you assist me please." He explained to everyone why that was. "Today is the Feast day of Saint Irene...she is the patron of miners and quarrymen, so it is a special day for them both."

Astrid

Outside Shelike there is a whole bank full of the funereal pyres, something only I, among the non-Havenites, am familiar with. They are common enough in the north where it is easier to burn your dead than to bury them in the frozen ground and sometimes safer.

From every place there wafts unfamiliar smells and I can see, in the streets, cattle roaming around untended. We are not overly pushing our speed through the increasing traffic on the river and this leg of our run is taking another four days.

Even more so than in Darkreach, it seems that once we have passed the border no one official pays the slightest attention to us. The only ones who acknowledged us in any way are a few small boats that come out from villages and settlement and chase us and try to sell us food.

Shilpa came to the rails and loudly told them to go away in no uncertain terms. They replied in kind. "I would not trust anything that they try and sell you," she told everyone. "The fruit may be fine to eat, if the skin is not broken, and you wash it, but that is all. The priests rarely come out to these people and there are many diseases among them."

Rani

I had not thought of that…the sight of the fruit made me homesick, and I was about to buy a basket to share with my wife.

Rani
33rd Duodecimus

In the distance…that long and wide island must be Jībha, the Tongue. There are now settlements to be seen on both banks of the river, as well as the island, and no obvious direction to take. Olympias looks at me. All I can do is shrug and direct us down the left-hand passage. I think that is widest.

Eventually, ahead of them they could see a vast jumble of islands and channels. *I am perplexed at what to do next. I am not actually sure of where to go from here. You climb into a boat and your boatman takes you to where you need to be. Parminder, in the bow, has no idea either. Before she was kidnapped, she had not been outside the city.*

Luckily, Shilpa (with her merchant background) is able to take over and give directions. She points out what we pass. Before they had finished passing Jībha they passed a small, and crowded island connected to the shore by a bridge. *It is covered in temples and is known as Mandira Dvīpa, or Temple Island.*

The eastern shore, or Pūrvī Taṭa, is covered in industry, mainly to do with shipping. I think that the Paścimī Taṭa, or western shore (now it comes into view from behind the islands) has establishments that are more to do with food and drink. Shilpa pointed them down a passage between two islands, as the actual shore of the river was lost behind them.

To our left is Lāṅga Ā'ilaiṇḍa, the Long Island, where many of the people live, and to our right is Hāthī Dvīpa, or Elephant Island, which had most of the military bases, and where many Kshatya, or warriors, live...including my family.

Staying part-hidden behind a sail she pointed out to her wife a large sprawl of buildings on the waterside with its own dock alongside it. *Looking at the place that I used to call home, I still don't know how I feel about talking to my family.*

Ahead lay Rājā kē Dvīpa, the Rajah's Island, where many of the rest of the higher caste people live. They could see a huge stone bridge connecting it and Lāṅga Ā'ilaiṇḍa. Shilpa steered them away from that channel, and pointed down between Hāthī Dvīpa and Rājā kē Dvīpa. Hāthī Dvīpa came to an end and another bridge connected it to a small island, "Ānanda Dvīpa" called Parminder happily, recognising something for the first time from the water.

"That is the pleasure island," said Shilpa dryly, as Parminder blushed herself into a deeper brown, realising what she had just said about herself.

"I used to work there," Lakshmi called to Harald, as she came down a ratline. "But I lived on another island that you can just see through that gap," and she pointed. "We will see it better later. I don't want to be seen there."

She has reconciled with her past, and has admitted to me that she does not mind mentioning it, as her current contentment with Harald stems indirectly from what she learnt there.

The pleasure island was connected by another bridge to a far larger island. On this massive island, except for a small dock closed off from casual entry by a chain, walls far taller than the masts of the River Dragon rose high straight out of the water. *It is all one massive fortification.*

"That will be a military base then...we have its like at home," Theodora, who had gone back aloft, called down from the mast. *She is obviously excited to be back in a real city.*

"Kilā Dvīpa," said Rani to those around her. "It is a Royal Armoury and the final refuge of the city. Only a small garrison actually live there, but most of the city is supposed to be able to fit inside, and it also has huge granaries with food held in reserve. Several Fire Mages of the sign of the Rat work there the whole time to keep the spells fresh."

"We are still on the main channel and you can see that there is no bridge here. There are many ferries of all sizes…" And she pointed at one that had an elephant with a load on its back on it. The elephant stood in the middle of a crowd of people, with both animal and people unconcerned about each other. It was very slowly pushing its own way through the water.

"In place of bridges, ferries connect Kilā Dvīpa with Rājā kē Dvīpa. Every other island has a bridge to connect it to the rest. Pavitra Phāṭaka is a maze of islands and bridges that make Rising Mud look like what it really is…and no offence is meant to you in this, Bryony…just a little village on a jungle river." *Her face shows that she thinks the same.*

Shilpa pointed ahead. "That is Vyāpārī Dvīpa, the merchant's island. It has the main markets on it, although many Sudra, merchants and clean tradesmen, live there as well. We are going to turn right down beside it and,"—she pointed—"you can just see Anta Dvīpa, where we are going, straight ahead there between Kilā and Vyāpārī. What you see there is the route to the sea."

Olympias headed them in that direction. When they came to the tip of Vyāpārī, they turned to starboard to head down the main channel. "That is Gantraj ahead. There are temples there as well, but not major ones, and lots of people, mainly Harijan, untouchables, and their trades. They are there on the opposite side of the city, where they will not pollute the Brahmin."

The wharves of Anta are now visible and so is the open sea beyond. As we come down the channel I can start to feel, for the very first time, the faint fore and aft rocking movement of the ship as it first encounters the slow surge of the low waves of the ocean that survived enough to come up the channel.

Olympias

I see where I want to go. She pointed it out to Astrid at the wheel. Denizkartal began to get his docking crew ready. *It is time to take in sail. Again, I think that we will use that southern wind to dock on our starboard side so that we can come in from down river and have our stern facing to the sea.*

By the time they came alongside the wharf, they just had their jib and the spanker up, and the spanker was down as soon as the first rope went across to the wharf, leaving Astrid to balance the ship with the jib until she was secured.

Astrid

The River Dragon is tied up much looser here than at Erave Town, as she will have to ride with the tide, and a gangplank has to be put across to the shore. Three hawsers were made fast from the stern and three from the bow.

I note that we are still at least a glass away from dusk when we tie up. We might not have been expected, but by the time Shilpa can make it to the docks there is a tax collector there waiting for her. A story had been prepared that would explain why they were there, and she was ready with it. *It is obvious that the River Dragon rides high and light, so it is one that is easy to believe.*

Her story is that she has fallen in with traders from upriver who want to make a run along the coast to Freehold. We are here to buy goods to add to the little that we already have. She is showing the inspectors the near empty holds with grain, flour, and a few small boxes, the saddles being hidden away in the concealed hold that led me to conclude that the River Dragon had been built as a smuggler.

By the time she has finished arguing, it seems that our charges for docking are fairly low. Now it is the time for Rani to stay concealed away from prying eyes, and for those from Haven who have lower castes to come out in public. Denizkartal began to move the stern ballista so that both faced the dock from the starboard side.

Chapter XXV

Basil
33rd Duodecimus

"Now that we are docked, it is time for Lakshmi and I to assess what lies around us." Basil left the boat first, as the most obvious target, but this time Lakshmi took the lead.

She has made herself up very carefully, and now does not even remotely look like herself. The very attractive young woman has gone, and she looks and moves like a much older person. I am not sure though that, on leaving, an old woman would wink at her husband in such lecherous way.

From what Conrad told us when he was questioned in Mousehole many months ago, I know that my target is somewhere near us, but I don't know exactly where. All that I am sure of is that it is somewhere nearby, and in the street that runs along the seafront—if he didn't somehow manage to lie against the truth spell that is.

The man never counted how far along it was, and from the look of it, the description he gave to us could possibly fit many of the places that I can see. What is more, we could even be under observation by someone who means us harm by now, and we would not know.

Basil followed Lakshmi's lead. *To all appearances, I am not with her, but just idly poking around, and looking at what is around me. In contrast, Lakshmi bustles along. She moves the whole time…as if she has a purpose as she quarters the island, just not reaching her destination.*

The pair did not head straight for where their target should be, but looked all around the whole island. Constantly, they checked on each other to see if anyone followed them.

At one stage, Basil found that he had a couple of people approach him from each end of a narrow alley, as if to cut him off.

Just a group of would be dacoit, street toughs, really. A quick flick out and in of my shortswords as I back against a wall, is enough to convince them that there may be an easier target somewhere else. They fail at being nonchalant as they turn around and leave…one pair each way.

They don't even think about Lakshmi, even though one pair had to push past her as they leave. She may not be familiar to them, but her type is, and she obviously has no money. I am unfamiliar, and being a well-dressed foreigner, obviously have plenty of coin. I may have money, but I have already realised that they are here and I am well armed.

As a trained officer, Basil noted what they looked like, and resisted the urge to follow them in turn and see where they kept themselves.

Basil
A few hours later

They returned individually after dark, and afterward Christopher prayed for the location of the pattern. They went below to confer, leaving a watch in the top and on deck. "Is it odd that we have so many guards?" asked Denizkartal. The Havenites all shook their heads.

Me first. "If I had a unit here, and could close off the bridge that leads to this island, I would be able to keep the arena schedule busy for quite some time. I watched purses being taken, goods being stolen from stalls, and so many people that almost had 'criminal' written on their foreheads that I cannot believe it."

"As for our possible target, we have the second docking from the sea. On the corner is a lighthouse. Strangely it is not as tall as that at Erave Town, but it is very solidly fortified, and well-armed and manned. It would be very hard to take. You can see that from the deck."

"Along the seafront from it some way, two hands of houses, is a house. It is large and it has guards. If that is not it, then there are so many candidates that I cannot list them all, but my money is on that one. It fits with everything Conrad said, and it just feels right to me. Lakshmi, what can you add?"

"I rarely came here," she said. "I worked on Kilā, we got a lot of work from the officers and soldiers there, on Ānanda, and on Rājā kē Dvīpa. This island has always been seen as dangerous. I know why now.

"I am glad that Ayesha has trained me and that I had Basil with me. No one seemed to follow us, or be more interested in us than you would expect… although Basil almost picked up four new close friends. I agree with what he said. That house is too well set up…and far too wealthy for Anta. I would expect it on Vyāpārī, but not here."

Father Christopher nodded. "I will have to go out with you soon later to confirm it but, from what you have said it is quite likely that is the one that I have picked up. At any rate, the pattern is somewhere in that direction, and you cannot go far in that direction without getting very wet."

"I have to agree with Basil about the people here," Christopher continued. "I spent a lot of time sitting on deck and looking at the people as they passed by. Most people are either only a little bad or a little good, but I have never felt so many thoroughly evil people in all of my life." *He is looking directly at Rani.* "Don't your priests care?"

Rani shuffles uncomfortably and speaks defensively. "They say that it is each person's fate to be what they are. If you are evil, you will come back in the next life as a lower form of life and that is its own punishment. If you are good, you come back as a higher caste and that is a reward. This is supposed to make people try and be good all of the time. For all I know, these people may be better now than they used to be, and their soul is actually working its way up."

Bianca

*N**ow it is my husband's turn to confirm which house we are looking for. He is travelling in a box of people, with Basil and Lakshmi in front and Ayesha, dressed in local fashion looking just like Lakshmi is. I am behind them dressed in a similar way, but even I know that I am not very convincing in my act.*

It almost seems that there are more people moving around at night then there were during the day. This must be the house…my husband looks silly dressed in a yellow robe and loincloth, and with his old staff and a bowl. I am sure that he is a too eager to seek alms…and his skin is very pale…but it is night.

He goes up to the guards and they push him away. Should I help him? No, it is his act. At least none of those at the house seem to notice me start forward. Once they were around the corner, Christopher, although obviously a little disoriented, started to head back toward the ship by heading determinedly around the block.

One by one, we follow his lead…except for Basil, who is staying behind near the house and on shore. The plan is that he will find a quiet corner and see if anyone is trying to follow us. So far, we seem unnoticed.

When they were all below decks, Father Christopher confirmed that this was indeed the house that they were looking for. "However, I am sure that what we want is not in the house itself. When I was at the door, the pattern still felt like it was a fair way from me, so it might even be in a building overlooking the sea."

"I made sure that I went up to the guards to see if I could feel how they were, and this time I felt them both strongly. They are both thoroughly evil men."

Rani lays out plans for tomorrow. Shilpa will set off to this Vyāpārī with money to see what can be bought. That will show to anyone interested in us that we are what we say we are. She will take some guards with her looking like mercenaries. At least my husband will not go this time. Rani has decided that we will all be from Darkreach.

If you included Theodora with her eyes changed to black, we have a creditable load of Darkreach travellers, assuming that any Havenites they encounter do not realise that Aziz is a Hob. As it is, we can do nothing about the house until my husband gets his mana back, and we need more information on what is there before we move.

Olympias
34th Duodecimus

Ayesha asked Olympias to take her fishing in the rowboat. *I guess that the shopping will have to wait until later, as I, with my greenish cast to my features, am supposed to be playing the part of a Darkreach merchant along with the Princess.*

Olympias pointed that out, but Ayesha quickly replied that: "It will be far less conspicuous if I get you to row me out there than if I get Denizkartal to take me." *That is very true. From a distance no one can tell where I come from, and his hair alone gives his origin.*

Olympias

After services, we made our short fishing trip. *It was short for two reasons: first, we quickly saw what we needed to see. The house has its own dock at the front…a large timber box with a gangplank connecting it to the house itself to make a floating pier.*

There is also a small shed backing onto the water with wooden rails coming down into the sea. The doors are obviously well battered by occasional storms, but still solid. That shed will house a small boat to enable them to get out to a larger craft if they want, or just to travel around Pavitra Phāṭaka. More interestingly, there is a room over the boat shed…one with a ramp leading to it.

A room like that would be a good fit as a place for a pattern. It is isolated from the rest of the house, and it is as far from anyone passing in the street as it is possible to be. The rest of the house is built against the street.

To the rear is a short wall, which I cannot see very far over, but which appears to have behind it a garden, and possibly grass at a level over a fathom out of the water. The tide marks on the boatshed rails indicates that the ocean is nearly at its highest point with the tides…and yet the boatshed is still well clear of the water. The yard might get a drenching if a southerly wind whipped up the waves and blows the crests inland, but otherwise it will be clear.

The second reason that the trip was short was that they caught so many fish that their boat rapidly filled, and their excuse for being there disappeared. Olympias looked around as they came back to the River Dragon. *I can see many fishing boats, but not one of them is in front of Anta near the house, not even when they see the results that we achieved.*

"I wonder if we went back there tomorrow," she asked Ayesha, "…would we experience some 'bad luck'? It looks like the real fishermen are not doing well, but they will not go where we were, and I am sure that the fish soon learn to stay in a place where no one will come to catch them."

Olympias

W̶e are only just back and already our grand shopping expedition is setting out to this Vyāpārī island. Shilpa is a Havenite merchant who is escorting Theodora and me. We are playing up the image of part-Kharl merchants from Darkreach. Astrid and Basil are emphasising their Insakharl heritage and Aziz and Denizkartal don't have to try very hard.

It seems that this Father Simeon is going along as well. He looks wild enough normally, but he has increased the stakes by making a voluntary transformation. He is now padding alongside us in his wolf guise as if he is a mostly tame animal. At least any street thieves will want to stay well away from his teeth.

He admitted that he could only speak a few words of Hindi, and in his animal form he could see, hear, and smell better, and still detect if someone is evil. They arranged a signal for him. He would put his nose in someone's hand if he needed to indicate the nature of anyone who came near. *A nose in the right hand will mean good, and one in the left will mean that they are evil.*

Aziz is carrying some clothes, and anything that might be needed in a pack, if the priest has to change back to a human form. The Khitan are coming along as well, because apparently everyone here is accustomed to seeing traders with Khitan.

Lakshmi and Ayesha also went with them, but not as a part of the group. *They are there to see if anyone is interested in us.*

The irony is that one of the few real Darkreach people, Nikephorus, has to be left behind because he doesn't look the part that people will expect to see. He is far too civilised in his appearance, in fact quite the dandy, and with what everyone west of the mountains 'knows' of us, no one will expect that. He is not happy about this.

Stefan organised the ship and the guards, who took their positions and waited. *Bryony, Bianca and Parminder are doing the babysitting with the children playing around them.*

Such a large armed group walking the streets means that most of the time we do not have to push through the people on Anta, a space opens around us automatically. However, the way is becoming more crowded as we approach the bridge to Vyāpārī. It is a bridge that is built of stone; nearly four chains long, but only two fathoms wide with pylons going deep into the river beneath.

As they went over the bridge, the Hob and the Boyuk-kharl took the lead, and they discovered that keeping a couple of cubits between them was usually sufficient to have people heading their way press themselves against the rail rather than get in their path. As they neared the end of the bridge, people delayed getting on it and as soon as they were off the bridge their clear space appeared again.

People coming too close were greeted by a glare from the two in front, or a smile from Astrid with her spear, or Basil playing with his swords. The Khitan just stayed in a tight group behind the merchants, and kept their bows in their hands, but without an arrow on the string.

Once they were among the shops and stalls, the 'merchants' started looking at what was available. *Shilpa says that it is some time since she was last here, and a few things have changed, but most things seem to be unchanged. This is good.*

She has led me directly to someone of great interest. I didn't know that Pavitra Phāṭaka has one of the greatest precision instrument makers in The Land. It looks like he makes anything that requires fine work, and I have bought an accurate clock, a mechanical one, in a glass case, a smaller timer, two telescopes, and two astrolabes—one a quadrant and the other circular.

The Princess has found a clock that indicates all of the items of astrological significance by little markers when their time comes. She bought it on the spot, although it will not work well on my ship as it relies on a pendulum. It is for the village apparently.

Oh Lord. How much are we paying? Shilpa looked like she bargained hard, but Theodora is paying up what she is told to pay without a murmur. The man has very little left in his stock at least. Have we left anything? The items were given to Hulagu to carry, but Anahita quickly took them from him…köle.

The rest of the expedition was not all that successful. *Most of the goods for sale in the market have been brought in from outside Haven. Shilpa says that seeing that we are going outside, it is not a good idea to buy them here, as the prices are higher.*

Our best items to purchase are a few tonnes of local bulk rice, faintly smelling of jasmine, although Shilpa has warned the merchant that she will inspect every sack when they are actually delivered to make sure they are the same quality as those he presents here, as well as cloth and spices. The cloth is silk, cotton, kapok, and even a little spilk, and will always find a market for those that we choose to sell. Even I know that.

They bought a large quantity of them with various merchants with payment only coming on delivery. As for the spices and such, Lakshmi had to duck away, after getting things from Aziz's pack, and come back looking very different, much more herself in fact, to do the buying. *If anything, she is more excited in a spice market than I was in the watchmaker's shop.*

When they left that area of the market, they had a porter with them who had a large barrow stacked impossibly high with boxes.

The pharmacopeia of Mousehole will never be the same again. Lakshmi has everything from the ingredients of potions, to incense, to poisons, to cooking herbs. As far as she is concerned, none of this will be traded away. With what she has on order from Carausius, and what we produced locally, she has most of what she thinks she should have in stock, although I am sure she will probably be happy to be corrected and to find more to buy.

The number of items that we are buying is sending ripples through the market, and people are starting to come to us to offer wares directly as we walk around. Apparently, most long-distance traders usually use caravans and have a more restricted load or else use much smaller, coastal traders without the capacity of the River Dragon. The size of our ship, although she is only a little one compared to the large supply vessels of the fleet, is not usually seen in Haven.

They let it be known where the River Dragon was docked, and that they were still interested in the right items at the right price and returned to the ship happy with themselves.

Theodora

They were strolling slowly to the bridge when a Havenite pushed past them. He looked pre-occupied and came closest to Aziz. As he did so he gave a jump, looked him up and down, and then looked at the rest of them.

That is the sort of jump which I give whenever I come upon magic unexpectedly, when I am preoccupied about something else. He is a mage. From what my husband has said about who lives where, I wonder why a mage is coming to this island. She waved Basil over and indicated that he should be followed. *Basil has made some hand gestures at his wife and slipped away, taking Simeon with him.*

They arrived back at the ship, and started stowing away what they had with them and arranging space for what would arrive over the next day. Anything that would stay on the ship for the village, and that would not be traded away, was put in one of the special places and hidden from most casual inspections.

Basil and the wolf-priest came back soon after. "He went to the house," he said. "And Simeon nosed me that he is evil. So, there is likely to be at least one mage there."

"A Havenite mage? What did he look like?" demanded Rani.

None of them can give her a description that doesn't fit at least half-a-dozen mages that she knows of. I know that she may have gone to school with him, but do we need to know his name if we are going to kill him?

When Father Simeon returned to human form, he confirmed his feeling about the man and added: "He smelt very strongly of blood, lust, violence and fear. He has taken a woman recently, and I smelt not just her scent, but that of her spilt blood on him."

Rani

They sat down and discussed what was ahead of them, as Rani listened to the reports and opinions. *I think that we are best to attack in two days, under cover of the New Year celebrations.*

"One feature of New Year is that it is a long tradition that all of the mages use their skills for the city. Everyone has prepared at least one spell that is only for show. You make up one, or use one you have learnt, that makes a display in the sky or on the water. There is an informal competition for who has the most spectacular spell."

"I always used to fire clouds of special fireballs of different colours direct into the sky, or along the water where they would explode and cast-off smaller balls. It is a huge waste of mana, but it is always fun, and it lasts for most of the night, as one person after another shows off their power and skill. Some people even make special wands just for the occasion."

"There is much music and drinking and people enjoy themselves. We have many festivals and celebrations in Haven, but this is our only non-religious one." *I am sounding quite wistful about it, aren't I?*

Rani

*I*t seems that the shoppers made quite an impression on the merchants with *their open display of wealth. The goods have already started arriving and are being stowed away. Now, other traders come from other islands to see us to offer more goods.*

In turn Basil, Lakshmi and Ayesha are keeping a watch on the ship from the niche that Basil used after the first trip out. Basil says that it is inconspicuous and offers a good look at anyone interested in us.

Ayesha

*O*ur watch is rewarded. There is a pinched looking man, but not a beggar, *slipping into a similar niche further up the row of buildings.* He stayed there for some time watching what went on, and the comings and goings from the vessel. When he left, so did she, waving at the watchers on the ship to indicate what she was doing.

He keeps checking behind him, but I thank Allah, the Giver of Skills, that I am better at this game than he is. She followed him back to the house, where he entered. *It took some time to attract their attention, so they must not have been truly suspicious, but the people in the house have finally noticed our arrival, even if it is only as the result of a chance encounter in the street.*

Basil

*S*eeing *that the occupants of the house have put a watch on us, however casual it was, I think that we will return the complement.* That night they put in place a watch on the house. They did it by climbing one of the neighbouring buildings.

It isn't the tallest here, so we cannot see everything that is happening inside, in fact its neighbours overshadow it, but that is one of its advantages. It provides a place to watch from that is hard to see into.

As a precaution, the person who would be watching was given the ring of no detection to wear. *It matters not if a mage sees through that enchantment, which they are unlikely to do due to where they are being watched from, because anyone who is picked up in that location can only be doing one thing and we need to do that one thing.*

Our watch place has another major advantage in its location. The building we are set up on is on the other side of the road from our target, not quite opposite, and deserted. We can enter it from the rear quite undetected. Basil, Ayesha and Lakshmi shared the watch in shifts, with the relief going up and waiting until the watcher there noticed them and took the ring off.

During the day that followed, they established that there were probably, judging by their dress at least, two mages who used it, as well as several others. *Some are obviously armsmen and guards. I have identified at least six of those, as well as the one who had come to look at the ship, and he has something in common in his look with the late un-lamented Vengeance.*

There are at least three servants. All of the people that they saw were male, and at least two of them were probably cooks from what they were carrying. *There is at least one girl, or woman in the building, and she is being abused in some way. We have not seen her, but Lakshmi heard a muffled cry of pain from there that can only have come from a woman or a boy.*

It will be hard to tell how many adversaries will be in the building when we attack, but at least we have some sort of idea now of what we will face. No one lives in the houses on either side of the target, and anyone who lives further down the road crosses to the other side of the street to pass the guards. They scuttle past with head lowered and eyes averted while the guards watch them intently.

*T*hey stayed for that night, and part of the next day before going back to the ship to sleep a little before the assault that had to go on that night.

Chapter XXVI

Rani
36th Duodecimus, New Year's Eve

The mage sighed quietly. *This will be a very dangerous assault and my best plan needs to have four parts. That many parts, however, make it harder to get right, and with more things that can go wrong, but it has the best chance of doing all that we want with the least casualties. Basil, who used to do things like this as a part of his work, says that it is a good plan.*

The simplest thing would be to just attack through the front of the building, but that allows for our enemy to flee from the rear if they wish. Our opponents have to be taken all at once from the front and the rear—and by surprise if possible.

The easiest part will be for those left behind. It will be their job to hold the River Dragon and to keep the children secure. I have told them to sail the ship away if it is needed, and at any rate to have it ready to sail without being too obvious. They also have to look for any move on the part of the garrison of the lighthouse fort, or anyone else, to interfere and to stop them if they can. It is a role of waiting, but it is also one that could be crucial.

The second most straightforward role will be for those who are going in directly through the front door. The guards of the day go inside at night, and the doors are secured unless someone uses the large brass knocker beside the gate. It will be the shore party's role to wait until they hear a noise from inside, indicating that the attack has become discovered, and to then force the gate and kill any of the residents that they find.

To this end, they have to somehow inconspicuously take a spare spar through the streets and use it on the front door. The gate that they have to force has a lock, and they could have had the magical lockpick with them, but more importantly, the watchers heard a beam being slid in place behind the door when it was closed.

The hardest part is left. This is our assault from the seaward side. There are two choices, using the saddles, or using either the small or the larger rowboat from the ship. I have decided that we will play it both ways. Seeing that there could be two mages, or even more inside, and the Master's servants have used a carpet before, we need to have a saddle available to us in case one of the mages tries to flee.

Theo-dear will thus ride a saddle. She will have Ayesha sitting behind her with her non-detection ring on, and given all that is happening tonight, this should at least keep them unseen by the lighthouse fort. Olympias and Denizkartal must leave first with the larger boat. They will take Christopher, Hulagu, Anahita, and Kāhina.

They will stay as close to the shore as they can, and row with muffled oars to try and avoid notice by the lighthouse garrison. They will land near the boatshed and the Khitan bows can pick off anyone who exposes themselves at the rear of the house. Their job is to isolate the boatshed while Father Christopher disposes of the Master's pattern.

As they are about to come ashore, Ayesha will be dropped off the saddle wherever she thinks that she can do the most good. That I leave to her judgement. My Princess can then land somewhere in shadow, and use her own spells or wands on any mages or anything else she thinks needs them. If anyone sees either of these groups and interferes, then we are lost.

Rani

Having established a plan, and set it in motion, Rani sighed. *Is the plan sufficient? What have I not taken into account? Will anyone outside the house among the neighbours do anything to interfere? I am about to find out. The fact that it is a very noisy mid-summer eve would help.*

As well, being mid-summer, it is the darkest night of the year. There is no light at all to be had from either moon, and it seems that tonight at least half of the stars are covered in a high cloud as it drifts across the sky, too high to interfere with the celebrations, but high enough to help block most of the light coming from above.

Stefan

I have my wife, Goditha, Parminder, Shilpa, Bianca, Nikephorus and Tabitha with me on the ship. I have assured Rani that I can do this, but I hope that I will not have to sail the boat anywhere. I can keep it secure, and even (though poorly) use the ballistae to interfere with the garrison, but sailing it anywhere is another matter.

I have placed axes near the mooring cables in case we have to quickly get away, but I am also hoping that that will not be needed. Everyone is in their place on deck, or in Bryony's case, in the maintop. I have Parminder below to care for all of the children.

Goditha and Parminder have their meagre spell books handy, and Goditha, the strongest of the apprentices, sits on the mage's hatch cover with a small bucket of pebbles and another of clay beside her. She is nervous. She sits and looks all around, and she keeps letting the pebbles run through her fingers with a clatter.

Astrid

It still lacks a glass before midnight when we move out. Harald, Aziz, and I have the spar, and Rani, Simeon, Basil, Lakshmi and Verily are moving ahead of us. Verily, Lakshmi and Basil will secure the area, and once the gate is opened, we are to go into the buildings and clear them.

Rani is our magical support and Simeon is again a wolf. That way he can use his nose to find out things that we might miss. It is not as subtle as in Rising Mud, nor are we as inconspicuous. What is more, I am a forest hunter in the middle of a city of unbelievable size. What could possibly go wrong?

It is hard to be inconspicuous when three of you have a small tree under your arms in a street in the middle of the night. As well, I am balancing a spear in my other hand, and Aziz and Harald have shields slung on their backs. It is a pity that my ring will not help. Hopefully, there is no city watch out on the streets tonight.

Shilpa has said there will not be a watch on this island, but I cannot imagine trying to explain ourselves to a unit of curious guardsmen. It is fine for Basil and Lakshmi, and even Verily. They are somewhere in the shadows ahead. I only occasionally see one.

Alongside Rani, Father Simeon is padding along like a good dog...and I am having trouble getting used to that as a thought...only he is a lot larger than the dogs I have seen around here. The local dogs know that he is not one of them and stay well away from us, turning tail quickly and running away fast if he is unexpectedly encountered. He is at least as large as the black wolves of the north…more like Hulagu's wolves, and I would not want to face his teeth without a magical or silver weapon.

They made it into the street that led off the wharf towards where the house was without anyone raising the alarm. By keeping to the more shaded side of the street we should be more inconspicuous now… More shaded? That is a laugh. Everything is shadow on this night.

There was a low mutter and lurch as Harald, who was at the front, slipped on something. I don't want to know what it is that he trod in. I just hope that I don't step in it as well. They were arranged with the shortest at the front and Aziz at the back. Harald will be standing on the steps as we swing the beam.

They came to a halt beside the gate. Basil and Lakshmi went ahead, and Verily took up a place behind them. We have all gone quiet and it seems to be silent inside. Now we can lean against a wall and wait until the fun begins from the sea. We are here for the assault on the building and the guards.

We have, except for thrown items and whatever Rani casts, no missile weapons with us, just muscle and all-out attack. No one is to get out past us. In the meantime, hopefully no one walks past and grows curious about this small army of foreigners standing in the street obviously waiting. Equally, I hope that no one looks out of a front window from the house.

Hulagu

*T*his is a new experience, and one I thought about before I left home. I have heard city dwellers compare the rise and fall of the plains to the sea, but I am not sure that it is a very apt comparison. I am rising and falling as the boat heads towards the sea, but the land of the plains is not likely to swallow you up if you somehow fall off your mount.

You can hide in the grasses and behind ridges on the grass. Here, you are open and exposed and at the mercy of whoever is moving you. Basil's sister and her green lover seem to know what they are doing, and they are admirably quiet, but I feel very exposed sitting in the front of this boat. He felt the solidity of the timber under his hand for support.

The rowers are behind me with their backs to me, and then there is Christopher, and finally my köle. We could have had many more people on board, and there is *space for four more rowers, but the woman just grinned when I offered to row as well.*

I can understand that and do not take offence. Even when standing at the long sweeps on the big ship we still tend to sometimes miss the water entirely with an oar, often falling over when we do. Rowing is not a natural skill for the emeel amidarch baigaa khümüüs.

We are moving away from the familiarity of the ship...and those were words I didn't ever think to have associated with myself...even if I mused about it when I first left the tents. Hulagu looked up towards the lighthouse keep beside him.

I know that others are worried about the garrison there, but I am not. The walled ones tend to think that they are invulnerable in their walls, and unless they are actually expecting something to happen, they do not use their eyes very well. They just look out and see what they expect to see.

At the most they will be looking at the horizon for an approaching fleet. On this night, most will probably be drunk. I am sure that I can hear some singing that can only be from the tower opposite. My people take advantage of this sort of laxness all of the time and the sentries usually do not live to learn from the mistake.

They rounded the point safely, and the boat rocked as the low waves hit them from the side. Hulagu looked right towards the horizon and swallowed. *When we finish here, we are going to go out on that in the ship. I really am not sure that I like that idea. Man is meant to ride to battle on a horse, not in a hollowed-out log with no soul. There will never be a totem of the ship. There is a breeze coming into my face, and I smell the salt, and the smell of what is, I have been told, rotting seaweed. That would indeed be right and fitting. Unlike the clean air of the plains, here the smell that the sea gives is not the smell of life, but of death and decay.*

It seemed to be ages, but eventually he saw what had been described. He had to get out with a rope, and hold the boat steady, and keeping low, he put away his bow in its case, and stepped firstly into the shallow water at the edge and then onto the land. He pulled the nose of the boat up a bit, and then held tight to the rope as the rest of the people got out.

Denizkartal took the rope from him and started to tie it off to something, as Hulagu drew his mace and unslung his shield from his back, and moved up the bank, following his köle as they took a position behind the seawall.

There is a small set of stairs here. He started to move up into the garden, his weapon in hand. *If she has seen us arrive, then Ayesha will be about to go into the shed above me and I should be ready to back her up. By the sounds above me, there are several people inside the building, and that will be a difficult proposition for one person even if, in theory, they are invisible.*

Theodora

I bring the saddle around the point, keeping close to the wall of the lighthouse fort and almost at sea level. *Looking back, the boat is only just breaking away from the ship. It was hard to see it in this light and, with everyone dressed in dark clothes, on this moonless night it is more like a patch of greater dark on the very faintly opalescent dark sea.*

She looked up. *I can see no one above me. Whichever of the watch are up there will probably have their night vision ruined by the glow from the navigation light itself. I have to stay down low with the saddle to avoid being lit up by the slightly smaller fort on the other side of the passage in case someone there sees us. We did not consider that.*

The light there shone brightly with a constant glow, but its beams did not reach down to the waterline. She looked back again. *I can see the boat clearly.* She looked up and to the right. *I cannot see anyone on the parapet, and they will be clearly outlined against the light if they are there. I will just have to hope that they have kept a poor watch at water level.*

Theodora moved the saddle along the waterfront below the houses to her left. *My husband had thought that this is an island of traders, but it seems that it is largely an island of shunned people. If it had not been for that, these houses would have been valuable. Once they must have been. I have seen foreigners among the people who use this street, and it looks like Anta, with the lower castes, is where they mostly live.*

I am glad that we have our own village, and I can now see how my husband grew up with the attitudes that she has. I am sure that the foreigners who live here will be charged plenty for the privilege, and have probably been convinced by those who rent to them that this is the best land and so must be highly paid for.

This must be the house. She felt a tap on her shoulder. *I am visible, even if Ayesha isn't, so I must keep low.* She brought the saddle over the wall, clipping the wall in the process. One of the bricks of the wall must have been loose. It fell into the sea behind them. *To me it sounds like the explosion of a war-rocket, but there is no reaction from the house or the outbuilding. I should practice more with the saddles. I am sure that Astrid would have done this so much more smoothly.*

She brought the saddle back into the greenery of the garden, turned it around and reversed it between two bushes. She brought it to ground and then looked around. *It will be some time before the boat is here, and it looks like someone is in the room above the boatshed.* A small window, high up on a wall, let light out. Around her, the rich and almost sweet smell of a Havenite garden wafted around with the warm breeze from the sea.

Looking from here you can see that the bottom of the boatshed is much closer to the waterline than the house is, and that the upper room is in fact slightly higher than the lawn by perhaps a pace and a half. The walkway slopes up with a rail on both sides. Light also spilt out from under the bottom edge of the door and a very low murmur of voices could be heard inside.

There is more noise from the house. It is the quiet noise of people talking that probably cannot even be heard from the street. It is being clearly heard here because the doors and windows on one side are open to the sea and light and noise spill out of them.

There are servants to the right…the east. She could see through the door that this was the kitchen. There are at least three people there. *If they stay inside, they will be left alone. Servants are not always responsible for their masters, or of the same mind as them.* There was noise of a brief scuffle from inside the upper room of the boathouse and then a slap, a short sharp cry *that was a girl and she objects to something.* The noise died down again with a few angry words.

I wish that I could hear more of what is going on, but the room is too well sealed, with only that thin gap at the bottom of the door. It is only a very faint noise that I heard after all. Keeping her eyes alert for any changes she settled down to wait for the boat.

After a while it struck her. *If the occupants are doing something in the upper room that may be illegal, immoral, wrong…whatever the word will be, the door is probably locked. Ayesha might not have time to pick the lock, even with her magic pick, and still surprise whoever is inside.*

She reached up to the hand on her shoulder, and leaning back, whispered. "When you go, stay clear of the door. It is probably both locked and alarmed. I will fire my wand three times, note that is three times, at it. Even if it is opened by the first, I will still fire through it. That should open it and it will perhaps give you a little more surprise than trying to pick it will."

The hand squeezed her shoulder to acknowledge that she had been heard.

Theodora

The boat is finally here. As Hulagu was preparing to get out with a rope, a squeeze on her shoulder told her that Ayesha was on her way.

She prepared her wand. *At this range it will be hard to miss, but I want to be sure. The question is whether to fire at the lock on one side, and try and break it open, or to go for the easier shot and try and break down the centre of the door. I have plenty of time to concentrate. At least I will make the first shot to be at the lock.*

She waited to allow time for Ayesha to get in position. *Hulagu is coming up beside the shed. He has his mace and shield out rather than his bow. He must have heard the people inside as well. One of the girls is following him with her bow. The wall must be too tall to fire over… It is time.*

She fired. It hit. With an air bolt it was often hard to see where you had hit, but it must have been at the right spot as the door simply flew open. *I can see movement inside, but no precise target.* She fired again. *This is one of the wands that I prepared for the dragon and is as strong as I could make it.* There was a male scream.

Something just flew away from the door to hit a wall. This time she saw a person…a man. She fired, and again there was another yell and her target again was moved backwards quickly. *It is now time to stop firing, but I will keep the wand in hand in case of need. It is now Ayesha's turn. At least she has some sort of surprise on her side.*

Astrid

The background noises of celebration from the direction of the University, and from Lāṅga Ā'ilaiṇḍa were interrupted by a noise from the other side of the house. It was as if a very large hammer had struck hollow wood. *It is time for us to move.* "Go." The three with the timber pole moved out to the street and prepared to hit the gate with it.

There was a second noise, more a muffled crump, followed by a truncated scream. They charged, and swung the pole at the large iron lock in the centre of the gate. The very first blow from the three of them was too much for the bar behind the gate, and with the sound of breaking timber, the two doors sprung open.

Simeon bounded between them and into the small courtyard that was now revealed. There was another noise and yell from the rear of the house as they dropped the pole, leaving it in the gap, and started to get their weapons ready.

I have to leap back to where my spear stands against the wall. Harald and Aziz are getting their shields off their backs before drawing. Basil and Lakshmi just pushed past them and moved inside. *Verily will be staying in the shadows at the gate to dissuade anyone from interfering, not that it is likely.*

Basil

T *here is a large door straight ahead.* Basil went and tried it. It opened. *Overconfidence…those inside did not lock it.* He looked at Lakshmi. She was ready to throw with a knife in each hand. He moved inside to see a surprised looking man coming down a set of stairs. *He is dressed for either travel or combat, and has a bag over one shoulder, and from it I can see wands poking out…a mage.*

Basil leapt at him, swords already moving. The man was reaching for the bag when first one knife, and then a second blossomed from his throat and then his chest. Basil, with no thought of defence, attacked with both shortswords. The left went into the stomach and the right was aimed up under the chin.

As usual, when this shot does go home as intended, it is fatal and the man shudders in death. Basil did not withdraw the weapon however, but kept it in place. He withdrew the left-hand blade, and keeping the man upright on the right hand blade, plunged the left under the rib-cage towards the heart. As he did so he felt the body give a shudder and saw the eyes open.

The man did have a contingency cure in operation. Basil withdrew the left-hand blade from the heart, twisting it as he did so and allowing the blood to follow. *The man's hands rise to weakly grab my arm with the blade fast in his brain before his eyes again glaze.* Basil kept the blade in place and stabbed again towards the liver with his left hand. *There is no more movement. One cure only.*

He felt people brushing past him as Lakshmi retrieved her blades. *One down.* He pulled his blades out and wiped them on the man. *He did not make a sound as he died, but he certainly made a smell.* Basil's nose wrinkled. Blood now covered his hands and ran over the floor. *My wife is going down a corridor ahead of me. Simeon is bounding ahead of her. Both leave a trail of prints on the wooden floor from the blood that they passed through. Harald is already climbing the stairs with Rani behind him, and Aziz has gone through a door to the right.*

"Laksmi, stay here and hold the door and the stairs." He headed to the door on the left. *Unlike Aziz, who simply charged the door ahead of him and pushed it off its hinges, I have to actually open mine with a handle, leaving blood on it as I do. The room is empty. It has chairs and a table with what looks like a map of the city and some goblets on it. There is another door.*

He continued through another room set up for dining with some food still out left as if waiting a return. *The next door is open, and I can see the kitchen beyond with servants milling around looking out of the open door to the garden.* He stepped to the door. *They are supposed to be left alive if they stay out of the conflict, but the four all have cleavers or knives in their hands. That is also one more than expected.*

"Drop those, close the door to the outside, and ignore anything you hear, and you will be allowed to stay alive. Interfere in what we do, and you will die. Which do you want?" The men took stock of the figure standing in the door to the main part of the house dressed in dark clothes and with two shortswords in hand, one held low and the other held upright with the point at eye level.

Blood is still streaked on the two blades and drips from my hands onto the floor. One of the men nervously looked out of the other kitchen door that led to the outside and two cleavers and a knife clattered onto the floor.

The fourth man flung his large knife inexpertly at Basil who merely had to put his right hand shortsword up to send the knife spinning back into the room ineffectively. Basil stepped forward and ducked slightly as the man, who had snatched up a cleaver as he moved, came forward swinging wildly with it.

Basil blocked with his right blade at the man's hand, using his momentum against him, and trying to catch the junction of blade and handle. With his left hand, he brought the blade up in a short arc that terminated with the point of the weapon lodged in the servant's heart. What had been a scream as the man lost several of his fingers became a gurgling sound as both hands clutched at his chest.

A surprised and hurt look has appeared on his face…death is always a surprise. Basil removed the shortsword through the man's hands, which clutched at it, and the previously whole hand began bleeding as it was, in turn, sliced open. He tried to say something as his mouth opened and closed a couple of times. Blood quickly appeared on his lips, showing that his lung had been opened.

A look of despair showed on his face as he looked at Basil pleadingly. He slipped to the floor as blood spurted out of his chest and from his hands, spilling over his clothes and then over the tiles. The others were starting to back up into a corner with expressions of terror on their faces.

"He made his choice. You still have yours." He paused. One of the men set up a keening as he sank to the floor in the corner and the other two fell to their knees, their hands raised in supplication as they pleaded for their lives. He stepped over the prone man.

He is not yet a corpse, but the blood is draining from his torso and hand as he vainly tries to staunch the mortal wound from the outside and blood pours into his lungs. Basil moved over and kicked the door closed. *Astrid is outside the door fighting someone…poor man. I still need to see if the rest of the house is secure.* "How many in the house? Quickly—tell me."

One of the men on the floor held up four fingers. "There are four, most noble lord," he said as he cowered back further.

Basil grunted and stepped back the way he had come. As he was about to leave, he turned back. "There are many of us. If you make no move from this room, you are safe here otherwise…" And he looked at the dying man behind him. The man was coughing his last as he drowned in his own blood.

He went through the door and closed it and listened. *There is noise from upstairs.* Basil quickly retraced his steps.

Astrid

*M*y husband has his matter under control, but looking up ahead of me, there are the backs of two men, large if they are from Haven, going through a doorway. There is noise from out there. They will be my problem.* She ran past Basil.

The two had made it out to the soft-lit yard when one of the men turned and shouted, and he blocked her charge so that her spear slid off a rectangular shield of cloth-covered wicker, and she had to twist it around to parry his return blow. She was then engaged, and with little time to look elsewhere, she was tied up in a serious fight.

The man is good. He is at least as good as Basil…and probably better. Even with my bracers to add to my strength and my torque to add to the speed of my attack, he is a good fight. She grinned. *I will take the practice and the safe option and abandon any thought of attack, unless he leaves himself open.* She started using her spear to simply block his attacks.

Time is on my side, and I can afford this and happily remain safe until he makes an error. Luckily, we are clear of the doorway and I can use the space to dodge his rushes. Eventually he will make a mistake. I just have to avoid him closing on me. She glanced to the side.

The other man is already down and clutching his leg. Blood is pouring from it between his fingers. His weapon lies discarded, as Simeon sits next to his head with bared fangs and a low and threatening growl. The man is too terrified to move.

Aziz

I am through the door and lying on the floor a couple of paces into the room. The door is still intact, but it lies under me. Lucky the room is empty. I am not used to fighting in a building. I didn't think of falling down when I did that. He picked himself up and looked around him.

The room is empty of people. It looks like it is an armoury or a stores room or something. There are lots of weapons and things ready to be taken up, but no enemies.

There is another door out of the room. Aziz kicked it hard near the handle with the sole of his boot. *That is just as satisfactory as, this time, the door flies open, and I stay up. Again, it is an empty room. This time it looks like a mage's study with two desks and some chairs. I have been in the Princess' rooms back home and they have the same look of books and paper and…things.*

He could hear combat elsewhere. *Why is everyone else having fun? There is yet another door to try out of this room.* Aziz kicked that. It gave but didn't open. He looked at it as if that would force it to open. It didn't. He tried the handle…*it is locked*…he kicked it again…again it gave. A cacophony of sounds has erupted from the other side. *I am getting impatient.*

Aziz backed up and shoulder-charged it with his shield side, trying not to fall through. This time it splintered and gave more. *This is a very solid door.* Another few kicks saw it sag open, with one hinge torn out of the door frame. Pushing it aside, Aziz went through. He entered a large room, which had many cages along the walls.

Another closed door to the left…it must lead to the yard outside. Some of the cages are empty, but most hold animals, all sorts of animals. Three of the larger ones hold, not animals, but naked women, all with their hands bound in front of them. All are cowering away from me. One looks like Bryony, one is from Haven, and the third has pale skin like my soft one, but could be from anywhere.

They all look terrified. He smiled at them to re-assure them. *That has the opposite effect to what I want.* The one from Haven screamed.

"Me not hurt you, me and friends here to help…to free…any bad men near?"

The tiny Hindi woman, although obviously not fully trusting him, pointed at the other door with her bound hands. "They took Rakhi. They are going to kill her." *She is pressed against the back of the cage, and looks ready to scream again if I move towards her.*

Aziz grunted and shrugged. "Friends there. If she alive, we keep safe. Now me keep you safe until others arrive." He took up station in the room. He looked at the cages the women were in. *They are locked. Lakshmi or Basil can deal with these when they get here.* He next looked around for something to give the women to cover themselves with.

Lots of animals and birds that I have never seen before. He turned to the women behind him and waved his hand. "They for killing too?" The women all nodded.

Harald

*B**asil obviously needs no assistance with that man.* Harald pushed past the pair and up the stairs. He rounded the landing and continued up as he heard a noise from above him and also the clash of arms rising from the garden below. He reached the top and looked to the right. *Damn. That noise came from my left, not this way.*

His shield came up just in time to block a blow from a sword. Harald's hammer swept around and found his opponent's shield, momentarily getting his weapon stuck into the timber. The two drew back and assessed each other. *My opponent is from Haven, and like me, fully clad in mail.*

He seems eager to get down the steps. That will not do. Basil will have difficulty with the armoured man. Again, they engaged. There was a passage of arms for several flurries and again they drew back and assessed each other. *I can feel a cut on my cheek, but he is limping from a blow to the hip. He has a grimace of pain on his face.*

Mail is good against swords, but provides little protection from the crushing impact of my hammer, and the several blows that I have taken have bruised me a bit, but most slid off. What is more I have the advantage in placement. We are both right handed, and the wall interferes with his blows while adding to my defence.

As they closed for another flurry of blows, Harald remembered the limp. He feinted at the man's head, and as he raised his shield Harald reversed the blow and brought the hammer down onto his knee. *My opponent has realised the blow is a feint and is trying to bring the shield down…too slow.*

With a crack of shattering bone, the hammer hit his knee. With a shriek the man started to collapse, as Harald used the momentum of the blow to bring his hammer around in a circle and down onto his head. *He must have been in a hurry to armour, as he has not fastened his helm properly.* As the man fell forward, his helm had managed to partly slip off.

The head of Harald's hammer came down messily into his skull. The man's downward motion continued, and he lay there twitching briefly as Harald pulled his bloody hammer out of the man's head and started searching the upstairs rooms.

Rani

I will follow Harald. My wife has the outside covered. I should look at the inside. She waited behind him on the stairs as he fought. *I was overruled by the others when I suggested coming armoured in case I was needed for physical combat. Next time, I will ignore them.*

She tried to get a clear shot at the armoured man with her wand but couldn't. However, Harald soon finished him, and they started carefully searching an empty upstairs.

Ayesha

The boat is about to land. Ayesha gave Theodora's shoulder a squeeze as she got off the saddle. *It is time for me to do my part.* She moved away from the direct line between the mage and the door, keeping on the far side so that she would be clear of those coming up from the shore. She reached a position near the door.

Allah the Just, let Theodora be accurate in her fire. Aid me in al-jihad al-Asgar. I can hear that there are several people inside. Invisibility is good, but in a small crowded and lit room it is not as good as in the open or against one person.

I will also not have an advantage of surprise the way I would like it. The blasts that will open the door will probably put my opponents on their guard, even if it does shock them somewhat into inactivity...I hope.

She felt the passing of the first air bolt as it hit the lock only two cubits from where she stood. *The lock didn't stand a chance. It has been punched out of the door and into the room, and the door swings open. Unfortunately, it is opening from the other side and I cannot see into the room, but there are still two blasts to come. The second must have hit someone... That despairing scream is not from a happy man.*

I have to be ready. Another yell...the third bolt must have gone straight into the room. She leapt around the corner and into the room. *There is a naked woman tied onto a bench and struggling. Beside her on the floor is a man dressed in a loincloth and with what looks like an obsidian dagger beside him. He is only moving feebly and blood flows from his head.*

There is another man in a pattern, a Haven mage probably—it is one of the Master's patterns, and there is one of the Masters visible in the mirror and looking at me from it. There are two other men that I can see. One, dressed normally, is drawing a sword.

The other, also wearing a loincloth, has a large flame-bladed knife in one hand, and one of those strange Haven things with blades coming out of it in several directions that are supposed to intimidate, to attack, and to parry in the other. It does very well in the role of intimidation, as all three of the men are looking straight at me...so much for invisibility. She moved towards the closest, the one with the sword.

He was able to get his sword out, and had raised a parrying dagger to knock aside one of her blades, but she was too expert for him as she drew the unblocked blade across his sword arm, trying to disable it. It streamed blood. *I have not put him out of action, but he is at least slowed.* She struck again with both blades before he could recover.

This time his arm hangs limp at his side, and he is weaving his parrying dagger around desperately as he tries to back away to get the other man between me and him. She allowed him to go as she turned to the Havenite with the odd blades. *He is obviously experienced from the way his blades and feet move. I wonder if he is my Haven equivalent...if ghazi meets thuggee.*

Before they closed, she caught a glimpse of the man in the pattern. *His eyes do not look human. They look as if they are as empty as the Master's sockets behind him. Merciful Allah...he has been taken over and the Master is casting through him.* She met the thuggee. "Allah 'akbar" she cried.

Blades flashed. *I am in a fight for my life and cannot pay any attention to the mage. Hopefully, someone else will deal with the others in the room.* Blades flew backwards and forwards and both took minor cuts, but they were a match in skill. The contest covered the entire floor as the mage chanted in the background. *From the time he is taking it must be a very major spell.*

Vachir Anahita Ursud

One of the men is down already and the wolf-priest stands guard over him, but Astrid seems pressed by the other, as she is not attacking. She looks for an opening, but is using all of the space so that she can parry and dodge his attacks.

Anahita waited with an arrow ready in case. *In the uncertain light, I do not want to fire into a melee. I will leave that choice to Kāhina and follow Hulagu. Father Christopher is already close behind me. He is very eager to get to the pattern.*

Olympias

*D*enizkartal and I just stand there. What have we been sent into? We may have been in the navy for some time, but this is outside our experience. There is nothing for us to do. Everything seems to be in hand. We are a reserve, and left waiting for an eventuality that does not look like happening.

She moved towards where Astrid fought the large man. *My brother has come out of the house and helped her deal with that issue. I cannot even help there.*

Theodora

*I*am supposed to stop anyone fleeing, but apart from this man, there is no one to stop and I cannot fire at this man without risking Astrid. At the same time, I could be following Hulagu to where there is fighting. Just then Basil appeared from the house.

Theodora sighed. *I will leave the resolution of that issue to him.* She hopped off her saddle and, leaving it backed into the bushes, ran towards the entrance to the boatshed.

Basil

*A*strid is still engaged with a man. She is parrying him with ease, but making no attempt to attack him. The man is furiously attacking. He realises that she is just using up time and almost playing with him.

"About time you arrived," Astrid said past her opponent as the dance of the combat brought her to face the house. "I have had nearly enough practice."

"Arrest or kill?"

"Your choice," said his wife.

I should knock him out. He may be innocent…no he isn't. He felt a nose touching his left hand. He looked down as the priest-wolf trotted back to his prisoner. *Well, that makes the choice easier. The man is evil.* Astrid, despite the man's best attempts to do otherwise was making sure his back was to Basil and Basil took advantage of that.

He is trying to glance back, but if he puts too much attention to me, my wife will skewer him like a wild boar. The man was only wearing street clothes, so Basil ducked low and with a swing of his shortsword cut at the back of his left leg. The man yelled in pain and tried to turn as his leg gave way. Astrid had been waiting for this sort of opening and thrust into his throat with her spear.

Their opponent fell and Basil followed him down with a suddenly reversed blade into the face. His body arced in a spasm, but he would not rise again.

Basil looked at Simeon and his prisoner. "You kept this one alive. I guess that he is not evil then?" The wolf nodded. Basil sighed. *I cannot just leave him there, even if Simeon says he is not evil.* "Put your hands behind your back and make no false moves." He moved behind the man. *I have started carrying at least one shackle at my belt out of habit and here I will get to use it.*

Wide-eyed, the young man had placed his hands there, but did not seem too happy with the prospect. Sticking his shortswords into the ground, Basil quickly leant forward and gave him no choice. Once he was shackled Basil rose and regained his weapons and looked around. *The action is happening at the shed, but there is no room for me there. Where are Harald, Aziz, and Rani?*

Just then Harald and Rani emerged. *He has a small cut on his face.* Basil made some decisions. "My dear, you stay with this one. Let Father Simeon do what he has to, and I will take Harald to replace Lakshmi as we start to search. Rani, come with me. I have not seen Aziz since we came in."

Hulagu

I cannot get into the room. There is a table with a woman strapped on it, a mage chanting, and another man digging through a bag with his left hand while his right hangs useless at his side. The room is full of combat.

A fully visible Ayesha is locked in combat with a man in a loincloth. Their blades are flying faster than I can follow as they spin around the room. There is no room for me to get past. What do I do? The man with the bag had found what he was looking for. It was a flask, and he struggled to get the lid off with his wrong hand without dropping it. *I know.*

Hulagu transferred his mace's haft to his shield hand, quickly drew a marto-bulli and threw it. He aimed at the man's head, but he missed. However, he was lucky in his miss, and the dart hit the flask. It shattered and liquid and glass sprayed all over. The man gave a despairing cry and started digging in the bag again, his face now cut as well.

Another man is sitting up from beyond the table. He was not visible before and he has a very strange expression on the ruin of his face. He doesn't look as if he is conscious of what he is doing. He must have been hit by one of Theodora's bolts. Perhaps he has been taken over… The man is bringing a wand up to fire.

Hulagu tried to push past the combat to get to him. However, he was too late. The man fired the wand, and a ball shot out of the end and both Ayesha and her opponent were enveloped in an expanding ball of water. Hulagu was able to dodge part of it, although only part. *I am badly hurt.* He kept rushing towards the man, trying to bring his mace around into him.

There was an explosion somewhere else in the room. *A wash of heat now… ignore it. Thankfully, my man does not seem to be focussed on what is about to happen to him.* The man fired again, this time out of the door, and before he could bring his wand around again, Hulagu was upon him. He struck down at his head and hit, crushing the skull.

He is dead, and yet the wand is still coming up. Hulagu hit again. This time he impacted on the shoulder. The man dropped the wand and collapsed. Hulagu looked down and contemplated him briefly. *By the Spirits…I am fast slipping into unconsciousness.* He struggled to stay awake and to get his own healing herbs out.

Anahita

*N*ow *Hulagu has moved, I can see clearly, both Ayesha and her opponent are down, and neither is moving. The mage looks like he is about to cast something…it is a good idea to fire.* She let fly at close range. *Shit…it is explosive.*

It hit the mage in the head and exploded. *His head has disappeared.* She moved. *A ball has flown out of the room from somewhere else, just missing me and exploding somewhere in the garden behind. I feel water.*

She grabbed another arrow. *I hope it is not explosive. I was lucky last time not to get backlash at that range.* She stepped forward. *There is a man straightening from a bag and he has a wand in his left hand. His right arm hangs useless, but he is otherwise fine. Hulagu is swaying and trying to get a flask out. His mace lies at his feet alongside another man.*

She fired at the man with the wand and hit. It is a normal arrow. *He has dropped the wand and is clutching his chest.* She put another arrow there, and as he looked down and raised his hand towards the arrow, another. *At this range it is hard to miss a man when you are used to hunting bouncing hares on the plains.*

I am firing from so close to my target that the arrows are sinking into his body almost up to their fletching—the points must be coming out of his back. She sent another. *The man has finally stopped pawing at the shafts sprouting out of his chest and is toppling backwards.* She looked around.

All of the enemy are down. Hulagu is drinking from the bottle. Ayesha is lying limply on the floor, perhaps she is even dead.

Theodora and Christopher are coming into the room and there is a naked Havenite woman tied with a limb at each corner to bronze rings on a table. She is trying to scream through her gag, and struggling to break free. Her eyes are as wide as the full moons. She stares to her left frantically at all that is happening.

Christopher

A *quick look...I need to act...I can do nothing about Ayesha. I have to save my mana for the pattern.* He called outside. "Simeon...You are needed... fast!" The wolf brushed past and looked around, and then moved aside and started to change.

Theodora

I stand useless in the entrance way, pushing back a shattered door that keeps trying to swing closed on me, and look with horror into the room. Anahita may have stopped the mage from completing his enchantment, but there has been a cost. His body, and his blood, now lies across the pattern and its containment is now broken.

If it is charged...I can see something red starting to boil out of the floor where the pattern is inscribed. It looks malevolent. It feels even worse to my senses. Free mana can sometimes do that. She was preparing to die when the thing boiling out seemed to look to the north. *It seems to be disappearing into the distance without actually going anywhere. I can see the wall behind it.*

In her mind she heard a thin scream of rage. *Someone, not me at least, is going to soon get a visit they won't like. Although I am grateful for it, I do wonder what just happened.*

She didn't wonder for long, however, as she started to assess the damage and say a prayer of thanks for their good fortune. Only then did she notice Ayesha's body lying on the floor looking like a wet and broken doll flung aside by an ill-tempered child in a rage.

Basil

*W**here is Aziz?*** Basil hurried through the house, leaving Harald at the door and gathering Lakshmi before she could make too much fuss over Harald's cut. It did not take long to find Aziz. *He is very glad to see us.*

"They not sure me here to save them or to eat them and me cannot get them out. You do that. Me cannot find clothes in room…maybe not got any… they say they for killing…another one to be killed now outside."

Just then there were a series of explosions from outside, and Aziz rushed for the door and wrenched it open. They looked out. *Kāhina is looking around at us with a knocked arrow, Anahita stands outside the shed looking in with another, and Simeon is bounding into the shed. Anahita just stands there. The fight must be over.*

"Do something about them," said Rani and ran towards the shed.

"You are freeing us?" asked a woman. *She looks a lot like Bryony.* Quickly, she held her bound hands towards Basil through the bars.

"It seems to be a hobby of ours wherever we go." He stepped over and used his bloody blade to cut the rope holding her. "Do you have any clothes?"

"Perhaps in that basket," said the woman pointing into a corner at a wicker basket with a lid.

Lakshmi opened one of her pouches. *She has what is needed in there, and although her picks are not magically enhanced, it didn't take her long to open the locks and release the women.* As soon as each one was freed, they ran over and began to dig clothes out of the basket and put them on. They do not appear to necessarily be theirs, but they are at least clothes. The Hindi woman drew away from Lakshmi when she went to comfort her.

"What is the matter?" asked Lakshmi.

"You are Kshatya and a warrior, and I am Sudra and a prostitute," said the woman, her eyes downcast respectfully.

"No," said Lakshmi with a snort. "The mage who left is, or was, Kshatya. I used to be lower than you, Harijan, and a prostitute as well. Now, I have left both caste and my old life behind. We will take you back to our ship, and if you want, we will take you out of Pavitra Phāṭaka when we go. It may still be dangerous for you here."

Hulagu

*N**ice that we all have this Sweet Ali potion…one sip and the room stops spinning…two and I can see straight…and three… That is better.* He looked around. *I am still very weak, but at least able to act. We seem to have won.*

He picked up his mace and then saw a naked Simeon, in human form, standing over Ayesha. *I caught the fringe of the water ball blast. Ayesha and her opponent have taken the brunt of it and they both lie on the floor. Neither seems all that damaged, but then neither is moving either. They just lie there on the wet floor.* He put his mace back into its holder and leapt to her side.

I am not a medic, but I can treat horses, and I know what to look for and she does not have it. There is no sign of life at all in her body. No pulse beats at her neck, her breasts don't move as she seeks air. All of that wasted time… and we have not even kissed.

He looked at Father Christopher…back at Ayesha…at the pattern on the floor…around again at Simeon. *He has turned to strip the wet loincloth off Ayesha's dead opponent. Can nothing be done?* Bleakly, Hulagu closed Ayesha's empty and staring…*beautiful*…eyes. He then gathered her body up into his arms, lurched to his feet, and staggered out of the room.

Anahita and Kāhina saw him and the limp burden he carried and began to ululate. Unseeing, unhearing, he moved towards the front of the house, moving unconsciously back towards the ship.

Christopher

"Theodora…" He spoke into silence. "I don't think that I need to do anything about the pattern. From the look of the blood across it, the enchantment has already been disrupted…the restrained mana made free. What do you think?" *Theodora is nodding.*

"I think that I agree," she held her hands out, palm down over the pattern. "I cannot feel the charging that I normally feel near one of these." Rani entered the room and she turned to her. "Come here and tell me what you feel."

Rani came over. "Nothing," she said and turned to Christopher. "Have you had time to cast your miracle already?" He shook his head and he pointed at the blood breaking the pattern.

"I am returning to the ship to see if anything can be done for Ayesha," Christopher said. He turned to Simeon. "Are you coming?"

Simeon looked around. "Is everyone else intact?" he asked, and then poked his head outside and repeated the question. Everyone nodded or signified assent. "Then I am coming."

They gathered Hulagu and his burden up and started guiding his steps. *We need to get him back to the ship. She has disappeared in his arms.* "Stop." *We need to remove Ayesha's ring from her hand. She has left the magic of the building.*

Other than that, it is more a matter of just steering him. He doesn't seem to be very aware of where he is going. Although he is careful not to hit Ayesha's limp remains against the remains of the door, he seems otherwise to be not very aware of the world. His face is a blank mask. Nothing shows on it.

Rani

*I*t is time to take charge again. The woman on the table was let free and clothed and reassured. *Next, we need to search the building…to loot it really, gathering treasure, and anything that feels magic.* The other women were reassured and gathered. *What we should to do about the prisoner I do not know.* She was going to set him free with a promise, but he refused to be set free.

"I am not from around here and these men had friends. If they saw me alive and knew them to be dead, I would be blamed and killed. Either kill me now quickly, or else let me come with you. I am new come here. I did not know about them when I came." He pointed at the women. "I was told that it was supposed to just be a job working as a house guard, and when I found out about the rest, I tried to leave but could not."

"Simeon does not think he is evil," contributed Basil, helpfully.

Rani looked at the gaggle of women crying and consoling each other. "Do you know anything about him?"

"He art new," said the second one with pale skin. "He hast not been a doin' anythin' to us."

"He gave us food secretly," said the first Hindi girl.

Rani sighed. "Bring him back to the ship...bring everything that looks useful...we need to be quick. Eventually, someone will raise an alarm or will look at what has caused the explosions." Just then there was an explosion, and a huge glow of light visible above the buildings from the direction of the University. "...Or maybe not."

With more fanfare than had heralded the advent of the Year of the Water Dog for them, it proceeded to slip away, and the Year of the Water Lizard came in being.

Chapter XXVII

Christopher
1st Primus, Year of the Water Lizard, the Feast Day of Saint Basil the Great

There is a miracle that will resurrect Ayesha. In theory it can be done. I have the required prayer written in my prayer book. Everyone does, and one day we all hope to be able to be strong enough in the Faith to be able to perform it. I am also sure that I am not strong enough to safely do it yet. Even with Simeon's help, I am not strong enough. Even with what I have stored... and with Simeon's help, I am not strong enough.

They moved back to the ship and Christopher looked at Hulagu sleepwalking beside him. Ayesha hung limply from his arms with one arm trailing loose.

Even in death she is a beauty. She enabled us to defeat the bandits in the first place and without her we might not have survived in Dwarvenholme. She could still be needed in our fight and there is only one of her.

I am just a priest. Mousehole now has three priests. Whilst Bianca and my children would miss me if I died or am unminded, I have a clear duty to try. I will not scare my wife by telling her of the risk that I face.

Simeon

Father Christopher is turning as I walk behind him in my loincloth. "You will hear my confession, and shrive me when we return, and I will then offer thanks to God for our work tonight before I do anything."

It is a statement, not a request. Simeon looked at the man beside him with reverence. I know what Father Christopher proposes. *He knows what lies ahead of him and the risks. The Gospel of John… 'Greater love has no man, than that he lay down his life for another.' Christopher exemplifies those words.* He could not speak in reply but only nodded in awe.

Rani

*T**he building is being thoroughly searched, and the pile of pillage grows in front of me. Gradually, most of it is put into the ship's boat. It will be more inconspicuously carried there than as if in a parade through the streets. The animals are looked at. Some we just free, but we will bring some of the birds and the sad-faced monkey back to the ship.*

Theo-dear was born of the sign of the Monkey, and has always wanted to have one of her own. The room of the Pattern is interesting, but we can do nothing with it. It looks like the spell that revealed Ayesha is built into its fabric. We can find nothing portable and the very room itself gives off an aura of magic.

Stefan

*I**t seems that we won. The rest of the people are beginning to arrive back at the ship. They have brought the spar that had been the ram, they bring more treasure, although at first not as much as we had got from Glyn. They bring magical items varying from weapons and lamps, to a quiver which had a pair of small oaken rods tucked into a pocket on its outside.*

Working out what they all do can wait until later. In many ways, more importantly than all of the magic and treasure they had found, they also brought four freed women and a prisoner. We need to stow everything and get ready to move quickly if someone wants to question us.

"Adara," said Bryony to a woman who looks a lot like her. *What?*

"Jennifer," said Goditha to another.

In their exchanges, it seems that we have inadvertently added my Bryony's cousin, and another girl from Deeryas to those on board. Those two want to know no more. They are intent on coming with us. The two from Haven are both from Pavitra Phāṭaka, and neither of them is willing to stay behind. They fear being taken again, although this Jennifer is sure that there are no more armsmen from the house left in the city.

"They doest lose two men when they doest attack the caravan I was working on, and this one…" said Jennifer, as she waved at the prisoner.

"I am Vishal, and there are others that they use and who run errands for them…" he said. *He is nodding in a semi-bow with his hands still bound behind him. I think that he is trying to be seen as a co-operative person, and not be just someone anonymous who can be tipped over the side of the ship without compunction to drown. Everyone is just ignoring him. He could run away but he doesn't.*

"…He wast a replacement. I doest look around the house afore we left. I hast been there the longest and there are no faces that doth live there that are not lying dead or who wast not in the kitchen."

She turned to Goditha. "Thee and me dost have a lot to talk about. Thou disappeared a-many years ago. Where hast thou been all of this time? Art thou captive as we heard? Art thou married? Art thou a sailor? Where is thine hair?"

She looked around her, giving special looks to Aziz and Denizkartal. "Doest this be a ship of war, or a pirate ship, or be it a trader? Why for art the four of us still alive and walk free?"

"Explanations will have to wait," said Stefan as he pointed people in different directions with their burdens.

Simeon

*F*ather Christopher is starting with a short service of thanks, addressing the Archangel and General of the Heavenly Hosts, Michael, who as patron of both graveyards and victory is appropriate, and in particular Saint Anne, both as patron of those who protect others against evil, and of those who return from the dead.

Ayesha's body lies limp and cooling in Hulagu's arms. He has refused to let her go, and Christopher has given up trying. He sits the man down in the priest's pattern with her limp form cradled softly in his arms. Maybe it is for the best this way.

Bianca has a worried expression. Christopher may not have told her what sort of a risk he is facing with this, but she is not stupid. She saw me confess him, and can see the rest of what he is doing as preparation. Anything that will steal a person back from the world of death cannot be trivial. As well, Father Christopher's concern is evident as he fusses around arranging everything to maximise his chance of success.

Having finished, he stood back and looked around him. *Everyone is standing there watching him.* "Is no one on guard?" he asked in mock joviality, as he went and hugged and kissed his wife before moving back to stand beside Hulagu. He put flasks of potion beside Hulagu and one in his hand.

"Listen to me…Hulagu…you must listen and hear me." Christopher shook Hulagu until he had his attention.

"Remember this," he said as the man's eyes slowly focussed on him. "If this works, she will be back, but will still be badly damaged and will die again…I cannot cure her as well…you will need to make her drink these immediately… she must swallow at least four doses…more will be better. She must drink as much as you can make her take…nothing else.

"If what I have been told is true, her soul may take some time to return fully to her body. The longer she is dead, the longer it takes, and it is nearly a glass now since she was killed. Do not expect her to return and be back instantly with us. It may even be some days before you can talk with her."

He stood and sighed, and looked fondly again at his wife and children. Bianca ran over and gave him a quick kiss. *Christopher has briefly raised his hand to sadly touch her cheek as he gave her a thin smile.*

Now I stand alongside ready to lend my support, as Father Christopher begins his long prayer for one of the greatest of miracles. I pray that he succeeds.

He has the mana from its storage and then all of mine, and I give a bit more. At last he speaks the final words of his prayer. He has collapsed boneless and drained, but Bianca is ready, and Bryony has sprung to help her. They caught him before I can even start and they move him aside.

Simeon checked Christopher's signs. He seems to be still breathing. He is just unconscious. It is now Bianca's turn to cradle someone. She sits on the deck holding her husband tight with tears mixed out of worry and pride leaking from her eyes as she watches Ayesha.

Ayesha

My eyes are opening. I am in Hulagu's arms and he holds a flask to my mouth. I am dying. I want to say that I love him before I go. He is trying to make me drink something.

She spluttered and then swallowed to get her mouth free to speak, but when she opened her mouth, he made her drink again, and again, and yet again. He kept doing it, and she tried swallowing so as to be able to speak and say what she needed to say.

Simeon

*S**he is trying to speak, but Hulagu is doing as he was told, massaging her
throat to make her swallow, and she has lapsed back into coma before
she can say anything. I need to check her signs. Although her eyes are closed,
her breathing is now strong, even if her heart is fluttering wildly like a caged
bird beating in her chest. At her throat the blood vessels can be seen pulsing.***

"She is alive and should eventually be back with us," he said.

Theodora

*W**hat do we do for Bianca, without being patronising? She has nearly
lost her husband, and it is far from sure if his soul or mind will be intact
even if he wakes again. Although mages can do such a feat as a conjuration, I
am not strong enough…and I am very powerful.***

*I could have brought Ayesha back as an undead. She would have had most
of the semblances of life, and even borne a child, but she would not have
been fully alive. My granther could have done what Father Christopher has
just done, but he is perhaps the strongest mage ever. I am sure that even a
Metropolitan would have thought more than twice about taking on such a
miracle, even with support handy.*

*Christopher is only a simple village priest. He is a pious and strong one,
but he doesn't have that much more power than any other…or he didn't. He
must have weighed up what he did have and decided that it was necessary.*

She settled for just patting Bianca in what she thought was a reassuring
manner, before moving on and organising them to be taken below to have
some privacy…and then turned to organising the same for Hulagu and Ayesha.

*In the meantime, I need to adapt one of my spells to cloud over our
involvement in what has just happened. I should have thought of that before,
and I think I already know how to do it…but I will need my husband's help.*

Bryony

"**I** must go back to Rising Mud with you," said Adara. "I now know who had you killed...kidnapped...whatever."

"It was Glyn, and I am sure that he probably also had you kidnapped by these men and he was trying to start a war."

"How do you know?" asked Adara, puzzled.

"Six weeks ago, we killed him," said Bryony. "And that is how we stopped the war with Haven just before it really started. This ship was bought with the money that he had with him to pay for the war. I saw his body and then, afterwards, I dropped his head into the river to be eaten so he could not be brought back.

"I am sure that you will be pleased to hear that, although it was quick, it wasn't a nice death. He is now rotting in one of the hells...hopefully in extreme and eternal pain."

Astrid

I can hear snatches of the conversations going on around me and I think that we are heading for the same trouble we had earlier at home. I need to, at least briefly, teach the whole story of the Mice to the new people all at once, even to our prisoner, rather than have them get wrong ideas and parts of the story in dribs and drabs.

Besides which, we still have a lot more to do on this voyage and we should get potential liabilities out of the way as quickly as possible. That means either killing them or letting them make up their mind whether to go or stay.

"All of you...the new people on board that is...we have a lot to tell you, and that you need to know about us. With the Princesses' permission..." She gave a bob. *I think Theodora understands. She is waving me on. Rani looks puzzled.*

"I will now take you aside and briefly tell you why you are with us now... and you can decide straight away if you want to get off the ship before we leave this city. You may now think that you will be safer with us than staying on the shore. You may decide very differently about this before I am through with my story."

Astrid
A few hours later

*I*t turns out not to be the case. Not only have they seen the people in the waterfront house, who had captured them, defeated so soundly, but they have just
seen a priest actually bring someone back from the dead, and some of them saw
other very powerful magic being used by the people around them.

I guess that the four women we rescued have all decided that they now have
some powerful protectors here, and they do not want to lose them. Our cursed
prisoner is even worse. He wants to learn from us.

Astrid
Early in the morning

A s they were preparing to leave, with the new additions to their number kept
safely below and out of sight, they had a casual visit from the watch. *They
are not coming directly to the River Dragon. From where I have sat myself,
I can see four men approaching from upstream moving down the dock and
talking to everyone they see.*

*I am guessing that they are asking about last night and if anyone has seen
anything odd from the number of shaking heads. Several people are waving
in the direction of the University. It seems that everyone from the area was
over there watching the celebrations last night.* Astrid sat near the gangplank
feeding the children. Denizkartal is finding some work to do near the forward
ballistae, rubbing wax on the deck, and others of the crew are dotted around
working and preparing to leave.

*Hopefully, we can do so quietly and peacefully. If the watch has seen what
was left inside the building, they will know that the dead people were criminals
of some sort. It remains to be seen if they were well connected criminals...and
apparently that is often very important in Haven.*

As she was sure everyone else in the area was doing, Astrid claimed that
the people on the ship had seen nothing. They had been preparing to go and
had worked hard until they went to bed. Even their watch had nodded off to
sleep after watching the display from the ship.

Either I am getting better at lying, or the City watch really don't care and

Theodora has wasted that spell she cast this morning. They were content to talk to just me, and accept reassurances that were as hollow as the ship.

Despite the implications of at least one thuggee being present in the house, it seems as if the Kali devotees are either not aware of what happened, or else their temple is truly not involved. Perhaps the watch has even been told to find nothing to prevent any embarrassment happening for certain people.

Astrid
A little later

*N*ow we can sail. Father Christopher has still not recovered. He still lies unconscious in Bianca's arms, although now they have been moved to the Princess' bed. He is breathing normally and there is no fever, and everyone on the ship is in awe of what he has done.

Hearing stories of people being returned from the dead in a tale is one thing. Actually seeing it happen, and having our own village priest perform the deed, is quite another. I am rather glad that I decided to investigate those wolves when I first left home.

Ayesha may not have woken up yet, but she is undoubtedly alive, and like Christopher, is breathing normally. She and Hulagu have been placed in a hold and she lies comatose in his arms as mind and body heal themselves back into one piece.

Bianca

*W*e have undocked, and are headed out to sea before the city of Sacred Gate is truly awake after the excesses of the night before. My husband has not yet recovered awareness, and I think that I need to talk to Simeon on my husband's behalf.

"I need to ask you two things," she said upon finding him. "Firstly, can you help me move Christopher out on the deck, and secondly, can you take care of the Services until he recovers please."

"But I am Catholic," he said in surprise.

"So was I," Bianca said dismissively and with a wave of her hand. "However, it will be either you or me that will perform the ceremonies…and you are ordained as a priest and I am not. My husband is a good man and he was content to be shriven by you. That is enough for me and I am sure that it will be enough for God."

Father Simeon took a passage from the Gospel of Saint John as his text and used Father Christopher's actions as an exemplar as he gave thanks that he had not paid the full price for his bravery, and gave further thanks for the miracle that had allowed Ayesha to return from the dead...and that they had all been present to witness to the power of their God.

It is a good sermon, even if my husband would be embarrassed at what was said about him.

Theodora

*W*e Mice now have to learn a bit more about these people who fate has decided to add to the roster of the village. No matter what happens, no matter how hard we try, it seems that Mousehole seems to always find more women than it finds men.

At least this time, as a minor bonus, it seems that Jennifer has been to sea more than once. Although, she is oddly reluctant to reveal why she left the village of Deeryas behind, it seems that she had been a trader's guard, and worked by land and sea between Haven and Freehold, with either horses or a boat as she could find work.

The prisoner, Vishal, also has some experience with working on the water. He seems happy to change who he works for, and to help work the ship. Indeed, he is more than eager. However, I still have not decided if he should be released from his bindings. On hearing me say this, he sat quietly and obediently by a mast and did not press the point...and that speaks in his favour.

Chapter XXVIII

Bianca
In the afternoon of 1st Primus, the Feast Day of Saint Basil the Great

*I*t is nice sitting here in the warm sun, cushions under me and at my back, against the raised quarterdeck. The River Dragon is carrying us all quietly over a smooth deep green sea. Under the quarterdeck are the only two small cabins that the ship boasts along with the galley and the tiny medic's room. Christopher's head is in my lap.

She held a hat in place over his face, shading it from the sun and looked lovingly down. *I had us moved up from the Princess' cabin once we left port. I think that the warmth and the noise above are better for him than the closer air beneath the deck. It is oppressive there, even with the stern windows open.*

I am concerned for him, but not overly concerned yet. He heavily overdrew his mana, and his spirit is wounded and perhaps wandering. He needs to recover. The healers on board assure me that his pulse is strong, and he is not running a fever. I worked that much out for myself, but it is nice to have confirmation.

He is, at least, in a much better condition than when he had to recover from the Sleepwell addiction. He is just unconscious. He mutters and turns away from smelling salts held under his nose, but he will not wake. In the meantime, we just have to wait and hope that he recovers before we reach Gil-Gand-Rask.

I have again asked Father Simeon to stand in for him and remind him whose feast it is today, and tomorrow is that of Saint Joseph…and there are many fathers on board to celebrate that one.

Olympias

*C*hristopher's healing has to occur naturally, so there is no need to hurry the pace. The River Dragon has a good supply of food and water, and so we can afford to take our time and dawdle along using just the natural wind. It is all good practice for my novice sailors.

The wind is coming gently from broad on the starboard side, but I am using the amount of sea that is available to vary the direction they sail and the rigging. I have even practiced them in climbing up and out to mount the studding sails for the first time, so as to pick up the lightest of the light breezes to make the River Dragon dance over the sea.

Rani

*W*e can use this opportunity to have intensive language lessons for everyone. The newcomers need to know all of the rules of Mousehole… including that everyone works, everyone learns, and everyone teaches, if they can.

The natives of Gil-Gand-Rask speak High Speech…the only people I know of to do so. I want everyone to have at least a few words of it. It also provides a good chance to get the apprentice mages back to work. I am surprised that Rakhi speaks the language well. She worked for a mage as a servant.

More surprisingly, the former prostitute Zeenat even speaks some that she had picked up from customers. It seems that the male mages are frequent visitors to the prostitutes. I had not been aware of that myself, but Lakshmi confirmed it.

It seems that even the highest of the Brahmins never ask too carefully after the caste of the woman that they have congress with, if she is skilled, and willing to do everything as they wish. Most of the women who ply their trade in the streets and rooms have at least one holy book that they are well familiar with, and it is the only one the mages ever want them to know about.

Rani

*T*he new women fit into the crew in different ways. I have grown used to being able to talk to all of the women, even quiet little Parminder.

I appreciate, in particular, what Shilpa and Lakshmi bring to the village and realise how much potential Parminder has as a mage.

Zeenat Koirala and Rahki Johar are unaccustomed to dealing with anyone outside their caste, except through their work, and I find it annoying now to be treated as I used to before I left home. They will not even let me test them to see if they can be mages as it would be 'wrong'. At my wife's insistence I have settled for just letting them 'find themselves', as Theo-dear puts it.

"After all," she said, "we have seen that even Make is starting to emerge from her shell and break away from the way that she was brought up. It has taken a long time, and I am sure that she does not realise it yet herself, but that is what she is doing. I am sure that these girls will eventually do the same if we just give them enough time." I hope that she is right.

Jennifer Wagg

I *am glad to see Goditha and hear that she and her brother are still alive, but I have some difficulty with her lifestyle. I like men. I like them far too much actually, and I refuse to settle down with just one unless I find the right one. I have admitted to her that this is one of the many reasons I left home.*

Once I discovered the pleasures of the bed, my parents quickly came to not approve of my constant seductions. They were continually surprised and relieved when I came to visit as I passed up and down the coast, and even more relieved when I left again, having once more outraged some one or another of the local women by borrowing a husband, or a son or two for the night.

I just cannot understand Goditha's choices. I already love Melissa and play with her, but I have a lot of difficulty with how she was born. Goditha is relieved that I have agreed to wait until the unconscious priest comes back to us and can explain an arrangement that is so far away from what I was brought up with.

I will listen well to what such an obviously holy man says. In the meantime, I am looking at the men on the boat. It is a disappointment to find out from Goditha that they are all, except for the second priest and the Havenite prisoner, very firmly taken...and that they all have very well-armed wives.

Adara ferch Glynis

It is good to see my cousin alive and to know that I am an aunt. My immediate family were also victims of the Master's servants, and I am firm in having no intention of leaving my cousin and returning home, despite the death of Glyn, in case the same happens to me. Stefan is discomfited and Bryony amused. If I cannot find another man, then what is good enough for my cousin will also be good enough for me. It can all stay a family thing between us. I have not told him the rest of why that is.

Bryony has told Stefan that such an arrangement is not uncommon among the Free for sisters and cousins to choose to take a husband between them, and she will let him know if it is going to happen. He will have little or no choice in the matter. He has complained about his parent's reaction to that. They were apparently very pleased with his one wife...but their reaction to two?

At least I know that apparently even this Father Christopher has already approved such marriages in their village.

Vishal Kapur

I have had my leg healed by the priest who tore it open with his teeth. Now I have to show myself to be useful to these 'Mice.' I was born Kshatya, but much lower in status than the Padma Rani, and I have no great expectations from my life.

I am one of many younger sons with very little in the way of prospects. My parents in Haven have set us all adrift in the world to do what we can. I can make my way as a guard, or in the army, and my parents only expect to hear back from me if I later become wealthy and am able to provide support for them.

Except for my training as an armsman, and my eagerness to do anything that is asked of me, I have gathered that I have little to commend me as a man that they would want to have living in their hidden village. I have quickly realised this, and I need to work hard to overcome my situation as well as my status as a prisoner.

I have tried to demonstrate this to the rescued women, but it seems to discomfit them. I suppose that they are also not sure about much that is happening in their life. Having a Kshatya serve them seems to them to be too much. Their Captain, Olympias, has taken great pity on me. Now I work up in the masts. It is not Kshatya work, but I have never cared too much for caste anyway. It has done me little good.

I am nimble and adept, and this Lakshmi woman watches me work. They have my weapons on board, but do not yet trust me enough to return them. As long as I know that they are safely held, I can ignore them and enjoy this scampering around the upper rigging happily learning what is wanted of me, glad to be alive and away from the men whom I was trying to escape from anyway.

Ayesha

I *am no longer dreaming of dying. My dreams are of being rocked to sleep in Hulagu's arms.* She snuggled around. *After all this time of dreaming of it, I really am lying in Hulagu's arms. The air is heavy here and we are both only just dressed. We are lying on some of the bales of cloth in a hold. Hulagu has me folded into his arms and there is a light blanket over us.*

I am feeling starved and very, very thirsty. Checking that she really was where she thought she was, she opened her eyes more fully and looked around. *Kāhina is sitting in front of us just looking at me with a smile on her face.*

"It is about time," she said standing up and stretching. "He only fell asleep less than a bell ago. I will get you both breakfast now, and then you can either go back to sleep or you can catch up on what my sister köle and I have been doing in your place for the last year. As he makes love to us, he whispers your name instead of ours. Now you can find that out for yourself."

"We are at sea. There is nothing else for you to do for at least two days but to recover. You are alive again…celebrate…" She turned at the foot of the ladder. "However, Shilpa said when we put you here that you are not to make a mess of the cloth, so that it cannot be sold, or she will kill you again herself." She climbed up and pushed aside the cover and left the hold.

Ayesha lay still and silent. *I have dreamt of being here like this. Now that I am, I still don't know what to do. From what Kāhina has said Hulagu must feel the same way. I have no Mullah here, I cannot marry, unless I get Christopher to do it. Christopher…where is he? I am sure that I remember dying…perhaps twice…and regretting many things as I did.*

Perhaps I was not that far gone, and the priest was able to revive me? But Kāhina just implied that I died. Hulagu stirred in his sleep and his hand moved across her chest. *I might be partly clothed, but there is at least one part where the clothing has somehow slipped aside, and his hand now lies there cupping my bare breast.*

She blushed both because it was there, and also with how it made her feel.

My nipples are traitors. They are starting to tighten of their own accord. Should I move his hand? No, he might wake up and we will both be embarrassed by it. I will just lie still and maybe he will move it.

The thoughts went around and around in her head until eventually the hatch cover was pushed aside and Kāhina came back down and someone...*the arm looks like Anahita's...*handed her down a basket.

It smells of kaf and fresh bread and other things. I really am starving. Kāhina didn't hand it to her. In fact, she has put the basket down well out of reach. *She has gone back to the hatch and been handed some cushions.* She came back to where they lay and bent down, and before Ayesha could react, twitched back their cover.

Ayesha blushed again as Kāhina grunted and nodded. Hulagu stirred and his hand and arm cupped tighter. She felt him move against her back and blushed at what she now felt behind her for the first time. *Now I definitely cannot move away without embarrassing him...and probably me as well.*

"I will go now, and let you wake him up," said Kāhina. "By the way," she said. as if in an afterthought as she turned away, "You might have noticed by now that when he wakes, he is almost always ready to make love in the morning and especially after a battle. This is both. Enjoy yourself."

Shaitan take her. She is leaving without even bothering to hide the grin on her face. Unlike when she had left before, this time she replaced the hatch cover very loudly by dropping it, and before Ayesha could work out what to think, Hulagu had stirred into being partially awake...*at least awake enough to be moving towards making love.*

His eyes are still closed, but he is murmuring my name and his love, although from what Kāhina said, he has been doing that for some time. How should I respond? The confident warrior was paralysed by introspection into inaction for at least long enough that the question of her immediate response became moot.

They did not emerge for some time, not until they needed more food and drink and to answer other calls. Timidly, Ayesha emerged from under the hatch to receive a loud cheer from Astrid. *At least I get hugs from the Khitan women who are normally reserved towards outsiders. I guess that I am no longer an outsider to them.*

She looked at Christopher lying there with Bianca, and went and kissed and thanked her. *I am rewarded with a wan smile, and an injunction from her to go back below and again enjoy what I now have.*

Over the next few days, Ayesha discovered she liked her new status, and that her dreams had been far too shallow and incomplete. *I still have not made up my mind how, or if, I will formalise the arrangement when we return to Mousehole, but I now know that our relations will be continuing in some form.*

Chapter XXIX

Christopher
3rd Primus

The peak of Tor Karoso, the mountain in the centre of the island of Gil-Gand-Rask, was just in sight on the horizon when Father Christopher woke up. *I am well rested, but both hungry and very, very weak.* As she fed him, tears of relief in her eyes, his wife filled him in on the gossip as everyone came past to thank or to congratulate him.

Ayesha came with Hulagu holding her hand and hugged him as she thanked him for her new life. *I wonder if I will soon be doing a ceremony, and if I am, what type it will be.* Father Simeon came to see him, and Christopher thanked him for acting for in his place.

Simeon acknowledged the thanks dismissively, and after a pause, went on: "That is something that I need to talk to you about. My Church has rejected me, and like you, I am now subject to burning if I am caught by them." *I hope that I am about to hear what I have prayed for.*

"I have to say that I was impressed by your deeds, and I have not found, in conversation with you or with Father Theodule any significant theological differences that make sense to me. I think it is about time that we had a discussion as to what Church I truly belong to." *I am hearing it. Praise God.*

"How do we go about that?" Simeon continued. "If I become one of your priests, do I have to marry straight away? Astrid heard me ask the Presbytera that question, and said yes, and offered to be my matchmaker. I perhaps think that she was in jest, but I am not sure, and your wife only smiled and said that Astrid had very good experience in that role and that I should take her up on the offer."

Christopher smiled. "She actually does have more experience than any of the rest of us, having, among others, gotten the Princesses together and found a bride for Hrothnog, and that was even a more interesting match than yours would be."

"She may have made the offer in jest, but why not ask her to look for you? In all seriousness though, you only need to be married if you are a priest. Were you not a monk? Have you thought whether you wish to return to a life of contemplation?"

"I have, and I don't," said Simeon. "I like the world…with all its faults. I was not made to withdraw from it. I only abandoned it to try and put limits on my lycanthropy, and in firstly the land of the Bear People, and then among the Mice, I have found people who accept me as I am and as they would accept me if I just had a different hair colour to them.

"Your children even like me better when I am in my animal form and gurgle happily when I change in front of them. After a life spent hiding away it is…refreshing. Why, even my whole home village where the condition is quite usual hides away."

"We accept you," said Christopher. "…as we accept Aziz, because in our experience we have learnt that real monsters are monsters of the soul, not of a mere externality like what skin you currently wear. Talk to Verily, if you wish to hear more on that subject. She is very wise in that area.

"We will have to wait until we can talk to one of the Metropolitans about your formal ordination, but I can see no problems for you. We will see Metropolitan Cosmas on the way back, and he will examine your faith before he says yes." Father Christopher paused and thought for a moment. "So, I guess that I had better get to work teaching you what you will need to know by then." He smiled happily.

Rani
Morning of the 4th Primus

The River Dragon came up to the reef that enclosed the north of the island of Gil-Gand-Rask. *The sea and the reef, like the mountains of the Mice, allow a degree of isolation to the people here. I am still not sure how best to approach the islanders. They have little contact with the rest of The Land, and it seems the most unlikely place to find a relic of the Masters.*

I would expect that, if they are under the sway of an evil influence, some rumour would have come out to the rest of The Land and someone would have heard something. Along with guarding caravans, this Jennifer has also sailed the southern waters as crew, and although she has not been here before, she has reported hearing nothing bad from rumours.

Surely, she should have heard something as idle gossip among the sailors. There should have been some talk of turmoil, of pirates, of...well, something other than the usual chat about a backwater island paradise with very unusual customs.

I have decided that we will be open in what we show here about ourselves and what we want. Gil-Gand-Rask is isolated enough that the truth will not be likely to leak out, and small enough that we can probably fight our way clear if I have made a miscalculation. The saddles were brought out from hiding and went into use finding a path for the ship.

The new people are astonished. Our riders started doing this on the river and this is good practice for them. They are darting out to take a sounding and then back to the ship with details for the ship's log, along with bearings and notes on water colour and currents.

The riders pointed and waved their arms around as they described channels through the reef and pointed out isolated pillars of coral waiting to trap the unwary. As they went, they were mapping out the channel into the lagoon.

Although they had the mainsail up, the breeze was light, and the River Dragon advanced slowly behind the saddles. Increasingly, it moved under the power of its sweeps as the sail began to flap, finally to be taken down.

A few small craft are out and about in the lagoon, but although there are more craft on the water near us than elsewhere, once they can see what is happening, none come close to us. It is as if the islanders are sitting back and evaluating us.

Not just the saddles give Olympias information. The masthead lookouts also call down what they can see with their new telescope and this is checked against our growing map. Stefan has already made a waxed waterproof leather case for the chart that is in use that attaches to the mast.

Now the glass is being used to describe what can be seen, the three long piers of different shapes with boats on both sides of them, the golden sands with grass behind them and then a short slope leading up a forested area with some windmills on it.

Lakshmi also gleefully called down that most of the women only had short skirts on, even if they were armed. This led to a scurrying in packs and a further session of being shocked for the newer people as most of the women put on their leather kilts, and Aziz adopted his normal clothing. *Mother Devi...do I have to do the same now?* Lakshmi also reported seeing, in the distance, what looked like a huge wall that appeared to run across the island.

Eventually, they made it through the barrier reef that seemed to circle right around the actual island and entered the lagoon. While still taking the depth, Olympias had the mainsail hoisted again. The wind had picked up a trifle, and they began to move, picking up speed, across the wide lagoon.

It is so lovely standing here in the warm sun, holding my wife in my arms, and having her lean back on my bare breasts, as we look at the scene before us. Around us seabirds fly, and others float on the surface and dive for fish. Below us is a pale-blue transparent sea. The fish moving beneath are as easily visible, and as clearly seen, as if they are birds in the air above.

There were rays and turtles clearly visible below among the schools of multi-coloured fish, and once even a huge shark with a head shaped like the letter 'T' moved through a shoal of small fish with them leaving space for the monster in their midst. *I just wish that I did not feel so vulnerable standing here half naked.*

The Mice moved towards the centre wharf where Lakshmi said some people seemed to be waiting for them. Olympias had the crew pull in the sweeps, and stand by the lines and began to furl the mainsail as she allowed the River Dragon to coast the last fathom in to the dock.

Theodora

*W*aiting on the wharf are a mixed group, some wearing just short skirts or shorts, others more fully clothed. Upon noticing the dress of most of the crew they seem taken aback and now there is much talking among themselves.*

"Greetings to you, wayfarers," said a man in the front in Hindi. He is short, no taller than Basil, and has very dark skin, much darker than that of Parminder, the darkest skinned of the Mice…almost black rather than brown.

He wears a long skirt of sh-hone and a loose shirt of the same fabric. Both are dyed in a sort of soft-outlined geometrical pattern. He has a necklace around his neck made of flowers. All of the people with him have the same colour of skin, and almost all of them, male and female, are dressed similarly. There is little evidence of weapons among them, apart from a single belt knife each.

"My name is Hlănelhane, and this is Şărnelşarn." He indicated the woman beside him. "We are the Speakers for the men and the women of the island. We ask why you come to visit us, and why you did not wait for us to approve you and to bring you in as others do."

He uses Hindi, but they are supposed to use High Speech, so High Speech it is. "If we have offended you, we ask for forgiveness. We have changed our dress to accord with what we saw of your people, but none of us have been here before and we seek to apologise beforehand if we transgress any of your customs.

"I am Theodora do Hrothnog and this is Rani Rai, and we are the Princesses of the village of Mousehole, which lies in the Southern Mountains. We need to enter your island as we are on a quest, and must eliminate a very magical and very evil Pattern that we know to be somewhere here on the island, although we do not know exactly where.

"This is our ship, the River Dragon, and I welcome you to it and ask if we can offer you refreshment. While we are here, we also seek to trade with your people. We have grains, flour, various materials and rose attar, but I will leave that matter to our traders."

"What is this pattern of which you speak?" The woman spoke. *She replies to my High Speech in the same tongue.* "We know of no major arcane symbols that would draw people to our island and that 'must' be eliminated. We do not know of your village, and your names are those of Haven and of Darkreach. What is more, many of your people appear to be from the same places."

"It is a pattern of magic..." said Theodora, "that we have found in various buildings and rooms, and dates back to the start of this Age or before. They are all tools of a great evil and they corrupt those who come across them. Those poor souls are overtaken by them and the so-called Masters who made them.

"As for our village, it is a community largely made up of slaves freed from the same great evil, and yes, many of those who were there, or who freed them, or who have joined us since have come from those lands. However, our residents are drawn from all parts of The Land, and now from another land as well." The two Speakers look at each other after that phrase. *That is... interesting.*

"We also aim to set up a school so that some of the best of the young from all lands may be educated with each other. This way they will learn the customs and languages of as many lands as they can, so that they may understand each other better when they are grown. We are also setting up, in opposition to Haven, a school for mages, and many of those with us are students there."

The woman nodded. "On this island, we do not build to last more than a cycle or two of years. That would not accord with our philosophy, which is one that emphasises the balance and the flow of seasons and cycles. The only buildings on the whole island that are that old are the wall and ruins that lie beyond it. They date from a much earlier time, before the burning and possibly from the age before the one we are in now. I must ask what makes you think that we would hold such a thing here?"

How much do I say? Too little may not give us the access we seek. Too much could leave them at the mercy of anyone here who is wrongly inclined.

"We have...documents. Some are only a few hundred years old, some may be far older or copies of ones that are that old. One of these, and in fact one of the more recently written, refers to various places and we believe that each of these places has a Pattern in it. We have personally investigated six of the twelve, and in all of them it is the case.

"Although it is a fairly newly written paper, it is written in Old Speech as if it is the casual jottings of a being to whom that is the normal tongue. It refers to places by their names in Old Speech and we can confirm that the names refer to the places we know. One of these names is Gil-Gand-Rask and it is one of the few that has not changed its name."

The people in front of me are all smiling broadly now. A couple give small chuckles. Have I somehow unknowingly made some sort of jest? What could be amusing in what I said? I will just wait on a response.

This time it was the man who spoke. "The name may not have changed, but the place has. Now the name is used to refer to the whole island and our town is called, by most, Freeport. For us, it is þoşÞãrntõ. Once Gil-Gand-Rask was the name only of the city that now lies in ruins"," he pointed inland, "and the island was just Gil-Gand."

"That means that your pattern is probably in the ruins beyond the wall. Anyone is, of course, free to go there and do as they will. If it represents a threat to the Balance and the Flow, we would of course welcome its destruction. Be welcome to our island, please trade, and enjoy our hospitality and we hope that your stay is pleasant."

His face is getting its smile back. "We will send traders to see your traders and I do hope that your young people enjoy running." *Now several others have the same smile, and on some of the young ones, particularly among the males looking at the women on the ship, the smile is quite broad.*

There is something here that I do not understand. That smile now reminds me a lot of Astrid without the sharp teeth. I will have to tell everyone not to accept an invitation to run until I find out what that means. "We thank you, and we hope that our customs do not offend you, and that we may be forgiven if they do."

Theodora

When the officials had left, she turned to the people on the ship and asked in Hindi: "Does any know what he means by asking if we enjoy running? We need to find out what it means in case it is a danger to us. Jennifer, you say that you have worked on boats in these waters, do you have any idea what it means?"

Everyone looked blank and Jennifer was shaking her head, but there was laughter from behind Theodora. She turned back to the wharf. *Either not every-one left or else one has just arrived without me noticing. It is a good-looking young man dressed simply in a loincloth. He heard me speak in Hindi, but he replies in High Speech.*

"I am Harnermês. We are a people who enjoy sports and games, and regard a person who is skilled in these areas to be blessed by the gods. If a woman likes a man, she will invite him to run for her to see if he is fit to mate with her. If she decides to enjoy some pleasure, a beautiful woman may have many men running and competing for her attention. Would you like me to run for you?"

Theodora opened her mouth to reply. *Oh dear…this child wants to have sex with me.* She blushed. *My husband just burst out laughing.* Rani had to explain to those on board, who did not have enough High Speech and were looking quizzical, what had just occurred. She left her spluttering wife to attempt to graciously decline the offer to run for her.

Jennifer came forward. "If'n thee dost not mind, canst thou tell him, please, that most of the women and men on this ship are already a taken, but that I would like to see how well he canst run against me. I hath been missin' some good exercise." Theodora looked at her, but translated. *It does not help that both Goditha and Astrid think that it is a hilarious answer.*

Harnermês laughed as well and said he would see her later, above the town, when the ship was settled and that she should wear clothes suitable to run in, not what she wore now.

He pointed to where a creek could be seen coming down the through the slope. A path ran beside it and seemed that this was where she should go. *I have never had to translate such a conversation before. I think that I have just organised for them to go and have sex.*

Jennifer is dressed in trews, a shirt and a jerkin with no shoes, good clothes for working on a ship, but even I know that they will restrict running. In Darkreach athletes are usually near naked. When the man had left along the pier, giving her a good chance to look at him, Jennifer turned to Goditha. She looked down at what she wore. "I doest wonder what runnin' clothes are?" she asked.

"I wilt loan thee mine leather kilt and binder," said Goditha. "That should doest thou."

Shilpa

A small group of men and women are coming along the pier. They are dressed much as we Mice dress for work at home, although there are even less sturdy sandals worn and the material is hemp rather than leather. However, their clothing is not a sign of poverty. Their kilts, and even their aprons, are covered in embroidery and heavily decorated.

They are here to negotiate with me in regard to the cargo. They had perfume, sandalwood, water tulips, sh-hone and kapok.

Rani is interested in them. The sandalwood and the dried water-tulips are both used as incense by water mages in ceremonies and the sh-hone is a cloth also used by water mages. And Hulagu, at least, is a water mage.

Theodora wants the kapok. It is one of the air mage cloths, as well as being useful for warm clothing, and while we had bought some in Haven it is very hard to buy in most of The Land. We cannot have too much of it. As well, near everyone wants to find out more about the perfumes. I wish the Princesses would be quiet and not seem so eager.

They have other goods with them. I regret not bringing more grain when I had the chance. Still, I have sold all that I want to sell. I am worried that I will have to dip deep into our coins to purchase everything that I want to take back home.

This proved not to be the case. She was buying now where these things were made — not in a market across the sea. *I thought that I had purchased a lot of herbs and spices in Pavitra Phāṭaka. I have bought even more here, where it seems that many I bought before may have come from, and I am paying less for them.*

We negotiate on cushions on the deck in the Caliphate fashion, with tisanes, tea, and kaf being served, and with Nikephorus constantly producing sweet things he has made and put aside over the previous few days 'just in case' they were needed.

Once the traders were gone a long string of porters arrived. They carried the grain and flour away with a sack balanced on each side of them hanging in a basket from a pole across their shoulders. *They arrive with goods and leave with more in bulk than they came with. It did not take long to empty the ship.*

Shilpa sighed as the last porter left. *If I were a real merchant now, two or three loads like this would have seen me rich. I am just bargaining to keep in practice, and as cover for what we really are about.*

Olympias

I can see what is coming to the ship and what was going from it. We will need more ballast before we leave. Cloth neither takes up as much space nor weighs as much as the same value of grain.

As the flow of goods dried up, she got everyone working. *No one is to go ashore until the ship is tidy to my standards. This means that the hold where the grain has been has to be swept and washed before the new cloth can be added.*

Basil

I look on in wonder. I have never before realised how much of a tyrant my sister is as a Captain. She does not have an easy-going side at all.

Jennifer

Finally, except for those who would keep a watch, they were dismissed. Jennifer started to head off towards the shore, but Goditha hailed her before she had gone more than a step on the wharf and made her wait while she kissed Parminder goodbye.

"Thou shouldst not run to get there…pray, I would have thee keep some decorum," she said, "although this is one place where a runnin' after the men doth make sense, thou needst not be seen too eager."

"But you don't like men."

"What doth make thou think that I won't run against them for thee?" *I had not thought of that. I must look completely horrified. Luckily, she has burst out laughing and hugged me.*

"Don't thee worry, I dost be happily married woman, and while Father Christopher, and even the Metropolitan, has approved these arrangements, I am sure that they rarely condone infidelity unless there be very good reason. In fact, I doeth know that. I be just comin' along to watch what doth happen. Some of our women might perhaps doeth worse than to do the same to men."

"That is right," there came a voice from behind them. Jennifer turned. *Astrid and Basil have joined us with a baby each and a basket. They both wear just short leather kilts, although Astrid is also wearing some fabulous gems, leather bracers and a golden arm torque, and Basil has shortswords and two arm torques.*

"That is why we are here. We are curious about it, as well. Most of the Mice seem well able to find the man they want, but one day we might have more men than women, although that does not seem likely at our current recruitment rate, and we might, one day, need a way to sort the suitors out.

"So, you should get a move on before the light goes. You may not need the light later, but you will to want see who wins the race, so you know which one to take to bed, unless you want more than one this time…and if you want that, why make them race?" *Astrid and Basil have not stopped walking and are now gone past.*

"You doeth mean that there mayst be more than one man there to run?" *I nearly have to run to catch up to the northern woman. She has flustered me completely.*

"I think it likely, but that is what I want to find out," said Astrid. "Ruth, she is our schoolteacher, will want to know everything about this when we get back. She always does. She even likes running. I am betting that there will be at least two men."

"From what we have seen," Astrid continued in the same tone, as if comparing two catches of fish. "Although you are only an average height among us, you are tall for those on the island…and you have nice breasts, and you have a very different colour skin to them, so you will attract at least some interest as an exotic partner."

"But what if I don't be a likin' the one who doeth win? *I may sound plaintive. It is because I am now worried by what I am committing to.* "What if he be ugly?"

"That is why you want it to be light when we arrive. I suspect that if you don't like the choices, then don't get them running. Goditha is learning how to be a mage. The Princesses have her learning these things and she speaks more of their language than I do. I can say please and thank you. Get her to ask them the rules."

Astrid

We have arrived above the village. To the left of the stream is a large, and elaborate, set of banks, standing stones, and circles, and to the right is a large flat space with some built up banks. There are a number of people moving around on it. Some are using bows and javelins and wrestling, and others sit and watch them and seem to be making bets on the outcomes.

A cheer and some groans could be heard from where a wrestling bout had obviously just finished. "I suspect that is their basilica on the left and we want that bit to the right."

This Harnermês boy is approaching us with a group of other young men. All of them wear just a loincloth or a short kilt. In addition, most wear some form of simple decoration…a necklace of shells, or a flower or shell in their hair. Their hair is black and worn as either very short tight curls, or else tightly bound back, or even teased out in a sort of halo that stands out a long way from the head.

He started talking and Goditha got him to slow down as she translated to Astrid. "He doeth want to know if thee are also to run, and why thou doeth bring babies unless thou wish to show that thee are a good breeder already, and he doeth want to know about Basil and me."

Astrid looked down at the young men. *Some of them are very openly admiring my breasts…and my rubies. That is fine…I am proud of both.*

"Tell him I appreciate the compliment, and I am sure that he is good in bed, but I am happily married and more than satisfied…I advise you to say something similar about yourself…and say that we are here out of curiosity as other lands have other customs…but that my husband wishes to run against them for the joy of it, and to prove his continued stamina to me."

My response has drawn a happy laugh…they laugh a lot…as the men look Basil over as a possible competitor. Harnermês started talking again. *We wait for the translation.*

"He doeth say that this be fine, and that he be glad he issued the invitation. Jennifer doeth be far more desirable dressed the way she is now than in all of those clothes she was in when we arrived and that they all doeth admire her beauty, and wish to thank her for allowin' them to run for her."

She has turned to her old friend. *Goditha is enjoying her discomfort at the open discussion. Jennifer may like bedding men, but she is not used to such an open approach.* "He doeth also want to know if it be thy intent to run agin them all. Dost thou think that thou will run so well that thou can best them all, doeth thee want them all to catch thee or doeth thee wish to only choose one?"

Jennifer

It seems that Astrid was right. She looked more closely at the young men looking back at her. *While not all are handsome, none are ill-favoured. In all my life, I have never had an opportunity like this. It is like a market day for choice.*

"Get thee to tell he that I will run and see how fast they doeth be," she said. "Then I will be a setting the rules for the final run, but unless they are all very, very good, I will probably only be choosing one of them…today."

An explanation came out about the course and Basil stripped off his weapons and jewellery before the islanders and the two from the ship lined up. *I think that they have asked Goditha to start us running. As he warmed his body up, Basil has told her what to say and she has confirmed it with the islanders.*

"Ready…set…go…" came out in High Speech *…And we are off. It was not a short sprint that we will run. The course runs for nearly a mile…a thousand fathoms.*

Astrid

"**I** would have thought such a course would wear them out rather than make them better in bed, but everyone has their own customs." She settled down with the babies on the grass and started to pull a picnic meal from the basket.

The watchers around the field can see the race, with its two pale-skinned runners among the dark, and I can see other people around the field stopping what they are doing to cheer on one or another of the participants and call things out.

Jennifer is a good runner, but she has several of the islanders ahead of her. Basil and Harnermês share the lead. "Well, if she takes on all that beat her, depending on her tastes she will either be very sore or very happy…or possibly both."

Leaving the children crawling around in the grass, Astrid stood with Goditha to cheer on the finish. *Jennifer has slowed a little and one more islander has passed her, but he looks exhausted by the effort. The winner of this race is Basil, but there are four close behind.*

Basil came over to his wife who was holding a beaker of drink out to him. "Well, Puss…do I claim Jennifer, or will you be happy with me?" he asked her.

"Oh, I think that I might keep you. Your sister looks to be good with that odd sword of hers and I would not want to upset her by sending you back." They kissed.

Goditha

*J*ennifer has given up on modesty and has removed the binding from around her breasts. She sits there panting and exhausted. "That," she said with venom, pointing at the binding, "doeth make it hard to run, but I suppose that it be better than the alternative." *Her breasts may not be as large as Astrid's, but she is not small either.*

Goditha translated that to the islanders to some laughter, and then after some talk, came the reply. "They doeth say that it be now time for the real race. They have decided that, if thou doeth approve; only those who doeth beat thee this first time will run the second race."

Jennifer has pushed herself and she needs time to catch her breath. She just nods. "They also doeth say that they all be glad that Basil hath ruled himself out of this race, or they could all be going home now." *Basil has smiled proudly and gotten another kiss from his wife.*

Quite a few of the other onlookers have drifted over by now, and it looks like bets are passing hands. One woman is smiling, patting Basil, and showing some money to him. She obviously won on him in the last race.

To ensure that the woman did not get the wrong idea, looking him up and down like that, Astrid has taken his hand and smiled widely at her. The woman has an expression of surprise on her face after seeing Astrid's feline smile.

Six men lined up for this race, and Jennifer took her place alongside the start and finish line. "It doeth be the last chance for thou to pull out...so to speak...doeth thou have any reservations?" *At least Astrid thinks it is funny and is laughing...Jennifer is just blushing and shaking her head. What would they say at home?*

Making sure that they all were ready she called: "Ready...set...go," and again they were off.

Astrid

"*I*t seems we be not too late t'en?" came from behind. *Stefan has joined us with Bryony and Adara on each side of him. Adara is holding Aneurin. At least it is probably Adara as she is fully clothed.*

"The finals have just started. Basil has already won me in the first race." She turned back to the race and turned to Jennifer. "It looks like you will not get Harnermêŝ." *One who had finished just two ahead of Jennifer is in the lead.* "I think that he was pacing himself for the run that counts…good tactics." She nodded.

The locals are jumping up and down and cheering and more money is being put down on the grass in little heaps. The runners round the outward mark and start back. Harnermês is slowly closing the gap, the others are out of it, and the one in front seems to be having more difficulty. It is a matter of seeing if he can hang on.

Close to the last chain they drew level, and just a few fathoms out the other runner ran completely out of wind. He had pushed himself to the limit and he nearly fell. Harnermês crossed the line less than a hand of paces ahead and came over to where Jennifer was. *Money is changing hands among the onlookers. Harnermês is out of breath and seriously exhausted.*

He got Goditha over and spoke to her in between deep breaths as he pointed first in one direction and then another. "He doeth want to know if that be to thy satisfaction." Jennifer nodded and Goditha listened again.

"Good, then he saith that what usually doeth happen next is that there doeth be a choice for thee to make. There doeth be a, I be not sure if the word be bathhouse, upstream and another one on the beach. Both are kept only for runners and be very comfortable. If I hast it right they doeth be sort of a holy shrine. I think that be right."

She listened and then continued. "There be always food and refreshment kept there if thou doeth wish to take a while at your reward. He doeth say that the upstream one it be closer if thee be in a hurry, but that the one on the beach be better if thee want to linger…to take a longer time with him such as over the whole night, and the moon doeth dance on the water, and the sun doeth rise better on the sea. He hath asked which of the two choices thou wilt prefer."

Jennifer is looking her prize up and down again. "I think thee and me will ha' some time by the beach," she said and Goditha translated. *More money is changing hands between onlookers.*

Astrid leant over to Goditha: "Can you ask them if they bet on everything?"

"Only on sports and on their results," the reply came back. To the cheers of the other locals, Harnermês took Jennifer's hand and gave her a kiss and with a wave they strolled back down to the village.

"Well, that is that." Astrid then looked beside her. "Of course, seeing that they are both here, we could get Bryony and Adara out there and racing and see what happens…" *Stefan has started spluttering, and the two girls are looking at each other and laughing.*

Theodora

The islanders treated the Princesses to a meal, but it was more an informal formality than a real one. *The islanders have their own set of manners and customs, but they are not the same as most other places are used to. Our entertaining skills fit in well and the idea of the guests at the high table... actually a coconut fibre mat spread on the sand facing the water...coming out to entertain the other guests sits well with them.*

It turns out that the island boasts two good bards of their own, and technically, both are far superior to any among us. However, we Mice are far more varied in our skills. Stories were told while they ate: the Quest and the recovery of Mousehole, the Finding of Dwarvenholme, and the Fall of the Masters.

After much prodding, I eventually force Astrid to get up and tell the tale of the Imperial Wedding. It amuses them a lot. She acts out the roles and tells the story in Hindi as I try to keep up a translation into High Speech, for those who lack that other tongue, retaining as much as I can of Astrid's unique way of looking at things.

Theodora, Shilpa, Bianca, Ayesha, Verily, Anahita, and even Stefan sang songs. *Most only sing a song or two. The islanders are isolated and many only speak their own language. At most, some have Hindi, of all the languages we speak. This meant that the songs, whilst appreciated for their music, are not understood well, although the bards who, as usual, do have several languages, like them.*

They have roast beast...pork at least, and other animals, as well as fish and roast vegetables. Most are served on large leaves and some seem to have been cooked in them. The drinks are something that tastes like a date wine, fermented and distilled coconut milk, and a strange white milky drink that tasted a little soapy, but that makes the head spin after a few cups. We drink from polished and halved coconut shells.

After the eating was finished, the women from Haven started with Parminder playing her sitar, with Shilpa playing tambouri and Lakshmi on drums. *Parminder then puts her sitar down and did a Haven dance, in which Rakhi and Zeenat nervously joined, before Ayesha and I show off Caliphate dance with Kāhina, Verily, Lakshmi, and Goditha on a variety of drums. Now we are shown the local dances and hear their tales and songs.*

I think that we will be not going to bed until it is very late.

Christopher

*B*efore midnight, and well before I go to sleep, and indeed well before the *feast ends, I need to check the village for a pattern of the Masters, just to be sure. After a good sleep, I will be able to cast again tomorrow. I want to trust what the islanders have said, but this matter is far too important for me to take on trust.*

To his relief there was nothing in the village that triggered an alarm in his probing.

Astrid
5th Primus

*T*he next morning, except for the watch, we sleep in. It is nearly noon before *we eat and begin to prepare to go for a look around the rest of the island on the saddles. Theodora insists on going along on the outing. I am only agreeing to let her go as long as she obeys instructions. Father Christopher, who despite Theodora coming, will still be the worst rider along, is not allowed to land at all unless I tell him that he can do so.*

Ayesha and Hulagu emerged from the hold, to ribald comment from the onlookers, both far too late to claim a place on the trip. *Anahita will be going as the archer and Aziz for any footwork that is needed. I will be in charge, as I always am when we are in the air.*

They were just about to set off when Jennifer and Harnermês appeared at the end of the pier. *She is obviously going to show him the ship.* With unspoken agreement, the departure of the saddles was delayed a little more. They drew closer to the ship as all conspired, with whispered comments and knowing looks, to ignore them.

To some degree of relief, from the appearance of Jennifer's face, she will be allowed to slip back on board her new ship without notice as everyone studiously ignores them. Unfortunately for her, I saw the approach. Everyone is prepared. The moment she set foot on board the ship erupted in clapping and cheers.

She may pretend not to hear any comments, but she has turned bright red. Seeing that she is still wearing just a kilt, as it is all she has with her, this is very evident. "How was the race?" asked Astrid. "Who came first?"

That has put a shocked expression on top of a face and upper body that cannot blush any more. Ayesha has helpfully translated for Harnermês. It seems he has only a bit of Hindi. I will bet that she thinks that such attention takes the pressure off her and Hulagu. Harnermês' face has taken on a smile of pride as he points at the woman beside him.

Jennifer

I am so embarrassed. This is not expected. I am more used to my behaviour with men earning censure than applause. To make it worse, the holy priest is clapping and laughing as well. I will have to find time to sit down and talk with him. At the very least I have a lot to confess.

It may have been a bad idea to show Harnermês the ship, but I did not want to let him go yet. Not only do I have to face the crew, but as well, if I wanted to show him anything, I have to have an interpreter. I might now be able to speak a few more words of High Speech, but the new words that I know are not for describing the parts of a ship.

She was just about to send Harnermês away when Goditha and Parminder, holding hands, arrived full of eagerness to come and help them. *They only make it harder.*

Chapter XXX

Astrid
Afternoon of 5th Primus

G
oing aloft with the saddles and swooping low along the beach is an *occasion of much pointing and open delight to the locals who are watching us...now to head for the wall in the distance. It is huge. Even Theodora admits that it is larger than anything in Darkreach.*

It is plastered, presumably over stone, and stands over two chains high with stairs coming up the back at intervals and with a seaward end that I can see stands a long way out into the lagoon. It does not seem to be garrisoned, but by its presence it obviously serves a purpose.

The islanders may not use stone for their own buildings, but they have a quarry somewhere and they keep the wall in good repair. Stacks of bamboo are ready as scaffolding, along with a pile of cut stone, and a work crew is already there on site working on a short section with a crack in it. They wave at us as we fly over.

Astrid first went along the entire length of the wall...*I guess that there are over sixteen miles of stonework*...and they found three sets of massive wooden gates set in it. *The islanders really only occupy one small finger of their island. The rest of it they wall off from themselves.* She next took them to the top of Tor Karoso.

The mountain is a tall oval that nearly splits the island into a jungle-covered north, part of which lies behind the wall, and a swampy south with daily doses of high rainfall, and according to what the villagers have told me, a reputation of being able to quickly kill the unwary.

The move from the heat and humidity to the chill of the heights made everyone glad that Astrid had insisted on them bringing the enhanced cloaks of warmth. Below them, as they circled, could be seen a bare stone summit of tumbled rocks.

It will be just possible to land the saddles on it, but inadvisable to move too far from them as it will be easy to fall off, and on all sides, the fall will most likely kill. "Father…when we land, do not move away from your saddle. You have to keep one hand on it at all times. I don't want to have to explain your falling off to Bianca."

They landed and looked around. To the north, well past the wall and the jungle, Zim Island stood out as a distant green blemish on an azure sea. *If the tales that I have heard are right, if there is anywhere that should have had a pattern…it is Zim Island.*

There had once been a city on it, and that city now lies in ruins and no one even knows its name. No one is sure how long the ruins have been there, but it has been the way it is from a time well before the Burning.

However long it has been there, there is very little space for much to grow there. The stark stone outlines of the tumbled ruins could be made out with the second telescope, which was passed around. It looked like the space between was densely filled with green. It would be hard to move there. In the far distance could be seen the mountains at the southern end of the Great Range.

Their base is lost below the horizon, but according to the charts it is over two-hundred sea miles away. Just think…to the right of them is where Basil's parents live…I wonder. Putting that thought aside, she turned around to the task at hand.

Below us lies the southern swamp. It is hard to see much as the trees obscure most of the view. Directly below us, I can see a ruined city. It is an odd city from what I can see, unlike any I have heard of. Visible through the trees are fallen walls and expanses of what had once been plazas.

That is evident from the stunted growth, as growing things have to force their way through stone, but what is amazing are the seven great mountains of stone. There are six in a pattern and one in the centre. They must be built by the same people that made the wall…only they are far, far, taller. The outer ones are all as tall as the Palace at Ardlark and the centre one is even taller.

They are so huge that it seems unlikely that people could have built them. From what I can see, at least three have stairs climbing them. The others might have them as well, but they will be facing the other way. Some plants cling to these giant man-made hills that make the tumuli of the so-called Funereal Hills look like child's sandcastles, but mostly they present just a bare stone mass.

"I guess that would be the city then. At least it was not hard to find. I am going to look from here for any threats, and then we will fly down to the central one of those stone mountains, and Father Christopher can cast a miracle and

tell us if he can find the pattern. Does anyone have any other better ideas?"
She looked around to see shaking heads.

Putting the glass to her eye she looked around. *That there is firm ground as well as swamp is evident from the number of the giant lizards that I see, their heads visible through trees. The giant flying furred lizards are also well represented. Usually they live on cliffs, and I can see several eyries below me on Tor Karoso.*

Here they also occupy the shaped stone mountains as well. They will be the greatest threat that we face. Each mountain has what looks like a building on top of it, and each of these buildings, and the flat space around it, is an eyrie of Giant Leather-wings, the furry flying lizards with a beak that is worse to face than a sword.

Despite this, we should be able to clear one of the tops, and that is because the field of view around it and the view it commands, is the best place to land. I can see that there is movement in the marshy spots, but I cannot see what is causing it, unless it is moving plants, and I still don't believe those stories, despite what Bryony insists on. At any rate, I don't want to land there if I can help it.

Looking briefly further she gave a start. *This is supposed to be the southern-most island, but I can see another island in the far distance. It is not very big, and it is very flat, except for some odd lumps, which I cannot make out at this distance, even with the telescope. It seems that there are boats around it, so there must be people there. Well, it is not important. I will ask the islanders about it later.*

Astrid got them to take off, and formed them to take the four points of a tetrahedron…one up and three down with Father Christopher in the centre. *I will keep everyone about thirty paces from the priest.* Astrid took the top point.

Theodora and Anahita hold the lower points at the front, and will use their bows to try and drive off the beasts. If they come too close to us, Aziz and I will use wands if we have to. Meanwhile, Father Christopher is under strict instruction to only use a wand if one of the lizards comes directly at him past the rest of us.

As they approached the stone mountains, the leather wings took off and rose to meet them. *It does not matter how small a leather wing is, or how large, they always challenge anyone who approaches their nest. The ones on the other hills circle their eyries, but the ones we are approaching come directly towards the threat, screeching as they come.*

Astrid halted the saddles in the air, and Theodora and Anahita began to fire. *These are nearly the largest type of the beasts, with a wingspan of two hands of paces. Although they are to be dreaded in large numbers, and when you are on foot near their nests, in the air and with arrows that explode they fall out of the sky easily. The problem is that they did not know when to stop. You have to kill, or at least knock out of the sky, every single one of them.*

What really worries me is that wherever they fall into the swamp underneath, it almost always seems that something, a creature that I cannot see properly, grabs them. They struggle and scream for only a brief span of time before falling silent.

Once the sky was clear, and they approached closer, it took only a minute to clear the juvenile beasts still around the chosen stone hill and then they swooped down to land. *We then have to clear the young, which although unable to fly, hobble forward on their legs and the elbows of their wings, their beaks stabbing forward like little bone rapiers.*

Astrid took over here. She landed and advanced with her spear, using it to engage them and tumble them down the slope in an indignant flurry. If any came back up, Aziz dispatched them. *With my spear, bracers, and torque I have the reach, speed, and strength to just lever them aside without any damage to myself.*

It did not take long for her to get rid of those that hobbled towards her. "You can all land now and Father Christopher can prepare to cast to find out where the pattern is. I am going to see if there are any inside here that need to be dispatched."

The top of the hill is over twenty paces square, and on one side has a set of steep steps leading up to it. A person climbing the steps would have to do so almost on hands and knees. The building occupies most of the top. Issuing from it there is what seems to be a trench cut into the stone and running from the building to the top of the stairs.

Sweeping aside nests and eggs, and baby beasts from the flat area to fall and tumble down the slope, Astrid entered the shade of the building at its entrance that faced the stairs and looked around.

The hair on the back of my neck is rising. In the centre is a stone table, like an altar, but dished in the centre with a continuation of the trench coming from the stair side. This was an altar for sacrifice, and from the size of it, probably human sacrifice. The blood would run around the channels, and then down the stairs to make them slippery as people go up and down, crawling through the blood.

They were not nice people who built this. Not nice at all. I can imagine a victim being forced to climb up the stairs, and as the knowledge of their fate grows in them, becoming covered in the blood of those who had climbed that way before them.

She looked at the rest of the building and gave a start. Using her spear to dispatch more of the furry leather-wing chicks and to clear the nests, she called for the priest, interrupting his preparations.

"Father Christopher…can you come here, please?" She cried out as she kept clearing. When the others entered, she pointed.

Surrounding the obscene altar, which I can now see is carved with represent-ations of worship, which includes the cutting out of hearts, and allowing the victims to bleed out, is a pattern. Here the trench draining the altar feeds into the pattern and is a part of it. The outside drain is only for excess blood. "Do you think that this is the pattern that we are looking for?"

"It could be," he said. "It looks like them, but none of them have been set up quite like this, although there is similarity to the one in Pavitra Phāṭaka that we pulled Rakhi from." He pulled a small book out of his pouch and began leafing through it, comparing what was in there to what was in front of him. "I would say that it is, but it is subtly different. I will still have to cast to see," and he returned outside and went on with his preparations.

Anahita and Aziz stood on opposite sides of the flat area on the corners. Only once did Anahita have to shoot down an approaching leather-wing that came diving at them from a distance. *It was probably a parent that was late in returning home. Now it is a dead parent.*

Christopher

I *have finished. We don't need to search any further.* "We will have to return here tomorrow. This is it. I am not sure why they set it up like this, but their spell must have used human suffering to give it power. That is necromancy of the worst sort. Simple necromancy, such as creating the undead, is one thing…and can be used for good or ill. This is pure evil. Usually a priest can only tell you if a person is evil. This very place is evil…horribly evil."

He waved his hand around to indicate the city. "The city has been abandoned a long time, but this altar has been used more recently… See?" *When I rub at the rock of the altar, there is still some residue of blood that sticks in the sheltered stone and comes off on my fingers. I will scrub them when we get back.*

"Someone has used it since, but I wonder if the Masters used this Pattern a cycle ago to recharge their entire network. At any rate, when I am finished here tomorrow, I will pray for the souls lost here. I would say that the men we killed could not get here easily, perhaps they were missing their carpet, and were about to sacrifice the women in Sacred Gate, for the purposes of re-charging or rebuilding their network. In my opinion we must be hurting them with what we do."

I am sure of that…now to note the details. He pulled out a pen and ink and began making more notes in the book about the diagram. *We cannot leave until I have drawn it completely.*

That is strange. "These patterns are more like those used by a priest than those of a mage, wouldn't you say Princess?"

"I have never seen a magical one like this," she said. "It is more complex and there is writing all over it. Magical ones are only patterns of focus for our minds. The patterns of priests have their Holy words on them and that is what this seems to be. Astrid, can you read them?" *She is tracing out what appear to be runes. I didn't notice them.*

"They could be six names, but they make no sense," she said. "They would sound something like this," and she started walking around and pointing them out one-by-one, as she read: "Khaarmal...Maarndrin...Togaath...Maarshtrin..."

"Stop, stop...my sense of evil grows as you say them. You are invoking them just by saying their names." He pointed outside into a visible patch of sky. "I don't know if you can see it, but there is already a circular cloud forming over us. I can sense the evil in it. This is a place of great power. Evil power indeed, but it is very great." He shook his head.

"They must have made very many sacrifices at this site over time for the power to endure over time. You can tell me the others later, and I will transcribe them one-by-one. I have written them down. I will have to look through our library at home and see if I can find any references."

"These names were not written in the pattern that we saw in Sacred Gate, but then the sacrifice was not done yet, and it would have made sense for them to have meant to be doing the writing with Rakhi's blood."

With that they had another look around and then flew back to the village. *Looking back as I go, the dark circular cloud that had so quickly and eagerly started to form above the mountain is slowly and reluctantly dissipating in the clear sky. By Saint Swithun, I had not thought that clouds could have malevolent intent before today.*

Astrid

*T*his night is far quieter, and we are all eating on the River Dragon. This *time the Mice are feeding some of the islanders. Jennifer didn't stop to eat with us, and she hasn't bothered to run a race, she has just dragged Harnermêŝ off somewhere else. Apparently, they cannot use the special huts, seeing that they have not run, but there are many other places in the village to tryst.*

*They started to go, and we started to make ribald comments…well, I did…
and the rest followed. Harnermêŝ, his face wearing a large smile, but not being
able to reply to what he assumed we were saying, simply mimed exhaustion
and age as they went, which again embarrassed Jennifer, but amused the rest
of us. After today it was good to have some hearty laughter.*

*In conversation, we have discovered that, although the villagers, partic-
ularly when young, go through gates in the wall to forage for rare plants and
to prove themselves, they almost never go near the stone hills and the city. It
has a fell reputation with these people. As a part of becoming an adult, a week
has to be spent beyond the wall surviving on what you find.*

*Some stay in the north and some climb the mountain. Some even go into
the south alone, but most of those few who boast that they will spend their
time in the city never return, or if they do, return changed to the extent that the
islanders eventually make them outlaw. They will end up leaving on a trading
boat or in a canoe. The islanders all know that something is very wrong with
the place.*

*Try as I might to find out about the island that I saw, I am getting nowhere.
Everyone I try to talk to either on my own, or through a translator, denies that
there is another island to the south of them. I notice that, although they are
direct in stating there is no island no one offers any other explanation, and
none try to deny that I saw something. They just will not explain what I saw
and soon change the subject.*

Astrid
Morning 6th Primus

*I just remembered what I read back in Mousehole about the Sea Nomads
and their floating towns. I wonder if that is what I have seen, but that still
doesn't explain the size of what I saw. It was larger than many of the towns
that are built on the land. How could such a thing float?*

*It is time to set out again. This time we fly directly to the central stone hill.
We only have to kill a few of the flyers this time, as no new ones seem to have
moved in. Looking south, I can just see the island I saw before. It doesn't seem
to be in the same place. It is further away. How could the Sea Nomads make
their island move? Maybe it isn't an island after all…but if it isn't that, what
is it?*

275

Christopher

This time Aziz had been left behind and Goditha was brought in his place. "Scavengers of some sort were at work overnight," said Astrid. "The bodies of the leather-wings on the slopes have been disturbed and something has even been up into the building."

I can see nothing…but now I need to prepare for my work. I notice that Astrid has brought a scrubbing brush and some water. She has started washing down the altar, trying to scrub away any trace of blood that remains there. I am ready well before she has finished, but I will allow her to continue. Her work may aid my casting and I have my own contribution to this work for later.

She seems to be satisfied with her scrubbing. Father Christopher set about casting the miracle that would disenchant the pattern.

This time it is easy to see the shape that rises from the graven design. It is winged and it has horns. It looks like an old illumination of the Devil would look. It is even deep blood red, unlike all of the others, most of which had a smoky greyness to them. It makes the same unheard sound in our heads as the others did as it rises into the sky and heads north.

Now that is finished, it is time for Goditha to get to work with her mason's tools. Each of the names graven in stone has to be obliterated, and the areas made flat, so there is not a trace of them left. Astrid sweeps away the chips and dust to the outside, so that they can blow away and do not just lie in the corners to be re-gathered by one of the Master's servants. It is my turn.

Father Christopher brought two large flagons out of his saddlebags. "We priests usually bless large quantities of Holy Water and carry it with us in case we cannot make more for some reason. This is my whole supply that I brought for this trip. I will have to pray over more later on. Give me a hand." The flagons were, one by one, upended over the central depression.

There is no physical reason for it to do so, according to Theodora, who is a more than competent alchemist, but the water fizzes slightly as if reacting with the stone. Astrid, after asking me if she can, applies her scrubbing brush again and covers the whole altar with the water.

I then allow the surplus Holy Water to run down the gutter and fill the pattern. As it goes it fizzes there as well and continues doing so as it begins to drain down the steps. It is only once that is done that we prepare to leave. We have been away almost the whole day, but the area somehow feels different to me.

Rani

*W*e are to leave early, so as to have good light to thread our way out of the lagoon and sail on. But before we can leave we have Şārnelşarn, the women's speaker, before us with two young girls.

"Your visit has been very different to the usual visits by traders," she said. "They come to try and bed our women without running for them and to trade with us at the lowest prices and no more. We tolerate them more than anything else, as we need what they bring, and they know that. You have joined in our customs and have shared with us. Since you have been here, we have been conscious that our world is very small. It may be time for that world to change.

"These are my twin daughters, Hailanmêŝ and Tarlanmêŝ. As you spoke of the school to us it seemed to me that this was a good thing for them to attend. They grow older, but are still young enough to learn. They are eight years old and I wish them to go with you. I have money here for them, and you can call here for more or I will send it through Haven."

She bent down to hug and kiss the two young girls. *It seems that our school will keep growing. All can see its need. At least the adults can. These girls do not look to be as sure about it.*

Theodora ushered the girls away to find them a hammock and show them around the ship. "Do not do that," Rani said. "Can you visit Darkreach?" There was a nod. "Astrid has convinced us to visit Southpoint. Her husband, Basil, has family there. We will give you a letter of introduction to them and let them know about you when we go there.

"It is closer, and I hate to admit this, but sending something through the people there will be a much safer way of getting money to us. If we have letters that are not urgent, we will also send them there. We have a trader from Darkreach come to us at least twice a year. If any of your people wish to come to see us, it is possibly best to travel that way as well. It will be far slower, but we know that it will be safe."

Rani

*I*t seems that there is likely to be one more addition to the ship before we sail. Jennifer is before us with Harnermêŝ. I heard Astrid speculating that this would happen. She will be insufferable about being right.

"I know that I be but new to thee, but I hath a great boon to ask. I canst not understand enough of High Speech, and I doeth not wish to ask Goditha to translate, but I do think that he wants to come away with thee and me. If he doeth want to, then I wilt be more than happy."

She is studying the deck and blushing. "He art very well-endowed, and what is more, he hath been the only man I have ever met who can outlast me. I doeth suppose that I hath really been looking for such a man for a long time, and if it be that he cannot come with us, then I will stay here."

Rani turned to Harnermeess and spoke to him in High Speech. "Young man, do you want to leave with us?"

"I do, or rather I want to leave with Jahnifer. If she is going, I want to go with her. If she stays I will stay with her. Our people rarely mate for life, but when it happens, the couples usually say that they knew straight away. I want to mate with her for life and to run for no other. We cannot speak well yet, but we are happy to just be together…not just in bed. I am useful. I can sail and fish. Will you take me with you?"

"She feels the same way," said Rani, "but before we take you, I have to explain a few rules about the way we do things…" In the end, he said goodbye to his family and re-joined the River Dragon with a small bag made of a beaten cloth by the time that it sailed out of the lagoon.

Once we are free of the reefs we sail for the north. We will now sail past Zim Isle, one of my reasons for deciding to go to Southpoint. Few get to see the place, and I am curious after all the stories that I have heard. Although its name has not come up so far in our quest, I cannot help feeling that one day it will, and I want to see what is there in the way of a harbour before we need it.

Christopher

I have the time now. I will cast a knowledge miracle and discover what the first batch of things that we picked up from the Master's servants in Sacred Gate is. Most are as they would be expected to be, but the quiver is interesting. It will repair arrows left in it overnight, and the rods allow you to locate lost arrows. The Khitan are very glad to be given those.

The obsidian blade from the man that Theodora killed with the blast from her wand is also interesting. Most blades are magically enhanced for combat in some way. This one is not. It is heavily enchanted, and designed to make the person it is being used on experience time differently to the rest of the world.

With horror Christopher realised its purpose. *Once a person has been given a small scratch from it, they will take perhaps an hour of their time to have their heart cut out, and while it is being done their soul will literally be eaten by something. I am not sure what that something is, but I have a feeling that those names might be connected to it.*

This blade cannot be left as it is. Even if I threw it overboard it could end up, some centuries later when we are all dead, in the wrong hands. The only thing to do is to break or to disenchant it. Good obsidian blades are rare and often useful, particularly for surgery. I will disenchant it as the less risky option. I cannot do this safely at present though.

The blade was carefully wrapped and put away into a secure spot where no one could accidentally cut themselves.

Christopher

*B*efore each of the last six services, I had Astrid recite one of the names and I wrote it down as it sounds. The names are: Khaarmal, Maarndrin, Togaath, and Maarshtrin, the four she uttered in the city, and Daahlgren and Tuurmaan, the two she had not.*

It may be overly cautious, but I made sure that Astrid confessed and had the sacrament after she pronounced each one of them. I fear those names, I have never heard them before. I don't know what they are, or even where they are from, but I fear them as representing some great evil.

I wonder if these are the names of the beings that stand somewhere in the Shadow behind the Masters. Conceivably these are the ones who created them and perhaps even direct them still. Perchance, they are some ancient and evil gods, just like the Baal of the Bible.

Chapter XXXI

Rani
9th Primus

Zim Isle is interesting, and yet it is not. I do not want to come too close to the land as it is possible that something, I do not know what, might try and board us. As we draw near, the water seems to grow darker, and the people Astrid is teaching how to fish catch fewer and fewer fish and those that they catch are...different.

The fish have things wrong with them...they might not be the same on both sides, or they might have an extra eye or a fin. Astrid showed some to Christopher and us. I have told her to throw them back. No one should eat such cursed fish. She soon stopped fishing entirely.

As we go, Olympias says that the ship is slowing, as if something is holding it back from under the surface although we can see nothing through the clear water.

The land itself shows signs of being entirely covered in ruined buildings of all sizes. There are no open spaces, but there is a good cover of plants forcing their way through stone, but they look unhealthy somehow. They are like the fish—wrong.

Most are not really green; both their leaves and flowers are of other colours. Blacks and purples—like giant bruises—are common among them. The flowers are often huge. There are few animals that we can see.

Even as we watch, a monkey, one of the few animals we have seen, is grabbed by something that shot out of a flower and wrapped around its body. With a shriek it is pulled in, and the flower closes around it where it can be seen briefly struggling and heard screaming.

The monkey on the River Dragon shrieked back from where it was on the mast. Other than that, everyone on the River Dragon stayed silent…and just kept watch.

There are several of the stone hills, but this time they lack the buildings on top of them, and they are entirely smooth with no apparent steps up them. Some of the buildings that I can see seem to have almost melted edges. It is as if their stone had become soft wax and run. Things seem to move in the undergrowth, but what they are is not clear.

There was once a harbour there, and it probably had been a good one once, but waving towards us from the water around it are tendrils of seaweed.

"Kraken weed," said Olympias. "I am not going near that without flamethrowers. Actually, I would not like to go too near that island without a large supply of flamethrowers and fuel and molotails and a flame dromond or two full of mages. That is a place to avoid."

I agree. We will just sail on past and hope that we never have to return here and actually land. As we sail away from the island, even I can notice that our progress is becoming faster. Even the water is somehow looking cleaner, but I notice that Astrid is still not fishing, even though I can see shapes in the water beneath us.

Olympias
10th Primus, the Muslim Feast of Ashura

I *have not been to Southpoint before. Our parents were posted there with my younger brothers after I left home to go to sea as a child cadet. Damn not having all of the charts available. Even though he lived here, my brother is useless for this, but Denizkartal has once come in here from the sea and he points the way.*

"Just look for the end of the range and the start of the jungle," he said. "Not far from where they meet there's a small bay with a large creek, and Southpoint lies up it a little way at a place where they could build a bridge.

"We will either have to use the sweeps or else use the magic wind to get up the creek to the dock. It is deep enough, but there is not enough room for us to tack. The wharf is usually only used for fishing boats and coasters. Larger ships, unless they use sweeps, oft anchor out in the bay and then come in to land by boat. It is a nuisance doing that and you're best to dock if you can."

Southpoint is supposed to be a walled village, more a fortification with some farmers than a real civilian settlement, although Basil loyally says that it has grown and there are many farms around it now, and gatherers and hunters range the jungles all around.

They sailed up across the small bay and up the creek with their own wind. *Denizkartal and I both have our uniforms on and are very visible, Denizkartal in the starboard bow and me on the quarterdeck beside Astrid on the wheel. That seems to be safest.*

My sister seems to be nervous…I really do think that she is actually nervous about the idea of meeting our parents. Well, at least there is something that can disturb the woman out of her usual irreverence and humour. That is news.

This is our fourth docking since our proper sailing from Evilhalt. My crew are getting a little more experienced at it. I thank my constant drills as the sails are furled smoothly. It seems that I am not going to be disgraced bringing my vessel into the port of my parents. Never mind that they are probably going to be working and will not see me arrive…but you should always act as if you are under review.

It was as well that she had taken it that way. She was both right and wrong. They were working and yet they were watching. As she drew up to the wharf, giving the orders to put out the lines and take down the sails, she had noticed the waiting official at the dock, but was going to take no more notice of anything like that until all was finished, leaving it to her supercargo.

The gangplank was out, and Shilpa, with Astrid to translate for her, had landed to see what fees were due. Olympias had not yet finished with the ship when Shilpa and Astrid reappeared.

"There is a woman who demands to see the Captain immediately," said Astrid. "I told her you were busy, and she said that you had better see her now if you wanted to land, so here she is…she says that her name is Anna."

"Mother!" Olympias turned quickly, and leapt to hug the woman. She then turned to Astrid, "…Astrid, this is our mother."

Astrid

*H*rothnog *had told Basil that the fortunes of his family would improve if he accepted the task he was given. He told me that he had taken this on faith, and it seems that they have. His mother is now in charge of the taxes for the village, and his father is in charge of the garrison. It is rumoured that one of them will be the next Governor.*

As visits of us Mice to a village go, this is an unremarkable one. It turns out to be just an opportunity to impress parents and introduce the Princesses and the grandchildren. Georgios Akritas was formally told he was Georgios Anoteron Akritas…the senior Georgios…and he was introduced to the junior.

At least he approves of the change. Why cannot my father be more like Basil's? Mind you, I know a bit of how Bryony was feeling in Evilhalt. Denizkartal may want to try and keep a low profile, but I want to spread the welcome around, so he can get introduced as well.

It seemed that everyone in the village had to be introduced to Tribune Akritas, and as it turned out when Denizkartal 'accidentally' let the news slip out…he used that to take attention from himself from the way he grinned at me…to Epilarch Akritina.

It seems that Olympias has been keeping it secret that she was promoted as well, and she is now formally in command of any Darkreach vessels found 'beyond the Great Range' as well as any ship that she is Captain of.

Basil has a big family. We get introduced to more brothers and sisters, and their partners and children, and even their partners and the grandchildren. I cannot remember them all.

Astrid tried to spread the load of greetings as far as she could, and even tried to drag Theodora along with her so that the adulation was directed elsewhere, but she lost out there to the local Governor, who wanted to show off her town and to find out what was happening in the rest of The Land.

It was the first time a member of the Imperial family had visited the village, at least since the beginning of the Burning, and once it was discovered that she was on board, the Governor was not going to let the opportunity to show off her charge pass her by.

She is so determined that even I have no chance of prevailing against her. At least Theodora looks more harassed than I feel, and she is now dragging her husband along as well to share the joy with her.

Theodora

I have set up a message line to take any communications from Gil-Gand-Rask, and assured the Governor that my Granther, the God-Emperor, will not mind if they use their duty boat to take messages to the island. Olympias has given them sailing directions, instructions and a letter of introduction as, apart from the local mages, there is no one in the village who speaks High Speech.

Taking advantage of all of this, the monkey, which had not been happy on a boat at sea, somehow escaped into the jungle.

It seems that I am the only one who misses him. The others all seem pleased and I wonder if someone was accidentally careless. He was getting better, but I believe that he had made himself a nuisance on the ship. I was told that he had to be watched all of the time around the babies lest he bite a nose or a finger.

Next day they set out back for Haven. *It seems that our school will grow further. We have with us an eight-year old Menas Climacus, one of Basil and Olympias' many Insakharl cousins, or nephews, or whatever he is, as a student at the school.*

One of the local mages thinks that he has talent and that, despite the scholarships, it is less likely that this will be realised down at the far end of the Empire. Apparently, I was asked before Astrid and Basil found out about this. They were quick to remedy this and have made themselves responsible for his tuition and care. He seems quiet like Basil and so should not be a problem.

Chapter XXXII

Olympias
13th Primus

From the moment they rounded the end of the Great Range they were running into the face of a storm coming up from the southwest and trying to drive them back onto the land.

There is little rain and the wind is only strong, rather than a gale, but it is constant. It does not slacken and the sea is building under us. Despite having the means to avoid a lot of the discomfort of this, my crew will do well to learn from this. Some are learning what the water looks like as you lean over the side.

The River Dragon was in no danger, but she would have to make a series of long slow tacks across the wide mouth of Iba Bay, where the sea lay between the mountains and the vast mud delta that made up much of the Swamp. They crossed in front of the delta itself, seeing the water grow muddy, even in the wind, as they traversed the outflow of the area.

Eventually, they rounded the delta and headed into Windin Cove towards Sacred Gate, now with the wind on their port beam and running on a long reach to the northwest with just the fore and aft sails up. The trip took ten days, and apart from the last leg, was very slow.

I am happy with how well they handled themselves, but several of the crew have been sick at different times. These are still not experienced sailors, and they are all glad to be reaching along the shores of Haven, particularly when we sight Sacred Gate again in the distance. They still regard shore as home. I need an experienced crew of my own, ones who think of the sea as home.

Rani
22nd Primus

*A*lthough there is some risk, we are again heading for the same wharf that we had docked at on the way out and will tie up there. Even though we may have left suspiciously close in time to the attack on the house, at least now we are coming back with a more convincing weather-beaten appearance from time at sea and with credentials as an established trader.

This leaves me with something that I have been avoiding…two somethings, actually. The first, and least serious, is reporting to the Maharajah. However, I can do that clandestinely through a letter. The second, and more serious, is my family. Do I go and see them? Do I introduce Theodora? If I do, how do I do it?

Theodora wants to meet them, and she has even anticipated some of the arguments that I was going to raise to prevent the meeting happening by bringing them up first. My Princess knows that the rest of my family are military, not serious mages, and she has prepared her own glamour. If she needs, she can appear as a Kshatya mage.

I haven't told her that my grandmother will probably see through it straight away, not because of a defect in the glamour, which seems perfect, even to me, but my grandmother will most likely know every man and woman of our part of the caste and what their relationship is. My family knew of my geas at least.

She eventually decided that she would tell them part of the story and just introduce Theodora as the co-Princess of Mousehole without mentioning their relationship.

I pray that Dharma will forgive my omission. It is cowardly, but it is going to produce less tension. I will compromise and talk more deeply to my grandmother and tell her the whole story. That way, if there are stories or rumours that come back, someone will know the truth and be able to speak it if it is needed.

Having made that decision, the next problem is how to get there. Should I use one of our own boats? Perhaps use the saddles? I should bring a servant, which means Nikephorus. Either Ayesha or Basil will demand to be there. I am sure that they know how apprehensive I am about this visit and will, in any case, worry about thuggee involvement and will want to protect Theodora.

Ayesha will be more acceptable, and less obvious in what she is. That will allow Basil to take Lakshmi and do whatever they want to do on Anta and beyond, to find out if there are any repercussions from our raid.

Perhaps it is time to put young Vishal to the test, and see if he will behave himself. He has spent as much time aloft as he can, becoming a sailor, but *now he can be a guard once again. He has an acceptable status; indeed, he is the only person on board who actually does, and he will know how to comport himself.*

Vishal had his two-handed and single-handed swords, his shield, and his bow returned to him, and he took up his duties and began to happily follow Rani around everywhere.

Vishal seems very happy that, if any of his family sees him, he now has a task of acceptable status that he is performing. I may not be as happy with this. Theodora made a laughing comment that now I can feel as she does, with Basil and Ayesha following her. She ignored me glaring at her and had the audacity to just smile broadly.

Shilpa, with Stefan beside her as a guard, was sent out to bring back an appropriate hired ferry.

She has taken a long time to arrive back with a craft...I should have been more specific about what I meant as appropriate. That boat is suitable for a much higher dignitary than I am. It even has an umbrella of rank as a permanent fixture.

She was roundly taken to task on that matter by Astrid as she tried to send it away. "You are our Princess. You are not going there as a cast-out member of their family coming home. You are paying a visit to them as our ruler and representing us. It would dishonour us before your family for you not to use this." Rani looked around her.

It seems, from the several nodding heads that Astrid speaks for them all... particularly those born here from the look on their faces. Why would girls who were born as Harijan care so much about my status?

Rani turned to Theodora for support and did not get it. "She is right. Whether you like it or not, you are not a private citizen anymore. How you appear represents the status of our whole village. What did I have to do in Southpoint? We are letting you off lightly by not making you visit this Maharajah of yours. Let us get going quickly before I change my mind on that one."

Theodora

I have prepared more than just a single glamour for this visit. I suspect that I know how my beauty will react to my other idea, so I am not bothering to ask her. It is often easier to ask forgiveness than permission and I hope...I trust...that she forgives me for what I am about to do.

She did however talk to Father Christopher who consulted with his conscience, and after asking Theodora's permission, with his wife, before agreeing to the rather unusual request that was made for special prayers.

He was reluctant, but my arguments about having more than one possible successor to us in case of, God forbid, an accident to Fear, did eventually persuade him. So it was that when Theodora succeeded in seducing Rani's brother in the gardens, a pregnancy was guaranteed.

Ayesha

*T*heodora *need not know that I am making sure that they are not interrupted. By Allah, the Protector, did she think that I was going to allow my charge to wander about an unknown area without me following her, and so failing in my trust?*

Once she saw what was happening, she quickly deduced the rest, and firmly made sure that the two servants sent to find them did not do so, but were directed elsewhere until it was over. *I didn't even have to harm a hair on their heads.*

Rani

*T*he *visit went better than expected in many ways, given that Theodora is not Hindu. My parents are even being coldly polite to her, even if they will not touch her. Sadly, I am now certain that they will never accept her true status. I have not brought it up, and neither did my Theo-dear. She just accepted the introduction that I gave of her as a ruler.*

She seemed to enjoy the visit, and even went off with my younger brother to look over the house and gardens, while I talk to my parents and then my grandmother. She came back quite some time later, seemingly pleased. At least that takes away a part of my sadness over my family and how they would feel about us.

I have to admit that the gardens are the nicest part of the house. It is easy to lose yourself in their serenity. Despite our cramped conditions on our ship, I will try and make up for my family's aloofness towards her tonight.

Basil

*W*e are already getting to be familiar with some of the area's most open talkers and where it is best to go to find out information. Speculation is still rife on the streets about what happened that night of the New Year. At least no rumours exist that might link the Mice to what occurred. Some of the speculation seems to imply that the Temple of Kali was involved, for some reason.

Even more importantly, although the people on the streets are still curious, the authorities seem not to have paid much attention to the incident. Apparently, they never do on Anta, as long as trade is not affected.

It seems that most have heard of what was found there, and apart from the rumour about the Kali worshippers, the consensus is that there was a falling out of criminals. The word is quite openly that some were mages, and another a thug. This just makes the authorities even less likely to investigate.

It seems that they do not like scandal that would make people question the status quo. Several people have died or disappeared since we left, and most of these happenings are blamed on a readjustment of the local criminal scene.

We have picked up nothing implicating any passing ships. That proves that either the people in the dock area really did not see anything or else they were just very good at keeping secrets from outsiders. I believe that it is the former, but even I cannot be sure of that.

Astrid
26th Primus

*T*he trip back up the river to Garthang took less time than they had taken going down as they went the whole time under a constant magical wind with no need to tack. *Those doing the sailing had little to do, but at least I am busy with the saddles, finding the way when we have no settlements in sight. We are still stopping each night to rest.*

It is a relief to stop and go ashore at Garthang. After here, we need take less caution with being seen. It seems that we have relieved the qualms of the Governor by giving him a letter to forward to the Maharajah, acquainting him with an outline of what had occurred, before we continue on our northward trek home.

Christopher
30th Primus, the Feast Day of Saint Gildas

I find now that not only am I not very good as a woodsman in the forest, but I not meant to be a sailor either. This leg to Erave Town took the same time going up as the far longer trip from the sea to Garthang. While we had a wind behind us, I am told that there was also more likelihood of mud-banks and treacherous waters and we had the current to face as well.

After four days they docked, and Father Christopher gathered Father Simeon and headed straight off to see the Metropolitan.

I can return happy to announce that Father Simeon is about to be ordained, and as a part of this, will conduct a service in the Basilica. He will henceforth be regarded as an Orthodox priest. I am inviting them all to attend. Perhaps our wolf-priest will end up as the chaplain to this ship.

Astrid

I am making sure that I am going to be there. Father Simeon has spoken to me about my role in his becoming a priest. I need to know as much about him as I can if I am going to work out which of the girls will best suit him. I have decided that I like playing this role. Not only is it needed, with no parents around to smooth the way for the girls, but also it is fun.

Olympias
32nd Primus

Sadly, my ship is emptying. Even as we still sail north over the lake, the process of leaving reverses itself. Riders start to fly up to the valley to let those left behind know what has happened, and to arrange to get the carpet, and to get most of the people back that want to be back. It is most of them who will leave.

At least we are not abandoning her. A small watch will be kept on the River Dragon, because the Princesses think she will be needed again and possibly soon, but this will be done on rotation. I am thinking that we should have at least half a dozen people on board most of the time. It is barely enough to sail her around the lake, but sufficient for some practice and to keep training going, and just enough to keep her maintained.

Shilpa

I need to fly ahead to Evilhalt and arrange for a carter to bring the cloth and the herbs and spices up to us in the valley. I wish that I had more confidence in the carters that I found there, all of whom are only used to going around the hamlets and leave longer distance travel to others, but I have to settle for what I can find.

It is a pity there is no one else in the mountains who would want to make the trip down to the lake, and none by the lake who want to risk the forest. They are all content to make their money closer to home.

Astrid

It is only on this final leg of the trip that I am able to get Harnermêŝ to open up about what I saw to the south of Gil-Gand-Rask. The reality of him leaving his home behind has finally sunk in as he sails up a vast river for over a week, and appearing and growing to his right, the range of mountains can be seen as they march endlessly northward.

As we come north, welcome snow, welcome to me at least, is now appearing on the tops of them, even in summer. I have been using Goditha to help me talk to him, but I need Theodora to translate, as I don't want to miss any of this. It seems that even the Princess is showing surprise at what is being revealed.

"What you saw," he said, "was a town of the sea nomads, the Kanak. When you were first seen it was thought that you might have been one of their ships, as we allow them to build some like yours on our island. However, we soon knew you could not be one of them, as you did not know the entrance channels and all of their ships have charts through our reefs to come in to see us."

"It is said that they grow islands out of seaweeds, and make gardens on them from timber, and then they sail these around the world. They never touch land with these islands, but trade with their ships. I think this is true according to what I saw, as I have been on some of their islands…their ships, and even speak some of their language."

"We…Gil-Gand-Rask, that is…are the only people in this part of the world that they openly talk to."

"What do you mean, 'in this part of the world'?"

"They tell tales of other lands," replied Harnermês. *He is still being evasive.*

I remember what we saw in the books. "Such as one that goes nearly from ice in the north to ice in the south, and one that never sees rain?" *I guess that I need to go and re-read them all, probably with Olympias, and take notes. Mind you, on my first read I thought that the mention in them of towns had just meant very large boats, not real towns.*

Harnermês wrinkled his brow. "They talk a lot about the first one, but I have never heard mention of the second one, but there could be one because they do not go far from the sea and there is one land which only presents cliffs to the sea, and so they never land." He paused. "How do you know about them?"

Astrid and Theodora looked at each other. "We learnt from the books that we took from the Masters. We like to learn things, as much as we can, and one day we may have to go to these places as it seems that perhaps the Masters were interested in them."

Chapter XXXIII

Astrid
32nd Primus

It seems that I will have less work before me as a matchmaker than I first thought. We have arrived home in the valley to the announcement that there are two weddings already in the offing and that the people involved are only waiting for the Princesses to arrive for the ceremonies to take place.

It seems that Aine and Dulcie have made their decisions. Aine will be marrying Aaron, to no one's surprise, and Dulcie has chosen Jordan and the men have agreed with the decision of the women.

There is some disappointment among the women that we have returned with four more women, but only two men, and one of them is spoken for already. The other two men left behind are not yet fully committed, but Elizabeth and Thomas seem to be paying attention to each other.

In addition, to the surprise of everyone, Arthur is paying court to Make… and Make seems to be responding. It is hard to tell with Make. It seems that her discovering that she can step outside herself with the dulcimer has made a big difference to her. It has made her grow inside.

As well it seems that people will not let Goditha and her skills out of the valley again for some time to come. All of the people with building experience in the village will be needed to work on the restoring of houses, workshops, and even the barracks and the school. What is more, everyone who has experienced a bathhouse wants our own as soon as we can have it.

Rani

*A*lthough there is no pattern of the Masters known to be there, I have decided that Wolfneck has to be the next visit on our agenda. There may be no pattern, but it seems that we keep finding references to it as a hub of communication, and to close it off we will not have to look far.

Importantly, we already know who to look for when we get there. Not only that, but we might obtain important information from this Svein, who Astrid talks about, about the two of the last areas that we know we have to go to in The Land, Freehold and the Brotherhood...both of which present their own special challenges, and that we know very little about.

The communication issue I regard as the most important. It is a nexus, and without strong magical devices to speak at a distance, messengers are still needed, and some seem to go there, for some reason.

What is more, we thought that we had largely dealt with what was happening in Haven when we executed Conrad, but when we arrived, we discovered that the Masters had a strong presence there again...or still. Like a hydra, the servants of our enemies seem to be able to sprout back into place even after they are beheaded.

I sometimes regret the way that we went about what we did in Pavitra Phāṭaka. Perhaps we should have tried to keep some of the people that were there alive to question, although, as it is, we nearly lost one of our people, or thinking of Father Christopher's actions in returning Ayesha to us, perhaps even two.

Maybe the regrowth of the evil that we fight will at least slow down now that we have eliminated the patterns in Haven, the Swamp, and on the island. That has to have hurt the Masters to at least some extent.

Astrid

*A*strid lay late in her own bed...*a bed and not a hammock*...and considered her options for Father Simeon's wife. *I wonder if I can look at one of the women who is not already Christian. No, I will lay that idea aside.*

None of them have shown the slightest interest in converting so far, and that is not something that can be forced, although perhaps I can sound out Shilpa, she has not made much noise either way on religion.

I think that I can, for the moment at least, leave out of contention the women that we have just brought into the valley, and I obviously can ignore

Jennifer and possibly even Adara in that regard, anyway.

So, by the look of things, I am left with Maria, Danelis and Tabitha...and I was so sure that Danelis would have been taken before now. I think that it will be best to sit each of the girls down and to see what they are looking for in a man...and if they are actually looking. Some people do not want a partner after all.

As well, it will take a special woman to marry a werewolf, especially knowing from his family history, that her children will have a good chance of being born as lycanthropes. That would mean problems for them in most places that I know of.

Whoever marries him will get a priest as a husband, and I can get Bianca and Ruth to talk to them about that role...if they have questions on that score.

Astrid chuckled to herself as she lay there in bed lazily speculating. *I once thought that I was going to be a hunter or a caravan guard. Of all of the roles that I could possibly have pictured that I would be in when I left home, being the longest married woman in a village—and its matchmaker—is not one of them. I am having fun with it, but I did not expect it.*

Astrid
34th Primus

The next day four people, two men and two women, all riding and with a string of four pack animals behind them, were seen on the Mousehole road. They had company with them, a file of Basilica Anthropoi, led by Praetor Michael.

Their smoke had been seen the day before, and there had been no attempt made by them to hide. They had just waved at Verily flying by on a passing saddle, but had continued on their way without expecting anyone to stop.

When I checked with a telescope, all four are older and the men are both armed, but even on the road and travelling, they have the look of priests. The women may have short bows tucked under their saddle girths, but they look like they will be more at home in a village rather than a battle. It looks very much like Metropolitan Basil's missionaries for the Hobgoblins have finally found their way into the mountains.

We may have asked them to come, but the soldiers will spread word of us when they return to their home. We need to show that we are strong...so I wait for them on a saddle at the valley gate and our four Khitan wait on horses. The military and the Khitan are looking at each other. These are the first foreign military to have been allowed in to the valley, and our Khitan are not quite sure how to react.

Bianca greeted them in the name of her husband, and they were conducted further into the valley to the village itself. At the village gate are the village priests and a crowd of curious onlookers. For the boys from the school, in particular, the Basilica Anthropoi are an eye-opener. Even Menas, although he came from Darkreach, had not seen their like.

Their local cavalry in the south were all kynigoi, the light scouts and skirmishers of the Empire. The kataphractoi were for open plains and grasslands. They were of little use in the jungles and in the mountain passes, and these riders were closest to them in the way they were armed and equipped.

The girls were less interested in what they saw. Those with martial interests were far more interested in Ayesha and Astrid, and the way that they fought, as their models than they were in the more conventional military.

Now we get to show them our hospitality. The priestly party have their animals taken from them and they are ushered inside. Michael and his men are shown the stable area set aside for their use, although their priest joins the others. We realise that, like Khitan, the guards will prefer to look after their own mounts.

The wives are taken aside by Ruth and Bianca and apprised of what they are getting into, and Zamrat is brought out of school to answer any questions that they may have.

Theodule

*I*t is time for what I have been writing down to actually be used. Tomorrow, the start of the first basic Hobgoblin dictionary, with its dedication to Saint Cyril and Methodius, goes on its way. With it goes a letter of introduction, a map, and instructions on how to paint themselves…and that is so important for a first-time visitor. They even have a large pot of paint made from ash and fat that we have made for them.

They had a promise that they would be flown over, and an eye kept on their progress. The Cenubarkincilari will also be told that they were coming. They are eagerly waiting on it, and I was, to be honest, getting exhausted with catering to two flocks so far apart.

I was also able to give them the good news that Dindarqoyun will probably go back with the troops to Greensin to train to become a priest. He is wavering, and with the right encouragement, seems ready to convert.

This is a matter of great excitement for all of us, as if it happens, it signals the effective end of the original faith of this Hobgoblin tribe. It will take some time for him to study and learn, but imagine what it would be like to have a Hobgoblin return as an ordained priest to the tribe.

However tolerant they might be of other religions, every priest of any faith wants eventually to see their own belief triumphant. As such, the conversion of the last druid apprentice in the tribe would mark a signal victory for the Orthodox priests. Without them even having to push, the rest of the tribe would invariably follow along behind him in the fullness of time.

Stefan
35th Primus

I *have looked at the new people in the village and what they can do with weapons. I am glad that both Jennifer and Vishal are actually quite good with what they use. Jennifer is very good. She has made her living at being a guard for a few years after all. Adara is about as good as Bryony was…a hunter more than an armsman.*

He was thinking about what to train the others in, and when he went out for a stint as the outside sentry, he was a little surprised to find that his wife and her cousin were coming along unannounced as well, bringing Aneurin with them.

They have a basket with them as well as their weapons. Bryony seems nervous, as if there is something she wants to talk about, but I realise that it will be best to allow things to come out as they may, rather than prompt for them. By not pushing things, and by waiting, I did bring her to marriage after all. Adara seems to be very tense as well.

They reached the lookout and accepted the handover, relieving Basil who prepared to return inside, giving Stefan a raised eyebrow as he left. Stefan just shrugged in answer, a communication that all husbands understand. Once he was gone, Stefan went through the routines of the new watch person, searching the horizon and nearby.

I am not going to neglect my duty in any way for what might be about to happen. He carefully looked all around. There is some quiet whispering going on behind me, not normal conversation, but it seems to be something they do not want me to hear.

Eventually it all goes quiet. I finished my fixed searches some time before, but now the two must have had time to decide who will speak to me. He turned. The girls are sitting beside each other on the bench, holding hands nervously.

"Stefan," said Bryony nervously. "I want you to hear out what Adara says, please. If, when we all go back inside the valley, your answer to what she asks is no, then there will be no more said. Until then, I ask that you will please be quiet and let us speak unless you have urgent questions that you must ask and cannot wait." Stefan nodded. *Am I allowed to say yes to that?*

Adara cleared her throat. *It is her turn to be nervous, and after a pause, speak.* "I didn't follow the same path of marriage that Bryony did, but there was a reason for it. My first love, when I was younger, much younger, was not a man. It was another girl...in fact, it was Bryony, and she loved me back for many years.

"However, after a time, she met Conan and she loved him more than she loved me, and so she chose him, and they were married" *She looks sad as she says that.* "And you know the rest of that. He was her first real male love, and she loved him then a lot more than she loved me.

"I do like men, but I like women as well, and indeed more than I like men... and I like Bryony a lot more than I have ever liked anyone else. Although I have had others, both men and women, I have never had another real love since I lost your wife to marriage...her first marriage that is." She paused and cleared her throat nervously.

I am trying hard to keep a non-committal expression on my face, but from the face of the girls, it may be a bit stern. I really am not sure where this conversation is going, and I am also not sure if I really want to know. I can see several futures ahead here and most of them are not very good from my point of view. I must be patient and wait and, oh Lord...I pray to Saint Dwynen for aid.

Adara drew a deep breath, glanced at Bryony, and then continued. "I realised that I had lost my life's love, and I was looking for something more than I had been left with when I was scooped up by our late unlamented friend, Glyn.

"Selling me was how he got some of the money you took from him, you could even call some of what you gathered from him my dowry. Finding Bryony again makes me realise how much I missed her, and how much I still love her. I should not have let her marry Conan without putting up more of a fight for her."

She is looking at Bryony, and my wife has tears starting to appear in the corner of her eyes. She is nervously biting on her lower lip, looking at Adara, and then at me, and back again. "She is torn. She has come to love you, but she realises that she also still loves me."

Bryony is now nodding, and the tears are starting to slowly make trails, un-noticed by her, down her beautiful cheeks. I have come to realise that I love her as well, and just want to rush to her and comfort her...hold still, you idiot.

"We have agreed that, if you say no to what I am about to say, I will go away from here and you will never hear about this again from either of us, because she has made promises to you and not to me." Adara drew a deep breath. *I suppose that this is where I find out what they have in mind. I hope that it includes me.*

"I want to stay with you both. I don't pretend to love you now, but if my love loves you this much, I am sure that I can learn to love you as well. I am also willing to leave my faith. It hasn't done us much good after all, and I will become a Christian and marry you.

"If you accept me into your family, however, you must realise though, that I will make love to Bryony at least as much as I will make love to you...but I also promise that neither will I turn you away from me in any way. What do you say? Can you share us? Can we all be happy together? Please?"

'Sblood. That gives me pause. I have no problem with women loving each other. I had better not in this village. What can I say? While Adara was speaking, what I really feared was that the two women were going to move in together, ignoring me, or perhaps even move away from Mousehole to leave me on my own, with or without my son.

I suppose that it will cut both ways. I will have to share Bryony, but then she will have to share me as well. Of course, just like my wife, Adara is very beautiful...I wonder if she is just as freckled? She is also good with Aneurin already, and she will probably make a good mother herself one day.

He looked at them both. *Sitting on the bench in front of me are two very beautiful women awaiting my answer. They are sitting there holding hands and huddled together in total misery. I must look very grim indeed, and they are obviously fully expecting me to reject what has been said, and so blight their happiness forever.*

I don't know anything that goes on behind their door, but Norbert, Sājah and Fortunata seem to be very happy together as a family. They certainly make it work. Even though it is outside anything in my past, and my parents will have kittens over it...it is not my parents who have an investment in this marriage.

If we all grow to love each other, there is no reason that this will not work for the three of us as well as it does for Norbert's family...or for any married couple. It will, at any rate, be up to us to make it work and no one else. I am sure that all marriages, in the end, are like that at least.

I wish that I could speak to Norbert for some advice on this, but I have been given a time limit. Oh well, it is time to decide. He moved towards them. *If anything, they look even more scared.* He tried to moisten his throat and speak.

"Can you both stand please?" They stood, leaving Aneurin asleep behind them. *Despite them being only cousins, they really are very nearly twins in so many ways. They are exactly the same size and, as far as I can tell with never having seen Adara naked, almost exactly the same shape, both very pale, both with freckles and green eyes and both with masses of red hair.*

To a casual glance, the only way to tell them apart is that Adara has much longer hair when it is not curled up tight as it was now. Mind you, I think that I am starting to recognise the patterns of freckles on their noses. He turned to Adara.

"Come, my betrothed, if that is what my wife wants, I think that it is time for you to give me a kiss, and then I guess you had better kiss your sister wife...I think that is what Sãjah and Fortunata call each other."

It is now my turn to be confused...having committed herself to marrying me, Adara does not seem to hold any reservations in her approach to me, and just like my Bryony, she tastes a little of cinnamon and other spices...and she is as voracious a kisser.

When they had eventually parted, she turned and kissed Bryony in the same enthusiastic fashion. *That is a bit of a surprise. I was expecting to feel a little jealous. Instead of that, I am actually feeling a strong sense of arousal just watching them. Maybe this will work out well. It is just as well that we have a big bed already.*

He then kissed Bryony as well. *They taste a little different, but not by much. Now I am definitely aroused, and I still have a full watch to put in.* "Well, what do we do now?" he asked as he held them both. *One woman is tucked under each of my arms. At the same time, I can feel that their hands are clasped both behind and in front of me.*

It turns out that, although the girls actually expected the worst, they hoped and planned for this result and we have a small celebration meal in the basket. I think that we had better all go and see Father Christopher as soon as I finish this watch.

As they ate, Stefan thought about his decision, and its ramifications, as he sat with a hand from each woman twined together as one on his lap. *Yes. I think that we can make this work. Admittedly it will be very interesting, explaining the way that things are to my parents.*

At least they should be happy with the possibility of even more grand-children...even if the circumstances are...unusual. Even more, and I had better not ever say this aloud, I am going to be very unlikely to ever have any incentive to stray with another woman.

Christopher

*W*hat with three marriages to arrange, and having to make sure that the
missionaries are settled, it will be a little while before we can set out
again. I have to impress that on the Princesses. We could have left on the tenth
of Secundus, but then Christmas will only be a few days off on the thirteenth,
so perhaps we should wait until the day after that. Hopefully then we can be
home in time for the Feast of the Magi and Twelfth Night.

Ayesha

*L*akshmi and I need to talk to this new girl, this Zeenat. She is staying quiet
and avoiding training in weapons as much as she can. It is time for that
to change.

"Lakshmi tells me that you were once a prostitute." *Embarrassed, the girl is
looking down at the ground. By Allah, the Compassionate, has she not listened
to the history of most of the women here? Her life has just started again.*

"Do not let that worry you," Ayesha waved dismissively. "We were
wondering…Lakshmi learned many useful things outside the bedchamber when
she was working in Pavitra Phāṭaka, and she did the same work that you used
to do. We want to know what you learnt. We want to see how you move, and
how you can use knives."

They were shown. *Zeenat is to be added to Basil's and my training group.
She moves well.*

Rani

*E*ventually, I have managed to have the two new Havenite girls brought in
to be tested for magic, along with the others we brought back. I should
have thought of this earlier. I asked Parminder to get them to agree.

*The little girl is one of the most stubborn and determined people that I
have ever met, and once she sets her mind upon a goal, it can be counted as
being certain, even if there is an elephant in the way. She should have been
named after Ganesh.*

*Both of the Hindu girls show potential as mages, and despite their object-
ions that they are not worthy to do so, they will be added to the list of apprentice*

mages. Zeenat, in particular, will become very busy I hear. Apart from those two, none of the other new arrivals show any promise.

I am becoming convinced that Haven is wasting something precious by ignoring those they regard as the lower castes. Is there any way for them to change what they do, and how they treat the lower castes?

I cannot think of any means of doing it without entirely destroying their way of life. By becoming so set in their customs, it is as if they have reached a dead end. They came so far, and now can go no further along that path without devastating what they have built.

Theodora
10th Secundus

Waiting meant that other things such as happen to normal villages had a chance to occur, and Carausius came back for another trip to trade with them and to also bring gifts, news and letters. She sighed deeply.

The gifts include the first two men to be sent to our village by Imam Iyād, and as if to counter them, four women who were sent by Metropolitan Tarasios who, it seems, had been told of the women that Iyād had rescued, and not to be outdone, has sent us three of his own flock who have experienced misfortune of one kind or another.

They are a very mixed group of men and women. The Muslim men are both older men and have lost their families. The older of the two, Asad ibn Sayf, a farmer, originally from the village of Doro on the eastern side of the mountains behind them, has lost his entire extended family through one of the last outbreaks of The Burning only a couple of years ago.

He has at least been given a pair of oxen, a plough and a small flock of mountain sheep to bring with him. They must have slowed Carausius' passage considerably.

The younger, Atā ibn Rāfi, is originally from Mistledross, in the south of Darkreach where he practiced the trade of timber cutting and sawing. He lost his family in a collapsed building in one of the earthquakes, which the southwest of Darkreach occasionally suffers. This one had been very bad, and the town was devastated.

Even I heard about it. It was so bad that many of the survivors did not want to try and rebuild when they had lost so much. His possessions fit on a single packhorse. Although not young men, both are still young enough to start another family. They are already causing more than a small amount of interest among the Muslim women of our village.

Of the women, Loukia Tzetzina had just become a journeyman woodworker when she lost her family to the same earthquake that had claimed the family of Atã. She is one of those who afterwards left the town. She has come with her friends: Zoë Anicia, a journeyman baker, and Verina Gabalas, a journeyman miller both of them with the same story.

They had all arrived in Ardlark to discover that, without more money than they had or at least without some connections, none of them could set up a business. Although attractive, none are really beautiful, and so even the option of selling themselves was not really a good one.

While it is hard for someone to actually starve in Darkreach, they were slowly getting poorer and poorer as casual workers, and starting to look at selling themselves when the Metropolitan decided to send them to Mousehole.

Verina has, as a gift from her sponsor, two halves of stone cut to make a small mill on one packhorse and Loukia and Zoë's tools occupy another. At least we need the skills that they bring, if not them as women.

The last girl, Ariadne Nepos, is most likely going to be the only unattractive woman in our village. She is an Insakharl and her Kharl heritage, from her size and strength to her brown skin with dark-green highlights, and even with tusks, is obviously Alat-kharl. She is bright for all that, and has a good measure of her artisan heritage and is a maker and layer of bricks and tiles.

Her parents were makers of fire weapons in Antdrudge and they were both lost in one of the many accidents that plague that industry. She had been on her way to learning to be a military engineer when, after their death, she had changed careers to something that she had always wanted to do. She is one girl who could have made a good living as she is in Darkreach.

Fortunately for us, she is restless. She saw us Mice when we were there, and listened eagerly to the stories that are already surrounding us. These had made her even more restless. She was looking for a way to find her way to the west, and was eager to leap at this one when she had eventually found Carausius. She has not been sent…she has brought herself. I hope that we do not disappoint her.

Aine

*A*t last we have a proper baker for Mousehole. Zoë was quickly taken away by Aine, and even before her friends noticed her absence, she was already being shown her new domain beside that of Aine next to the village wall.

The workshop bakehouse is already being used, and the roof is snug and secure so it can all be used, but the rest of the building is still just an empty shell. Still, it is far more than she could ever have hoped for in Darkreach.

She has taken one look at the generous kneading trough and the tables, and went quickly to fetch her clothes, paddles and loaf moulds from where their packs had been put. I like her already. Greetings and being shown around can wait until tonight. Men and the future can wait as well.

She has a lot of work to do in order to have fresh bread ready for everyone tomorrow, and that is all that matters to her for the present. Her main concern now is that her carefully tended yeasts in their sealed pots have survived their long trip. At least our local sourdough is a good one.

Theodora

*A*lthough it is still small, our little village now has over sixty free adults living in it. With eighteen young ones here for the schooling and the new children, it will not be long before we have a hundred people living here. In fact, even without any new arrivals… Theodora unconsciously rubbed her stomach …*the next round of pregnancies will probably get us to reach that point.*

Mousehole has grown and changed a lot over the last year and a bit. No longer is it a hidden bandit den with a few oppressed slaves living in fear and silence. It has a certain vibrancy and life in it, singing is often heard as people work and the sounds of happy children are a frequent background sound to what goes on here.

Basil

*C*arausius has become aware of his animal handler's designs on Theodora Lígo, but then she was not adverse to the idea, and Carausius is clear to me that he thinks his worker is a little more than he seems and that he thought this enhanced his prospects, after all…and he nudged me confidentially… *look at the rank that I have from my work.*

I sometimes wonder just how secret the secret police really are. It doesn't seem to be hard to work out who is likely to be one, at least one who is senior or fairly active, even Ayesha had been easy to discern as not being what she had said she was as soon as she tried to do anything that did not fit exactly with her cover.

It applies on all sides though. Look at how few professional thieves there really are, in Darkreach, if not in Haven. It seems that all it takes in an open society is acquaintance and the possibility that there might be someone around who is not what they seem to be to work out that someone is either a criminal or a lawman.

Perhaps Carausius might not have realised Candidas' role if he had not been aware of mine. Oh well, He is likely to be a safe person to know the secret anyway…especially if he does become Candidas' father-in-law, unless his pride makes him boast to someone, and he is not likely to want to endanger his trade connection to us.

The dispatches that came with him told the story of the location of the Master's pattern in Antdrudge, and how following up on it had led to a network of corruption and possible treachery in the whole organisation to do with the production of the fire weapons…and with undeclared links to the west.

It seems that Darkreach has not realised that they have been exporting a lot more molotails than they had known of for many years. The whole network has not been closed down yet and Strategos Panterius is asking me when I think it will be a good time to strike.

Basil thought on this and wrote out what had occurred since the last time, with an emphasis on the events in Gil-Gand-Rask and Haven, and the likelihood that there was an attempt being made to re-establish a series of powerful patterns.

I need to point out that we are about to fly north to take out one end of the message and smuggling chain at Wolfneck, and that now might be the time to hit their contacts at the other end of the line in Darkreach…before they grow wary and try to hide or cover their tracks.

He emphasised that even once a pattern was cleared, it would be a good idea for the priests who have learnt the locating spell to do regular checks in every location to see if another had been created somewhere nearby.

Rani

*I*t has not taken long for me to realise that it is just as well that my wife insisted on everyone in the village learning Darkspeech as one of our basic tongues. With the places people are coming from, it will soon be the most common language in our polyglot village…although every tongue can be heard here, and the children at the school seem to be, despite Ruth's best efforts, establishing their own argot out of everything they are exposed to.

Their trade words are mostly Hindi, the religious ones are Greek or Arabic, those used for building are Latin, those for hunting and some of the trades are Faen and Darkspeech, while anything remotely to do with domestic animals uses words that are Khitan. Those for war are Darkspeech and Dwarven.

Words from Bearen, Hobgoblin, Sowonja and other tongues are scattered through it seemingly at random. Already they have made up their own grammar and only the young ones can follow each other's speech as they switch languages four or five times in one sentence. To them it is all a game and a fun one at that. I wonder what will come of this.

Theodora

*A**tã will be starting to clear some of the timber outside the valley, rather than destroy the woods that are within, and Asad, after checking with me if this is allowed, has decided to ask him to clear an area he has looked at, so that he can farm outside the valley below the road in the direction of the Bear people.*

He wants land of his own to pass on to his children, and the good land is starting to fill up in the lower valley itself, and it is now regarded as common land anyway and the top meadow is only suited to summer grazing.

There is plenty of land outside the valley and it is not hard to walk out to go to work. Asad says that it is just the same as walking out of a walled village to work in the fields that surround it. I suppose that he is right in that. He seems not to be worried by the hard work of making a new farm or of being exposed.

He will take his bow and spear with him each day, and he will be building something again. He also expects that others will soon join him and indeed, on hearing his intent, Arthur declared that he will be doing the same, and that with the two of them working on clearing for each other, it will make it easier for both of them.

Verina is looking around the whole valley for the best place for her to set up a permanent mill to work in. Apparently the first thing that she has to decide is whether to use wind or water to drive the mill. I know nothing about these things, but apparently, I am supposed to give advice. I will just keep nodding and seeming to be deep in thought.

It seems that each has its advantages. I do know that, seeing that we are all currently grinding flour by hand in querns, the villagers are all hoping that she will not take very long to work this out and to get set up. Everyone is well and truly sick of having to do that backbreaking work.

I am excited to discover that we now have a timber cutter in the village. It gave me the chance to unveil what Dulcie has been working on for me since before we left for Haven and I have just finished casting for. It was prompted by Astrid using the carpet to carry a log. It has taken me nearly a week of casting, and Dulcie has been working on it for far longer, but I am able to unveil something that is even more unlikely looking than my saddles, if that is possible.

It sort of looked like the skeleton of a dray, with a flat floor, but it had no draw bar and no wheels. The uprights could be tipped or folded away from it in order to roll something on to it and whatever it held could be tied down.

The whole thing will, if someone is keeping hold of it, or even if they are riding on a small platform at its front, fly at the speed of a very slow walk while it is holding several tonnes. It stops exactly where it is if you let go. It is perfect for carrying timber or stone around the area…and it will save the poor carpet.

Ariadne timidly asked if anyone could use it. Of course…a brick-maker cannot make bricks and tiles without clay, and there is not enough in the valley that is useful and that which is now coming down from the upper valley is apparently better for pots than for construction. She will have to find a new supply and bring it in from somewhere outside. With the use of the sky-dray, she can even look for deposits that are not at ground level.

The girl started going out when the hunters went out and while they sought game, she looked at the ground. On the first of those expeditions she took along a rope and a large satchel, and it was found that they had someone who could keep teaching what Thord had started, in terms of climbing, when he was not there.

Rani

*N*ow that I have some more free time, who do we take with us into the north? Astrid and Basil are going, of course, as are my wife and I. One advantage of waiting before going out again is that Astrid will have enough time to finish weaning the children so that, for once, they will not be going into danger with her.

Olympias has volunteered to take them on the ship, but I have decided that Valeria will be caring for them in the village. When we leave, we will take all of the saddles, so there will be little chance to communicate.

This leaves me to work out who will be the other six to go. Astrid has convinced me that, given the folklore of her people, Father Simeon might be of more use in Wolfneck than Father Christopher. He is not as strong in the faith, but there will be no pattern to get rid of that we knew of, and hopefully, there will be few casualties.

That means that Bianca can stay home as well. Stefan can bring his new wife Adara with him. To the rest of us, she and Bryony seem to be interchangeable nowadays, something that is not helped by Adara looking after Aneurin as much as Bryony does, and by the two women wearing each other's clothes.

I am not sure that I understand that relationship fully. Do the girls like men or women? It is very confusing to an outsider. At least they all seem to be happy together and that is the important thing, after all.

Hulagu and Ayesha will both come, they are both formidable as mounted archers and lastly, I think that Shilpa can come, and perhaps Vishal. Why should Astrid have all of the fun in matchmaking? The new girls are going to take a long time to wean away from the idea of an appropriate caste relationship.

Shilpa is well beyond that, and as the last original Havenite in Mousehole without a partner, deserves the first try at him if she wants it. She is older than him, but not by that many years. Rani was chagrined to be approached by Astrid with exactly the same idea before she could say anything.

At least Astrid has said that she will get to work and get him dressed ready to go. The cotton lungi, the kilt, and pyjama trousers that he wears, and are all that he has, lack even a shirt, and even in summer the nights can be cool in the north.

He needs at least a kurta to go on his top with the pyjama and indeed, just some northern clothes...something warm...and boots. He cannot go just with sandals or bare feet. He may end up dressed in an odd mix of styles, but at least he should be warm.

Unfortunately, Astrid had to remind me that Simeon and Vishal couldn't use the saddles. However, with a grin she had pointed out how Vishal could go the whole way with his arms around Shilpa on the same saddle. She had thought ahead. If we take both Danelis and Maria, they can share Simeon between them.

They are both small enough to carry him, and he is not little, on a saddle. As well that will give us two mage apprentices, Hulagu and Maria. The apprentice mages each only have one real spell apiece, but it could still be useful if we need support. Also, Danelis can use a hammer and shield, and Maria can use a horse bow, and Ayesha will be there anyway with her skills.

Without trade goods, babies or luxuries, we can just fit thirteen people onto the ten saddles. "Having a man's arms hanging tight around her waist, with him close behind her, or with the girl on his lap, and his head on her shoulder for a whole day will have to give the girls an idea if the man is interested in them," said Astrid with a grin.

"When they land, if the man isn't interested, then they will not have been trying very hard. If need be, we can get Maria and Danelis to toss a coin and see who gets first try at the priest. I will talk with them."

Chapter XXXIV

Rani
14th Secundus

I *have decided to make the trip to Wolfneck in three stages with two stops on the way. We will not arrive tired. The first leg is the long one to the northwest from Mousehole to Greensin that we have taken several times before. At least this time we have saddles rather than the far slower carpet.*

It is there that we will see the Metropolitan, Basil Tornikes, and introduce his new priest to him. Several months ago, he also promised to give us a letter to take to Father Simon in Wolfneck, instructing that he give his co-operation to us when we needed it. Finally, it has come time for us to ask him for it.

As they were close to passing high over Evilhalt, Astrid swung over, and loudly and innocently asked Stefan if he wanted them to pause briefly, and drop in so that he could introduce his new bride to his parents. *I was about to say something to object to this introduced diversion, but Stefan has hurriedly said no and taken on a faint blush.*

Adara smiled, and gave him a kiss from where she rode behind him. *Astrid did that quite deliberately. She was expecting him to say no, and was trying to see how he would do it. Astrid is also trying to work out exactly what is happening in that family. Unlike me, she has both no shame about this curiosity, and an almost total lack of inhibition to go with it.*

Simeon
15th Secundus

It is odd to no longer be celebrating the Feast Day of Saint Denys, but my new Church has never even heard of him. I have now met the Metropolitan and apprised him of my antecedents. I am relieved that he so quickly pronounced that, although such a priest was unheard of, as far as he knew, the matter was one of faith.

He said that if the person is truly good, and that cannot be doubted with so many priests and monks around to sense if it were otherwise, then what is important is a person's faith, not their heritage. I have already accepted the faith of Darkreach—which land I was brought up to think of as the enemy. How different can it be to accept as simple a thing as a being of a different race—admittedly one he was not used to accepting as one of his flock?

"That is good," said Simeon. "You should soon have a Hobgoblin here as a student priest when the cavalry return, and Aziz is in two minds as to whether he wants to take up the cloth as well." *I am glad to see that, although he has sent missionaries to them, the idea of a priestly candidate coming so soon is a shock to the Metropolitan.*

He is pleased that two of the men that he had sent are already married, and the third appears to be well on the way to that state. On the other hand, he is alarmed over the deception that had been practiced upon them by Ulric, and has hurriedly produced the letter for Wolfneck.

It seems to have been written for some time, and awaited but a signature and a date. I have been instructed, in no uncertain terms, to render all assistance to the Mice, and am given the power to threaten excommunication to any who stand in their way.

Theodora

It may be too late perhaps, but I now realise that perhaps it had not been a good idea to talk to the Metropolitan about the girls arriving from Darkreach. I can already see him going over in his mind the number of girls lately who had been made orphans, and wondering which ones from here might also be sent east.

He can see one of his flock...one who has experienced such a loss...in front of him as a possible partner of his newest priest, and he has realised that circumstances might offer less for them in the home villages of the girls.

I have tried to repair matters by stressing that the girls must fit in with those already there in terms of their attractiveness and other attributes, but I am not too sure of the effect of that. My husband has also realised my error and she is giving me a look.

I need to change tack and get his mind on other things. I will talk about the school and what we intend with it. That, at least, proves to be a good distraction, and I can see that at least he has now started thinking along the very different lines of the children who can profitably be sent to Mousehole instead of more women.

Rani
16th Secundus

*W*hen we set off for North Hole, we return towards the mountains and fly just north of east on the second leg of our trip. It is not quite as long as the first leg, but North Hole, a Dwarven village, is located in the mountains of the north near Lake Orroral.

Apart from Thord's occasional comments about its ruler, Baron Cnut Stone- cleaver, and its layout, we know little about it. I suspect that the village will already be smaller than it used to be, due to the number of Dwarves that are leaving all of the settlements to go to Dwarvenholme.

I wonder on the effect that will have. From the air it is easy to find the village inside its hill to the south of the lake. It has some fields about it as well, and is one of the few clearings we have seen in the forest up to this point.

Thord is right. Upon entering the village, it is easy to see that there is a similarity in concept to Dwarvenholme, and even to Kharlsbane, that can be readily observed. After talking to the guard to the right of the entrance, they left the saddles in the stables to the left and continued along the corridor to the concourse.

Although it is also round, it is far smaller across than that in Dwarvenholme. It is also only two levels tall, although it is deep enough down to allow them to add more if they want. What is more, there are many gaps in the circles among the trades and shops. Many are gaps that look very recent. Marks can be seen on the walls and floor where things have been removed and taken away.

Despite this, there is an atmosphere of excitement, and you would have thought that they are growing rather than losing people, but losing people they are. Even as we are being shown in to the Baron, a group of dwarves can be seen packing goods into packs to be put on ponies that will soon leave, presumably for the long trip south.

Far from being despondent, the Baron is actually jovial towards us as assistants to the great dwarf Thord in his finding of Dwarvenholme. Theodora smiled to herself. *I have always suspected that this is how tales and legends came to be, and how we come to have differing accounts of events. The listeners only hear what they want to hear and ignore or downplay the rest.*

In a few generations, we Humans and Insakharl might disappear from the Dwarven stories entirely, and only Thord will be left in the tale, or we may change to being Dwarves in the Dwarven version of the stories.

Just as towns seem to change their names over the cycle of ages, I wonder what my Dwarven name will become, or if seeing that we already have similar names, if Thord and I will become the same person in the tales. How they will explain the spell-casting shepherd, I don't know. For some reason spell-casters are far rarer among the Dwarves than they are among other races.

Baron Cnut is not pleased to hear that the menace of the Masters may not be fully dissipated. He is eager to suggest that the Mice should come around to check his area for signs that the Masters may be attempting to take over his village.

I have promised to get Father Christopher to eventually do a tour of the whole area to check and see if they are trying to return to the Dwarven areas. Thinking of it…it is something that their enemy seems to be trying to do, and so, spending some time checking over the supposedly clear areas might well be a good idea to catch them before they get themselves established somewhere else.

Chapter XXXV

Astrid
17th Secundus

*T*he next day we head north. First, we go over the lake, and then we follow the Methul River downstream towards the sea. I came south to the west of here. The Methul rises in the slopes of the Darkreach Gap and ends in the Northern Ocean at Wolfneck. Most of the people who live in The Land don't even know of it and yet it is one of their great rivers.

I have only been this way once before, but I know my way. At first, the path north from North Hole goes over forests that soon clear into vast heath lands that lie between river and mountains. As we fly, we go over the herds of mammoth, and the many other types of the animals of the cold lands that can be seen beneath us. Eventually, we rejoin the river on the flat lands to the west, as the mountains curved east towards their end. I have missed these lands.

Often, particularly after we pass where the Bowyanga River joins the Methul from the mountains, the river seems to almost disappear into vast cold swamps as it winds through numerous small lakes and over the flat ground. To the west, the forest has become an endless expanse of pines with little in the way of gaps.

When I fly us near enough to one of these gaps, it is to find yet another small lake in it. At least they can see now why my people rarely used horses. There is so little clear and solid ground around for them to travel on. The path back to the south sometimes disappears completely, and it is apparent that travellers must often make their own tracks, and in summer will have to sometimes travel over fallen timber instead of on dry land.

Eventually, the river reappears from the morass as large clumps of trees reappear on the east of the river, and the boreal forest begins to take over the whole landscape. The endless green sea that I am used to…all the same trees…the same colours.

I am flying lower and lower, eventually just clearing the pines as I make them travel in single file. I have the lead well ahead of the others, but make sure that others were keeping watch to the sides. There could be Rangers anywhere out here, and they watch the sky as much as they watch the ground. I am heading up the right-hand side of the river, on the opposite side to Wolfneck and its cleared land. There are fewer outlying hamlets here.

When the first clearing appeared in the tree tops on the west of the river, and before the farm within it could be seen, I have slowly brought them down under the canopy, and for the rest of our travel we will move at the same height as a horseman and will slow down our speed.

She had the mounted archers fly with an arrow knocked. *Although to the others, the endless trees with an occasional outcrop of rocks will all look the same, I know exactly where I am and where I am headed.* Eventually she came to a dense thicket of larch, and she rose higher over brambles and fallen timber before bringing them down to a halt near one of those outcroppings of rock in a clearing in the centre of the thicket.

"If you listen you can hear an axe… We are only about two hands of chains to the east of Wolfneck and directly across the Methul, so you will need to stay fairly quiet and you can light no fires. I want you to all stay here. You can eat and rest safely here. Few come across the river unless they are Rangers on patrol."

She looked around. *They are all listening to me.* "Try and avoid killing any Rangers if they come near you…use a sleep spell if you can, as most of them are friends of mine. I will take Ayesha on one saddle, and find a spot near the village to land. Then, with the Metropolitan's letter, I will try to find Father Simon and scout out what is happening.

"Ayesha has her ring and can disappear when I leave her. I will wear mine as well…and I will know where she is. I will come back to her once I have been into the village, and we will return and tell you what is happening, then we can plan what to do from there."

Theodora

I hate being bored. For those of us who have been left behind it is a quiet day…a very quiet day. Astrid has told us that the northern forests are quiet, and she has not lied. What little noise there is ends up being eaten by the trees that closely surround us.

The noise of the axe stops, and little else disturbs our rest except for an occasional bark from a dog or two, and the buzz of the giant mosquitoes from the unending bogs. What the mosquitoes have to live on when there are no Princesses to prey upon, I cannot work out, but they, along with gnats and midges, are here in quantity.

Now we know why Astrid had gotten small pots of dadanth cream, made from what they had returned from Haven with, and why she made us rub it on all of our exposed skin. Despite the constant drone from the clouds of insects that fly around us incessantly, few are being bitten at least.

Astrid

*I*t is getting to be late in the afternoon when I get Ayesha to let me off. Astrid watched Ayesha disappear, noting carefully where she was, and then she leaned her spear against a tree and put on her own ring. She took up her spear again and headed in. She found the well-used trail that she had looked for and jumped onto it.

Looking back, I can scarce see where I arrived. Unless someone goes looking, which no one is likely to do this close to the village, if they are given no cause to do so, the tracks I have just left are not likely to be seen, and even if they are, their significance will most likely be missed. I doubt that even the best will recognise my prints after all of this time.

Spear in hand, she headed in. Once she had to step off the track to avoid someone coming the other way and she had to keep a good eye out for any of the local mages. *They, at least, have a chance of seeing through the ring's glamour. I already have my cloak pin on as well, in case someone is seeking me magically, but I don't feel anything from it.*

Once she was in the village itself, she had to increase her vigilance as she moved towards the wooden palisade holding the riverbank that made up the local wharf.

In particular, I now have to keep a very keen eye out for the mages. There is not much room to dodge one coming around a corner. Occasionally, she was at risk of being run into by chickens or dogs, but otherwise no one disturbed her passage. Astrid reached the wharf.

I am relieved to see that Svein's boat is not there at its mooring. He is somewhere out at sea. Good, we will have to wait, but perhaps we can lay a little trap for him when he returns to the village.

Next, she headed for the church of Saint Fergus and for Father Simon, the head of the parish. *I realise that Christopher is getting me to pay a lot more attention to the Saints, but Saint Fergus has special care for Wolfneck and its inhabitants as he is the patron, generally speaking, of all Greenskins…those people with ancestry that is Kharl, or part Kharl, or any of the other similar races.*

I suppose that it is a good chance that the first real Hob church will end up with a dedication to the same Saint. It is nice to see my old church again. I am still not used to the stone churches of the south. This one, built in timber, with a roof that rises in layers, each of which has soaring eaves like the prow of a boat and tipped with a dragon's head, means home to me.

I am surprised how small the church actually is. It will not house even all the people of Wolfneck, and I cannot remember it ever being full, even on a major festival. It will just about take Mousehole a couple of times over and in our valley, we are already laying out the lines of a far larger building than this just to start with.

Ducking into the church, she was left with the problem of her spear. *What do I do with it when it is not being used? It is hard to slip through a door or under something low, but if I put it down, it may not be there next time I look if someone finds it. Normally, I just prop it in the entry chamber of a church, but I might need it here.*

Father Simon is not visible. The newer priests, Fathers Maurice and Bjarni, are fussing around near the altar, and someone is talking quietly in the confessional, and I can hear a person talking out though the door that leads out of the side of the apse, even though it is closed.

She waited. I am a hunter. I am good at waiting. Eventually the person from the confessional left and then the door opened, and Father Simon came into the body of the church.

Behind him is a young face on a big body…well, that is a surprise… Thorstein, the youngest of my brothers, and the only one younger than me, has become a priest. Who would have believed that? That would mean Father Fergus is in the confessional. Unless there are more Vocations newly declared, that should account for all of them.

She moved towards the side, so that she would not just appear in front of them and looked around. There are only priests in the building now. She leaned her spear against a wall, got the letter from her pouch, and removed her ring. *There is no way to do this without startling everyone so…*

"I need everyone to stay calm and just accept that I am here." She moved into the light. *My brother has taken one look at me and fainted. The others just stare blankly.*

"Father Bjarni," she said. "Just accept that I have the authority to ask this of you, please, and go and close the door and secure it. Make sure no one comes in until I have finished what I need to do here. Metropolitan Tornikes has given me this letter of explanation, and I act in his name."

She walked over and handed it to Father Simon, who opened it and started reading. "And thank you all for congratulating me on being alive." She grinned and moved towards her brother, who had started to recover. He looked up and saw her standing over him and promptly fainted again.

"Come on, you goose. Wake up and pinch me." She shook him. "Seeing me alive cannot be a bigger shock to you than me seeing you as a priest." She picked her brother up casually and took him to a clear spot and put him down again, going back to retrieve her spear.

"You cannot bring a weapon into church," said Father Maurice in a shocked voice.

"I will tell that to my village's chief priest when his wife comes into a service covered in blades and possibly even a bow...mind you...I have to admit... unless it is a special service, there is always a chance that he has forgotten to take his mace off as well, because he really is very absent-minded. In our village of Mousehole, we don't really worry about such things."

Father Simon had finished the letter and come over. "Well, he says nothing really, except to do as you say, and to listen to your story, and that you are going to kill or arrest Svein and his men, and anyone who objects can be sanctioned to the limit of the power of the Church. I have to say that I have no problem with that part...what is it that you want us to do?"

"I was going to tell you the story...but why don't you like Svein?"

"He has always avoided me and coming to Church," said Father Simon. "But since you...since you were supposed to have died while running away, he has gotten worse. I am hearing rumours..." His eyes betrayed how, as he glanced towards the confessional. "...that he is trying to bring back what he calls the Old Gods of our people."

"He is away now, and apparently he is bringing back a priest for them. It is rumoured that they will have a sacrifice when they return...a Human one according to the person who told me. They had listened to Svein with interest as he talked of this Turman and his co-gods..."

Astrid held up her hand to stop him. "Did you mean Tuurmaan?"

Father Simon looked curiously at her. "That may be what it is supposed to sound like and there are others..."

Again, she held up her hand "Do not say them...and do not ever allow anyone to say them. They are evil names. If my little brother has recovered..." she turned to Thorstein, "I forgot to tell you...you are now an uncle twice over." *He is looking at me in surprise.* "You will get to meet my husband later...now shall we all move to near where Father Bjarni is, so that you can all hear me as he guards the door and I begin the story."

Astrid

"We had heard rumours, but when Ulric was sent to ask the Dwarves about it and did not return, we decided that it was all just rumour," said Father Simon.

"We executed Ulric. I killed him myself." *My matter of fact tone has led to a shocked reaction.* "In our village, we follow some Darkreach customs, and one is that making children into sex slaves gets you executed. Ulric confessed to that, and much more than that before we executed him. We have killed several slavers for that now.

"Now we need to act before Svein returns, so that we can take him easily. We have found that it is safer to dart around into different places and to nibble at the enemy, rather than hit them all at once in the open when they can all fight us at once. There are not many of us, and we like outnumbering and surprising them. It is far safer for us, if we do it right.

"Can I bring my friends in openly? Does Svein have supporters? Do we need to take anyone prisoner first? How do Magnus and Leif stand?" *I have just named the two most powerful of the local mages and their reaction is very important.*

"Magnus is getting old and he holds himself away from Svein. Leif wants to be the most powerful local magus, but he does not either like or trust Svein. However, Ketil…" *He names one of the next strongest mages.* "…is one of his most influential supporters. The others seem to be waiting to see what happens."

"I am sure that we can deal with Ketil. We are experienced with controlling mages. We have killed over a hand of them who follow the Masters. Our mages are far more powerful, and we are a lot sneakier. I walk around with more magic on me than anyone in Wolfneck has now, except some of the mages.

"Until I come back, I want you to keep away from his supporters, don't talk to anyone if you can avoid it, and I will come in from the water after midnight service with the others into the rear courtyard. You should all stay at the church, bring your wives and put the children to sleep somewhere, if you wish to keep them safe…and tell people you are doing a special service for Saint Peter's Feast."

There are again surprised expressions on the faces of the priests. "You are surprised that I know whose feast it is? In our village, our priests make sure we know. Before I left Wolfneck, as you may remember, I might have been to church once a month. Now, on a busy day, I go to church only once a day. Sometimes I go two or three times a day.

"We have to try and keep up with our Muslims, and they pray six times a day. Besides Father Christopher speaks well, even the Muslims say so, and we have nice music and... Did I tell you that he brought someone back from the dead a few weeks ago? But he is not with us this time...and please be nice to the priest we have with us, he is a shape-shifter...a wolf, and we only just stole him from the Catholics."

The priests may as well keep a permanent expression of surprise on all of their faces. I had better give them a few more and get it over with. "I should also tell you that our Princesses who rule us are both married, and to each other. One of the men with us has two wives...let us say that life is different in our village.

"All of the Metropolitans we talk to, Basil, Cosmos and Tarasios, he is the Metropolitan in Ardlark, all of them know what we are like, and all of them have given us their blessing. With this many of you, even if most of you are young, you should know by now that I am not evil, so you just have to trust me.

"I will be back after the service...now get ready to open the front door." She went over and took hold of her spear and put her ring back on and disappeared. "You can open it now and I will go." Father Bjarni crossed himself and opened the door, but just stood there looking out. *I have to move him sideways myself.*

A strid reversed her route in, and reaching somewhere near where Ayesha should see her, she took off her ring. *Ayesha is alert, and has immediately taken off her ring so that I can see the saddle.* Then, being cautious and keeping low, they flew back to where the others waited in the larch clump.

They arrived near to dusk, and as they ate, Astrid drew things in the dirt and the situation was explained and plans were made. They settled down for some sleep before the night's work began.

Astrid
The morning of 18th Secundus, the Feast of Saint Peter

O ur takeover of the village is quiet and efficient. None of the precautions that we have taken are needed. Our presence is unsuspected. Ketil woke up with a sore head, as he hung naked, except for a loin cloth, from a timber frame used for stretching leather and already enchanted. He was made to expend and overdraw his mana uselessly and then questioned.

He had to endure this in front of the village. He was indignant at his treatment, and it turned out, was as yet innocent of any actual crime. However, he had been given promises, and he had made promises in return. He was able to point out several among the onlookers who had done the same.

They were taken in hand by the Mice, as were several who tried to slip away once they realised what was happening. Some try to object, and being armed, have to be subdued by force.

We do it so easily. For the first, I use my spear to block one man's sword and then fell him cold with one blow of its butt to his groin. Ayesha slips behind another and knocks him out as Basil blocks his attack. It becomes easier as we go on.

With only a little persuasion, they discovered that the new religion was to come out into the open with the return of Svein. *The sacrifices have been decided. The idea of a sacrifice is news to the village as a whole, and particularly to the town leader, the Captain, Siglunda the Wise.*

She is to be the first, followed by some local leaders, including Father Simon and the other priests, as the new priests dedicate their altar and make a new Pattern. Wolfneck may not, as a whole, be a very pious place, but they do take the idea of their priests being sacrificed to a pagan god without the whole village being consulted as a very serious insult to the community.

Once Ketil had been emptied of any useful information and taken down again and firmly tied up, Astrid hopped up on a chest, so that all could see her and called on Siglunda. "You have heard what he has told us. You are the Captain here, and yet you have let it get this far. What are you going to do about it?"

"You cannot talk like that to the Captain," said her father, Tosti. "You are a brainless chit who ran away from a good marriage, and left your loving family to fend for itself, without a woman to cook and mend for them. How can we trust you? You have left everything behind and are nothing now. You may as well be outlaw," he finished dismissively.

He must not have been paying attention to what has been said by our captives…and I am angry with him anyway…I have been angry with him for years.

"My loving father speaks," Astrid's voice was scathing. "He was going to sell me to the animal Svein…I am nothing now?" *I may be a little wound up, but too bad.* "Let me introduce you to my husband. He is the one handling the people who are too close to Svein. His name is Basil Akritas, and he is a Tribune, that is a very high officer, in the army of Darkreach…wave at my father, dear.

"We are the ones who found Dwarvenholme, killed most of the creatures who held it, and gave it back to the Dwarves...you see the lady...our Princess with the golden eyes...her name is Theodora do Hrothnog and she is a very powerful mage. Last time I met Hrothnog, her grandfather...yes, that Hrothnog...I gave him a kiss and he did not complain.

"We have killed creatures of the Masters, the ones that own Svein, and have done so for many years, all over The Land. Oh, and you are a grandfather and they do not take after you...they are handsome children, you have the nerve to call me nothing...you...you..."

It was her brother, the novice priest Thorstein, who moved to calm her down. "Sorry, I have to let Father Simon speak, and then our Princess Rani, who is a Battle Mage from Haven, and then I am sure that Siglunda will then tell you to do exactly what we say." She looked in a meaningful way at the Captain, and stood aside before going over to stand with Basil.

Siglunda the Wise

I may look at Astrid a trifle nervously. I wonder what has happened to the shy and blushing young girl who ran away rather than fight against a bad marriage. I admit to already feeling intimidated by this new Astrid.

It is perhaps a good idea to do what has been suggested to me. The new Astrid is right. I have obviously failed as a leader. She ordered Svein's supporters to be locked up 'for their own good' until he was arrested, and Ketil was told, in no uncertain terms, as he stood there shivering in the cold, what will happen to him if he tries to give any trouble.

He can be tied up, and stay that way for as long as is needed and he will be kept where he can be watched by people with wands. We will make sure that he is drained of power regularly. I will quietly ask one of these strange Princesses what else I need to do.

Father Simon

I am still not sure how I feel about all of this, but the letter makes it very clear that I should co-operate. At least this Krondag night, I have the fullest church for a service I have ever had, without there being some special occasion such as a big wedding or a major Feast. Somehow, I found the special patronage of St Peter, evangelism, an easy area to warm to today.

Chapter XXXVI

Astrid
18th Secundus, the Feast Day of Saint Peter

I have organised a watch to be kept on the sea with a telescope, from a saddle so high up that the saddle looks like an eagle in the sky…just a faint circling spot. From where we are keeping watch the island of Neron, where Skrice is, can be seen far in the distance with the bare and uninhabited island of Ovington to the north and left of it…only just sometimes visible as a smudge on the horizon.

The smaller dot of Durham Rock—the Shunned Isle—is too far away directly north to make it out in the surface haze. However, it is from that direction, not one of the other islands, that eventually a small dot appeared. That is odd. Stefan, who saw it, has come down and brought Rani and I up to see. They flew into a small huddle and talked earnestly to each other.

"That will be him," said Astrid. "And he has an air mage or priest on board his ship."

Rani is looking at me. She looks curious. "How do you know that? I am a mage and I cannot tell that from here."

"You are also not a sailor. Look at him. He is steering straight for Wolfneck… now look beneath us…the waves are indicating that the surface wind is from the south-west."

"And that means?"

Astrid sighed. "He has a magical wind. That is what the River Dragon looks like from the air when it uses its own wind to drive it. He is cutting across the real wind, and if he were actually using it, he would be beating to an angle that we might get to with the River Dragon, but that his drakkar cannot do and the sail on it is square to us, not set for beating against the wind at all."

"So, he has access to an air mage…now weren't the Masters air-based mages or priests or whatever?" Rani nodded. "Quod et demonstratum." *I am learning my languages well. Now I can sound smug in Latin.* "We may have a Master on board Svein's boat. He is coming to consecrate a new Pattern in the name of his gods.

"At any rate, it is as well that it is summer, and the day is at its longest. He is around fifty leagues away from us, and I am guessing that he will be a bit more than six hours getting here at the speed he is making, which is very fast even for a drakkar, so he will be in Wolfneck sometime after dinner tonight." She grinned.

"Now I have given you all of that, it is up to you to work out how to deal with Svein and his crew, a Master and possibly a priest as well…unless the Master is the priest that they are expecting, and I think that being a village priest would be beneath them."

Rani

*T*his gives me another problem. Capturing a boatload of people is only moderately difficult. Including a mage or a priest as a part of the package to be wrapped up makes that task far harder. Having a Master on board makes it very hard.

If we just wanted to destroy the boat, we can have done it at sea with very little risk, but I realise that for Siglunda to try and regain control of Wolfneck, it will have to be shown that Svein really is what we know he is.

There are too many people in the village, and Astrid's father is typical, who have not been convinced by what they have heard so far, and will not be convinced until they hear it with their own ears. Astrid is right about her people being stubborn and hard to win over. From knowing Astrid, I should have guessed that myself.

Rani and Astrid went down to Wolfneck again, and although the lookout was replaced every hour, there was no change in the speed or direction of the boat. *Astrid is sure that it will definitely be coming in near nightfall.* Preparations continued in Wolfneck.

Ketil, who has been thoroughly drained of mana, has been given a part to play, and is left in no doubt that how he plays his role in the performance, will help decide his eventual fate. He has a couple of like-minded accomplices, the ones who were supposed to actually meet the boat, to help him.

They have been told, in no uncertain terms, that there is an archer aiming at each of them, and them alone. Ayesha even took Astrid, Adara and Vishal up to them and introduced the targets to their archers. She pointed out that, at the first sign of treachery, their personal archer would fire at them and would keep firing until they were dead, ignoring other targets.

It was explained that each archer had magically-enhanced heads. It will not take long to kill them. The targets had not liked the idea at first and liked it even less as they thought about it. It seems that, being introduced not only to the person, but even the actual arrows that are being aimed at you made it seem far worse for them.

Astrid thinks that it is hilarious, but I think that now the main problem might be one of them giving it all away, not by treachery, but simply by doing something like fainting or by being too nervous. Ayesha may have taken intimidation a little too far.

Wolfneck is an almost square village. It is walled, and the boats dock along almost the whole riverside across a wharf area of around a chain of twenty paces in width and over six boats in length. Rani stood there giving orders and people jumped to complete them.

Siglunda stands beside me to give a semblance that this is an action by the village, but generally she stays silent, just hurrying people on if she feels that they are being too slow to help. By moving boats around there is now only one place that Svein can come ashore without staying a boat or two out from the dock.

With this in mind, barrels and other objects have been moved around so that there is plenty of cover on the wharf for the ambushers to hide behind. The best archers are placed behind those objects and in the houses with openings that faced the dock. Others are placed guarding the people who are regarded as being possibly untrustworthy and the families of those on board Svein's boat.

Ayesha is to go aboard the next boat upriver and keep still and hide. Hopefully, if there is a mage on Svein's craft, and he comes close enough to her to pick up her magic, they will think that it is a part of the boat. Strict instructions have been given, if it is needed for people to shoot at them, to only aim at the legs of the crew. They are needed alive for questioning.

I hope that will not be needed. Theodora is preparing to cast a spell that should, unless the Master interferes somehow, make all them unconscious for several minutes at least. It is targeted only at crew, so it will leave everyone else from the village standing as well as any passengers on the boat. That way the magic resistance of the Master will not affect the chance of success of the spell.

It will require a lot of preparation, but my Princess has a diagram drawn out and charged. She stands in a street leading to the dock behind a lightly made barrier where she can see to cast, but will hopefully not be seen until it is too late to do anything about it. If the crew all fall, the archers can then all target the Master.

The crew can then all be secured before they wake up. It is a simple and elegant plan…at least in theory. I will be in hiding down another street with my wands. This time my wife and I both wear our armour. At least everyone has their weapons from Dwarvenholme with them, and can fight a Master hand-to-hand if it is needed.

Father Simeon interrupted the orders being given out. "Before I left, Father Christopher wrote out some miracles for me. Normally, I could not cast some of them, but the Father realised that I would have lots of support to lend me strength," he waved at Father Simon and his attendant priests. "I expect to see everyone in Church well before the boat can see the wharf area."

"It will be near sunset and we will be conducting Hesperinos. After that service, we will be seeking a miracle to give everyone the luck that the Mice enjoyed when killing the dragon." *I happily agree to that addition. We can always use luck being on our side.* "After that is done, I will change shape in case I am needed in that form. I also brought Sleepwell potion if it is needed by Father Simon to help him cure those who need it."

"In that case," said Rani, "I had better get Astrid to announce to everyone about your appearance." Astrid nodded.

Astrid

"Listen up," Astrid called as she jumped up on a case, and cried out in a voice loud enough so that most of the village could hear. She waited for heads to turn in her direction. "Our priest here," she waved in Simeon's general direction, "… well, he is a real priest, but he is more than that. He is also a shape-shifter and a wolf at that." She looked around.

They are murmuring and muttering among themselves and looking in Simeon's direction. It is not hard to see that I judged the people of my old village correctly. My audience are clearly impressed by this revelation, the old legends run deep here. There is no wonder that Svein had found a ready audience for what he said about the Old Gods. Having a priest on your side is one thing. Having a priest who can also shape-shift? Well, that is powerful stuff indeed.

"Once he has cast his blessing on all of those who will be fighting, he will change into his wolf form, so do not be surprised if there is a real fenrir fighting on our side to slay the servants of these evil so-called elder gods." She smiled inside. *That well fits some of the tales the skalds tell.* "If he appears, do not be surprised and accidentally shoot at him."

Astrid
Just before dusk

*H*ulagu is the last rider in the sky and he reports that he had to fly far inland *before coming down. The ship should be just outside the mouth of the* river now, and no more than half an hour away. The priests gather the archers and others into the church and begin their short service. Father Simeon draws on the power of the village priests and uses the local icons. He has a smug expression on his face when he finishes and pronounces the benediction.

"I could feel that work…I am sure that it worked very well. God approves of what we do," he said as he rubbed his hands together and began to strip off his borrowed vestments and then to change his skin.

Quickly everyone took their places and hid. *The signal for them to emerge will be Stefan firing the first enhanced arrow at Theodora's command. Until they hear that explode, all of our people will stay hidden out of sight.*

Ketil and his friends are urged towards the dock. They do have their weapons on them, but it will take a very keen eye to see that these are tied firmly in place and will need to be cut free in order to be used.

"Remember," Astrid told the mage, "my arrows have your name on them if we are found out. You may remember what my archery is like, I hope. I have gotten much better since I left. It is having more live and dodging targets to shoot at that makes the difference. Remember that, once we start firing, it will be up to you to keep out of the way, but do not dodge until then. Because if you do, then you will be my first target."

She smiled warmly at Ketil, showing her teeth as she did so. *He is one of those who had spent a lot of time looking at my growing breasts and following me with his eyes as I grew up. I didn't like that, or his remarks back then, and I am really starting to enjoy this part.*

Astrid
A short while later

*S*vein's ship, the Blood-drinker, nosed its way up the river. *It is a long and low drakkar. It is built for speed and for raiding isolated farms along the coast rather than for much serious trading or fishing. By Saint Swithun, the ship is* *keeping its wind with it all the way, and I can feel it rushing past, changing the direction of the light evening breeze.*

I can see that whoever is steering—damn that, I cannot see past the sail!—is bringing it under sail almost to the dock. A man stands in the bows with a rope. He threw it to one of the waiting men, and words were exchanged in a low voice, and the man on the dock looked around.

Whatever he said has not raised any suspicions, as the sail has come down smartly and the crew are starting to stow everything away. I recognise all those that I have seen so far. A group stand up in the boat and move to the side to start climbing up onto the dock. These are the ones I want.

The one in the lead is my beloved Svein. The next is cowled like the Masters in Dwarvenholme, and the last one is a Human. He is dressed the same as the Master, but his cowl is thrown back and he has a real head and a face. As the Master passes by the crew, I can see each one slightly draws away from him.

The ship was secured to the dock, and soon Svein and the other two had climbed up and were standing on the timbers of the waterfront.

Ketil and his friends are more than keeping their distance from them. They do not want to be hit by accident, but I think that it is starting to raise suspicions. Looking around, Svein said something to Ketil in a slightly louder voice. *I think that is a name and a question, but I cannot quite make it out. I hope that Theodora acts soon.*

I think that…ahhh, now the ship's crew are starting to slump to the deck or the ground.

In a moment, the Master and his servant were staring at Svein lying at their feet, and she saw Stefan's arrow on its way. She didn't wait for it to hit, but fired immediately at the Master. *At least two others have done the same.*

The first arrow hit and exploded. The second two did the same, and Ketil and his friends dived away. *One is calling something… Loose…*

A cloud of arrows come in. One of the targets has a charm of protection from un-enhanced missiles in operation, as most of them fall from the air, but there are far too many enhanced ones for him to do anything about… Loose …

The Master started to raise his hand. *It has a wand in it, but again there are far too many shafts and now a bolt from Rani. Simeon is darting out at the priest, who is trying to cast a spell of his own, but he has several normal shafts in his legs distracting him… Loose…*

The Master shuddered and dis-corporated to the sound of the same faint shrill scream wavering behind him in the air that they had heard from the Masters at Dwarvenholme as they died.

It starts to fall, but this one obviously has a contingency in place, a moment later it is standing again as another round of arrows come in. Loose…

It has dropped the wand from its hand and has to scramble for it. Loose…

Simeon has struck at the priest and jumped up on him, seizing his right hand in his jaws and knocking him to the ground. Most of the villagers have stopped firing now, as they realise that their shots are useless… Loose…

The Master is trying to open a pouch on its belt, but it doesn't have the time… Loose…

Another round of shafts hit the Master, at this short range all seven of us who fired hit. Again, Rani has let lose a fire blast, and Theodora has probably joined her as well, as the fire that sprang up on the cowl was almost instantly snuffed out as if by a mighty wind and the robe flew in the air…and I need fire no more.

The Master had again made that thin eerie scream sound in all of our heads, as again it died. This time there is no return for it. Suddenly, apart from a snarling wolf-priest with bared teeth, and the frantic noises from the man that he holds down, there is a silence over the dock and no movement, apart from Ketil and his friends crawling rapidly away. It is very tempting to use a normal shaft and put it right up his arse.

Now it is time to tidy up. "Everyone move," she called out to the villagers. "Tie up the prisoners…make sure you get Ketil and his friends, as well. Hurry now." The wharf sprang into life. Astrid reached where Simeon sat on his prisoner.

A low growl is rising from his throat, and his open jaws are poised only a few fingers from the man's face. His front paws are planted on the man's chest. Well, that is truly an expression of terror that is plastered on his face, as he looks up at the teeth bared and poised a scant hand from his face. I can even think slavering jaws, as the priest is drooling on the man.

Astrid

A strid called Ayesha over from where she had emerged, unneeded. "Hello lyubov', my love." She smiled at the captive priest. "I am going to get you tied up. The lady beside you is a ghazi, an assassin from the Caliphate. I will bet that she can remove your tongue before you get a chance to make any sort of casting. Now Simeon will get off you. He does not like you. You must stink of evil."

She nodded towards Basil, who was now beside her. "This is my husband. He is going to tie you up, and then we will question you." She smiled her broadest smile. *He is looking from Simeon's teeth to mine.* Basil had brought the gag from Mousehole, and the captive was stripped and quickly and securely trussed.

Simeon padded quickly over to the church to resume human form and to dress. *The uninvolved villagers, now emerging from their houses to watch, are giving the huge wolf a wide and respectful berth as he goes.*

The captives are divided into three groups. The first is a group of two: Svein, and the un-named priest. We have them tightly bound and gagged, and they will be kept under a constant guard. The second group are also tightly bound and guarded. It is made up of Svein's crew.

The last are Ketil and his friends. They have lost their weapons again, but they are only given bound hands and a single guard. Due to the villagers being familiar with me, Rani is allowing me to decide how to proceed here and I know just what we are going to do next.

Astrid
Half an hour later

Wolfneck lacks a large hall and we cannot fit them all in the church. Astrid had moved everyone to the area where traders set up just outside the walls to the west to see the interrogation. *No one is allowed to miss this.*

To the light of some enchanted sconces, everyone looked at the prisoners set up in the front. Siglunda sat in a chair along with the Princesses, Father Simon and Father Simeon. The Mice were scattered around the crowd where they could keep an eye on everyone, and what they were up to. I have set up the skin-stretching frame that we used on Ketil earlier. Svein is being shown it first.

He may be ugly, but he is a big, strong man and he tries hard to struggle, but between Basil with his experience, and me with my enhanced strength, we have hung him up in it with as much difficulty as if he were a little child.

Astrid then turned to the crowd. "You will all remember me. I ran away from here, because my father over there was going to sell me to this beast as a wife. My younger brother went another way and ran off to the church, but I went even further, and I found a husband and children and a new village. We didn't have time earlier, but now I am going to introduce you to some of my friends here."

She pointed people out as she spoke. "The two ladies over there are the Princesses of our village of Mousehole. You will notice that one of them has golden eyes. She is called Theodora and she is Hrothnog's granddaughter. Her partner is Rani, and she was a senior Battle Mage from Haven.

"This is my husband Basil…he is also a Tribune in the Darkreach army, but is on loan to us. Some of you will have already met Father Simeon…he is a fenrir—a skin-changing wolf—as well as a priest. He is not from The Land, but from another place far to the west. Some of you may have heard rumours of it.

"Stefan here, was from Evilhalt, and he threw the blow that slew the southern dragon—a real fire-breathing, full-sized dragon, biggest I have seen, far bigger than the three to the east of us that hunt in the sea. Shilpa and Vishal are from Haven. Adara, from the Swamp. Ayesha is a woman ghazi from the Caliphate, what we would call an assassin. Hulagu is Khitan, and a mighty warrior, despite his youth. Tabitha is from Erave Town, and Danelis is from Warkworth.

"We come from all over, and we, and some of our friends, have made it our mission to kill all of the creatures that Svein is a servant to. We eliminated one more today. We eliminated a lot more when we found and cleansed Dwarvenholme…you might have heard rumours about that. We have stopped a war by killing the ones who wanted it."

I have started counting things off on my fingers as I go. "We have cleansed the islands to the south…we have killed the dragon of the southern mountains, and slain many bandits and other evil men, and freed their slaves. You will probably hear the story in full tonight from one of our skalds. Now, at my urging, and it seems to be only just in time, we have turned our attention to the north and my little home village of Wolfneck."

She paused and looked around with a stern look on her face. "Tonight, Svein and his friends were going to allow that creature from the north to kill Siglunda and your priests, as a sacrifice to their dark gods. Once that was done, you would have woken up, and all of you would have been their slaves, and every decent hand in The Land would have been set against you."

"No woman, or even child, would have been safe against the priests and slaves of these dark gods and their lusts. Some of you may remember Thorkil as a bad thought from the past." She paused and looked around. *Some nod in response. Others grimace at the recollection.*

"Until we killed him, he was one of these beasts, so we know all about this, and I will get Danelis and Tabitha to talk to the women later about them and what they did. In the meantime, we will be starting to question these guilty men. We know they are guilty already. We need you to hear them explain why. We will use magic, and we might use physical persuasion as well." She looked towards the prisoners and smiled at them.

"I sort of hope that we have to do that. Our expert at that is not here, but she did tell me what to do…and my husband holds his rank as one of Hrothnog's secret police. We have questioned many people and gotten their stories. You will remember Ulric. He came to spy on us without knowing that I was alive. He is now dead for his crimes.

"Many of these men that we now have bound will be executed. We know that already. All that is to be determined, is how long it will take for them to die and how it will be done. If we want, we can easily make it last a year or more. If they are good and answer us honestly and fully, we will be merciful and quick when we kill them."

There was another pause as she moved closer to where Svein hung and pulled out a sharp blade and began roughly cutting away his clothing so that he would hang there naked. As she carelessly cut away, she began to talk to the crowd again.

"I am going to start with my former betrothed. Some of you will have heard him boast to Ulric and everyone else how he was going to make me share my body with other men, and he was going to break me. He told Ulric that he was going to then send me away to other evil men to have me made into a slave for sex. Many of you will have heard him talk like this…particularly on the night before I…disappeared."

She threw the last of his clothes aside. Svein hung there naked as she cut away some leather holding some necklaces of coloured stones and glass around his neck, and the beads fell around his feet in the short grass and bounced on the hard ground. "He is one of those who are going to die." She now turned to Svein, and went to remove his gag as she kept talking.

"If he does not talk now, tomorrow our mages can cast a spell on him to make him talk, but now, I am going to be spending the night with him as he wanted, but I won't be doing to him what he wanted me to, and if he does not tell me enough, he will not enjoy the experience at all." She smiled bleakly at her audience. "You will all stay here and listen to what he has to say."

Astrid turned to Svein as she finished taking the gag off him. "Start talking. We already know a lot about what you have been up to, from different places, so if I catch you in a single lie, well…" She began to move the tip of her knife around his body, lingering in sensitive areas with it, to press a little and just break the skin.

I am doing just as Bianca told me to. I need to use the appearance of terror, and build on his in-built fears, and what he would do to someone else if he had them in the same situation. "I am not hearing your confessions…start talking and make sure that everyone can hear you." She was behind him at the time she said that, so she leant down a little and put her hand between his legs and squeezed hard on what was conveniently at hand.

Looking past him at the villagers, I can see shock on many faces. Svein screamed loud and long and fought against his bonds. "Don't be such a baby. That was only a gentle squeeze. Wait until later." Astrid reached up and past him and patted his cheek.

"Our torturer told me that building a slow fire under there works marvellously. She said it was the combination of the pain and the smell that works best, and you can also use the same fire to heat up metal things to stick in interesting places…and I forgot to tell you something else. Dharmal didn't want to talk at first, because of some nonsense about having his soul in torment.

"You might like to know that I introduced Hrothnog to his new wife, and kissed him goodbye when we left Darkreach. Do you want to bet that I cannot arrange a worse eternal torment for you than the Masters can?" She slowly started to push her knife into the area between his scrotum and his anus trying to exert pressure there without yet breaking the skin too much.

Svein is trying to turn to look at me. His face has a growing look of horror on it. With the mention of Hrothnog, and the growing pain between his legs he began weeping and broke. He occasionally spoke too low for people to hear, or stopped for a little while, and Astrid had to prompt him to speak up.

Astrid just leant forward and stoked a vulnerable area with a blade or gave a little playful squeeze. He told of how long he had worked for the Masters, he told of people killed who were supposedly lost, he told of helping Thorkil escape from Wolfneck and of sending him to Dharmal, he told of how he met the Masters, when he was driven to Durham Rock, the Shunned Island or Arnflorst, for he called it all three.

Basil is writing as fast as he can. It was not long before even my father is turning pale in the lights that are making this place bright, as Svein tells of what he had planned for me, and how even though he wanted to possess my body, he only wanted to marry me as a way of breaking my father. He started to tell about the priest with him, who started struggling and trying to make noises through his gag. Astrid left him. She went over to the bound priest and stroked his cheek.

"Don't be impatient, lyubov…your turn will come later. Vishal…Stefan… can you come here and take him where he cannot hear what is said. Keep a close watch on him. That way we can check what one says against the other later. You can organise for his crew to be gagged and put somewhere else as well. We want to check what everyone says against all of the others. We wouldn't one of them trying to minimise what he did by lying would we?"

She went back to Svein while the removals went on. "I am so sorry that we were interrupted, my former betrothed." *I stroke his cheek again in a mockery of affection. He looks terrified…oh…look at the growing puddle… I look at it and then at him. I hope that I look disappointed. He looks thoroughly miserable in his humiliation.*

"You must keep talking as there is so much more of the night to fill up with your tales. You want to keep telling me new things until at least midnight. There are still hours to go yet. It would be horrible if I grew bored…for you that is…I am sure that I will have fun."

Svein launched into more detail. He went back to the priest. He told of how Skrice, on Neron Island, was now devoted to the new religion or the old religion. He kept changing which one he said. He started to say the names of the gods. *I will stop that right there. No one needs to hear them invoked, and naming them might give them some power here.*

He talked of his visits to the Masters and taking them packages. He told of slipping east with three Masters and stealing past Cold Keep, the northernmost settlement in Darkreach, and how he had dropped the Masters north of Antdrudge.

There had been people to meet them with horses. *Basil will have that information sent in as soon as he can.* He had been there before with money and with packages, and he had brought messages and boxes and packages back, including lots of molotails over the years that he had sold on through his contacts.

He even has a contact among the Walrus Clan at Shastrii-lo-pesti-song in the Northern Waste…it is a pity that he always kept his hood up, but Cloikchu will not be too hard to find. For a start there are not many of the Saelk-le-ibri, the Walrus clan, living there. I do not know him, but most of my time there has been with the women. Still, Mathanharfead will track him down.

He told of meeting Brother Job and others of the Brotherhood. He faltered about telling more about his recent trips and had to be prompted heavily by Astrid. *It seems that he still hopes that protecting some secrets could help him.*

Eventually, he confessed that The Brothers believed the Masters to be archangels who came to visit them and tell them the wishes of God, and they were about to launch a holy war aided by magical weapons given to them by the Masters that Svein had carried there from Arnflorst. There were three of these weapons. He had been told that these weapons could destroy whole armies.

I am sure that to our mages these weapons sound more like machines rather than honest magic, although how machines could do that much damage, I do not know. They sure sound that way to me at least.

While all of this is going on, most of the village just sit still and listen. Sometimes people mutter in anger at what they hear, as events touch them or their families. They are riveted into their places by these events that have been happening around them, without them knowing. They have only just avoided being an unfortunate major part of the story.

Svein kept going until after midnight. To do this, he had to talk about crimes going back to his youth, of murder and robbery, and of rape. *There is a growing number of gasps and mutters from the audience as long-held mysteries are solved.*

Several girls had to be comforted by families, as at long last their stories came to light, and the threats that had held them silent for years were rendered nugatory. *People who aided him are being named. Fathers are starting to finger weapons, and some are beginning to look in the direction his crew have been taken.*

He spoke of enslavement and debauchery and of his secret desires, what had been planned for Astrid, and what he had been told would happen and what he could do when the Masters triumphed. All of the time he spoke Astrid moved around him and prompted him to keep talking. Sometimes that prompting led to cries of pain interrupting his tale. He finally sagged in relief, an empty sack when he realised that he had made the time.

"We are going to check what you have said. Then my husband is going to cut your balls off, because he promised them to me as a present, and after that you will be killed. My Confessor will have words with me about that. He counselled against this, but I will still do it, and regret the act afterwards. Now, if you want, you can talk to a priest, but your soul is so corrupted that I doubt that you could ever be sincere."

Svein is looking at me with an odd mix of hatred and fear on his face. I think that I like that. He began reviling and cursing her until he was gagged. He was cut down and trussed and the priest brought out. He was put up in the drying frame in the place of the ship's captain.

Astrid
Just after midnight, 19th Secundus

*T**his is where it gets really interesting.* "Hello, Iorund. Svein has been very helpful for us. He has told us a lot. We are going to take your gag out and you are going to tell us even more. We have already killed most of the Masters where they were hidden away in Dwarvenholme, and now we have killed yours. We are going to kill every last one of them.

"We have killed many of their servants in The Land and we are rooting out the rest—wherever they may be—and then we are killing them. They are a dark shadow on the world, and the shadow will be lifted... Now, speak to me about your deeds."

There is a mad light in the man's eyes as he speaks. "It matters not how much it seems you are winning. You will fail eventually. The Speaker for the Gods has told us that there are blasphemers who are seeking to undo their plan for the world. The Gotterdammerung will come. It is prophesised that the world will descend into war and we alone, the servants of the Gods, will survive in eternal glory to rule over a world of slaves."

"So, you only exist to start the final battles and then you will be rewarded?"

"That is right. You can do what you want to me. The Old Gods will succour me, and I will tell you nothing, and I will be rewarded later. As witness to this and to aid me, I call up Khaarmal. I call up Maarndrin." If anyone had chanced to look above them, the night sky was starting to darken further, and all could feel a chill seeping into them already. "I call up Toghmmmpf…" *He can speak no further. I have jammed the gag back into place. Now he can neither bite his tongue nor speak.*

Astrid turned to the mages. "Even Bianca cannot break open the mouth of a fanatic. I will leave this one to you when you have slept and recovered your mana. Do you want to go on with the minor ones now, or when we have all slept?" *The Princesses look at each other and at Siglunda and at the villagers around them.*

"These are evil things that are being discussed. Let us hear them in the bright light of day, I think," said Rani after briefly glancing at the swirling clouds above. *Christopher obviously told her about them after Gil-Gand-Rask. I am glad that she doesn't think it is a good idea to proceed further in the night. The other two are nodding as well.*

Astrid turned to her audience and spoke in a much louder voice. "You have heard what has been said tonight. If I were you, I would spend some time examining your conscience. I would then be going to see Father Simon tomorrow if you think that you need to. Our guards will continue in their places tonight."

She looked around her, trying to look at the eyes of those she knew had family under arrest. "If anyone is under arrest, you will now understand why, and you will realise that the best that they can hope for is outlawry.

"For those who have family who are under arrest, you might want to pray for them as well. You can talk to them tomorrow, if you wish. I warn you that anyone attempting to rescue them will be killed without warning. You have a couple of minutes to get home, and then until dawn we will assume that anyone on the streets is trying to rescue the prisoners."

She looked pointedly at some of the men fingering their blades. "Even if they just want to kill them themselves, many of our people do not speak Darkspeech well, so you may not be able to talk to them to convince them you are innocent and meant to do something else. Go to bed now and we will see you all in the morning."

People begin to disperse. I note that some of the girls I grew up with are looking at me as if they have never properly seen me before, or as if I had suddenly grown wings in front of them. Some of them are still crying and are being comforted by their mothers or sibs.

The Princesses seem to have left things to me. She organised a roster of guards and took over a tavern for the Mice and their prisoners to sleep in. *There are several as good as one another, but we will take Brodir Lind, the Brother Shield, as the closest to where we are questioning everyone.*

She cleared the stables as much as she needed, and put the prisoners and the saddles in there. There had been only one person staying there and she sent him to the Oka Heimili, the Mist Home.

Astrid
Morning, 19th Secundus

*I*t is well and truly light outside, and we have well broken our fast, before the *first cautious heads appear from doorways. The time has come to talk to the priest, the crew, the mage Ketil and his friends and to pass judgement on them all.*

As Astrid was preparing to move the prisoners out for questioning, Rani and Theodora came up to her. "We have decided," said Rani, "that you only have Svein as your responsibility to cast judgement on. Siglunda should make the decisions about the fate of the rest. It is her village after all."

"We won't tell her," said Theodora. "But if she is too lenient, we will take the prisoners back from her and make up our own minds."

Astrid nodded in relief. *I have been harbouring the feeling that my responsibility for the village was going to extend to passing judgement on the captives. I am glad that it isn't. I grew up here and know all of the prisoners. Admittedly, I don't like any of them, but I do like some of their cousins and sisters, and that will probably get in the way if I am ordering someone's brother put to death.*

I saw Gudrid watching as her brother was bound as one of Svein's crew. I then saw, but pretended not to, when Gudrid turned to stare dully at me with pain on her face. I was expecting her to come and plead for his life. I don't know how I would answer that. I know how I should answer, but I am not a ruler and it will be Gudrid, for the Lord's sake. We played with dolls together for half of my life.

I am not supposed to make decisions like that. That is why the Captain of Wolfneck is chosen for life, or until they resign, and they don't have a lot of friends while they hold the job. They have to make the hard decisions…Good… Siglunda hasn't done her job before. Now let her do it when it is even harder.

Astrid

After breakfast, the minor captives were sat down in a row, while the pagan priest was brought out and Astrid went around the village calling on people to come out. She did this and hit doors with her spear butt until everyone was there.

Svein is still tied and gagged. I doubt that he has been fed or given a drink. He is lain down on the ground where he can be watched. The priest is stripped and fastened up into the frame. His skinny body shrinks in on itself in the chill morning air. By the time Wolfneck has gathered, Theodora is ready with a pattern and a truth spell prepared. She is working in High Speech.

To make sure everyone knew what she was saying, Astrid had Magnus translate what was said to the villagers. *Everyone gets on with Magnus. They should trust their own elderly mage to get right what is being said.*

The spell was cast, and once he had been told not to kill himself, or to utter the names of his gods, Iorund had his gag removed. He told of how some of the people of Skrice, including himself, had been approached. He told of how some of them had then banded together and risen up and sacrificed most of their priests in front of the village, and how they now ran Skrice for the Masters in the name of their Gods.

I can see that he is trying to avoid saying something, even under the spell. He is hiding something. Now to see what it is, by asking what he is hiding and by finding the right question that he cannot avoid answering…

Astrid

So, *some of the mages, as well as the island's bards and sages, have fled with the one surviving priest and are now outlaw on the island. The Masters are waiting for winter to come to hunt them down. They believe that the fugitives cannot escape off the island and that they seem to have little support… Or so Iorund believes. I guess I know where we need to go next.*

He told of the arrival of three Masters in the great ship, and how there were now Kharl living on the island. Basil came up to question him on that. *Iorund cannot tell the difference and does not know the names of the different tribes, they are all greenskins, but they sound like mostly Isci-kharl. There are also some of the giant Insak-div among them.*

"They only have the least bright with them," said Basil. "That is some consolation. The kind of people who spread hate do not seem to appeal as much to the bright ones, just to the slow, the lazy and the evil. I am going to have to report this to Hrothnog." He turned to Rani. "Work out if you want me to ask him to not involve himself, and let us solve it, or if you want him to take the island, but I do have to report it when Carausius comes next."

Rani nodded. "I think that all of the islanders will fight against him if it is Darkreach who come in force. If it is only us who do it, some may side with us, so they will not be united."

Having worked that out, it is time for Iorund to tell us more. Once Wolfneck was brought over to the Old Gods, Svein was going to go back, and the great ship was to come here with more people, and they were going to use it to move along the coast attacking the towns as they went.

So, they were going to start taking over the north, and then the Brotherhood was going to move against Freehold. With the north in hand they were then going to move down the west of the mountains. He speaks as if it is inevitable and his capture is only a temporary setback.

Astrid realised something. *He has the same fanatic confidence that Dharmal exhibited right until his end, despite all of the evidence before him. He has seen his gods in action after a sacrifice, and he thinks that nothing can stand against them. The more believers they have, and the more sacrifices that they are given, the greater grows their power.*

Now that they have the people of Skrice and the Brotherhood to draw on, they are powerful indeed. He doesn't think about the reverse...how what we Mice are doing is cutting back on their power now. He doesn't know of the losses of patterns in the south, or of the servants there, or even of the taking of Dwarvenholme.

Eventually, he ran out of things to tell them and started on his own personal reasons for being a target to be recruited. *I am revolted. I may even need a sauna to get clean from standing so close to him. He is a foul creature and it seems that neither a young boy nor his sheep are safe from him.*

Astrid quietened him up and turned to Siglunda. *I was watching Iorund and didn't notice her near me and listening. She, and indeed most of the village, have shocked expressions on their faces. Even some of their new recruits, bound nearby, have the same look.*

"I don't think there is anything else that we can get out of him of interest. He has not contradicted anything Svein gave us, but he is yours to condemn. I get to execute Svein, and my husband and I want to get that chapter of my life closed."

She spoke up so that all could hear. "Svein is about to die. If there are any of who want to watch his death, or who wish to say anything to him before he loses his mind, then you should follow me now." She turned to the priests. "Just in case he truly repents and wants one of you, can someone come with us please?"

Father Simeon nodded. "Christopher told me of these confessions. I told Christopher it was my turn to bear the burden of one. I will come with you." Basil and Astrid went over and picked up Svein and took him down towards the river.

A few of the local girls are following, making comments about his manhood and his alleged prowess in bed, and even some abusing him for corrupting their brothers, or in the case of two women, of corrupting their sons. Three fathers and some sons are coming as well.

They may want to have a hand in his death for what he and his men have done to sisters and daughters, and have covered up, but I am refusing them. This is something I have promised myself for a very long time. The men can watch on as he dies, but that is all. They will just have to be content with seeing him die badly.

Astrid

Once they were at the riverbank, Astrid removed Svein's gag. He started to curse, and Astrid slapped him…hard…hard enough to draw blood.

"You will shut up. The only reason you have the gag off at all is so that you can confess to Father Simeon, if you have the balls to tell God all that you have done and to abjectly crave forgiveness. If you are going to do this, you had better do it soon. You won't have any balls attached to you for very long."

Svein cursed her again. "I will be safe. The Servants of the Old Gods told me so. They looked at my future. I should not have been weak last night, but I have found my faith again. You can do your worst. Kill me now, and I will live again and come back only stronger. I know this in the name of Khaarmaamfpl."

Astrid was quicker this time, and using her enhanced strength and speed, she grabbed hold of his tongue and hung on to it hard, pulling it tight from his mouth while pinning him by the throat with her other forearm. He was already squirming with the pain of that and having his tongue nearly pulled from his throat added to the agony.

"Very well," she turned to Basil. "Time to make him less of a man, and we will see how his gods help him then. We will give him a little time to appreciate his situation, and then we will cut his throat and tip him in the river."

Basil drew a sharp knife and knelt behind the naked and bound man, who started struggling even harder. Basil reached between his legs and grabbed. He didn't try for any subtlety, just grabbing the man's sack, pulling it tight, and with his other hand, cutting it off with a stroke.

Svein's attempt to call on his gods became an inarticulate scream, and his body started a series of frantic spasms, like a stranded eel, as he tried to reach the source of his pain with his tied and pinioned hands. Astrid let go his tongue and his incoherent screams grew louder and shriller.

Basil moved around him and, opening his hand, picked out his testicles from the rest of the mess in his hand and dangled them in front of Svein. He offered them to Astrid, who nodded towards the water. Making sure that Svein could see what was happening Basil threw them in.

There must be something swimming there in the way of a large fish, as there is a swirl of water and a splash…as something seems to have swallowed them instantly. Svein is still screaming and writhing on the dock in pain, the blood streaming down and pooling around under him. Basil pulled his head back and slashed his throat like an animal being slaughtered, but not as deeply.

His screams have turned into a continuous wet bubbling sound, and behind me I can hear at least one of the women that are still watching among the gathered crowd being sick.

Once Svein had stopped moving they tipped his body into the water, watching the blood spread and seeing a further commotion in the water. *Making noises of approval, the small crowd are starting to disperse back to where the others of the crew are being listened to before being judged.*

"Father…" Astrid turned to Simeon, "Can Basil and I see you, please? Now that is over, we both have sins to confess, and we need to see about our penance. I think that I can already safely say that I won't be doing that again."

Astrid

*W*e *are just in time to hear the rest of the judgements.* Iorund had his head cut off and was thrown in the water, as were most of Svein's crew. Some of the crew, and most of Ketil's people had a geas of service placed upon them and were allowed to live…and others of both groups were made outlaw and exiled. Three were made slaves, and would be taken and sold far away from Wolfneck.

They might end up in Darkreach, or among the Khitan for all that I know. Ketil is one of them and he does not look happy at all. Life can be hard for a mage that is made a slave.

The outlaws were told by Rani and Theodora where they could and could not go. Unless they could prove they had jobs that temporarily brought them that way, they were not to be seen in the north at all. They were told directly that it would be in their best interest to go to Freehold, and to somehow go away completely to the Newfoundland that Father Simeon had told them about.

Theodora

W*e have told them an invisible mark is being placed upon them, so that we Mice will know if they break these conditions in any way. I thought of making a spell that would leave such a mark…a sort of geas mark…but I don't have one yet. The outlaws don't know that. I just mutter over them in High Speech…actually a recipe for a healing potion…before they go on their way in fear.*

The villagers around them, although some may have tears in their eyes, hold away from them. No one offers to go with any of them into exile. The first is released and with only a plain dagger, the clothes he wears, and a few days food, he is driven out of the village to live or to die.

One by one, the rest will suffer the same fate and they know it. None of them dare even wait for one of the others to be released after them. If they are seen their lives are now forfeit. All they can do now is run south and hope they do not meet anything too large and hungry before they find safety among other people.

Rani

S*iglunda has a lot of work ahead of her healing the village of Wolfneck. What is more, she now has to keep a watch out for a ship from the north. Any people coming from Skrice, instead of being welcome traders as they once would have been, now have to be thought of only as spies and possible invaders.*

The drying pool of blood from where Svein was killed remains plain, soaking in to the timber and staining the wood of the dock as a reminder to them all. None seems to want to clean it away, at least not while Astrid remains in the village. By the time she leaves, it will probably be too late and the blood will end up staining the dock as a permanent reminder.

"We will return," she said to the assembled villagers. "We should send a ship to you before winter, and when it comes, we expect you to provide people to go with it to Skrice and perhaps further. We will need armsmen, mages and priests. Hopefully, this will be our final task, but we have much work to do before we can even think of that."

Astrid

I am not reconciled with my father, or indeed with most of my brothers. They were well on the fringe of what happened, and all have escaped any punishment, but I cannot yet find it in my heart to forgive them fully. Among other things, it was fleeing from the direction that the rest of our family were heading that drove me away from Wolfneck, and Thorstein to the church.

Astrid went to see Father Simon. "I am sure that you agree that Thorstein would be better away from the male part of his family."

"You may be right, but I am reluctant to send him on to Greensin. I do not think that he is at all suited to be a monk, and we have done his teaching here so far."

"Well, send him to me down in Mousehole. I have two nice girls in mind for him as possible wives. One is called Zoë and she is a baker, and the other is a miller called Verina. They are both from within Darkreach.

"It is good to have a priest in the family, but, without our mother to do this, it is my responsibility to see him married properly, and these girls have been approved as good matches by Metropolitan Tarasios in Ardlark. I also still have Maria and Tabitha available and both of them are good girls as well."

In discussing them like this, Astrid managed to conveniently ignore the fact that Tabitha was older than her, and Maria and the Darkreach girls were the same age, while Thorstein was several years younger than any of them.

"We have Father Simeon in hand, although he needs that less than the others of our village priests. He has more common sense than Father Christopher and Father Theodule do. We love Father Christopher very much, and he is a very holy man, but he really can get lost in a walled field. What is more, we need a junior priest in the village to help out with the duties there."

"You have too many juniors here for you to teach properly on your own, and we have three senior priests in our village, and as yet, no junior ones, although our Hobgoblin may end up entering the priesthood one day. All of our priests are good teachers and Thorstein will end up with a good education with holy men."

Father Simon

I look at Astrid and think for a bit about how this little girl has changed.
Once she would only speak to me in the Confessional…and that was rare.
Now she offers religious advice to her old village priest uninvited. Mind you, I
do have to admit to myself that she makes sense.

"It is agreed then," he said. "I will wait a week or so, until the first outlaws
have had a chance to move some distance along the roads south out of the way
and then send him south to you. They will soon be clear of the area and will
probably head east anyway. Hopefully there will be a trader I can send him
with, but the outlaws should move far faster than he will anyway."

Father Thorstein Tostisson

I am not sure if I want my life to be so organised for me, but with my sister
and my superior set on it so, I do not seem to have a lot of choice about the
matter.

I suppose that it is an advantage that at least I don't have to now marry one
of the local girls. I grew up with them all, and I don't really like any of them
very much. What is more, I think that my relation to my sister would make a
relationship difficult with any of the ones who are near to my own age.

Astrid

We leave very early on the next morning, heading south in one long
flight. That is a nasty season in my life over for good. I can now put it
behind me. Maria was supposed to be carrying Simeon on this second leg if it
were to be needed, but it seems that Danelis has made her decision.

From what seems to have happened last night, it is also obvious that Shilpa
has made a decision as well. She has taken the younger man with her well in
hand. During breakfast, Shilpa had a very smug expression on her face and
Vishal looked more than a little stunned. We get used to that look on the face
of men in our village.

Cast

Aaron Skynner: in his 30s, a tanner and widower from Glengate, comes to Mousehole seeking a wife. He marries Aine.

Adara ferch Glynis: cousin of Bryony from Rising Mud and in love with her. She was rescued from the Master's servants in Pavitra Phāṭaka.

Aine Bragwr: a woman of around 30-years from Bloomact in The Swamp, she is now the brewer and distiller for Mousehole. Marries Aaron.

Amos Ostrogski: younger brother to Stefan, leatherworker in Evilhalt.

Anahita of the Axe-beaks: in full Vachir Anahita Ursud. A Khitan girl from Mousehole and Hulagu's köle, she is the mother of Būrān.

Andronicus: secretary to the Metropolitan of the North for Orthodox.

Aneurin ap Stefan: son of Bryony and Stefan.

Angharad ferch Kessog: ten-year-old daughter of the Orthodox priest of Rising Mud, sister of Cadfael. Student at the school.

Anka Ostrogski: Stefan's mother in Evilhalt.

Anna Akritina: mother of Basil, customs official at Southpoint.

Apinaya Sarin: Subadar of the River Patrol of Haven.

Ariande Nepina: Insakharl (part Alat-kharl) from Antdrudge. She is partly trained as an engineer but wanted a quieter life as a brick and tile maker and layer after her parents are killed in an accident. She moves to Mousehole.

Arlene Caelfinddottir: nine-year-old female Bear Folk student at the school.

Arthur Garden: farmer and youngest son (of 4) from Evilhalt. He comes to Mousehole seeking land and a wife. He was talked into coming by Ulric. He ends up courting Make.

Asad ibn Sayf: a widower from Doro. He is a farmer and becomes the husband of Hagar and Rabi'ah.

Astrid Tostisdottir (the Cat): a part-kharl girl from Wolfneck, in the far north of The Land. She is married to Basil. Her children are Freya Astridsdottir, 'the Kitten' and Georgiou Akritas. Attractive but for a strong jaw & lengthened incisors (she has a strong bite). She is tall and statuesque, with pale blonde hair and dark green eyes. She can lap up drinks & purrs when having sex. Her youngest brother is Thorstein, now a priest.

Atã ibn Rãfi: a widower from Mistledross. He is a timber-feller. He becomes the husband of Umm and Zafirah.

Ava: servant at 'The Dead Enemy' in Evilhalt.

Ayesha bint Hãritha: a ghazi or assassin of the Caliphate assigned by a Princess to guard Theodora. She is one of the rare women of that culture who is allowed independence and has received an education at Misr-al-Mãr as a ghazi (holy warrior). In return she must obey any order of those who are placed above her. Part of her education is to give her cover as entertainer. She is the minor daughter of Hãritha, the Sheik of Yãqũsa. She is short, slim, very attractive, bright, ambidextrous and good at it and has superb senses & a beautiful soprano voice. She has black hair and eyes and a tiny waist. Good at climbing & tracking, can ride well. Usually uses knives (including to parry), can use bow & horse mace.

Aziz (Azizsevgili or Brave Lover): Hobgoblin captured during the attack on Mousehole. He falls in love with Verily and converts to the Orthodox faith and marries Verily. Their sons are Saglamruh (Strong Spirit) and Sunmak (Gift). His former name is Saygaanzaamrat (Plundered Emerald).

Basil Akritas or Kutsulbalik (nickname from great-grandfather): is a mostly human (one sixteenth kharl) who appears as a youth just out of his apprenticeship (although he is ten years older). He is an experienced secret police officer of Darkreach and of the Orthodox faith (as it is practiced in Darkreach). He comes from Southpoint from a military family and is now married to Astrid and living in Mousehole assigned to guard Theodora by Hrothnog. He has black eyes.

Basil Tornikes: Metropolitan of the North at Greensin.

Bianca: foundling from Trekvarna now living in Mousehole and married to Father Christopher. Their children are Rosa and Francesco. She can smell treachery and can make herself do things she really does not want to if she has to. Sings in a husky contralto and has pale blue eyes and blonde hair.

Bianca Fletcher: daughter of Robin and Eleanor.

Bilqĩs: a tiny girl, from a trade background in the Caliphate, she now lives in Mousehole as an apprentice mage. She has some ability as a glassblower.

Bjarni, Father: a young Orthodox priest in Wolfneck.

Boyǫkųrek (Great Heart): head woman of the women's circle of the Cenubark-incilari hobgoblins. She is also Aziz's mother.

Bryony verch Daffyd: a freckled red-head from Rising Mud in the Swamp. Her husband (Conan) and father were killed at her wedding and she was brought to Mousehole. She now lives with Stefan and her son is Aneurin ap Stefan. She is cousin, lover and sister-wife to Adara.

Cadfael ap Kessog: twelve-year-old son of the Orthodox priest of Rising Mud, brother of Angharad ferch Kessog. Student at the school.

Calgacus: Chief Magister (leader) of the Bear Folkings. He is a shaman and shape-shifter.

Candidas: animal handler for Carausius from his second trip on. He is also a member of the Antikataskopeía and will be marrying Theodora Lígo.

Carausius Holobolus: Darkreach trader in fabric, spices or anything else. His guards are Karas & Festus, animal handler is Candidas, his wife is Theodora Cephalou and his daughter is Theodora Lígo.

Cathal: Magister (leader) of the Bear Folk village of Birchdingle. He is a shaman and shape-shifter.

Christopher Palamas, Father: the chief Orthodox priest for Mousehole and husband of Bianca. Their children are Rosa and Francesco. He is a very holy, but diplomatic, man and a dedicated healer.

Cloikchu: Svein's contact among the Inuit at Shastrii-lo-pesti-song. His name means 'Stone Dog'.

Cnut Stonecleaver: Dwarven Baron of North Hole in the Northern Mountains.

Cosmas Camaterus: Metropolitan of the Orthodox Church for the south of The Land (from Evilhalt and including the southern independents). He is based in Erave Town. He is tall with a large beard. He is usually happy and smiling.

Cynic the Smith: Mayor of Erave Town.

Danelis: from Warkworth, she now lives in Mousehole where she usually helps Harald in the mine. She also helps on the farm. She has a minor ability with telekinesis and is short with silver-coloured hair. She marries Simeon.

Denizkartal: coxswain to and lover of Olympias. He is a Boyuk-kharl, the largest and most intelligent of the Kharl races.

Dharmal: Dwarf and leader of the brigands who attack Bianca's caravan. He ruled Mousehole and acted as the main servant of the Masters in The Land. He was executed after the Mice overturned him.

Dindarqoyun: last druid apprentice of the Cenubarkincilari, the southern hob-goblins. He had not yet chosen his adult name and his child name means 'Pious Sheep'.

Dulcie verch Mari y Saer: from Bathmawr in The Swamp. She is now the Mousehole carpenter and marries Jordan.

Eithear Reodarson: male bard of the Bear Folk.

Eleanor: caravan guard from Topwin in Freehold she now lives in Mousehole and works as a jeweller. She is married to Robin Fletcher and is one of the first in the village to fall pregnant. They have adopted Aelfgifu, Gemma and Repent and have a daughter Bianca.

Elizabeth: an orphan from Trekvarna in Freehold who now lives in Mousehole after being a slave there. She is a skilled musician and assistant brewer.

Fãtima: comes from an unknown background in the Caliphate, she lived in

Mousehole as an apprentice mage and assistant cook. As Fatima bint al-Fa'r (Fatima daughter of the Mouse) she is now married to Hrothnog as the Empress of Darkreach and Ambassador of the Mice.

Fear the Lord Your God Thatcher: seven years old, she is the adopted daughter of Rani and Theodora.

Fergus, Father: Orthodox priest in Wolfneck.

Festus: part-kharl & guard for Carausius, a Darkreach trader in spices etc.

Fortunata: Dressmaker and embroiderer for Mousehole. She is the first wife of Norbert and her son is Valentine.

Freya Astridsdottir: twin sister of Georgios Akritas, daughter of Astrid and Basil. They were the first children born in Mousehole to live. Loves cats.

Fullon Ógánson: eight-year0old male Bear Folk student at the school.

Gamil, Chief Predestinator: local leader of the Shing-zu, the builders of Vhast

Gemma: nine-year-old child, adopted daughter of Eleanor and Robin.

George Pitt: son of Lakshmi and Harald.

Georgios Akritas: twin brother of Freya Astridsdottir, daughter of Astrid and Basil. He is named after Basil's father. They were the first children born in Mousehole to live. Good at fixing things.

Georgios Anoteron Akritas: (the senior) Basil's father, husband of Anna. Guard commander at Southpoint.

Giles Ploughman: farmer at Mousehole. He is married to Naeve and their daughter is Peggy.

Glyn ap Tristan: a mage in Rising Mud and servant of the Masters. He has one of their patterns in his outbuilding.

Goditha Mason: sister to Robin Fletcher and married to Parminder. She is the mason of Mousehole and an apprentice mage. She is regarded as the father of Melissa Mason.

Gudrid: girl of Wolfneck, greenish skin, friend of Astrid. He brother is one of Svein's crew.

Gukludąshiyicisi (strong carrier): a mature hobgoblin of the Cenubarkincilari and a carter around their tribe. He becomes their first trader to the Dwarves. He decides to call himself Guk outside Dhargev.

Gurinder: eleven-year-old child and sister of Parminder.

Hagar: from a farming family outside Dimashq in the Caliphate, she lives in Mousehole as the village butcher.

Hailanmês (Hail-an-meess): eight-year-old girl from Gil-Gand-Rask at the school. Her name means 'Curious Butterfly'. Twin of Tarlanmês and daughter of Şärnelşarn.

Harald Pitt: miner at Mousehole. He marries Lakshmi and their son is George.

Harnermês: (Har-ner-meess) A young man from Gil-Gand-Rask. His name means 'Curious Dolphin'. He becomes Jennifer's lover and joins the River Dragon.

Hlãnelhane: male Speaker on Gil-Gand-Rask. His name means 'Blue Ocean'

Hrothnog: the immortal God-King of Darkreach and great-great grandfather of Theodora. He is now married to Fãtima.

Hulagu (Tokotak Hulagu Jirgin): A young Khitan tribesman with ten toes. His tribe and totem is the Dire Wolf. He becomes a part of Mousehole. His daughters are Khãtun (with Kãhina) and Bũrãn (with Anahita). He marries Ayesha, Aigiarn, and Alaine and becomes Tar-Khan of the re-born Clan of the Horse.

Inis Éadoaindottir: female bard of the Bear people.

Iorund: a man from Skrice who was supposed to be the priest of the 'Old Gods' at Wolfneck after it was taken over by Svein and his men.

Ir Baethson: ten-year-old male Bear Folk student at the school.

Iyãd ibn Walĩd: Imam of the main mosque in Ardlark.

Jacob Majewski: Master boatwright in Evilhalt, built the River Dragon.

Jennifer Wagg: young woman, guard and sailor, from Deeryas. She was rescued from the Master's servants in Pavitra Phãṭaka.

Job Sword-of-God, Brother: Second Disciple of the Brotherhood and head of the Flails of God.

Jordan Croker: a journeyman potter from Greensin. No more potters were needed there and he came seeking a place to settle and a wife. He marries Dulcie.

Kãhina of the Pack Hunters: Hulagu's köle and mother of Khãtun of the Dire Wolves.

Karas: part-kharl & guard for Carausius, a Darkreach trader in spices etc.

Kessog, Father: Orthodox priest in Rising Mud.

Ketil Edvardson: a Fire Mage from Wolfneck and supporter of the 'Old Gods'.

Lãdi: From the Caliphate, she is the chief cook at Mousehole and very skilled.

Lakshmi Brar: former Havenite, she has converted and is now Orthodox and married to Harald Pitt. Their son is George. She is the apothecary and midwife for Mousehole.

Leonas of Goldentide: a mercenary from Freehold who is Captain of Militia in Erave Town. He is the father of Stefano of Erave.

Loukia Tzetzina: cooper and cabinet maker from Mistledross. She lost her family in an earthquake and has moved to Mousehole.

Magnus: an elderly mage in Wolfneck.

Make me to know my transgressions: young woman from the Brotherhood brought as a slave to restock Mousehole.

Maria Beman: a kidnapped woman from Greensin, daughter of Johann Beman, brought to Mousehole by slavers after it was freed.

Masters, the: animated skeletons of the old Dwarven Druids with the ability to use magic as air-mages. They may now longer exist, or there may be more somewhere.

Mathanharfead: the name Astrid is known by among the Inuit. See the short story *Astrid in the White World*. It means 'Killer of the Mathan'. A Mathan is a type of giant bear in their tongue.

Maurice, Father: an Orthodox priest in Wolfneck.

Melissa Mason: daughter of Goditha and Parminder.

Mellitus: Insakharl customs officer at Mouthgard.

Memrin do Modlin: a Kichic-kharl Primus of the Border Regiment stationed at Forest Watch.

Menas Climacus: eight-year-old Insakharl cousin (or nephew) of Basil & Olympias.

Micah: a man in the Brotherhood in charge of taxation. He finds people who owe taxes who may sell the women in their household as slaves.

Michael: a Praetor or leader in the Basilica Anthropoi who escorts the missionaries to the Cenubarkincilari Hobgoblins.

Mü-lin do Taraz: Kichic-kharl, Second Sergeant of the Border Regiment at Forest Watch.

Nacibdamįr (noble iron): young Hobgoblin and chief of the village of Dhargev and of the Cenubarkincilari, the southern hobgoblins.

Naeve Milker: former Freegate dairymaid who now runs the herds of Mousehole. She can become catatonic under stress. She becomes an apprentice mage and marries Giles. Her daughter is Peggy Farmer.

Nargrit dol Katuch: Kichic-kharl Sergeant of the Border Regiment in command of the Forest Watch garrison.

Nikephorus Cheilas: now married to Valeria and father to her child. He was an upper servant (Praetor koubikoularios) in the Palace at Darkreach.

Nokaj: grandfather of Hulagu, senior shaman to his tuman.

Norbert Black: he is skilled as a blacksmith, weapons smith and armourer. In Mousehole he marries both Fortunata and Sajãh. His sons are Valentine (with Fortunata) and Bishal (with Sajãh).

Odhamnait Teítldottir: female bard of the Bear people.

Olympias Akritina: Basil's sister, a junior officer in the navy in charge of a small fast scout and messenger boat and later the Captain of the River Dragon. Her lover is Denizkartal.

Panterius, Strategos (General): he is in charge of Darkreach Intelligence or the Antikataskopeía.

Pąrlakmugąni: bard of the Cenubarkincilari. His name means 'Bright Singer'.

Parminder: assistant cook and sometimes dressmaker at Mousehole, she marries Goditha and is sister to Gurinder. She becomes an apprentice mage and is a xeno-telepath. Her daughter is Melissa Mason.

Penial Denton: a Freeholder who has worked in a shipyard and as a sailor. He was brought to help build the River Dragon by the unknown person who commissioned her.

Rabi'ah: a poor spinner and weaver from Ardlark. Her drunken father sold her into slavery. She is sent by her Imam to Mousehole.

Rahki Johar: Harijan servant from Haven. She was rescued from the Master's servants in Pavitra Phāṭaka.

Rani Rai: a former Havenite Battle Mage and now co-Princess of Mousehole. She has broken caste and is married to Theodora and has adopted Fear.

Repent of this thy wickedness: 6 year old slave brought from the Brotherhood to help restock Mousehole. She is adopted by Eleanor and Robin.

Robin Fletcher: Fletcher and bowyer for Mousehole. He is married to Eleanor and they have adopted Aelfgifu, Gemma and Repent and have a daughter Bianca.

Ruth Hawker: former Freehold merchant and now teacher of the village children in Mousehole. She is married to Father Theodule and their identical twin sons are Joshua and Jeremiah.

Saglamruh: son of Verily and Aziz, brother to Sunmak. His name means 'Strong Spirit' in Hobgoblin.

Sajāh: from the Caliphate, She is the Seneschal of Mousehole under the Princesses. She is second wife of Norbert Black. Adopted mother of Roxanna and Ruhayma and mother of Bishal.

Salimah al Sabah: Theodora's alias when she is not being herself.

Şārnelşarn (Shaarnel-sharn): Women's Speaker on Gil-Gand-Rask. Her name means 'Hidden Path'. Mother of Hailanmêŝ and Tarlanmêŝ.

Shilpa Sodaagar: former Havenite trader and now assistant smith in Mousehole. She takes Vishal as her partner.

Sigihevi the Short: Human Mayor of Evilhalt.

Siglunda the Wise: a mage and midwife, Captain (village leader) of Wolfneck.

Simeon Alvarez, Father: Catholic cleric and werewolf who is born in Xanthia in the Newfoundland. He flees there and ends up in Mousehole through the offices of the Bear people. He changes to being Orthodox and marries Danelis.

Simon, Father: senior Orthodox priest in Wolfneck.

Simon of Richfield: a traveller and chronicler from before The Burning and even from before the Schism of the Church. He wrote a book called 'My Travels Over the Land and Beyond'.

Sonia DeMage: older woman and most powerful mage in Evilhalt. She is the grandmother of Tiffany.

Stefan Ostrogski: a young soldier from Evilhalt. He is now in charge of the militia of Mousehole and is married to Bryony and her cousin Adara. His son is Aneurin ap Stefan. He is also a leatherworker and has an inherited magical sword called Smiter and another, anti-dragon sword called Wrath.

Stefano of Erave: son of Leonas of Goldentide, student at the school.

Sunmak: son of Verily and Aziz, brother to Saglamruh. His name means 'Gift' in Hobgoblin.

Svein: man of Wolfneck and 'suitor' to Astrid. He is an ugly (kharlish appearance), violent drunkard and around 40 years old. Owns a ship and is a rival of Astrid's father. He is the Northern agent for the Masters.

Tabitha: born in a farming hamlet near Erave Town, she now lives in Mousehole as an assistant carpenter and cook. She has one green eye and one blue one. Cats like her.

Tarasios Garidos: Metropolitan of Ardlark.

Tarlanmês (Tar-lan-meess): eight-year-old girl from Gil-Gand-Rask at the school. Her name means 'Curious Flower'. Twin of Hailanmês and daughter of Şärnelşarn.

The Vengeance of the Lord is Mine Quester: Brotherhood scout and Inquisitor from the Flails of God who comes to Mousehole to spy on it.

Theodora Cephalou: wife of Carausius.

Theodora do Hrothnog: great-great-granddaughter of Hrothnog. She is not entirely human, a mage and, at 120 years, is far older than the late teens that she appears to have. She is now Princess of Mousehole with her husband, Rani and their adopted daughter Fear.

Theodora Lígo: daughter of Carausius.

Theodule, Brother: a former monk and now assistant to Father Christopher at Mousehole. He marries Ruth and their identical twin sons are Joshua and Jeremiah.

Theophilus, Abbot: in charge of the Orthodox monastery situated at Greensin, that of Saints Cyril and Methodius. He is also in charge of the training of new priests and monks.

Thomas Akkers: a younger son and farmer from near Bulga. He comes to Mousehole seeking land and a wife.

Thord: a shorter and broad humanoid of the species locally known as a Dwarf. He comes from Kharlsbane in the Northern Mountains, but is now Mousehole's Ambassador to the Dwarves. He rides a sheep called Hillstrider.

Thorstein, Father: priest in Wolfneck and youngest brother of Astrid.

Tiffany: six-year-old granddaughter of Sonia DeMage from Evilhalt, student at the school.

Tosti: father of Astrid and Father Thorstein.

Ulric: one of Svein's crew. He poses as a suitor from Warkworth to gain access to the valley to spy for the Masters. He is executed.

Umm: slave of the bandits from a poor farming family in the Caliphate, she is now a spinner and weaver in Mousehole and helps in the kitchen.

Valeria: 17-year-old from Deeryas on the south coast, she is now the servant of Rani and Theodora and has married Nikephorus.

Verily I Rejoice in the Lord Tiller: a former Brotherhood slave and, now an assistant cook and apprentice mage in Mousehole. She can 'smell' magic and has married Aziz. Their sons are Saglamruh (Strong Spirit) and Sunmak (Gift).

Verina Gabala: an Orthodox miller from Mistledross. She leaves Darkreach after she loses her family in an earthquake and ends up in Mousehole.

Vishal Kapur: young armsman from Haven. In the pay of the Master's servants, he is captured and then joins the Mice.

Yumn: orphan carpet maker from Ardlark who became a prostitute to raise a dowry or get enough for a loom. She is sent by her Imam to Mousehole.

Zafirah: a poor spinner and weaver from Ardlark who sells herself into slavery to pay the family debts. She is sent by her Imam to Mousehole.

Zạmratejedehar (Emerald Dragon): known as Zạmrat. Hob and daughter of Guk, a student at the school. The 'ạ' is a long 'aa' sound.

Zeenat Koirala: Harijani, former prostitute from Haven, rescued in Haven.

Zoë Anicia: an Orthodox baker from Mistledross. She loses her family in an earthquake and ends up in Mousehole.

Glossary

Aemigdius, Saint: Christian Saint, Feast Day 22nd of Undecim, he is the patron of protection from volcanoes and earthquakes.

al-jihad al-Asgar: an Arabic phrase 'the lesser struggle', the general fight against what is bad in the world.

Alat-kharl: one of the Kharl tribes of Darkreach, they are usually found working in the trades.

Allah 'akbar: 'God is Great', both an affirmation and a prayer.

Ānanda Dvīpa: an island in Pavitra Phāṭaka, the pleasure island with brothels and gambling.

Anne, Saint: Christian saint. Her Feast Day is 25th October and her patronage is of those who fight the undead and protect against evil, and also of those who return from the dead.

Anta Dvīpa: an island in Pavitra Phāṭaka mainly inhabited by the lowest castes. Its name means End Island.

Antikataskopeía: the 'secret police' of Darkreach.

Arnflorst: see Shunned Isle.

Arthur, Saint: Christian Saint, Feast Day 18th Undecim, he is the patron of orchardists.

Barbara, Saint: Christian Saint, Feast Day 14th Duodecimus, patron of engineers and ironworkers.

Bean, Saint: Christian saint. His Feast Day is the 12th of December and he is the patron of potters.

Bear-folk: a group of humanoids who have a high number of bear-based lycanthropes among their number. They live just north of the Swamp.

Birchdingle: a Bear-folk settlement.

Bowyanga River: a large tributary of the Methul that flows down from the Northern Mountains.

Brahmin: the highest caste of Haven society. It is made up of priests and money-lenders (often through intermediaries). They are forbidden any physical labour.

Brodir Lind: The Brother Shield, a tavern in Wolfneck.

Brotherhood, The: The Brotherhood of All Believers are militant semi-Christians of an extreme Puritan type.

Bulga: an independent village on the north coast of The Land.

Burning, the: a dread disease that causes people to go mad and destroy things. Less than one person in twenty survived the years that it raged.

Cat's Argument, the: a tavern in Rising Mud.

Cecilia, Saint: a Christian Saint, Feast Day 23rd Undecim, patron of bards and entertainers.

Cenubarkincilari: a small Hobgoblin tribe in the southern mountains. The name means 'Southern Raiders'.

Coins among the independent towns: the smallest is the copper deci-follis, ten of these make a tin follis, the standard coin. Fifteen follies make a silver/copper alloyed milesaria. A quarter of a milesaria is a bronze trachy, ten milesaria (150 follis) is a silver solidus. Three solidus (450 follis) make a gold hyperion, a gold talent is 2,000 follis and a platinum eagle is 22,500 follis. Astrid hands over f5,350 as a deposit.

Coins in the Swamp: The smallest coin in the Swamp is the 'mote', a copper coin. It is a tenth of the standard coin, 'ten motes' or 'tens' which are made of tin. A penny is a silver and copper alloy and is worth fifteen ten mote coins. A farthing is made of bronze and is worth a quarter of a penny. Other coins are a 'tenpenny' (150 tens, made of silver), a guinea (3,300 tens, made of gold) and 'ten guineas' (33,000 tens and made of platinum).

Confederation of the Free: see The Swamp.

Cosmas and Damien, Saints: brothers and Orthodox Saints, Feast Day 7th Duodecimus, patrons of medicine and surgery.

Cyril and Methodius, Saints: Christian saints. Their Feast Day is 11th Quinque and their patronage is conversion of the heathen, defence of the faith and translation.

Dagh Ordu: Khitan name for a monolith in the Southern Plains. It has a ruined city on the top and a resident dragon inside.

Dating: Years run over a 48-year cycle; with the twelve zodiacal signs that are used on Vhast along with the elements of Earth, Air, Fire and Water. There are twelve months of equal length, each having six weeks of six days. The first parts of the story take part on the Year of the Water Dog. A year thus has 432 days so a year on Vhast is nearly a fifth longer than a Terran year. A person who is fifteen on Vhast will be eighteen on Earth.

Diwali: 'row of lamps' a Hindu Festival celebrating the killing of the demon Narkasura.

Devi: a major Hindu goddess, the mother principle.

Dhargev: a Hobgoblin village in the Southern Mountains. The main settlement of the Cenubarkincilari tribe, the name means 'Our Home'.

Dharma: Hindu God of Truth.

Doro: a village in the south of Darkreach. It is one of the last places to have experienced an outbreak of The Burning on a few years before.

Durham Rock: see The Shunned Isle.

Dwynwen, Saint: Orthodox Saint, Feast Day 25th Primus, patron of both lovers and sick animals.

Dzlieri Guli: Khitan for 'Strong Heart'. It is the name of the packhorse used on the raid on Rising Mud.

Emeel amidarch baigaa khümüüs: a Khitan phrase, literally 'people who live in the saddle' for themselves.

Enchanted Bed, the: a tavern in Rising Mud.

Epilarch: a Darkreach naval rank usually held by the commander of a small flotilla or temporary formation.

Erave Town: a town on the southern shore of Lake Erave.

Evilhalt: a town at the very northern tip of Lake Erave.

Fabian, Saint: Christian saint. His Feast Day is 20th Primus and his patronage is of Holy Martyrs.

Fergus, Saint: Christian Saint. His Feast Day is 27th November and his patronage concerns all dealings with 'Greenskins', the Kharl and Kharl-related humanoids.

Fisherman's Arms, The: a tavern in Erave Town.

Flails of God: Brotherhood Inquisitors.

Forest Watch: a Darkreach outpost on a large hill in the Great Forest. On a clear day it has a view of most of much of the central mountains area and, in particular, the approaches to the Darkreach Gap.

Freeport: the main settlement on Gil-Gand-Rask. In High Speech it is þoşÞǎrntõ (Port of the Free) (Thosh-thaarn-too).

Ganesh: elephant-headed Hindu god. He is often called 'the remover of obstacles' and he rides a mouse.

Gantraj Dvīpa: an island in Pavitra Phāṭaka.

Gasparin: a hot spice.

Gil-Gand-Rask: a large island in the Southern Seas.

Gildas, Saint: Christian saint. His Feast Day is 29th Primus and his patronage is given to those who fight monsters of the oceans.

Glengate: a town to the west of Lake Erave.

Greensin: a town north-west of Evilhalt. It is the home of the senior of the western Metropolitans of the Orthodox Church.

Harijan: the lowest caste of Haven society. It includes all of the less prestigious occupations.

Hāthī Dvīpa: 'Elephant Island', an island in Pavitra Phāṭaka. Site of most of the army bases.

Haven: a nation at the mouth of the Rhastaputra River.

Hesperinos: performed at sundown, this is the beginning of the liturgical day for the Orthodox.

Hilary, Saint: Christian saint. His Feast Day is 14th Primus and his patronage is lawyers.

Hillstrider: Thord's Mountain Sheep that he rides.

Horse and Imp, the: a tavern in Rising Mud.

Iba Bay: a broad and deep bay formed to the east of the vast delta of the Swamp rivers.

Insakharl: this is not a distinct race, but a name given to those who have part-Human and part-Kharl ancestry.

Irene, Saint: Christian Saint. Feast Day is 32nd Duodecimus. She is the patron of miners and quarrymen.

Iwerddon: one of the hamlets of Rising Mud.

James the Less, Saint: Christian Saint, Feast Day 18th Duodecimus. He is the patron of siblings.

Jībha: 'the Tongue', a large island in the Rhastaputra upstream of Pavitra Phāṭaka.

Jude, Saint: Christian Saint. His Feast Day is 17th of Undecim and his patronage is towards those who have forlorn hopes.

Kharl: one of the races of Vaast. They are the most common form of humanoid after Humans. They vary greatly in appearance, but often have some animalistic features.

Kilā Dvīpa: an island in Pavitra Phāṭaka. It is a massive fortification.

Köle: Khitan term that means something similar to captive or slave. It is for a term that is usually five years.

Kshatya: an upper Havenite caste. It consists of warriors and rulers.

Kyrielle: a name taken from the lines 'Kyrie eleison, Christe eleison' (Lord have mercy, Christ have mercy), the first lines of a sung mass. Its form is the base for a type of poetry and some secular songs.

Lāṅga Ā'ilaiṇḍa: 'Long Island', an island in Pavitra Phāṭaka.

Leidauesgynedig: see Rising Mud.

Lyubov: a Darkspeech word, it can be sincere or mocking if it is said right; 'my love'.

Mandira Dvīpa: also known as the Temple Island in Pavitra Phāṭaka.

Maskirovka: a Darkspeech word, in the Wolfneck dialect, meaning a tactic of deception.

Mistledross: a village in the south of Darkreach. It is in one of the few parts of The Land that regularly experience earthquakes.

Monica, Saint: Christian Saint, Feast Day 16th Duodecimus, she is the patron of those in difficult relationships.

Neron: an island in the north, the last inhabited island. The village of Skrice is there.

Orroral, Lake: a lake to the west of the Great Divide on the Methul River.

Orthros: first Orthodox service of the morning. Usually starts before sunrise.

Ovington: an island in the far north. It is the second island in the chain that runs from the Northern Mountains and is uninhabited.

Padma: the Hindi word for the Lotus blossom. It is also used as an honorific for a female noble.

Pair of hands filled: a hand is six; a pair of hands is twelve. A pair of hands filled is the square of twelve. Astrid is indicating that she thinks there are at least 1,728 Hobgoblins in the valley.

Pandit: a Hindi honorific used for a wise person, teacher, or mage.

Paradēśī: Hindi for an outsider, a foreigner.

Paścimī Taṭa: the western shore of Pavitra Phāṭaka.

Pavitra Phāṭaka: also known as Sacred Gate. It is the capital of Haven.

Peter, Saint: Christian Saint. His Feast Day is 18th Secundus and his patronage is to evangelists.

Pūrvī Taṭa: the eastern shore of Pavitra Phāṭaka.

Rājā kē Dvīpa: also known as Rajah's Island, an island in Pavitra Phāṭaka.

Rangers: what passes for a military in the village of Wolfneck. They are scouts and hunters more than anything else and fight from cover with bows if forced to fight.

Rhastaputra River: the main river draining the mountains and area just to the west of them.

Rising Mud: a village in the Swamp it is called Leidauesgynedig in Faen.

Sacred Gate: see Pavitra Phāṭaka.

Seytanyi: Hobgoblin word taken from Arabic, it means demons or evil spirits.

Sezni, Saint: Christian Saint, Feast Day 4th Duodecimus, Patron Saint invoked for dealings with Lycanthropes.

Shaitan: Arabic word for the devil.

Shastrii-lo-pesti-song: a village in the Arctic. It's name means 'Place of Fire'.

Shunned Isle: it is also called Durham Rock or Arnflorst (its original name as a city). It is the furthest north of the chain running up from the Northern Mountains. It has a fell reputation.

Skrice: a village on Neron Island.

Southpoint: the southernmost town in Darkreach.

Spanker: a large fore-and aft sail, like the mainsail on a modern yacht.

Sudra: a Havneite caste of merchants and most of the more profitable trades.

Swamp, The: the common name for the Confederation of the Free.

Swithun, Saint: a Christian Saint, his patronage is the weather and his Holy Day is the 15th of Undecim.

Thug or Thugee: an assassin of the Temple of Kali.

Tor Karoso: a mountain on Gil-Gand-Rask.

Trekvarna: a city in Freehold.

Ursula, Saint: patron of Virgins, Feast Day is the 6th of September.

Varuna: Hindu God of water and oceans.

Vidvānōṁ Dvīpa: also known as the Island of Scholars in Pavitra Phāṭaka.

Vitalis, Saint: A Christian Saint, the patron of merchants and traders, Feast Day 34th of Undecim.

Vyāpārī Dvīpa: the Merchant's Island in Pavitra Phāṭaka.

Warkworth: a free village in the west of The Land. It lies between The Brotherhood and Freehold.

Week: each week on Vhast has six days. Generally, across The Land, these are given the names: Firstday, Deutera, Pali, Tetarti, Dithlau and Krondag. Kron is the name given to the sun. The definitions and roots of some of these names are unknown.

Windin Cove: a wide bay more than a cove, at the head of lies Pavitra Phāṭaka.

Winifred, Saint: Christian saint. Her Feast Day is the 19th Primus and her patronage is healing.

Wolfneck: a part-Kharl village in the north of The Land. It is home to Astrid.

Yadci: Hobgoblin word that means 'strangers'.

Yµmµkimṣe: Hobgoblin word, literally 'Soft One', it also means Human.

Ynys Cyslltu: the central island of Rising Mud. In Faen its name means 'Linking Island'

Zangindoyµshzcu: the largest Hobgoblin tribe, who have several villages in the Northern Mountains. Their name means 'Rich Warriors'.

Zim Island: An island in the south that is completely covered in an un-named ruined city. It has dense jungle between its buildings and Kraken Weed around it.

Details of Mousehole

The characters in my books have detailed descriptions that have been used to help write their stories. Only a few of these are mentioned here. The 'Q' level is the level of quality of goods produced by the person with Q3 being a journeyman level. A 'C' is how many competencies the person has down a career path. Again C3 would be a journeyman. A person can have two or more indications beside them. A sage score indicates a person's knowledge in four areas: Biology, Alchemy, Physics and Humanity. A score of 'E' is 14 and very high. Theodora has $C11^{20,AD}$ as a mage and Rani has $C9^{19,FD}$. This means that Theodora is an eleven competency mage with a psychic ability of 20 (extremely high) and is of the sign of the Air Bird. Rani is a nine competency mage of the sign of the Fire Dragon. Her psychic ability is also very high. Every town and village in Vhast is treated in this way.

Mousehole

This (overleaf) is a snapshot of the village at the end of 'Engaging Evil', not as of this book. Most of the people not mentioned here are still living in the Hall of Mice or the old barracks. Most of the houses are empty at this stage and only those listed are repaired enough to be lived in.

The village was known in Old Speech as Muzel. All of houses around the edge that back into the surrounding cliff will extend into the rock wall. Some go back a very long way and will be used, eventually, for maturing cheese and other activities that need a constant temperature. There is around 3m of elevation between levels. All of the buildings in the front and middle rows have two levels. Very few of the last row are more than one level, but may be the same size as the others due to being build well back into the cliff.

1. Watchtower on the wall

2. Wider section of wall around gate

3. Smithy and residence: Norbert Black (blacksmith Q5, weaponsmith Q5,

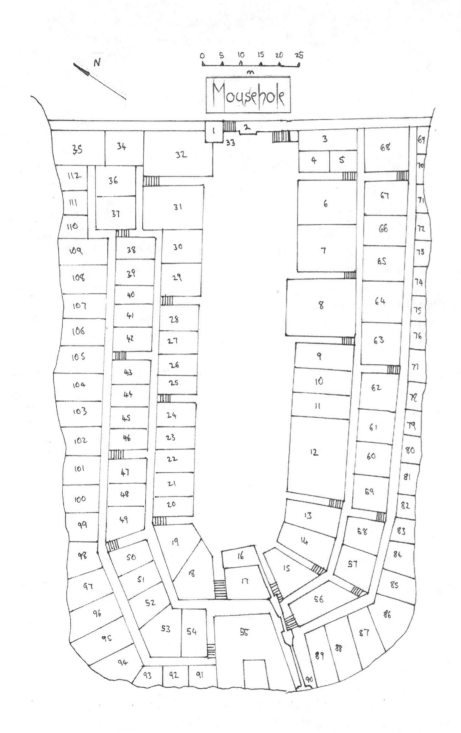

Mousehole

armourer Q5), Sajãh bin Javed (housekeeper Q9, administration C3
Fortunata Belluci (dressmaker Q6, embroiderer Q5, her workshop is at [...]

6. Stable (extends under next level)

7. Bandit Barracks: Thord Arnorsson (Shepherd C4)

8. Hall of Mice and residence: Father Christopher Palamas (Cleric [...]
Presbytera Bianca Whipple (she does not know that this is her surna[...]
(Vagus C4), Father Theodule Panaretos (Cleric 7[15]), Presbytera Ruth Haw[...]
(sage 6F36 & teacher C4), Togotak Hulagu Jirgin (Tribal C4), Vachir Anah[...]
Ursud (Tribal C3, Vagus C1) & Bodonchar Kãhina Juyin (Tribal C2, Vag[...]
C1)

11. Kitchens, run by Lãdi al-Yarmũk (Q9)

12. Village hall

16. Pool of fresh water

19. Apothecary's workshop for Lakshmi, and healing chapel used by her and [...]
the priests

22. Leatherwork workshop and residence: Stefan Ostrogski (Armsman C5,
Leatherworker Q4) & Bryony verch Dafydd (scout C4, vagus C1)

23. Dressmaking and tailoring (used mainly by Fortunata & Astrid)

26. Residence for Harald Pitt (Trade C9, miner), Lakshmi Brar (Illicit C5,
physician Q4, sage E400)

27. Residence: Giles Ploughman (farmer & husbander C4, cheese-maker Q4,
cheese at 110) & Naeve Milker (husbander C5)

28. Workshop and residence: Robin Fletcher (bowyer Q5, fletcher Q6),
Eleanor Perrot (Armsman C5, jeweller Q7)

29. Brewery: Aine o Bloomact (brewer Q7, distiller Q3, vintner Q3)

30. Bakehouse, there is no skilled and specialist baker in residence

31. Barracks that was used as the slave quarters

32. Guard room and armoury

33. Short flight of stairs up to watchtower from the wall

53. Residence for Goditha Mason (mason Q3, mage C2[17E?]) & Parminder Sen
(Mage C2[16S])

55. Princess' House: Theodora do Hrothnog (mage C11[20AB], noble C5, bard
C4) and Rani Rai (Mage C9[19FD])

62. Verily I Rejoice in the Lord (Vagus C4, Illicit C1, mage C2[21F?]) and Aziz
(Armsman C4)

90. Spring emerging from cliff

94. Residence for Basil Akritas (Armsman C4, Vagus C8) and Astrid the Cat
(Scout C5, tailor Q4)

110. Cheese-making and storage for Giles.